DARK MOTIVES

ENDORSEMENTS

I first became aware of Zanne Dyer's writing at a writer's critique group and was instantly impressed. Had the privilege of critiquing several chapters of *Dark Motives* in that group and can now happily commend the finished result. It's a fast-moving, clean mystery-thriller that harkens back to the old film-noir style. A fun read.

—**Dan Walsh**, award-winning author of *The Unfinished Gift*, *The Reunion* and the bestselling Jack Turner Suspense series.

Fast-paced and hard hitting, this debut novel brings a strong new voice into the suspense genre. This multi-layered story leaves the reader continually surprised by the nuances of the evidence and the unexpected twists as the plot thickens. Readers will find themselves staying up late because they are unable to put this book down. These characters leave an indelible impression that demands a sequel. "

—**Cindy Champnella**, author of *The Waiting Child* (St. Martins Press) and *The Twelve Gifts of Life* (Ambassador International)

Thrills, chills, kills, and strong wills churn through this fascinating and compelling novel lacing fascinating plots, subplots, characters, and danger. Truly an edge-of-your-seat kind of read. I'm so excited about the beginning and the continuing career of this new novelist. Where has she been

hiding this great talent? I don't know but I'm so glad she has come out from the dark with a ground breaking first novel.
—**Kathy Collard Miller**, co-author with her husband, Larry, of *God's Intriguing Questions: 60 New Testament Devotions Revealing Jesus's Nature*.

There's a new star on the writer's horizon and her name is Zanne Marie Dyer. *Dark Motives* is a real page turner! I'm amazed this is her first novel—such a seasoned writer. The plotline is layered with intrigue and murder clues are cleverly hidden. Even the detective's name—Jet Wholeman—seems to hold meaning. You won't be able to put this suspense novel down as you seek justice for the murder of a little girl. Job well done. I'm ready to read her next novel.
—**Donna Collins Tinsley,** former President of Word Weavers Volusia County Group, creator of Somebody's Mother Online Prayer Support Group, Radio host on WAPN 91.5 for Prayerline, Holly Hill, Fl.

DARK MOTIVES

Zanne Marie Dyer

ELK LAKE PUBLISHING INC.
Plymouth, Massachusetts

Cover and Interior Design: Derinda Babcock

Editor(s): Sue Fairchild, Deb Haggerty

PUBLISHED BY ELK LAKE PUBLISHING, INC., 35 Dogwood Drive, Plymouth, MA 02360, 2020

Library Cataloging Data

Names: Dyer, Zanne Marie (Zanne Marie Dyer)

Dark Motives / Zanne Marie Dyer

402 p. 23cm × 15cm (9in × 6 in.)

Identifiers: ISBN-13: 978-1-951970-55-0 (paperback) | 978-1-951970-56-7 (trade paperback) | 978-1-951970-57-4 (e-book)

Key Words: crime, mystery, terrorists, detectives, Al Qaeda, murder, relationships

LCCN: 2020937717 Fiction

Dedicated to Craig St. Clair Dyer,
Rose, Jesse, and Jo-jo

ACKNOWLEDGMENTS:

My husband, Craig, was a lifeline in the writing of this book. As a criminal trial lawyer, he was a treasure trove of knowledge for legal and criminal procedure. It wasn't easy for him to sit still while I conducted brutal data extractions from his frontal brain files. But he did it. And despite his aversion to domestic chores, he even jumped in to help with those. In times past, I cooked meals. But for the last two years I've had him on a diet of crime questions for lunch and suspense for dinner. He never complained.

A special thank you goes to Philly Rose, the first to read my early work, and the first to encourage me to finish.

To Jordan of *Ello Creative* who worked after-hours to design my fabulous website and other creative strategies.

I am deeply grateful for Eva Marie Everson, President of Word Weavers International—the first professional writer/author to see value in my work and to inspire me to continue.

A big call out for Jessica R. Everson and Sue Fairchild, who both worked patiently with me to polish my manuscript.

To author Dan Walsh, who offered mentoring through my Word Weaver's critique group.

To my friend Frank—my first bona fide groupie. He read *Dark Motives* twice in a two-month period, because he "couldn't put it down."

To Sergeant A. Hairston, who so graciously made suggestions concerning police protocol.

To my beta readers: Gary, Gail, Frank, Carol, Tammyann, Leon, Cindy, Pierre, and Linda.

To my book elves: Bethany, Josi, Maggi, Rosa, Angie, Donna, Pam, Gail, Sasha and Sebastien.

To my son, Jesse, who has always believed in me.

CHAPTER 1

The unexpected wind and rain pelting his truck windows brought a welcomed camouflage to the night's mission. As he turned off the truck lights and made a left turn onto a dark residential street, he uttered a quick prayer of gratitude. With deep calming breaths, he turned his attention to the rows of familiar houses. He had surveyed this area several times over the past weeks, but he could not afford any surprises. He had to make certain no one was out braving the thunderstorm. A quick glance at his watch revealed the time to be just after midnight. The timing could not be better for this wet and windy weather—merciful and beautiful rainfall he knew must have been sent to cover his tracks—and that of the sleeping girl beside him. He looked down at the trash bag on the passenger seat—still as death. He thought of her angelic face. All was going according to plan.

He slipped the automatic transmission into neutral, turned off the ignition and coasted onto the grassy shoulder between two houses. He double-checked the landmarks he had surveyed days before and, feeling assured, put the truck into park and removed the key. He sat for a minute, unmoving except for his eyes, which scanned the doors and windows of the surrounding houses.

His grip on the steering wheel tightened with anticipation—the climax of his operation neared. Time to make his move. As he reached toward the bag beside him, a loud buzz jolted the silence. He looked to see his phone, lit up and throbbing, on the center dashboard. Before the phone could make another sound, he silenced it with one swift move. The screen revealed a familiar number, one that must be ignored.

Confident no one on the street had been aroused, he pushed the plastic trash bag from the seat to the floorboard. His steel-toed work boot connected with the small bundle of flesh and bone and brought forth a moan. She was still alive—this certainty sent an unexpected thrill up his spine.

He squeezed the phone as it lit up again. Why would she call at this late hour? Reluctantly, he stabbed the green button.

"What do you want?"

"I know what you are doing."

"Keep your mouth shut, or I will silence you myself."

He heard her suck in her breath. "But you could destroy everything we have worked for."

Still holding the phone, he looked around. All remained still. "Do not forget your place, woman."

He hung up and stuck the phone in his pants pocket. Working to steady his rattled nerves, he clenched his fists. No one would be allowed to interfere.

With a final check of the surrounding area, he looked closely at the property line between the two houses. All clear. He eased open the driver's door in darkness, his interior light having been disconnected, and slid out. He leaned back in and grabbed a small bag of tools and shoved it in his other pocket. Closing the door with only a tiny click, he moved around the side of the truck until he reached the passenger side, and gently opened the door. He froze as a bolt of lightning lit up the sky. The flash captured his gloomy silhouette in a blaze of light, but his dark clothes melted against the black truck, disguising him. When darkness was restored, he reached inside the truck and dragged the bag to the door's edge. Maneuvering the bag to the right position, he easily lifted it out of the truck. Fortunately, the load was light.

With barely a sound, he closed the truck door, moved around the rear of the truck and strode across the sandy, weed-choked yard. The falling rain absorbed the sound of his boots as he moved into the shadows between the houses. He stopped momentarily to check for any sounds. Some distance off, between the crashes of thunder, he heard a dog barking. But the noise was too far off for concern.

He moved to the backyard toward a grassy corner where he had pried open a wooden fence weeks earlier for a quick entry. This site had been chosen carefully.

A tight smile crossed his lips as he relished the thought of his plan unfolding with perfect precision. He had spent months laying out the details of this mission—one that would bring down the most influential religious zealot in the state of Florida. Paradoxically, the fragile innocence cocooned within this bag would serve to destroy the faith of thousands, if not millions.

Once through the broken fence, he moved to the back of the house and stepped onto a shabby concrete porch. An unlocked utilities door awaited him, exactly as he had intended.

He placed the plastic sack on the floor just inside the door and grabbed a long combat knife from under his shirt. Pulling his phone from his pants pocket, he turned on the flashlight mode and slowly proceeded into the adjacent kitchen. He closely inspected each of the rooms as he moved. Only one was occupied.

On the floor, in what he supposed to be the living room, was a sleeping man, curled up in a fetal position. He did not care who he was or what he looked like. He only knew the stranger could not be allowed to awaken until he was long gone. He reached down, one hand holding the knife, and rolled the man onto his back. The stranger grunted but remained asleep. Standing up, he shone his light on the body and viciously kicked the stranger squarely in the temple. There was a sickening, and satisfying, thud. From his training, he knew the sleeping man might never awaken. If he did, he would never be the same.

He returned to the bag, lifted it from the floor, and moved down the hall to the closest bedroom. The first room on his left was strewn with filthy debris. He stepped carefully around the trash until he reached a small closet. He leaned down and placed the increasing weight of his shouldered load onto the floor. This was the moment he had waited for. Laying his phone down, its light pointed at the ceiling, he grabbed the sealed end of the bag, untied a knot, and dumped out the contents. A dull thud sounded in the silence.

He picked up the light and flashed the beam downward to find the young face of the sleeping girl. Her face lit up like a porcelain doll, and he felt himself wishing she were awake so he could see her clear blue eyes. He knew her name was Mary, nothing more ... nor did he care. He did wonder, however, if she felt fear or sensed her approaching destiny. He lowered himself to his knees for a closer look. Strange. She had a hint of a smile on her lips.

Without knowing why, he felt compelled to lean in and whisper, "Why do you wear that silly look of contentment? What is it you see?" He would never know, and the unknown bothered him.

He sat back and studied her.

A wave of disappointment hit him as he realized she was older than he first thought. Although small, the lines beneath her loose-fitting clothing revealed an older girl, closer to fourteen or fifteen years old. No matter, he assured himself. There was a divine reason for all.

Her chest heaved for another breath, but he would not allow it. Her death was quick and merciful. He smiled at his own benevolence. She was indeed fortunate to have been chosen for this mission, and the surge of power he felt to have such charge over human destiny thrilled him.

He considered two thoughts. The first was regret. He wanted to do more, to beat someone to death, release the anger and frustration welling within him. But a soldier must practice restraint. The second thought was of the victory he would feel when Pastor Bill Williams was arrested and charged with the murder of a young girl. A shameful shepherd, who all would believe had killed one of his own sheep. His huge church would wither and die, and he would be strapped to a gurney and sent to hell.

Yes, the heathen zealot and the dead girl might be considered a small victory to his superiors or even a distraction from the focal mission, but he had a much larger vision. His would bring national or international exposure of the lies and hypocrisy of Christianity. As the Americans would say, "One small step for man, one giant leap for mankind."

His comrades and brothers might not agree with his methods, but they would applaud the results. With only a few minor details left to be dealt with, he would soon return to the comfort of his tent to enjoy a hot meal and a restful bed.

When he had completed his tasks, he collected the small bag of tools—used to make a minor alteration to the dead body—restored them to his pocket and slid back into the wet night. As he headed for his truck, determined to focus on the second mission, an unforeseen thought crept in. Maybe this particular operation did not have to be the last one. After all, he need not answer to anyone for his actions. These people were unbelievers, mere dogs. His mouth watered at the idea, but he shook the idea away. No, he must concentrate now on the mission for which he was sent—the destruction of an evil empire and, of course, the business of evading the pesky American police.

CHAPTER 2

Dunkin' Donuts is not the best place for a serious conversation. The jabber of hyped-up customers getting their late morning coffee fix fills the air in a steady hum, while two lines of customers wait at the counter. I can only imagine the cars backed up around the building, waiting for their turn at the take-out window. All but one of the tables is full, so I scramble to grab a chair for my wife Sydney, who now has the job of securing the spot. I plant a quick kiss on the top of her head before making a beeline for the check-out counter. A coffee and sugar fix are the order of the day.

Back at the table, with my bag of donuts, a honey bran muffin, and two hot coffees, I'm ready to take on the world. Between gulps of black coffee and mouthfuls of double-chocolate donuts, I surreptitiously look around at the sugar-stuffing community around me. Double chins and ballooned bellies seem to be in full bloom, but so does the lively animated chatter. Looking across the table at Sydney, I watch as she samples the stiff-looking bran muffin, probably gluten free, then returns the baked good neatly to her plate. She looks up and gives me a disapproving eye as I lick the sticky frosting from my fingers. Somehow that bran muffin reminds me of an only child who doesn't quite fit in with the other more robust children. How she manages to eat something healthy in a sugar palace like this is just another mystery in our relationship. I quickly assure myself that all of us wheat-eaters are happy and healthy enough. The gluten-free craze will pass. After all, for all we know, all those people are in a cult.

Sydney's soft voice drones on about something, but an annoying thought distracts me as I look down at the two remaining donuts: Will I someday look like these folks around me, with a belly so large I can use it as a table? I compartmentalize that thought, reminding myself I'm still young, fit, and squeezing into a size thirty-four pant. Besides, my job keeps me on the go. I take a satisfied, guilt-free bite of my frosted pastry and escort it down with steaming coffee. It's good to be alive.

I'm brought back from my thoughts when I hear Sydney, from across the table, utter one word. One name. *Andria.* The name slices the amiable chatter around us like a single tart bite in a sweet, soothing snack.

"Jet, did you hear me?"

I look up to see her penetrating stare. "I'm listening, honey." Stalling for time, I pick up my phone with an apologetic smile and check for messages. The direction the conversation has taken dampens my high spirits a bit. The only Andria I know is a local, tough-minded journalist, who is often looking for scoops on some of our department's major homicide cases. She's a sore subject for both of us.

I lay the phone down, giving a quick glance behind me, an old habit. Turning back, I look her in the eye. "Okay. You have my full attention. What were you saying?"

"If you listened instead of canvassing the place, maybe you'd know."

"All part of my training." I give her a wink.

Wiping my mouth with the back of my hand, I do a quick study of her body language. Stiff and defensive. Shoulders back. Elbows locked. Chin tucked. After ten years of marriage and two kids, it's obvious something is wrong. I detect the first dark clouds of a gathering storm.

She takes a distracted sip of her vanilla latte, still eyeing me, and leans forward in her seat, eyebrows raised in a silent question.

I squirm under her stare.

"Well?" She lifts her open palms. "Have you been listening to me?"

"Andria," I parrot.

"Well?"

Her steel blue eyes penetrate mine and I realize how great she looks today. With only the slightest hint of makeup, her face is luminescent, her thick auburn hair falling in waves.

"I want to know *now*," she says in slow monosyllables.

I'm hoping, on some subconscious level, whatever she'd said is about to pop back into my conscious awareness.

She blows out an exasperated breath. "Well, say something."

I tap my fingers on the table again. "Are we talking about the same Andria?"

Her lips are pursed a little now, and her eyes are getting steely, but as a trained police interrogator, I'm not overly worried. Time to change tactics, get off the defensive, and pull out my bag of tricks.

I look into her eyes, putting on my best Ryan Gosling smile, with a little George Clooney thrown in. This look always works on women. Leaning toward her, I whisper, "You know, sweetheart, your eyes look stunningly blue today, and I like the way you're wearing your hair."

She narrows her stare. "This is the way I always wear my hair, and you're changing the subject."

I gulp. "Well, it works for Clooney."

"This is no time for acting. I'm serious."

Suddenly, as if on cue, my police radio band chirps. I eagerly grab it from the table. Lady Luck is on my side.

Pressing the transmit button, I speak into the radio. "Go."

A response quickly crackles over the speaker. "Jet. Call in."

It's my partner, Tina Serwathka.

"10-4." I hit the disconnect button.

With another apologetic glance, I set down my coffee cup, grab my phone, and punch the speed dial. Tina picks up.

"Jet?"

"Hey, Tina, can you give me a sec? I've got Sydney here. Getting coffee."

"Sure. But make it quick. We just picked one up. Homicide off Oakland and Sistrunk."

I hang up and turn to Sydney. "I'm sorry, honey, I've gotta take this. Just got called in."

"I know." She glances off into some distant place. With a singular sigh, she quickly checks her purse, stands, and gracefully angles herself over to my side of the table. She leans in, and for one sweet second, I think she's going to kiss me. Instead, she picks up my napkin and brushes powdered sugar from my chin.

"You're a mess, Jethro." She gives a maternal shake of her head.

When she calls me Jethro, she's not happy.

"I have someone coming over to tune the piano this afternoon, a student at four, and the boys' soccer game at six. I'll see you tonight." Moving to leave, she adds, "That is, if I'm still awake."

"I'm sorry. I really am, honey." As she walks away, I call after her, "If I don't make the game, tell the boys to knock 'em flat."

Nodding over her shoulder, she moves toward the door. A young man jumps to hold it open for her with an admiring glance.

I guess I should be bothered by his admiration, but truth be told, his attention causes my heart to pound. My wife is a beautiful woman who deserves looks of admiration. I just happened to have married the Venus de Milo with arms, and art is made to be admired.

As long as they don't touch.

Her parting look of sadness tugs at my heart. I silently vow to make it up to her. Plenty of time for that. The Rolling Stones song "Time Is on My Side" rolls through my mind as I watch her open her car door, slide safely in, and pull away. I make a mental note to change the oil and tires on her SUV.

Bad things happen to good people—but not on my watch.

With my phone now heavy in hand, I press the speed dial. Tina picks up.

"Jet?"

"Yeah," I respond, a bit too loudly. "Can't a cop get a break? I'm on donut time."

Several curious people turn their heads toward me with smiles of understanding, allies in the brotherhood of sugar-munchers.

"Jet. We've got a kid in an abandoned house on Forty-Fourth and Pine. Watch commander wants us there, now." The moment she says *kid*, my breath catches.

A child.

Images of the last juvenile murder investigation flash through my head. The emotions crash around—anger, frustration, sorrow. The slaughtered lamb, the loss of innocence. Familiar feelings of anger wash over me as the mind-boggling, age-old question emerges: If there is a God, why would he allow such bone-chilling crimes against humanity?

I feel the coffee acids mix with my rising stomach bile. "What's the address again, Tina?"

I repeat the location back, submit the streets to memory, and end the call.

Moving a little too quickly, I stand up, gulp down the remainder of my coffee, spilling some down the front of my shirt. Wiping off with one hand, I angle toward the exit door and wave to a familiar face behind the counter. She hurriedly gestures me over, holding out a tall coffee to go.

"Lieutenant Wholeman, you take. No? One Grande Americano, double shot espresso for good policeman." Her short rotund body presses against the counter as she leans toward me.

I hustle over and, with a wink, take the coffee. "Nobody knows the way to a man's heart like you do, Nita."

She waves, casting a crooked smile.

Some people actually respect cops.

I push through the exit door, and as I pass the trash can, I ball up my paper cup, get my bearings, and toss the paper over my head in a perfect hook shot. Right in the can—*bull's eye*. Lady Luck strikes again. But this perfection can't last ... not where I'm going.

Already I can feel a strange mix of adrenaline, fear, and excitement running through my veins. Hunting bad guys can be exhilarating but can bring out something ruthless in the best of us when it involves a child.

With only ten steps to my department-issued Dodge Charger, I'm making a U-turn on Broward Boulevard and heading west toward I-95 within seconds. The sky is darkening, sending the first drizzle of rain to my windshield. I hit the wipers and turn on the headlights. Somehow, this gloomy weather seems in sync with my assignment, but the soft metronome thump of the wipers is oddly comforting as my mind searches for a sense of normalcy in an upside-down day.

I quickly key the address into the center-console GPS. I know the area, but the Australian female voice droning in the background tends to relax me. I turn up the volume of the tactical radio to pick up any scuttlebutt about the incident. According to the voices reporting to dispatch, the area has been secured and the crime scene preserved by Sgt. Jose Martinez. Martinez in charge is a good thing.

Pushing the accelerator harder, I'm thrust back into my seat as the car lurches forward. As I weave in and out of the light traffic, I'm wondering if Martinez has seen the body yet. He has kids, so this won't be easy for him either, but he's still the best one for the job.

Martinez has the reputation of being a master at preserving a crime scene and its evidence, and unless the first officer at the scene really messes things up, everything under Martinez's care moves only with his permission. Both a stickler for rules and a perfectionist in working a crime scene, Martinez is a top cop. On a personal level, he's frankly a pain in my rear. As I jump onto the interstate and accelerate north bound, I'm still thinking about him. I've known Jose since our early days in the academy.

Admittedly, I was a real jerk back then, and for whatever reason, he got under my skin from the very start. In a tense moment, I called him "Hoser." He's probably never forgiven me.

I exit at Oakland Park Boulevard and turn west. Getting closer to my destination, my stomach begins to knot. My hope is this murder is not connected to Mary Ford, the young girl who was abducted four days ago from a local church. The church happens to be the same one Sydney attends. I hate to mix business with personal and plan to avoid that scenario as much as possible.

Turning off the main road into a residential area, lush green trees appear in abundance. In these older developed areas, I realize, about the same time the trees finally mature to royal beauty, the houses reach a point of decay. Just up ahead there's a beautiful old oak with a trunk as wide as a water barrel. Moving closer, I see the trees limbs are filled with young children, looking happy and carefree. As I automatically scan the faces, hope shines. Maybe the body isn't Mary Ford. She could be found any day now, restored to her family and, like these kids, lost only in a world of play.

The map on the screen shows fifty feet to my destination. I slow the vehicle and observe the ever-deepening trees hugging the aged houses. These old oaks seem to offer sheltering shade to the many homes that have lost the care and maintenance of their owners. Sadly, it probably won't be long before developers come in and scrape the ground flat. Making a final turn onto Forty-Fourth Terrace, I remind myself new trees will replace old, jobs will be created, and life will go on. At least for some of us.

"You have arrived," announces the Australian voice.

I steel myself for whatever awaits me.

CHAPTER 3

Without killing the engine, I look to my right where there's a rundown, boarded-up house. If concrete structures had faces, its expression would be forlorn and abandoned. Just a few yards ahead, Martinez stands in the middle of the road, waving directions to officers and support staff. Standing at only about five-foot-six, his erect posture and air of authority still suggests he's a force to be reckoned with.

I pull up alongside Martinez and open the car window.

"Hoser," I call out, and quickly correct myself. "Jose."

Okay ... so I'm only a recovering jerk.

He turns a rigid face to me, neatly re-tucking his clean, heavily starched uniform shirt into his pants. Despite his best efforts, the blue shirt is showing signs of melting under Florida's brutal heat and warm drizzling rain.

He gives a cursory nod. "Lieutenant Wholeman."

"Martinez, glad to see you're on the job. What you got?"

Stepping closer, he bends down, sticks his head in the window, and speaks in hushed tones. "This could be the Ford kid."

Frowning, he stands back up. He pulls off his bill cap, grabs a handkerchief from his shirt pocket, and wipes his forehead as if he wants to wipe away the possibility. "The techs and Missing Persons Unit arrived about ten minutes ago," he continues, "but I've kept everyone away from the room with the body. It's up to you now." His Spanish accent is always stronger under pressure. He obviously doesn't like this type of crime any more than I do, but we can't control everything.

"Good job, Martinez. FBI involved yet?"

"Yeah, they've been called. They plan to send someone out here if this turns out to be the Ford girl. Security has been posted at the door. Washington was the first officer on the scene. Based on his report and what I've heard, I think the clothes will be a match."

Precise and to the point, as usual.

A mental image of Mary Ford flashes across my mind. Her picture has been plastered on the front page of every local news source for the last three days, including major television networks. They all display the same picture—a fourteen-year-old blonde with a beaming smile, dressed in a pink T-shirt with the words "Daddy's Girl" on the front. The article always also explains she's intellectually disabled and has a defective heart, but except for being small, could pass for any other child. I let out a long, slow breath. The poor kid had been easy prey.

Putting the hard, cold facts aside, I'm tempted to believe the pink shirt, the mushy slogan, and the hallowed place she disappeared from are all something out of a sappy dime store novel, penned to ensure tear stains on its pages. But this is all too real. The young girl was at church with her family— where they regularly attended—and disappeared after a trip to the bathroom. Ironically, her father had been the one to escort her to the bathroom. He stepped away for just a minute—one minute too long. She never came out of the bathroom … he never saw her after that. The heartsick dad was left to deal with not only the trauma of her abduction, but the parting memory of her in that pink T-shirt, the slogan forever emblazoned in his mind. Sadly, he probably blames himself for not having protected her. At least that's how I would feel.

I'm short on time and have to get to the crime scene fast before anyone tampers with the evidence. The Ford case is high profile, and the media will soon descend like vultures.

"Listen, I've gotta go. I'll get a full report later." The engine in neutral, I rev the engine a little. "Gotta beat the media mayhem."

Martinez backs away from my car and points to a location just three houses down.

Taking my foot off the brake, I roll into an opening in the swale area and pop the car into neutral to do a quick study of the surroundings. The neighborhood street has two rows of flat-roofed, old Florida homes, all embedded in heavy tropical foliage, ripe banana trees, tall palms, and vibrant purple bougainvillea. The lot houses are made of predominantly gray concrete, except for an occasional structure in lime green or pool blue. The yards are mostly dirt and weeds with splotches of choking grass. A few of the yards are decorated with card tables, folding chairs, and even an occasional sagging sofa, giving the appearance of a perpetual garage sale. I can't help but think the scene is oddly refreshing after dealing with homeowners' associations.

I kill the engine, taking a deep breath to mentally prepare for what's ahead. With one motion, I grab my crime scene bag from the passenger seat, sling a digital camera over my shoulder, and slide out of the car. Moving quickly toward the house, I flash my shield to the officer standing at the checkpoint entry.

As I approach the decayed structure—its perimeter sectioned off by orange cones and yellow crime tape—my steps slow and my legs begin to feel heavy—they don't want to go in there anymore than I do. I set my focus on the front door. The grayish, slab-like appearance reminds me of the entrance to an abandoned tomb. A dead structure hiding death. The windows have been covered over with now grayed plywood in several places, the wood layers flaking away. Faded graffiti covers much of the wood and mottled stucco walls. Gang signs, profanity, and declarations of affection compete for space.

All my senses are on red alert as a powerful smell of human decomposition hits me. There is no other smell like this smell—thick, wet, shockingly sweet, and yet distinctly bitter as bile. I remind myself if it is Mary Ford's body in there, it has nothing to do with her sweet life. I don't know where she is now, but she's not in there.

A storm of flies buzz in the late morning heat and humidity. The uniformed officer, looking fresh out of the academy, stands watch at the door, frantically waving the bugs away. He's a pale-faced, skinny kid, with chunks of toilet paper jammed up his nose and a smear of Vicks VapoRub just beneath. He looks like a scene from a comedy mistakenly pasted into a tragic movie trailer.

I flip back my suit jacket to reveal my shield. "Detective Lieutenant Jethro Wholeman."

"Gotcha." He flashes a smile and looks down at his notepad. "Lieutenant Jet Wholeman, Homicide." He scribbles my name on the form attached to a log pad, checks his watch, and records the time of my arrival.

While he takes notes, I open my bag, pull out a stash of rubber gloves, paper foot coverings, and a medical mask.

"Kept the house secure, officer?"

"Yes, sir. No one's been in there except three designated technicians, and they have instructions to stay out of the room—the one with the body."

"Good work."

20

With my face mask on, I move to the gloves. I catch the rookie looking up at me with a hopeful expectation, like a bell boy waiting for a tip. Then the realization hits me.

"Jimmy." My voice is muffled through the mask. "I didn't recognize you with that tissue disguise." Leaning down to pull on my foot coverings, I glance back up. "So, pass the detective's exam?"

He beams. "Yes, sir, Lieutenant. Second from the top."

I stick out my hand in congratulations and he gives it a vigorous pump that almost cuts off my blood supply. His enthusiasm reminds me of Batman's young protégé, Robin. I half expect him to yell, "Holy Homicide," but there's nothing holy about this place.

I turn my attention to the fractured front door which bears the distinct markings of a forced entry. Bending down for closer observation, it's apparent the damage is old. The scuff marks and scratches around the lock and doorknob show entry was probably the result of a couple of good, stiff kicks. Exposed, splintered areas near the base reveal pitted brown discolorations of wood rot, suggesting the damage happened months earlier. I maneuver my camera in and take a few shots. The camera only has eighteen megapixels and lacks the magnification power the forensic photographers carry, but suits my purposes. Having plenty of pictures is the best way to capture a crime scene for later review.

Jimmy leans over my shoulder to watch. "I hear you're the best homicide detective the department ever had." He leans in closer. "Looks pretty banged up."

Ignoring his less than sharp observation, I shift my attention. The odor of decomposition emanating from the entryway registers on my olfactory nerve as approximately days. The medical examiner will probably agree on the general time of death, though his configurations will be much more scientific.

I stand up, ready to face the inevitable. "Think I can borrow that flashlight?"

Jimmy fumbles with his utility belt to remove a heavy Maglite and eagerly hands it over. "Anytime, sir."

I open the door. Armed with a flashlight and a firm sense of resolve, I step through.

Though the time is now approaching eleven, the interior is shrouded in darkness. The gloom is eased only by thin beams of light penetrating the plywood covering the windows, and the sharp slashing movement of a flashlight swung by a crime scene technician. Even in the semi-darkness, the Mag is too much. I bag it and pull the mini-mag flashlight from my belt instead. Flicking the mini on, I join the stream of light with the other beams moving about the almost-empty interior.

"Hey, has anyone thought to get some lights set up in here?"

One of the techs looks over at me.

"Roger that. Lights are on the way."

I stop to get my bearings and look around. The baseboards are blanketed in thick films of dust and filth. Several old, tattered mattresses are lying about the floor in the middle of what would have been the living room. Empty beer cans and liquor bottles are scattered about, and mounds of similar trash are piled into several of the corners. Cigarette butts cover the area, ground into a carpet that once served as a convenient ashtray. Near one of the floor mattresses, my flashlight captures something. I squat down for a closer look. There's a box of tinfoil, baking soda, and a Bic pen. In a different world, this could be the innocent byproduct of a to-do list or recipe for chocolate chip cookies ... but I know better. I pick up the pen and examine it. The pen has been hollowed out, rendering it a possible low budget tube for the inhalation of cocaine that's been mixed with baking soda. The tinfoil was probably used for meth, hot-railed.

Through the entryway and into the living room, I find myself walking on badly stained and matted carpeting. Out of the corner of my eye, I see something ghostily luminescent moving toward me. I turn to see a white figure dressed in biohazard coveralls—a forensic tech. I signal to him, pointing to the foil collection on the floor.

"Okay, I'll bag it." He squats down, picks up the materials with a gloved hand and places them in a sterile container.

"And have that pen tested. Might give up some DNA if you're nice to it."

I look toward the kitchen on my left, but a sudden movement from the right catches my eye. Turning, I see another young, uniformed patrol officer in the semi darkness. This one female. She has a paper medical mask over her nose and mouth but, before lowering my light, I catch a glimpse of her large mournful eyes.

She acknowledges me with a nod.

"Which room is the body in?" I ask without ceremony.

Twisting her upper body toward a door directly behind her, she points. "In there."

She swats at something in the darkness. Death and summer in south Florida are a rotten combination.

I move toward the guard stationed at the bedroom door. "No one's been in or out, right?"

He nods silently, struggling with an obvious case of nausea, gulping back a couple of spasms.

I know how these officers feel. Creating a professional demeanor in the face of death has taken me years of practice, but even those of us who do this kind of work well have our moments. I ignore the first rumblings in my own stomach and harden my resolve.

I step into the bedroom.

This room seems even darker with only shafts of light piercing cobwebbed corners. With four steps, I'm at the opening of a small walk-in closet. In the center, under the ambient light, is a small mass. Aiming the light at the figure, my heart misses a beat. The shape is a human, a child, and obviously no longer alive. In fact, the mass is very dead. My mind blinks with the realization that I'm thinking of this poor child as an *it*—pathetic attempt to distance myself. *Focus, Wholeman.*

Four days of decomposition.

I check Amber Alert details, still fresh in my head.

Blonde?

I aim the light beam at the head. Check.

Blue eyes?

Maybe. Hard to tell with loss of pigment.

Female? Check.

Fourteen? Maybe. She looks closer to eleven or twelve.

Last seen wearing?

Could it be?

The periphery of the flashlight beam finds a cloth-like wad of material in the corner of the closet. I lean in. Yes, it's pink.

I can't see what's printed on the shirt, but I know the writing is there.

Here lies Daddy's Girl.

Gulping down a new flood of acidic bile, I silently whisper to the dead form, "Who did this to you, little girl?"

I squat down and move the beam of light around the inside of the closet area. Farthest from the door is the pink shirt and, beneath it, what looks like one white sock. Moving the light back to the body, a white sock still covers one foot, the other is bare.

"Jet?" I look over my shoulder to see Tina moving in from behind me toward the closet entrance. There's sadness in her eyes, the only part of her face showing outside the mask.

"It's her. We need to get started on the photos and sketches."

Tina stands in silence.

"I know this is hard for you, Tina. It's not everyday someone from your own church is abducted—"

"I'm okay."

I wipe my brow with my sleeve. The day is getting hotter and the humidity is a damp weight, gluing my shirt to my skin. This room will soon be a small oven.

Tina leans in closer. "Are you sure it's the Ford girl?"

I stand and face her. "Pretty certain. Size seems to be about right—a teen, small for her age. Description matches." I flash a beam of light in the closet corner. "There's the pink shirt. No sign of her shoes, though. Ask around, would you? See if anyone's found a pair of pink tennis shoes."

"Will do. Does the shirt have any lettering?"

"Let's take a look."

Still on my haunches, I lower to my knees and reach for the pink shirt. Trying to disturb the evidence as little as possible, I lift one corner. There it is. The white lettering.

"Daddy's Girl," Tina reads aloud, her voice barely a whisper.

A bit startled, we both jerk our heads around as a clank of equipment sounds behind us. Maggie, a young crime-scene investigator, stands at the door's threshold, wide-eyed. She normally has a way of bringing levity to the most serious of cases, but she's not smiling today.

"Hey, Jet. Tina." She gives us a somber nod and glances toward the closet. "Ready for me to get started?"

I nod up at her. "Yeah, Maggie, go ahead. The ME is late but do as much as you can for now."

She removes the large camera slung over her shoulder and puts her leather bag on the floor. Squatting next to the bag, she opens it, pulls out specialized lenses and attachments, and begins to make some quick adjustments to her camera. "Okay, I'm ready as I'll ever be."

We part to make room for her as she moves in and positions herself near the body. She systematically snaps pictures from every direction, periodically changing out lenses to emphasize areas of greater interest. As her petite frame maneuvers nimbly about the closet, she makes routine comments about angles and magnification techniques she's using. I'm glad for the narrative, a helpful distraction. All the many routine steps to a crime scene investigation, with its varied fields of expertise, help lend an air of objectivity.

Maggie pauses to make some lens adjustments and zooms in on the body where bruises are visible on the small neck.

"Could have been death by asphyxiation, strangulation," I note. "Sure wish the ME was here for some input."

I point to some dark bruising around the wrists. Maggie targets the area and continues rapid-fire pictures.

"Someone sure had a tight hold on her." My teeth begin to clench.

"Don't worry, Jet, you'll find the slime that did this." She stands up. "Well, that about does it for now."

Maggie moves out of the closet and begins to pack up her camera equipment. "I'll get the rest of the angles when the ME gets here. Time for some fresh air and maybe a shot of something strong."

"I could use some air too," Tina says, joining her. "How about a shot of black Cuban coffee?"

"That'll do it for me."

They head for the door, and as they leave, I hear them exchanging small talk about other crime-scene techs who had or had not been called in. Maggie always keeps the mood light.

My job is not over yet. The room is burning hot, but I'm determined to stay and get a few pictures of my own. I start snapping, focusing on the general positioning of the body, systematically moving to all four corners of the closet. I'll study these pictures later in my office, where I can be more objective.

Right now, I'm finding it hard to think, uneasy about the details of the crime scene. Nothing seems to fit together, or maybe they fit together too well. There's no time for overthinking.

Back on automatic pilot, I keep moving.

Five minutes later, just as I'm about to exit the bedroom door, the ME, Dr. Richard Causeway, makes a no-nonsense entry and a beeline for the closet.

"Hey, Doc, hope we didn't take you away from anything pressing."

Ignoring my sarcasm, he hurries past me.

"There's been no real attempt to hide the body." His forehead wrinkles into a scowl as he stares into the closet.

"Maybe he was in a hurry."

"Or maybe he wanted her found."

"My first guess," he continues, "is that the body has been here at least four days."

"My guess exactly. Well, hate to leave you, but I'm done in here for now. The tech just finished up the preliminary pics and I'm about to go take a look around. Call me if you need me."

I turn to leave, but Causeway remains fixed at the closet entrance.

"Poor kid," he mumbles, shaking his balding head.

Doctor Richard Causeway is normally clinical and emotionless. This sensitivity is something new.

He spits out a couple of curses. "May the guy who did this have a painful journey to hell."

It was the closest thing to a prayer I'd ever heard him make.

I don't stay long enough to say amen.

I move on, flashlight leading, looking for anything and everything. I feel like a kid in a cemetery on a Halloween scavenger hunt. I turn down a narrow hall, stopping at a small bathroom entrance. There, a crime scene tech is squatting over the toilet, collecting things like hair follicles, urine droppings, and, if he gets lucky, maybe even a saliva sample. Of course, that's on the off chance someone hugged the porcelain bowl after a combination of say, eight balls, beer, and a pepperoni pizza.

Without looking up he gives me a nod.

"Is that you, Mike?"

"Yep, it's me." With a pair of tweezers, he picks up a hair from the toilet seat and places the evidence in a plastic bag. "You know I always wanted to be a plumber."

"That and a wanna-be golfer. You up for a game next week?"

"Got it. But you better work on that slice of yours."

I continue watching him. "Find anything of interest?"

"Nothing but bathroom sludge, hair, and toilet paper. All the things that talk to me."

A glint of something catches my eye from behind the toilet seat. I move my flashlight, lighting up a broken light bulb. A seemingly benign article, but more likely a makeshift device for heating and smoking drugs.

"Grab that would ya, Mike?"

He leans in and retrieves the bulb with a gloved hand. The upper end of the bulb is shattered, and the interior is a burned brown. With a knowing nod, he silently bags it, then returns his attention to the ignoble toilet seat. "You know, Jet, this seat might turn out to be a great undercover snitch. The one that gives up the secrets of all its former compadres."

"And I'm pretty sure they're all dopeheads."

Even Jimmy, our soon-to-be rookie detective, would be able to recognize the signs of a well-used crack house. I can almost hear him saying, "Holy Crack House, Batman." But again, there's nothing good in this god-awful place.

"Talk later, Mike."

He nods as he scrapes some green slime from the floor and examines it.

I head for the exit, in desperate need of some fresh air. Time to find my partner.

CHAPTER 4

I don't have to look far. Tina is leaning against an old oak in the front yard, the branches still dripping water under the warm sun and clearing sky. She and a few other milling officers are borrowing some coveted shade from the tree canopy. Tina isn't difficult to spot in a busy crime scene, standing at five-foot-eleven-inches tall, reed thin, and with a head of red hair, you can't miss her. As she scribbles notes on her notepad, the aura of strength and competence she exudes is hard to overlook. She's been in the homicide division for four years and my partner for the same, but despite being given a couple of opportunities for transfer, she's firmly turned them down. For this I'm thankful. We make a good team.

"Tina?"

She brushes away a strand of red hair as her forehead knits. I don't know how she always knows—the years of working together I guess—but her expression tells me she already knows what I'm about to say.

"Sorry, Tina, I need you to get back in there and monitor the scene."

Tina's face flashes anger followed by determination.

I know she's not angry at me, more likely the situation. Nevertheless, spending time with death isn't a job people rush to sign up for.

Feeling a stab of guilt, I look for a diversion. "Wish I'd had a jar of Vicks last week, when I was crawling around for hours under a house looking for evidence. Only thing I found was a dead raccoon." Scanning her face for some sign of sympathy, I find nothing but a set of shrewd eyes.

"Don't worry about me, Jet," she says with a smirk. "A woman will get the job done right."

I ignore the jab. "Make sure you observe everything Causeway does in there. No room for mistakes on this one." She steps out of the sheltering shade into the brilliant heat.

"Got it, Jet," she growls over her shoulder. "I'm not a rookie anymore."

As she leaves, it dawns on me she hadn't been talking much—no wonder I can hear myself think today. Tina would be the perfect partner if she weren't such a chatterbox. Every sort of trivia, on any subject imaginable, is downloaded from her brain to her mouth, like a walking Google head. At times, her information is helpful, or even interesting, but mostly I tune her out like I would the background whir of a ceiling fan. Watching her walk unwaveringly toward the house, I almost miss her customary chatter—*almost*. Still, talk or no talk, she always gets the job done. Today will be no different.

I glance around and spy Martinez, still guarding the middle of the street, invoking his position as Crime Scene General. Pulling off my paper mask, I shuffle toward him, shoving my hands deep into my pockets.

"Hey, got a couple minutes?" I ask through a dry throat. I could sure use a cold drink about now.

"Yes, sir. Over there looks like a good spot." He points to a tree near the sidewalk.

As we head for the nearest refuge of shade, I make a last-second sprint to claim the oak, lean luxuriously against it, arms across my chest. Jose frowns at me as he closes in, and I smile back wickedly. "Can't help it if I'm faster than you, buddy. So, ready to give me the scoop?"

"Okay, so here it is," he says, all business. "Officer Washington responded to a citizen's complaint about a bad smell. He met with citizen, Mrs. Bertha Washington, who lives right next-door, house number 18006—"

"Hold on. They aren't related by any chance, are they?"

"Yes, sir. She's Officer Washington's grandmother. As I was saying, she took him to the house and pointed out where the odor was coming from. Of course, Officer Washington didn't need any help with that." I roll my eyes, nod in agreement, and lean down to pluck a blade of grass. I stick the blade in my mouth and suck the juice out of the root end. Jose looks at me, unable to hide his disgust. "That grass could have pesticides or . . ."

"Live on the edge a little, Martinez. You might enjoy life more."

He takes a moment to adjust his cap, straighten his utility belt. Wiping his brow, he opens his mouth and closes it again, looks down, and begins to study his meticulously spit-shined shoes, as if trying to locate a flaw.

"Sorry for the interruption, Martinez. Go ahead."

He starts up his report and stops. "This is one of those times when I hate the job," he finally sputters. "I have four daughters under the age of ten ..."

I reach over and put my hand on his shoulder. "I think you're speaking for all of us, Jose."

The gesture felt good. *I'm really not such a bad guy.*

Jose lifts his chin, seemingly encouraged, and continues his clipped, monotone report. "Washington saw the house was deserted, the front door showing signs of forced entry. He proceeded to enter, weapon drawn, and found his way to a back, bedroom closet where he discovered a dead body, a young girl. He immediately exited the premises and proceeded to vomit his lunch in the yard."

"Uh, you can leave that part out of the report."

Martinez straightens his cap again, scribbles on the page, and clears his throat. "Good man, Washington. He took it hard. He has a little sister about the same age as the kid inside. Crimes like this make you feel like no kid is safe ..."

I stop listening. Martinez is breaking my personal rule—Don't mix family with business. Not on a homicide crime scene. This rule acts as a safety barrier. Despite my best efforts, thoughts of my boys, Shane and Max, steal into my mind. Unfortunately, I might have to miss another soccer game tonight. I picture them running carefree in the lowering sun, the other fathers yelling from the sidelines. A wave of disappointment strikes, and I make my second vow today to be a better father. But I can't think about that now. There's always a tomorrow. Then, I think of that young girl entombed in the closet. There's no tomorrow for her.

I wish I had a silver bullet to protect my children. I wish I could protect them all.

Martinez goes on talking. "My little one, Josita, is a friendly little thing. Has no understanding of the word *stranger*. She tries to wander off in a crowd."

My mind wanders too, finding no safe place.

It's times like these I'm glad for the safety rules Sydney and I've put in place for our boys. Shane, at nine years old, is pushing for more independence, and Max, age seven, is ready to follow his brother anywhere. When they go to the neighborhood park or to a friend's house, we always make sure they employ the buddy system and carry cell phones for emergencies. We feel bad about the whole "stranger-danger" concept with all its incumbent lack of natural friendliness, but we enforce the idea just the same. Though most parents have rules, I guess you could say I've taken things to the next level.

Sydney was a little nervous when I first started taking them through simulation drills designed to teach the proper response to specific life-threatening situations. One of my personal favorites was the vehicular trunk drill—the boys got a real bang out of the exercise. I can still see them howling and laughing as they climbed into the trunk beside me to learn how to disconnect the brake lights, then use those same lights to flash an SOS code for help. Granted, it's not every day a kid, or anyone for that matter, gets locked in a trunk, but there it is, the hyper-vigilance that comes with the job.

One of their favorite drills was the one where I snuck up behind them, grabbed them in a mock abduction, allowing them to kick, scream, and punch me with all they had. I instructed them not to give up, to fight every second of the way—too many kids go willingly, paralyzed by fear, missing all the important opportunities for escape. Sydney originally protested these drills, arguing I was making both her and the boys paranoid. Personally, I'd rather them be paranoid than dead, like Daddy's Girl. A father can't protect his kids from every harmful possibility but, at the end of the day, I only have myself to rely on. I don't share my wife's trust in a higher power.

An image of the small pink shirt, wadded up in the closet corner, creeps into my mind. I inwardly cringe and shut the vision down.

Another officer approaches Martinez with a crowd-control problem. I call it Morbid Curiosity Syndrome. Taking a couple steps away to let them talk, I look around. Crowds of people are calmly milling around, like they could be getting ready for a picnic. Hard to believe someone's child has been murdered. Not with all this sunshine around.

Without warning, a sense of helplessness washes over me—a feeling that visits occasionally, like an unwanted houseguest. I know only one way to get rid of this feeling—work and more work.

My attention is grabbed by Martinez yelling to an officer and waving him toward some rubberneckers gathering too close to the cordoned off section along the road. When he's accomplished that task, he walks back over to me, resumes his oral report. As he talks, I stretch out my back and neck, thinking about how badly I could use a cold soda.

"Washington called it in, and the perimeter was established," Martinez finally finishes.

"When did you arrive on the scene?"

"8:46."

"Which one's Mrs. Washington's place—the lady who called it in?"

He points to the house next door.

Looking over there, I notice the surrounding crowd is finally starting to dissipate.

"Well, I'll get on it. That about does it for me, Hoser—I mean, Jose."

He flinches.

I put my hand on his shoulder, give it a squeeze. He seems embarrassed at this lame attempt to apologize, so I take my cue and head off in the direction of the witness. With a backward glance, I catch him doing an almost ritualistic straightening of his utility belt.

My conscience questions me. Why do I pick on him? He's not such a bad guy. Except for his anal attitudes, robotic behavior, and strict adherence to rules, that is. They're the type of things that serve to make the rest of us look sloppy. And then there's all those weird compulsive things he does, which shouldn't bother me. Those things don't seem to bother anyone else. Tina, in one of her trivia modes, told me once she thinks Martinez's ritualized perfectionism is OCD.

Obviously, a morsel of knowledge she'd picked-up from some website, Twitter, or infomercial. But compulsive disorders, as far as I'm concerned, are just more psychobabble.

Sydney has accused me of having something she calls a critical spirit. I told her the phrase sounded more like a terminal illness than a trait. Seeing the best in people comes naturally to her, but Sydney majors in music. I major in crime. The way I look at things, my personal grudges and criticisms can be put on or discarded at whim, but a good cop is in it for the long haul. We are in the business of enforcing penalties for mistakes. Mistakes that must be identified. At any rate, psychology gurus have always annoyed me, with all their song and dance about a poor criminal's childhood. For me, anything or anyone who stands in the way of proper consequences is a handicap to society. Back in college, my philosophy professor would have said I sounded a little like Nietzsche, but I'd like to think my philosophy is more a combination of Bruce Willis in *Die Hard* and Tommy Lee Jones in *Men in Black*. Now *there's* some philosophy.

Then there's Tina. She once called me out on my intolerance of psychology pimps. She reminded me that our own department uses a psych profiler to assist in murder cases. I explained to her that was different. A profiler uses an exact science designed to decode the disordered and perverse mind. She countered with, "So science can only be applied to a very twisted mind? What about the mind that's just a half a bubble off the mark?" The way she looked at me, I had a sneaking suspicion she had been referring to my own fine mind.

I'd quickly moved off the subject.

Halfway up to Bertha Washington's yard, I'm now dripping with sweat and unbearably thirsty. An older woman standing in the yard immediately spots me and locks eyes with mine. She is a short, gray-haired lady, skin as dark as night, looking around ninety years old.

Leaning heavily on an aluminum walker, she motions me over.

I introduce myself to her, and as she reaches for my hand, I meet her sad eyes. Before I can divert her, she proudly points out her children, grandchildren, great-grandchildren, and a few great-greats, not to mention some curious neighbors. In the background, their voices reverberate through the air with the telling and retelling of the story of the dead child found next to Granny's house.

Without further delay, I begin the interview, but I have trouble getting control as each family member jumps in, eager to contribute. Their "testimonies" are only hearsay, with a few of their own theories and speculations thrown in.

Trying to hide my annoyance, I suggest to Mrs. Washington the conversation be moved to her porch for some privacy. After I help her up the three porch steps, she painfully lowers herself onto an old, rusted glider chair.

"I'll just sit myself down a bit. Have a seat, Detective Wholeman." She gives me a sad smile.

I pull up an old wooden rocking chair, looking comfortably padded and covered in a brightly colored quilt. My guess is this is her customary seat, which she's offered up to me.

The glider begins to slowly rock with her movement. She gestures a weary arm to a small metal tray beside her topped with a green pitcher and some paper cups.

"You like some lemonade, detective? The lemons come off my own tree."

My mouth waters. "Sounds great. Thank you, ma'am. I can certainly use it."

She pours a glass and gives it to me with steady hands. I take a long drink, draining the glass. "That's got to be the best lemonade I've ever had," I say, wiping my mouth with the back of my hand.

She smiles as she tops off my cup and hands it back to me. I drain that one too, set the cup down, and grab my notepad. "Mrs. Washington, can you please start from the beginning? Tell me what you saw at the house next door." I nod toward the crime scene.

"Why, I'd be glad to. I got nowhere I have to be. Like I said, just yesterday I call the city because all kinds of sordid people were coming and going from that house. Of course, the city never calls me back, so I call Officer Washington. He's my great-grandson." Her chest swells perceptibly with pride.

I smile and nod. Washington's reaction makes sense now. This is his home turf.

"Dayton Washington is a good boy, son of my first grandson, Lincoln, who be the son of my first—"

"Aside from the smell and people coming and going, was there anything else unusual about that house?"

She looks at me with a shadow of disappointment. I had no doubt derailed the tale of the family tree. I have no patience for small talk. Sydney, on the other hand, would have listened until the cows came home.

She sighs. "I been complaining 'bout that house for goin' on two years now. All kinda riffraff been comin' and goin', all hours of the night. I always say, no good comes out of anything that can't be open to the light. Police shows up, arrests some people, and before you know it, they're all back again. Told the city they best bulldoze that house down. I feel something evil coming outta there."

She peers at the house like she's struggling to see through the walls. "I felt something brewing in that house. Four days ago, a great sadness descended on me, so I prayed like never before. I knew evil had visited that house."

"And how did you know that?" I pause to observe her face.

"No one come around again for the last four days."

Bingo. Four days.

She looks up at me, eyes misting. "They all musta seen what was in there and wanted no part of it. That poor little child. But don't you worry none, she's with the Lord now." She reaches over and pats my knee.

Bertha looks out at her family, all still huddled in the yard, then back at me. Her eyes are penetrating in their sadness. I squirm a little under her scrutiny.

"Just a matter of time, you see." She looks upward, as if seeing something of great interest.

I look too, but seeing nothing at all, remain silent.

Slowly, she turns her stare to the house next door. Her ancient, clouded eyes survey the abandoned structure. "Just a matter of time," she repeats, ominously, sounding like a wizened old prophet.

"Matter of time until what?" I try to hide my impatience.

I follow her gaze to the front of the house, then past toward the street where the television news crews are arriving in polished vans. "Well," I say, clicking my pen and returning it to my shirt pocket, "you can choose to be a celebrity"—I nod at the approaching media crew, their cameras already pointing in our direction,—"or you can hide in your house. They'll be over here in less than a minute. Media can be friend or foe, depending on how you look at it."

She pushes herself out of the glider and up onto her walker, waving off my attempt to help her. "I'm going on ninety-six years, Detective Wholeman, but I can still stand on my own. Like they say, use it or lose it."

"That's what my grandmother used to say." I smile.

Smiling back, she announces in cheerful tones, "I best be makin' some pitchers of lemonade for the family, before they get heat stroke. Maybe some for the camera folk too. Come to think of it, I better get some pies in the oven."

"You sure you want to talk to them? The news teams?"

She opens the screen door, shuffles through, and says over her shoulder, "They're friends as long as they tell the truth, but only the good Lord knows what that be anymore."

She turns and closes the screen door behind her. She looks back at me one more time. "Now, you remember my Dayton." She points off to the side yard where Officer Washington stands talking to a couple of neighbors, his face solemn, intently listening.

"He's a good boy, my grandson Dayton, and a good policeman. He like everybody and everybody like him, and that be a gift from the good Lord." I nod distractedly as I look away and back again.

Suddenly, her eyes seem to narrow, like they're burning with emotion. I try to look away but feel compelled to return her stare. With a deep, raspy breath, her voice resonates through the heavy air.

"You best *duck* when you is *told* to, detective."

These words echo around inside my head like sound in an empty bell.

"You *duck* when you is *told*," she repeats.

An unwelcome chill creeps up my spine. Her unnerving stare is followed by one of those sixties, déjà vu moments. I have the odd sensation I'm a kid again, standing before my Grandma Elsie, a notorious Bible-thumper.

I wasn't exactly scared of my grandmother, but I sure as heck respected her. There was this time she chased me two blocks because I'd fed one of her famous apple pies to my beloved, but slobbering, mange-covered dog, Mugs. I thought the nutritious fruit and corn syrup filling would put some fur back on his haunches, but Grandma didn't see it that way. She pulled me all the way home by my shirt collar and thrust me into a kitchen chair. Sitting there, I'd imagined some pretty ghastly scenarios, but she surprised me. Making her way over to the oven, she removed a second pie. She slid the sweet-smelling concoction onto the table as if she was tossing down a gauntlet. "You stole from me, Jethro Caesar Wholeman. This deserves a punishment. Instead, I'm going to forgive you. Forget it ever happened." She paused in her dialogue, looked up like a pilot waiting for audio transmission from an air tower. Her eyes burned with intensity as she began to talk. And talk. Unfortunately, or fortunately, depending on your take, I can't remember anything else she said. I do remember I kept nodding and unabashedly stuffing my face with apple pie. For the first time, I feel kind of bad for not having listened. As fate would have it, she died the next day. Those were the last words she ever said to me, and I can't remember them.

With a jolt, I find myself nodding to old Mrs. Washington, feeling like that same guilty, pie-faced kid again. She smiles a sad smile from behind the screen door.

I return the smile. "You know, you remind me of my grandmother."

"Then I'm sure she's told you about the power of the cross and God's forgiveness." She stares at me. Waiting.

"Those pies wouldn't happen to be apple, would they?"

She chuckles, slowly turns, and walks away.

I stand there alone on the front porch, feeling a bit unsettled. *Duck* when I'm told to? What's that supposed to mean?

I shake off her strange warning and blow out a breath, the one I've apparently been holding. I smile, feeling like I've just been held captive in a parallel universe—a *Twilight Zone* moment—where the odd wanderings of an old woman portend a mysterious message.

I scribble some notes on my notepad and look out at the crowds. What a circus.

Stepping off the porch, I make my way past the knot of media collecting around the reluctant Martinez. I can hear him sternly directing all their questions to the public information officer expert, Leon Karza, who stands calmly in the shade, responding to a couple of reporters. Despite the shade, he's sweating profusely in his shirt and tie, his attention obviously grabbed by the shapely female reporter approaching him, her long graceful arm holding out a cold can of Coke. She's looking suspiciously cool in a white skirt and jacket as she smoothly slides past the other reporters— reminiscent of those cheerful Disney characters who, while waving at families in the blazing summer sun, are enjoying hidden cooling systems beneath their heavy costumes.

Looking closer, I realize the woman is the infamous Andria Wilson. She's one of the city's most competitive reporters, notorious for her feminine wiles. The PIO she's busy schmoozing is well trained, but I doubt the strength of his stamina in the face of his seasoned interrogator. The new trend to have an expert handle, or should I say *outwit,* the professional media, not only complements the department but gives everyone a big break. Cops, especially me, have no time to babysit the press.

Andria catches my eye and smiles. I nod and keep moving. I don't care to be waylaid by a reporter—*any* reporter.

Several other journalists start toward me, but I signal them to stop with an outstretched arm and a disdainful shake of my head. I move on, knowing the wave of reporters will soon surge past Martinez and me and wash up against the Washington family, whose numbers have now swelled to about fifty. The Washington clan in Bertha's yard is busy expressing familial camaraderie. There's back slapping, hand shaking, and heads pressed tightly into one another in comfortable discussion. Despite the darkly oppressive matter that has called them to this undeclared reunion, they seem oddly content, as if they draw light and strength from one another. Like another Florida sun shower.

I think of my own family and how much I need them.

Wiping away the accumulating sweat from my brow, I can't seem to wipe away the nameless, uneasy feeling clinging to my spine.

CHAPTER 5

Notepad in hand, I return to shade of the tired old oak, lean against its trunk, and scribble some final follow-up details from Bertha Washington's interview. Then, I give a tired huff. The day seems to go on and on, and I'm thinking I could use a Red Bull right about now. Sometimes Martinez has a cooler of them, compliments of his wife. I head out toward him. Just then, I hear my name.

"Jet. Jethro Wholeman." A woman's voice, one I know well. She yells to me from across the yard. "Hey! Jet."

I feel my diaphragm flex.

"Don't ignore me, Jet." Irritation is evident in her voice as she approaches.

I come to a reluctant stop and slowly turn.

Andria Wilson has obviously targeted me and is trotting in my direction. I huff a little and make a show of looking at my watch.

Andria and I had dated, ardently, for about six months before I ever met Sydney. But now, many years after the breakup by some weird twist of serendipity, we find our careers crossing paths.

"So, Jet, you're looking good." She shifts her weight to one hip as she tucks a long dark strand of hair behind her ear. "We missed our usual lunch yesterday. Maybe we can catch up tomorrow?"

"Busy. This case has me on the run."

"Of course. But you can still give me an update, right?" There's a microphone in her hand, hanging conspicuously at her side, just in case I decide to spill the beans.

"I'm sorry, Andria. You can see I'm crazy busy." I turn and walk away.

No doubt, Andria is quite a woman, but eleven years ago, we concluded our fiercely competitive natures and mutual obsession with our careers were not a recipe for long-term happiness. Admittedly, the physical connection had been powerful, but the real fuel on the fire was the mental chess game we had going. One of us had to have the last word, the final answer, or the winning move. Even a simple Scrabble game or an evening game show could become a war of wits. The real kicker came with rifle marksmanship. I consider myself fairly good with any type of gun, having won multiple medals in marksmanship during my military service, but it wasn't long before I discovered Andria had some natural skills herself. Her weapon of choice, a 9mm Baby Glock, was dead on at the range. She was also pretty decent with a twelve-gauge shotgun. I worked at hiding my annoyance, but her skill rankled me. The smug smirks she made when the paper targets were brought in let me know my feelings weren't a secret.

"Jet," I hear behind me. "Can't you just give me a minute?"

I keep walking, tempted to look back, but I don't. When Andria and I were dating, there had been a definite temptation to keep things going between us, but common sense won out. We ended up going in our different, tangential directions. As fate would have it, however, Andria's journalism career has recently brought her back into my neck of the woods. I don't really want to work with her, but journalists are a necessary evil. We meet at a coffee joint or some other arranged place every other Tuesday to exchange information on local crime. The meetings are purely business.

At least for me.

She trots ahead of me and once she's made some ground, turns and plants herself squarely in front of me. A playful smile flashes across her face as she reaches into a white leather bag hanging from her shoulder. She slowly pulls out a tall can. I instantly weaken. A can of Red Bull, still perspiring cool beads. I reach for the can, but she pulls it away with a look of mischief.

She whispers, "Is it Mary Ford?"

"Isn't it too soon to be harassing me?"

"But you think it's her." She gives me a sideways look, tucks the can back in her purse with one hand, still holding the mic in the other. She flips her hair back and looks at me hopefully.

I watch her with a certain practiced detachment, but some unwanted memories begin to pop up—evenings at her place, cuddled up on the couch, sharing our dreams of future conquests, the sound of her voice as she'd whisper sweet nothings into my ear, the way she would tuck and re-tuck a strand of raven hair behind one ear. As if reading my mind, she takes a strand of hair and begins to twist it around her forefinger.

"Andria. I'll get back with you later. It's too soon." I turn on my heel and can hear her footsteps following.

Everything about this woman is an assault on the senses—soothing one moment, an injection of adrenaline the next. Even now, her energy seems limitless, but back then her vigor was almost bionic. I never could keep up with her. To my amazement, despite the daily demands of her journalism career, she had been able to keep her apartment ordered and pristine. In fact, she managed to keep everything she owned that way, including her personal appearance, which was, well … immaculate. I don't know why, but her inflexible routines used to both annoy and fascinate me. Tuesdays, she'd pick up her business attire from the dry cleaners. Wednesdays and Saturdays were for yoga classes. Friday afternoons, pedicures. Saturday mornings, the hair salon. Basically, every day was an Andria day. Like clockwork, she started her mornings with a jog along the ocean bordering her condo. After a quick shower, she'd do a routine perusal of the newspaper and sip her steaming coffee—timed to percolate at exactly 7:00 a.m. A coveted treat.

A woeful voice calls after me. "Jet, let's just chat awhile. Catch up on things." The tone is soft, pleading. A new strategy.

I ignore her and keep moving, not sure where I'm going.

"Jet. Give me just one minute. I deserve that. Would you stop? Do you realize we've just walked in a complete circle?"

"Like a dog chasing its tail." I yell over my shoulder.

Does this woman ever get tired?

As my steps quicken, memories keep coming. In our dating days, I'd felt annoyed when Andria would return from a long workday ready for another jog and a twilight swim. As for me, I'd just want to kick back and watch some TV with a cold drink and a box of fried chicken. Andria's idea of an evening of relaxation was vigorous exercise followed by an hour of research on global news.

Despite the trillions of gigabyte storage in the human brain, having devoted any bytes at all to this woman bothers me.

"Jet, would you look at me?" Her voice crashes my thoughts. "I can't understand why you're holding back like this. It's not like you. I thought we were friends. What's going on with you?"

Her annoyance is turning to anger. She's always been able to read me like a poker player, studying an opponent for *tells*. I can feel her now, reaching inside my mind for an extraction. It's a sort of sixth sense at work—what makes her a great reporter as well as a royal thorn in my rear. A homicide detective takes pride in his ability to hide his hand and keep information to himself, but when she's around, I feel like I'm in a hot game of Texas Holdem with someone looking over my shoulder.

I stop abruptly and turn to look at her. "I can't talk to you, Andria." I pinch between my eyes with my thumb and forefinger, warding off the first twinge of a headache. "And put that mic away. I'm in the middle of an investigation. I've got nothing to say."

"You always do that thing with your eyes when you're lying."

I pivot sharply to walk away. Done.

But she's not.

"Jet, you may have a No Comment Policy now, but when the time comes to make a press release, you'll remember me first, won't you?"

I keep walking.

"Jethro? Wait. Don't you want your Red Bull?"

Coming to a halt, I turn back to grab the can from her hand and spin on my heel. Done for real.

"You jerk, come back here."

I walk faster, popping the lid of the can, and take a deep, refreshing swallow. The sugary liquid dribbles down my chin in cool rivulets. As she calls my name again, I wave the back of my hand at her and continue up the street, enjoying my can of cold liquid caffeine.

I reach Martinez who is busy scolding another patrol officer—something I assume comes naturally to these guys with a Napoleon complex.

"Jose," I interrupt, "how long have we been raiding this house?" I nod toward the crime scene and glance back long enough to see Andria still standing in the street, boring holes into my back.

Martinez stops, dismisses the officer with a wave of his hand and pulls a pen out of his pocket, all in one smooth movement. He begins to click the pen in his hand, like some type of Morse code, then slides the utensil neatly back into his front pocket. "We were out here about the last six, seven months. Last time was about four or five days ago. Procedure is to have the investigating or arresting officers search the entire house. If the child was in there, we would have seen her."

Four days. So, close and yet so far. A near hit.

His gaze goes past me, down the street to Andria. He looks an instant too long, his brow furrowing in what could be either interest or distaste. My guess is the latter.

I clear my throat. "We must have had uniforms out at this place just before the crime went down. My best guess is she's been dead four days."

"Yeah," Martinez says, taking the pen back out of his pocket. "That's reasonable." He takes another long glance at the house, a red flush creeping up his neck. "This might have been prevented if there'd been proper follow-up."

"Hindsight won't help, buddy. Let's keep our eye on the ball. I'm going to review the reports from the last couple of weeks, and I'll have Tina talk to the responding officers."

I look around at the milling people while Martinez turns his attention to the roadside. His eyes are fixed on a couple of patrol officers, laughing and backslapping.

I give an exaggerated cluck of my tongue. "That's a real bromance going on over there, Martinez. You better go take care of that."

He grimaces and excuses himself. He's off to rid the world of the misdemeanor of callous, agency mirth.

I turn and see Andria heading toward Bertha's house. I snicker inwardly. I don't want to go anywhere near there, so I figure now's a good time to find Tina and get an update. Before I have a chance to track her down, the FBI arrives. I can easily spot them by the shiny black Chevy Suburban, plain steel wheels, black tires, no logo lettering, and dark tinted windows. The vehicle doesn't have the usual white government plate, just a regular Florida tag—a pathetic attempt to travel incognito. I laugh to myself. They could have spray painted *G-Men* on the side and been less conspicuous.

The door opens, and Special Agent Vicki Anderson steps out, a familiar face from the Fort Lauderdale federal office. We've run into each other on a couple of prior kidnapping cases and high-profile robberies. She's in her mid-forties, average height. Her matronly build is accented by a dark, frumpy suit. Despite her meek appearance, I instinctively know she wouldn't hesitate to pull her sidearm if she had to.

"Wholeman," she yells as she climbs out of the Suburban.

"Hey, Vicki," I return with a wave. "So nice to see the FBI has nothing better to do."

Working with the Feds has always been a total pain for local law enforcement, including me. They come in demanding the lead whether they know what they're getting into or not, and they carry their attitudes in a holster of supreme arrogance. Vicki, however, is more tolerable than most of them.

She approaches with a quick, no-nonsense step.

"Yeah," she grumbles. "We *do* have something better to do. Don't you read your DHS notifications?"

"I've sort of been busy solving a murder crime. What's it about? Some senator's latest affair?"

She huffs a chuckle and extends her hand in a perfunctory greeting. "Seriously, Wholeman, you really need to read your notifications. The terror threat has been elevated to orange in the South Florida area."

Extending my hand, I give her a nod. "Same wildfire threat, I suppose."

She looks back at me with a confused expression.

I look out at the skyline. "We've had rain, but the fires are still a hazard."

She shakes her head. "No, Wholeman, you have some catching up to do. We have reason to believe a religious fundamentalist group is planning something big in the area."

"Really?" I motion her to follow me. "Any *particular* fundamentalist group," I ask sarcastically. "Anyways, nothing of any great importance goes on in South Florida. Haven't you heard? The Great Satan is up north, not down here in the Sunshine State. We only have the city that cocaine built and a potential graveyard of retirees."

Vicki stifles another laugh. "Maybe they think South Florida is the soft underbelly of an evil empire, decadent and worldly. After all, *you* live here, don't you?"

"You sure know how to hurt a guy, Vicki."

I come to a stop, digging the toe of my shoe into the ground. "So, you're here about the Ford case."

"You're a smart one, Wholeman." Her smile vanishes. "So, is it the Ford kid or not?"

"Yeah," I say, rubbing my forehead, "I'm pretty sure it is."

She sighs. "Is the body still in there?"

"Yeah, but the ME is probably packing things up by now."

"Well, I'll have a look." She's all business now.

We move to the front entrance of the house and put on paper masks and foot coverings. Inside, we find work lights have been set up and crime scene techs are still working feverishly in the heat, dripping with sweat.

"Hey," I yell out, "make sure the sweat doesn't contaminate evidence. Try to keep dry."

Vicki huffs. "Get an air conditioner in here before you ask the impossible."

The fans running on a portable generator have reduced the strong odor, but it's still there.

I lead Vicki through the living room and toward the back bedroom.

"Hey," barks a voice, thick with irritation.

We both turn to see Charlie York, the forensic crime scene investigator, chest out and face blood pressure red. He's emerging from a dark corner of the living room.

"This is *my* crime scene," he bellows.

Typical Charlie, a bully every chance he gets. *He* runs the crime scene, and he wants everyone to know this fact.

As Charlie moves toward us, Vicki flashes her credentials. "FBI," she states flatly.

"I don't care what you are."

I quickly intervene. "Come on, York, the FBI are brothers." I pause. "And sisters." I give Vicki a wink. "I mean, siblings of the law enforcement community."

"FBI ain't any sibling of mine." He steps forward, closing in on my comfort zone, so I put out my hand, straight-arming his chest.

He stops cold.

"Shut up, Charlie." I calmly lean in and give his shirtfront an almost imperceptible twist, leaving a clear message. "Go about your business before you say something you may regret."

Vicki takes a step toward us. "I don't have time for your Neanderthal humor, boys. Cut it out."

I let go of his dress shirt and, without a backward look, lead Vicki away.

"Wholeman," he calls after me.

"Later, Charlie."

I hear some snickering and unintelligible whispers from onlookers.

"Get back to work, all of you," Charlie yells.

As we continue toward the bedroom, I inwardly smile, hoping I left some wrinkles in Charlie's shirt. Or, better yet, his ego.

Over the years, York and I've come to realize we've got no fuzzy feelings for one another—something the whole department has picked up on. Long ago, I decided York was incompetent and capable of overlooking crucial evidence. From the first case we worked together, I didn't trust him. Since then, our approval rating for each other has hit a record low.

As we walk down the bedroom hall, Vicki gives me a smirk. "You both get along so well. How long you been married?"

I chuckle. "Believe me, I've tried to end things. But the divorce drags on. He's a jerk with tenure, protected by the union, and—" I cut my opinions short, knowing I've already said too much.

We turn into the bedroom. There, in the middle of the room, stands a metal gurney. On top lays a standard-size body bag, not even half filled.

Vicki shakes her head and blows out a heavy sigh. "Too small. Too innocent."

Movement catches my eye, and I see Dr. Richard Causeway backing out of the closet. He turns, his face grimy and running with sweat.

He looks over at Vicki. "What do you know. The FBI is paying us a visit. How are you doing, Special Agent Anderson?" He snaps off one of his latex gloves with a loud pop.

"Hello, Doctor. So, what did you find?" She attempts to peer around him into the closet.

"Probably the Ford girl." He snaps off the second glove, then drops them both in a disposal bag. "We'll have to complete the ID process, of course."

"I'd like to see the body." Vicki turns toward the body bag.

Causeway hands her a pair of gloves. "Wouldn't dream of stopping the FBI."

The doctor opens his notebook to make some additional entries, while Vicki moves to the head of the body bag. She slowly pulls down the heavy metal zipper. Vicki takes a deep breath and opens the bag. The child's face is revealed.

"God help us," she says under her breath, her body stiffening.

She quickly re-zips the bag and turns to me. "Well, Jet, I don't envy you. I hope you find the dirtbag who did this as soon as possible. It's a shame the death penalty is so slow to be implemented in Florida."

She's right. In Florida, there are people who've been on death row for over thirty years—who will die of old age before the injection ever has a chance to kick in. Meanwhile, there are juveniles serving life sentences who never had the chance to mentally develop or be rehabilitated. The system has flaws, but it's still the best there is.

I finally respond. "Maybe we'll get lucky. If he's transferred to general population, his roomies will take care of him." It's well known within the criminal system that prison inmates hate child molesters—the state has to segregate them for protection.

"Hah," Vicki snorts. "You have a better chance of getting a death warrant signed by a California governor."

Causeway looks up from his notepad. "Of course, he may have a terrible accident during the apprehension process." He gives a wicked smile that Vicki ignores.

"Well, boys, I've seen enough to last me a lifetime." She turns to leave, and I follow, leaving Causeway to finish up.

"Scene's all yours, Wholeman," she says over her shoulder, moving quickly toward the front door. "And this is no longer a suspected kidnapping. That means the FBI will be getting out of your hair."

"Ah, shucks. I'll miss you and the rest of those stuffed shirts." We pass a few stragglers still examining evidence and move outside. Vicki keeps to the sidewalk, walking in a controlled run.

"So, Vicki, off to bag your terrorist?"

She stops, turns, and studies me for a moment.

"I'm not joking, Wholeman. This terrorist warning could be the real thing. Make sure everyone in your department keeps their eyes open."

I hold up my palm to stop her. "Not my job."

She waves me off in irritation and walks on.

At the end of the walk, we step on the grassy swale and stand silent for a moment.

"I've done a few kidnappings, Wholeman. I know how tough they can be, especially when the victim is this young. Work it fast, follow the evidence, and let it go. You can't win them all. You have to move on and live your life."

I stop short, a little taken aback. Who made her my shrink?

She climbs into her vehicle and turns back toward me, a current of anger in her eyes. I realize her lecturing is just as much to herself as to me.

"Don't worry. I'll get this guy," I assure her. "I'll follow the evidence right to his front door if I have to. Hopefully, he'll try to escape." I mimic the motion of firing a gun.

"What a cowboy." She shakes her head and starts the engine. "And keep an ear to the ground about my terrorist. I have a feeling about this, and it's not a good one. Nothing's been the same since that Hamas missile strike just outside Jerusalem. Escalation is to be expected. From all I've heard, they could be right in our backyard."

I give her a quick salute. "On it, Special Agent Anderson."

I turn to go. She can chase the terrorists—I have a murder to solve.

CHAPTER 6

Hakeem Ahbad stepped onto his vehicle's back bumper and hauled himself up onto the bed of the truck. From there, he grabbed the roof rack and swiftly pulled his full weight up onto the cab's roof. He stood and looked out at the orange tree orchard, rich with fruit, and thought of the many bags of ripe oranges stored in his tent. He would delight in their sweet taste for weeks to come, but this land would serve a higher purpose than the production of food.

He took in a deep breath of the sweet-scented air, relishing the feeling of ownership. This tree farm was his coveted inheritance, passed down from his Uncle Omar, who had invested in the land many years earlier. His uncle's son Wajid had been bypassed in the will because of his heathen interest in the art of dance. His young cousin had formed an underground theater club that had dared to orchestrate a performance for hundreds of young college students. The audience had been bussed into a secret place in the desert, but the location was betrayed by a fellow student, and Sharia enforcers showed up. His cousin and all of the dancers were executed on the spot. This was a monumental day for Hakeem. Their foulness meant he would be gifted with the Florida orange orchard his cousin had thrown away along with his heathen dreams.

He scanned the area within the orchard and mentally paced off distances, calculating the many rows of space between the trees. He stretched up on his toes, to see over the endless tree canopy. His gaze froze as it came to rest on a wisp of steam, rising distantly into the air. He knew the vapor came from the cooling towers of the Turkey Point Nuclear Power Plant, just over eleven miles away. In his mind, he could imagine the steam cloud darken, thicken, and engulf the area with radioactive dust and debris.

A broad smile spread across his face.

He turned, hearing the rear doors of the semi-trailer being pulled open. From within, his men—his workers poured out, shielding their eyes from the sunlight. They began milling about, pointing in various directions.

He climbed down from the truck and barked at them in Farsi. "Do not stand around. What do you think you are—tourists? Get that equipment out of the truck." With quick strides, he moved to the back of the trailer and began waving his arms in the air, now yelling in English. "Faster. Faster. Let us get moving."

Hakeem strode off into the field from the rear of the open trailer, repeating the same search he had conducted just a day earlier. He quickly located the marker stones he had set among the trees. "Over here," he commanded, waving his arm. "This is where the first corner must be located." Hakeem became more animated. "Faster, faster. The sooner the tent is erected, the sooner we can commence the digging."

Six men quickly went to work removing canvas and poles from the rear of the semi-trailer. Another three began gassing up chainsaws. Hakeem joined them, shouting commands, even though they knew their jobs well.

The roar of chainsaws filled the air as the men cut down the fragrant trees that stood in their way. Soon, a large tent would be erected in their place.

Two hours passed before the necessary trees had been reduced to short stumps. The dead remnants of the once magnificent trees were dragged away to dry and wither. Another hour, and the large green-khaki tent was fully erect, and a compact front loader was driven down a ramp from the back of the trailer. A forklift extension grabbed and moved a portable toilet and placed it inside the tent. Several more maneuvers offloaded light fixtures, a diesel generator, refrigerator, dirty-water pump, tables, and palettes of foodstuff and water.

The men ignored the hot Florida sun, working diligently, until a beeping tone sounded—the announcement for prayer. Immediately, the men abandoned their work and retreated into the tent—quickly retrieving their prayer rugs.

Hakeem stood in astounded disbelief. The work needed to continue, and prayer was now interfering. He quickly recovered his broken composure, knowing this frustration must be crushed. This was a holy mission, and prayer would be rewarded. The fire in his heart caused him to want to rush forward, to teach these Americans a lesson on both economic and military levels. But he must also go about this plan according to the holy book.

A tall, skinny man named Basaam asked in a timid voice, "Where is east?"

Hakeem paused for only a second and, with a quick turn of his body, pointed over the back of the tent. "Mecca is there."

The men diligently aligned their prayer rugs upon the ground and commenced praying.

Hakeem joined them, slowly and reverently.

Just moments into the prayer time, however, there came the thumping sound of an approaching helicopter. Hakeem jumped to his feet and sped to the open tent flap door, the other men quickly straightening their backs.

Hakeem stood in the doorway listening, silently gauging the location of the sound. He slipped out of the tent and moved along the southern sidewall. Peering down the row of orange trees, seeking after the horizon, he saw, about a mile away, an aircraft flash by, moving west to east. He quickly ascertained it as a private helicopter. As he listened, he felt assured the craft had not deviated from its flight path.

Hakeem's shoulders sagged in relief as a wave of victory washed over him. He threw out his chest and marched back to the tent opening, counting his steps as he went. Forty-four more steps toward success. He tapped his forehead four times. A sense of calm swept over him.

Six apprehensive faces greeted him inside the tent.

"It is nothing," he said dismissively, giving a wave-off with his hand. "Let us return to prayer, and we will be given a victory over the Great Satan." Before his knees met the prayer rug, he added, "We must hurry, brothers. The truck must be moved. It might attract attention."

Everything will be on time. Just as it has been divined. He smiled broadly. He knew his name would soon be great in paradise and in his country. And one day, the world.

CHAPTER 7

Jose Martinez heads for home, feeling the tension slowly fade from his shoulders as he passes the familiar, well-tended yards of his neighborhood. He carefully aims his cruiser into the driveway of a small, three-bedroom house, parking it as close to dead center as he can get—three feet from the garage door, as always. *Home. Finally home.* He blows out a steady stream of air, releasing the breath he'd been holding. He begins to hum as he heads for the front porch. The front door bursts open, and four small girls rush toward him.

"Papa, Papa, *Recogerme, Papa.*" The girls squeal in delight.

"English. In English, girls." Jose chuckles.

"Pick me up, Papa," they repeat in unison.

He scoops up the two smallest girls, one in each arm, while the other two hug his legs. Jose lumbers into the house, the giggling girls still clinging to his legs. Despite the weight they've added to his step, he marvels at the sensation of feeling physically lighter. His daughters' presence always has a way of diminishing the world's problems.

Once in the living room, he drops his giggling bundles onto the living room couch. The two older girls scramble off to the kitchen to retrieve their mother.

He watches as his dark-haired wife emerges from the kitchen, wiping her hands on a worn yellow apron tied at her plump waist. An eager look is in her eyes. Jose can't help but smile when he sees her face smudged with white flour, bright against her brown skin. A wide smile lights up her countenance, chasing any trace of plainness from her face.

Jose, still grinning, remembers the first smile she ever gave him—eleven years ago—at the Florida immigration office. She was seeking American citizenship. He was waiting in line, trying to help his cousin Fabian from Cuba, when he first noticed Angelina standing in the same line. She looked so lost and alone. He was too shy with women to talk to her, but Fabian was the bold, friendly type. Before he knew what happened, his sly cousin had them both talking like old friends.

Angelina could not speak a word of English, but his first language was Spanish, and despite her Mexican dialect, they were able to adequately communicate. Conversation had never been his strong suit, but she made their chat so easy with her encouraging nods and smiles, her eyes wide with interest at his every word. One year later, they married, and Jose had never regretted a moment of those ten years.

"Angelina, *mi bonita esposa*." He wraps his arms around her.

With a laugh, she playfully pushes him away, waving her hand in dismissal. "Go now. Get cleaned up. You smell like old burrito, too much in the sun."

"Okay, okay, but better the smell of a working man than one without a job, his feet always up on your coffee table." He winks at her and turns to leave.

"Ha. Then I would have you out cutting the grass, painting the house. I make you a big sweetie-do list."

Jose laughs over his shoulder and moves toward the bedroom. He can hear his oldest daughters, Aida and Jamalette, chattering as they run to help their mother set the table. At ages six and seven, he is proud they are already behaving like mini versions of his wife.

The familiar distaste of his soiled work clothes, clinging to his damp body, makes him increasingly anxious to shower and put on fresh clothes. He can feel his teeth clenching. Just eighteen more steps to the dresser, twenty-three steps to the shower door ... *ten, eleven, twelve, thirteen* ... He snaps the rubber band on his wrist, barely feeling the usual sting. Quickly opening his dresser drawer, he finds a fresh T-shirt and jeans, neatly folded and sorted by color. As he grabs the clothes, he turns to see his youngest child, Josita, peering around the corner of the bedroom door.

"*Hola*, baby girl. What do you want?"

With her pudgy legs pumping quickly toward him, she points at his head. "Me do, Papa. Me do."

"Again?" He laughs as he lowers himself to his haunches, bending his neck low so she can reach.

Slowly, Josita takes off his police cap, carefully removing it by its black bill. He watches as she brushes the cap twice with her small dimpled hand, walks to the dresser, reaches up, and places the cap carefully on top—precisely center. Jose freezes.

Oh, Lord, not my baby. Do not let her be like me. She is not yet four years old.

With a forced smile, he gives her a playful pat on the bottom. "Gracias, my little *bambina*, now go play. Go on," he says. With a heavy sigh, he grabs his clothes and heads for the shower.

Jose, elbows resting on the dining room table, watches his girls chatter and giggle between mouthfuls of chicken and rice tortillas. Angelina tilts her head and watches him. "Jose, you so quiet tonight. Come now, you tell us about your day, no?"

"Ahh, it's nothing to speak of." His voice is sullen as he waves a dismissive hand in front of his face. "Today was not a good a day. I'll tell you about it later."

Angelina narrows her eyes at him but says nothing. She gives a clap of her hands, with instructions to the older girls to clear the table and attend to their homework. With much clattering of plates, they quickly obey and head for their bedroom.

Josita stays behind and climbs into his lap. He strokes her soft hair and holds her against his chest. *Oh, heavenly Father, please guard my little Josie. Never take her from me. I could not bear it. Protect all my children.*

"What is wrong, Jose? You are sad, I know."

The child's head pops up, large brown eyes questioning. "Daddy sad?"

"No, *chica*, Daddy is happy because I have you."

He sets her down on the ground. "Go play with your sister. Rosa loves to play dollies with you. Mommy will be putting you both to bed soon."

Before leaving, Josita reaches over and snatches the dinner napkin from his lap. She shakes it twice and attempts to fold the linen into a small square before placing it in the center of his plate.

When she is out of hearing distance, Jose says between gritted teeth, "See what I have done to her?" He picks up his napkin and throws it on the floor. "What kind of father am I?"

"Stop it, Jose. You are a fine father. If our little girl grows up anything like you, she will be a great lady. She only copies what her eyes see. It is good for a child to copy a good father, no? She copy her papa's prayers too. She copy his kindness."

"I want her to be healthy and happy like you."

"Me? With my bad English? Oh, Jose." She shakes her head. "And you know I never have a father's love, like our daughters. My papa ... just a bad memory I try to leave in Mexico. You like how I turn out? Then you will much more like how our girls turn out. You are a strong man. Good policeman. You love the Lord. No child can ask for more."

"*Mi amor*, Angelina. You are my pearl. I thank God for you, but you only see me through the eyes of love."

She smiles and grabs for his hand. "I see you through the eyes of God. Now, no more foolishness. You tell me about work."

He takes a deep breath, then blows out. "We found the young girl. Mary Ford. She was in a crack house off East Oakland Boulevard, stuffed in a closet. Dead. But I don't want to talk about it. I want things to feel normal, just for a little while. Let's talk about something else. Let's talk about your day."

She waves away his comment. "This is bad, Jose. Talking is good. Who is the wicked person who did this?"

"We don't know yet. But we have the best detective in the force on this."

"God is best detective. I will say prayers tonight for the child's family. The mama and papa suffer, but little Mary ... she is happy now." Angelina tilts her head to one side, studying him. "But something else is wrong with my husband. Why so worried about Josita tonight? You have seen these things before, no?"

"I just had a bad day."

"You have *problemo* with that detective ... what is his name ... Jet?"

"How did you know?"

"Hah. This is nothing new. He always tries to make you feel low. He call you, how to say, *Hozer*?"

Jose leans back, crossing his arms on his chest. "Why should it matter? Cops talk junk all the time. It means nothing. I don't know why his attitude bothers me."

"Maybe it is because you respect this detective? You want him to look up to you?"

Jose gives a bitter guffaw. "Look up to me? He is a giant of a man, and I'm just a shrimp in its shell to him."

"No. He is nothing but *la Goliath*. You are like David. A mighty warrior."

Jose's shoulders straighten a little.

"And your quiver of arrows is full. You have four children, he only has two," she says with a laugh.

"Two sons," he mutters, dropping his chin. A few seconds tick by. With a huff of disgust, he sits up and hits his forehead with the palm of his hand. "I am a stupid man. Who needs sons when I have four perfect girls?"

Angelina leans toward him. "One day, we have boy. You see, Jose."

"I don't care about that. He just always makes me feel like … like what I am. Short."

"You are, yes … short. But not small. You are a big man to me. I show you tonight." She teases him with a wink.

He tries not to laugh, but he feels the rumble, deep down from within his soul.

CHAPTER 8

The day's not over, but I'm still wired with adrenaline. As cold and colorless as the morgue is, with its white walls and slate-colored freezers, the cool is almost a welcome relief after the day's scorching heat. Almost.

Keeping a safe distance, I watch the medical examiner as he leans over the frail body on the gurney. I don't want to see any more than I have to.

The medical examiner, Richard Causeway, zips up the body bag. Just the sound makes me flinch. "Have the parents identified the body?"

"The mother's brother and his wife came in on their behalf. Positive identification. Mary Ford. She died of asphyxiation caused by strangulation." His tone is clipped, clinical. "Ligature marks around the neck."

I nod, remembering the marks at the scene, hoping beyond hope the poor kid didn't suffer much.

His eyes lock on mine as if he's reading my thoughts. "I don't think she suffered much. There are heavy traces of chloroform. She was most likely unconscious from the start, and with a weak heart, she would have gone fast."

An involuntary gush of air leaves my lungs. I must have been holding my breath. "Any defensive wounds?"

"None."

"That means she was too scared to fight or trusted the guy."

He waves me closer. "I want to show you something." He unzips the body bag.

"I can see from here," I say, a wave of nausea threatening.

"Have it your way. This girl is a most interesting phenomenon. She is what we call an elf. A rare genetic mutation on Chromosome 7. It's believed to be the source of mythological elves in history. You know? Like the ones at the North Pole?"

Poor guy. He's sniffed too much formaldehyde.

He points to her face. "See this? She has all the features. A flattened nasal bridge with a small upturned nose. Large open mouth with prominent lips. Puffiness about the eyes. If the eyes are blue or green, as in this case blue, the iris typically has a starburst pattern. Quite beautiful, actually."

"Are you for real, Doc?"

He opens the mouth of the body with his gloved hands. "Small, widely spaced teeth, as you can see, slightly pointed. And here we can see the typical long neck, despite the small stature. This used to be called Elf Syndrome but is now referred to as Williams Syndrome. It's almost always accompanied by a heart disorder."

Leaning in just a bit, I've got to admit I can see the elfin-like features. "So, does this syndrome account for the mental disability also?"

"Absolutely. Mild to moderate intellectual disability but with strong verbal abilities. This syndrome is a real study in genetics and has disclosed many new ideas about how the brain works. These children have mental deficits, revealed as inactive areas in SPEC scans, but when it comes to music, the brain lights up like a Christmas tree. They are gifted in that area, and some are musical geniuses. Oddly enough, they are called the happiest people on earth."

"Oh, come on. I know fact is stranger than fiction, but this is sounding more and more bizarre."

"I'll agree with you there, Detective. They also have difficulty processing negative emotions. They simply do what comes naturally."

"And what is that?"

"Being happy. Simply happy. The downside is they lack natural fear and social inhibitions. No one's a stranger. Everyone is friendly, trustworthy, and—"

"Hold it right there. What do you mean, no one's a stranger? Like, she'd be the type of kid who talked to strangers?"

"More than that. A child with this disorder will walk away with a complete stranger. Something in their neural pathways that imprint for social fear is somehow missing."

I step back and let out a low whistle.

My mind races to fit this newest piece of the puzzle. This news would certainly explain why there were no signs of resistance.

"There's more. Definite signs of sexual assault. No sign of the perpetrator's body fluids, though something may turn up in serology. This is the odd part. These injuries occurred postmortem. The yellowish hue of the surrounding wounds suggests the tissue never had a chance to respond to injury. Probably inflicted after death. Serology results will confirm that too, but we'll have to wait."

"Hold it right there. Did you say postmortem? She was sexually assaulted, but *after* her death?"

"That's what I *implied*," he corrects.

I exhale slowly, fighting the shiver crawling up my spine.

He snaps off the latex gloves, disposes of them in a biohazard trashcan and moves to the sink. Methodically soaping his hands, he continues to discuss his findings. "This kind of thing is occurring more often. Used to be a case of this magnitude happened maybe once in a career. But now … full moons, changing tides, whatever it might be—something out there is changing."

I wait without comment.

He dries his hands with a paper towel. "Speculation is one thing. I prefer facts. The physiological findings show she was chloroformed, strangled, and sexually assaulted, postmortem."

Anger wells in me. "If there's a hell, it better have an especially hot furnace reserved for the pervert who did this."

The doctor looks at me blankly, as if he's trying to understand my emotion. As far as I'm concerned, these medical examiners are all genetic throwbacks from the Vulcan race.

"Detective, I'll spare you the details, but the wounds involved in the sexual abuse don't appear natural, but deliberate. It'll all be in the report."

"Deliberate?" I repeat, taken off guard. "You mean like these wounds could have been done to *appear* as if she was molested?"

"Could be."

"For what reason?"

"I deal in science. Reasons and motives are your job."

"Causeway, help me out here. I'm not sure I see the difference between a sexual abuser, and one who wants to *look* like one."

Causeway scratches his head. "Speculation is not my strong point, but I'll give it a go. At the end of the day, I suppose they're both the same, but the difference is in the intent. This guy's goal may not have been to achieve arousal, but to make it appear that someone else did."

I drop back into my seat. My earlier instincts about this case were right on. This is not the simple crime scene package all tied up with a bow it first appeared to be.

"The guy is sick." I almost spit the words. "A freak. A necrophiliac."

The doctor shakes his head as he turns his attention back to the gurney. With a couple of quick, mechanical moves, he slides the small body bag back into the freezer.

I sigh an almost unconscious wave of relief. With the gurney out of sight, it's easier to imagine the girl somewhere else—laughing with other kids in some sort of after-life paradise.

"Necrophilia is very rare," Causeway says flatly as he moves to pack up his medical tools. "The obsession is indeed a bizarre phenomenon. Dates all the way back to the fifth century BC. First recorded by the historian Herodotus. His writings say the Egyptians would not hand over their most beautiful and well-known women to the embalmer for four days to make certain they weren't violated."

I wince. "Aren't necrophiliacs predominantly white male heterosexuals?"

The doctor raises his eyebrows in surprise. "Been doing your homework, I see. Yes, ninety-two percent are male, eighty-four percent are Caucasian, eighty-two percent heterosexual.

"I don't know whether to be impressed by your knowledge or worried." This guy may be creepier than I thought. "So, Causeway, I take it this happy hodgepodge of information is just another hobby of yours?"

"If one wants to be more than mediocre at his job, the study of supporting subject matter is essential." He gives an indignant sniff. "And Criminal Psychology was my minor."

"Well, then, while you're on a roll, what is the psychological makeup of these wackos?"

With a snort, he folds his arms across his chest. "These monsters want a silent, unresisting partner. They crave total control to satisfy a complex set of fantasies and impulses."

Trying to take this in, I stand up, massage my tired neck. "So, to put it in layman's language, our murderer is potentially a white, heterosexual male under the age of sixty. A control freak who doesn't like women or conversation."

"Now, hold on a minute," he says, beginning to pace, his hands behind his back. "A scenario involving necrophilia would be extremely unusual. We can't be certain yet."

"So, you have a background in criminal psychology ... with the set of findings you've given me, what would you determine to be the motive? Hatred of women? Revenge of some sort?"

"As I said, motive is not my line of work. I will defer to you on that one."

"Okay. My guess, off the cuff, would be a setup. Someone creating false evidence. After all, you said the alternative is very rare. I'll go with something more likely."

"Could be." He frowns.

I move toward the door and lean up against the adjacent wall—its surface is surprisingly cold, almost soothing after an intense day of heat. With my arms crossed against my chest, I shift into a reflective mode.

Experience has taught me, all too well, there are some crimes that reveal no true motive, only random acts of cruelty. In my mind, the murder of a child makes it difficult to ignore the stark reality of evil, lurking out there, waiting to pounce on the innocent.

I catch Causeway's eye. "Doc, do you believe in evil?"

"Not really. I think it's all genetics."

"Hmm. So, you subscribe to the Bad Seed theory?"

"Exactly." He shakes his head with a crooked smile. "The movie on that one is a classic. Remember that poor guy Leroy, the landscaper? He figured out the young girl of the family he worked for was a killing machine. So, the kid decided to get rid of him too. Set him on fire."

"How could I forget? Leroy's famous words: 'There are small electric chairs for children—blue ones for little boys, and pink ones for little girls.'"

Causeway laughs, a little too hard. "My mother kept me in line with that quote."

"Can't say I'm surprised. Not with the line of work you chose."

"My work is a science, not a fetish. But I do admit it's fascinating."

I shake my head. "You know, Causeway, you might just be a high-functioning sociopath."

"If I were, I'd have nothing to be ashamed of. Sociopaths don't choose their condition. The movie, *The Bad Seed*, did an excellent job of making that point. These emotionless people are mere victims of their own chemistry. Naturally, there are childhood experiences to be weighed into the whole equation—"

"That's a pile of horse manure." I rein in my anger. "Evil is a choice, not genetics. And as far as childhood experiences go, evil can be birthed from a happy home as well as a dysfunctional one. I've seen it all. Cops know this better than anyone else. The criminal's childhood doesn't make them cruel. Sure, it contributes, but that's not the entire equation. I've seen just as many people from horrendous backgrounds choose to take the moral road as those who didn't. Pop psychology is always touting the idea we're all just pitiful victims of our past experiences. Well, I don't buy it. The word *choice* is fast becoming some sort of modern-day religion, but

I rarely see the concept applied to those who steal, abuse, and slaughter others—don't they have a choice too?"

Causeway looks at me with fascination and taps his lips in thought. "I suppose even a genetic sociopath has a choice. A good theory."

"I don't have to theorize. I'll tell you what I know from years of boots-on-the ground experience. The world has more than its fair share of murderous slime, all closer to zombies than to humans. And yes, you and I've seen stuff no man should ever have to see, but obviously we've come to polar-opposite conclusions. I may not be able to explain what generates evil or where it comes from, but I know it exists. And I may not be sure of a god, but I'm certain there's a devil."

Causeway scratches his bald head. "The supernatural is not my field, I'm afraid. I'm a scientist." He moves toward the door and I follow. As we step into the hall, the door closes behind us with a heavy thud. Causeway leans against the wall and removes his iPhone from the front pocket of his scrubs. "I'm about to order out for some Chinese. You hungry?"

"Hungry? Are you even human?"

He dials up a number. "Last chance, Wholeman."

"I like you, Causeway, but not that much. I have a wife waiting for me."

A flash of the conversation Sydney and I had earlier over coffee intrudes on my thoughts. Almost instantly, the discussion looms, like a dark cloud, waiting. Suddenly, Chinese takeout doesn't sound half bad. But being the responsible guy I am, I say my farewells and head for the back door.

The parking lot is unusually dark. One of the halogen street lamps is out. I pat the Baby Glock on my hip and flick the locks open on my car. Leaning up against the car door, I pull out my phone, hit the speed dial, and wait for Tina to pick up. As usual, she connects promptly, her no-nonsense voice sounds.

"Serwathka here."

"Hey, partner. I know it's been a rough day, but can you get the ME investigation reports on my desk by the time I get to the office?"

"Already got them."

"And I need the reports of all violent crimes ever reported at that church."

"They'll be here tomorrow with the two o'clock courier."

I take a breath and think—she is one great partner.

"Also, cross check the names of any local pedophiles or allegations of sexual abuse with a list of all church members. See if there are any matches."

"I'm on it."

"Later, partner."

I end the call. Right now, all I can think of is getting home ... for better or for worse.

I exit the lab parking lot and accelerate onto East Davie Boulevard, the windows wide open. The phone rings. Tina again. I pick up.

"Talk to me," I yell over the rushing air.

"Got some news."

"Better be good."

"Not a chance. A rep from Victims Advocacy just called. He said the aunt and uncle who identified the body of Mary Ford, Donna and Frank Delzin, have requested law enforcement presence when they notify the parents."

"What? That hasn't been done yet?"

"No. Not only do they feel the need for added support, but there's also a medical concern. Apparently, the mother is a diabetic, and they're afraid she could go into medical shock. They want someone with first-aid training on the scene. That would be me." The last word sinks an octave lower.

"I'm sorry, Tina." I hesitate. "I'll go with you."

She lets out an audible sigh of relief. "I was hoping you'd say that. The address is 130 South West Eleventh Place, Plantation. The Delzins will meet us there."

"Okay. Meet you there in twenty."

I thought the day couldn't get any worse. I was wrong.

CHAPTER 9

Tina and I stand at the door of the Ford home, Frank and Donna Delzin beside us. The porch light is on, but the house is dark. Drapes drawn. All is quiet. Part of me wants to get this over with, the other part is hoping no one is home. Frank raps twice on the door and slowly opens it to a dimly lit room. Peering in, we can just barely make out the forms of Mr. and Mrs. Ford sitting silently in the gloom.

"It's just us," Frank calls out as we all step in. The Fords stare up at us from their place on the couch, holding tightly to one another's hands. I look at them, trying to communicate some sort of compassion, but only fear looks back at me.

Frank gestures toward us. "These are the detectives assigned to the case—"

"Was it her? Was it our little girl?" Mrs. Ford tries to stand but drops back into her seat.

"I'm so sorry." Frank begins to sob.

Donna rushes to Mrs. Ford, takes her hand in her own, but Mrs. Ford shakes Donna's hand away and bolts from her seat as if she wants to escape the news. As she blindly passes me, her legs give out. I catch her just before she falls. Mr. Ford jumps from the couch and takes her from me in his large arms, holding her close. He's a big man, at least six-foot-three and broad. She practically disappears in his embrace.

"I've got you now, honey. Just hold on. We'll get through this together."

Tina steps in. "Mr. Ford, let's just get her comfortable on the couch. I have first-aid training, and I'd like to take her pulse, make sure she's okay." She turns to Donna. "Could you please bring a glass of orange juice or something similar?

Tina crouches down beside her and then checks her pulse as she talks soothingly to her. Donna moves to the kitchen, flips on a light, and, within moments, returns with the juice. Tina gently presses the glass to Mrs. Ford's lips. She obediently takes a couple of sips but then, pushes the glass away. "Thank you, officer. You are very kind. I'm okay now." Her voice sounds pleasant, but her eyes look empty.

"She's such a happy girl, you know. Always singing or humming." Mrs. Ford speaks without looking at anyone in particular. "Even her dreams were happy ... except that one."

Mr. Ford steps forward and puts his hand on her shoulder. "You mean the nightmare ... that one where the man was chasing her?"

"Yes. A man with a beard." Her head sags forward.

My inner antennas go up. "Mr. Ford, did Mary or anyone in your family know a man with a beard?"

"No. I don't think so."

I say nothing more. Now's not the time.

Bob Ford sits down beside his wife, Melanie, placing his hand on her knee. She looks toward me, our eyes meet. I know she's looking for someone in authority to confirm her worst fear. I swallow hard. There's no way to soften the blow. It's best to be very direct in these situations.

"I am so sorry, Mrs. Ford. Your brother, Frank, did make a positive identification. Mary is dead." I wait a minute to make sure my words have sunk in. "We are here for you. If you like, we can sit down with you and your husband ... answer any questions you may have."

They stare at me without expression. Their state of shock is apparent.

Bob speaks out, to no one in particular. "This is my fault. I should have protected her."

I lean in and place my hand on his shoulder. "No. It's not your fault. No father can be there every minute. We can only do our best."

Mrs. Ford lifts one arm, listlessly reaching out to me. "Did she suffer?"

I take her outstretched hand in mine. "She did not suffer." I say the words firmly. "The medical examiner stated it's likely Mary never regained consciousness from the start."

Her eyes brighten a bit as she releases my hand and leans into her husband's chest. Mr. Ford gently lifts her chin and looks into her eyes. "My love, this is answered prayer."

I watch in amazement as they take hands and join in an audible prayer of gratitude. I look over at Tina in surprise. Prayers of thankfulness seem out of place, but Tina looks back at me undisturbed. In my book, this odd turn of events is a symptom of shock.

Donna busies herself, turning on a couple of low-wattage lamps. As she moves toward the kitchen, she turns to us with tear-filled eyes. "I'm about to make some hot tea, would you like some?" We decline with thanks.

Bob stands and extends his hand to mine. "Thank you for your time. We know this was difficult for you also." He places his hand on Tina's shoulder. "Thank you for your kind attention to my wife."

Tina chokes up and simply nods.

As we hand him our cards, I reassure him once again. "Please feel free to call us if you have any questions. Day or night."

He smiles weakly and sees us to the door.

Once outside, I turn to Tina. "You did good in there."

"You too, Jet." She looks out into the night. "Time to get some shut-eye. We need to get to the office bright and early tomorrow."

"You lost me after the shut-eye."

CHAPTER 10

Finally, home, I find the house a little too quiet. From the door, I can see Sydney's back as she unloads the dishwasher. "Honey, I'm home," I call jokingly.

"Hello," she says without looking back.

"Today's been one long day. I'm exhausted and dirty as all hell. Gonna take a quick shower and see ya in a couple."

No answer.

I finish taking my shower and flip on the exhaust fan to remove the moisture from the bathroom. I hear someone enter the bedroom. I turn, peer around the door frame, expecting one of the boys eager to tell me about the soccer game—to go over it, play by play, but Sydney enters. I watch her settle down on the edge of the bed and angle herself toward me. Giving her an apologetic smile, I grab my shorts from the door hook. I'm certainly not shy about nudity, but for some reason, I have a sudden urge to cover up. I work fast to get them on, almost losing my balance as I stuff my second leg in the shorts.

"Hey," I say, "sorry I couldn't get home earlier for dinner."

She waves her hand in dismissal. "It's okay. I kept it warm. The boys ate and went straight to bed. They were exhausted."

Dressed now, I step toward her. "Wow, I forgot how late it was. Did they win the game?" I'm hoping to keep the conversation light.

"I'll let you them tell you about it tomorrow. Have a seat." She pats the bedside. "I'd like to talk." She thwarts my next move like an expert chess player.

I remain standing. "That shower felt great. Been looking forward to it all day."

She gives me a weak smile.

I notice my clothes have already been neatly laid out for me on the bedside. I also notice how freshly inviting she looks, so attractive in a white cotton sundress. The intoxicating blend of her shampoo and tea-rose perfume fills the air. I'm tempted to forget how tired I am, forget dinner, and take her into my arms. Instead, I move past her and grab my clothes.

She reaches out and touches my arm, meeting my eyes with a silent plea. A beat of time. I look back into her eyes with a flicker of hope. Maybe she's forgotten her earlier irritation and is giving me the go-ahead signal, the one that would cause me to close the bedroom door and forget everything but the aroma of her warm skin. But I'm getting a different signal.

Her stiff demeanor makes it obvious she's ready for the talk that's been so neatly sidestepped. Was that only this morning? It seems ages ago. I remember the parting look of disappointment in her eyes as she left the coffee shop. I know I'm in some kind of trouble, but which one of the many possible offenses I committed isn't registering.

Before I can stop myself, I blurt out, "What's the matter, honey?"

"I think you know. We need to talk." Her voice has a firmness that defies argument.

"Right now?" I can imagine that stupid husband look on my face. The day has drained me, and the last thing I want to do is talk about personal problems. There's nothing like the death of a child to sap your energy.

She looks up at me, her back ramrod straight, arms locked against her body. She's wearing the same expression I wear when cross-examining a suspect.

"Yes, now."

"But what about that dinner?" All I can think about is sneaking in to kiss my sleeping children good-night and then seriously vegging out in front of the TV.

"I need to know, now."

Sinking down on the bed beside her, I can't quite hide the huff of air I let out.

I do a quick review of possible domestic crimes I've committed. She mentioned Andria, but I'm certain there's more. She's the past. I do a quick review. I missed three family dinners this week, there's the Baby Glock I put on credit, and the recent increase in Netflix use.

I assure myself I'm not one of those deadbeat husbands, locked in escape mode. These crime related TV shows are a sort of career resource for new ideas. Granted, most of the action is pure Hollywood, but something can always be gleaned from it. Well … at least some of the time.

That must be it. Too much TV. Women need conversation. Relief floods me. This is something I can fix. She loves that chick series *Downton Abbey*. I could pull up some old episodes to watch with her. Out of the corner of my eye, I manage to check the time on the wall clock. 8:52. I do some quick calculations. If this conversation is tied up, in say, ten minutes, I'll be able to grab dinner and be planted in front of the TV by nine for tonight's episode of *Sherlock Holmes*.

Negotiation time. Ready to make some major concessions, I strategically place my hand on her knee. She strategically removes it.

"Are you seeing her?" Her voice cuts through my thoughts.

"What?" My face pulls back in surprise. Something about the way she intones the words, *seeing her*, holds a sexual implication.

I look away and back again. "What do you mean, *seeing her*? Seeing who?"

Why is it hard to breathe?

"Have you slept with Andria?" She's watching my every reaction.

"Dear God, Sydney." I rake my hands through my hair. Words escape me, though my mouth is open wide.

"You used to date, and you're seeing her again." Her voice is thick with accusation. "Even our friends have seen you together." Tears begin to fall down her cheeks.

"What friends? I deserve to know my accusers, Sydney."

She doesn't answer, but a recent memory of a lunch at Pizza Hut does. I was sitting at a table with Andria Wilson when Gail Summers and her sister Pam walked in. Those two are real talkers. Gail's son is on Shane's soccer team. The rumors must have started and spread from there.

"No, honey, you got it all wrong." I reach out to touch her arm, but she jerks away, her body rigid with anger. "We were just grabbing lunch, discussing cases."

"So, you admit being with her." She shoves tears away with the back of her hand.

"Of course, but Andria and I—"

"Don't you dare say *that* name in my house."

"Okay. *That* woman and I—"

"And that wasn't the *only* time you've seen her," she cuts me off again. "You've seen her other times. Admit it."

I hang my head, pinching the bridge of my nose. I did nothing wrong, and yet, I feel guilty. Yes, I admit to myself. I saw Andria a few times, but those meet-ups were just business. I kept it that way. Andria would have liked our relationship to be more, but I had drawn clear boundaries. I kept our conversations short and to the point. I never discussed anything personal, never gave her any indication there could be more.

"Sydney," I plead, "I only met with her to talk shop. I never—"

"Did you sleep with her?"

"I can't believe this." I jump to my feet. "What is happening here? Am I convicted before trial? Have I been sentenced too?" I begin to pace, massaging my tightening neck. "You're not giving me a chance to explain. The answer is no. I did not touch that woman!"

She puts her finger to her lips to silence me as she rushes to close the bedroom door. "Keep your voice down. I don't want the kids to hear this."

I lower my voice to a whisper. "I didn't do anything wrong."

"You've been seeing your ex-girlfriend. People have seen you." She moves closer, her arm makes a slight forward jerk, and I think for one incredible second she's going to reach out and slap me. But she freezes, her eyes locked on mine. With a sigh, she sits back on the bed.

"It's not what it looks like. I swear, Sydney, I did not sleep with her." I sit down beside her and put my hand on hers. She removes my hand, but her eyes are a shade less accusing. She scrutinizes me, using her feminine intuition scanner.

"Okay," I breathe out slowly. "Yes, I dated her, a long time ago. Before I even met you. It's over. Done with."

She studies me. I'm on her polygraph.

"I only met with her to discuss cases. To get information on investigations, and she wanted the same from me." Then I say something really stupid, right up there with my other Darwin Awards. "Honey, we were just using each other."

Sydney draws back, her mouth open. "How dare you be flip with me." She jumps from the bed, leaving the room with a slam of the door.

Feeling as if all the air had been sucked out of me, I sag under the pressure. I can hear the clock ticking as I aimlessly finger a yellow flower pattern on the bedspread. Pathetic.

Enough. I jump up, ready to prepare a strategy. I'm not known in the department as a problem solver for nothing.

An absurd TV show comes to mind—*Dr. Bill* ... or was it *Dr. Phil*? Anyway, he said married couples often grow apart. Busy lives and demanding schedules eradicate intimacy and may prompt one partner to outgrow the other. I wonder now if this is true of us. No. Sydney and I are both mature adults who find time for each other when it counts.

No more thinking. What's needed now is action.

I change into jeans and a polo shirt, just in case I get thrown out of the house. At this point, who knows? My heart plummets. This could be rough. I remind myself that plenty of mountain camping trips with the boys have prepared me for anything. Let's just say, I know how to pack a bug-out bag. But then again, I could always shack up with my buddy, Mike, in his beach condo. I grab a few essentials from my dresser and head for the kitchen.

I find Sydney standing at the sink, washing the dishes. Even though it's mid-summer, the room seems cold.

"Honey, isn't that what the dishwasher is for?"

She answers without turning. "I *am* the dishwasher."

Her statement seems to have a double meaning.

My skin prickles. There's a feeling cops gets when there's unseen danger—one that keeps them on high alert. The one that makes them move for their weapon. This feels like one of those times, except I've no defense.

Even my usual charm seems stuck like a jammed bullet in its chamber. I'm beginning to feel a distinct fear that my marriage is in danger. Family vacations come to mind. Camping, fishing, boating, lazy days on the beach. I think about the little things like our quiet chats before we fall asleep and our morning coffee together. All these happy images of family life cascade through my mind, all made vulnerable by a terrorist attack of gossip and rumor.

I sink down on the kitchen barstool, waiting for her to open the conversation. Minutes go by as she knocks suds around in the sink.

She finally speaks. "Friends who saw you together said the little rendezvous didn't look like business to them." She turns and fastens daggered eyes on me. "They said you looked cozy, whispering to each other."

I throw up my hands. "Those meetings were simply an exchange of information, confidential material, that's *all*. Our conversations are not the kind of stuff you want busy bodies to overhear. What were they doing there anyways? Weren't they missing a *Young and the Restless* episode?"

She pauses, thinking of her next angle no doubt. Meanwhile, I'm thinking about Andria. Yes, I admit, taking things further with her had crossed my mind on a several occasions. But I didn't. I might have communicated a few involuntary looks of appreciation, ignored too many of her flirtatious touches, but things never went further.

"Honey," I say softly. "I never touched her. You have to believe me."

"There was a time you did."

"I can't erase history, Sydney."

She turns her back to me, slamming the dishes around in the soapy water, bubbles flying.

I can see now this isn't going to blow over like our other minor marital squalls. This is a hurricane force storm.

CHAPTER 11

Hakeem quietly shut the apartment door and turned the dead bolt lock. Covered with dirt and caked mud from the Homestead job site, he focused on getting into the shower—a hot American shower. On the drive back to Ft. Lauderdale, he imagined feeling the hot, soothing water washing away the day's sweat and labor.

He swiftly turned as a penetrating voice came from behind him. "What have you done? You have compromised our mission."

He snapped around to face Meeka. "Do not speak to me like that, woman."

"Speak to you like what?" she continued in English. "I am talking to you as someone who has acted like a complete fool."

The anger flushed red in Hakeem's face. He fought to keep control but could feel his fingernails cutting into the palms of his hands. Back home in Syria, he would have beaten her senseless and then accepted the praise of his brothers. But here, in this American cesspool, he would find himself arrested. He had heard of this kind of incident before. A neighbor would call the police, and they would demand entrance to inspect the woman for injuries.

He inwardly boiled over the nonsensical laws of this satanic country. He must do nothing that might bring attention to himself.

He lowered his voice. "Remember your place, woman." He hissed the words across the room, his neck muscles corded, his chin jutting forward.

"My place?" Her voice contained a strong authority, one that stemmed from familiarity with western cultures. Unfortunately, she knew American laws protected women. She also had extraordinary combat skills, something few women could boast of.

"My place is making sure this mission meets with success." Her voice was shrill in his ears. "Your killing of that girl has nothing to do with our mission."

He sucked in his breath. "It is *my* mission," he hurled back at her. "And you are breaking with your teachings, your trade craft." He lowered his voice menacingly. "We were to have no contact. You were only to use the drop location. You have broken protocol."

She did not respond but stepped silently toward him. "We are here to prove they are vulnerable. We are here to instill fear. We are here to distract them, to turn their attention back to their own defenses. We are here to serve the holy one. We are *not* here for personal missions. Did you think I would not discover your shameful act? Or your schemes performed in that house of squalor and drug use? I am a trained agent. You forget this."

"Silence." He keeps his voice low but knife sharp. "You have been trained to follow instructions without question. If you speak of this again, I will make sure you are the one who lies on the American execution gurney. It is my calling to show the world the infidels are led by evil men who call themselves pastors and priests and yet murder their sheep."

Her face showed disgust. She knew he was referring to the death of the child. She started to speak but stopped.

"Bah." He huffed. "Why do I waste my time on a woman?" He turned toward his bedroom. "We shall blow up or fracture the atomic reactor, yes, but I shall also bring down the biggest church in this city of Sodom."

He turned and raised his hand and shook his fist at the window of the apartment. "Soon, they will arrest this priest of hell, and all of them will see who the true god is."

"This is not the way. Children should not be sacrificed."

His hands shook with rage. Fighting for control, he clenched and unclenched his fists, four times.

He took a deep breath. "That man is a Zionist leader. He must suffer the consequences. And you will suffer consequences if you do not obey. You should have great shame for the western clothes you wear about like a harlot."

"I must fit in. That is my training."

"Hah. Even the brazen women at that church do not dress as you do. You are drunk with the attraction of men's lust."

She gave a thin smile. "You have shortened your beard. You look more western now."

He clenched and unclenched his fists four times. He knew she was baiting him.

"There is one way, woman, you can put your brazen ways to good use. Find out what the police are saying, who are snooping around the church. Pay close attention to anyone who speaks directly to the pastor."

She nodded, just barely.

"Now. Answer my questions. Where is the boy who assisted in the laboratory's medical transport service?"

"Young Kazim is back in Daytona's aeronautics school. His job is done."

"Did you report the graffiti on the bathroom wall as I instructed?"

"Yes. It was painted over last Wednesday morning."

"Did you instruct the landscaper to keep the hedges high on the west side?"

"Yes."

He rubbed his palms together. "You are dismissed."

Things were coming together nicely. Between the fresh paint and the high hedges, his patchwork had been well disguised.

Before she left, she tossed a thin stack of stapled papers on the countertop. "Here is the information you requested."

He turned away and with his back to her, gave his final orders. "Use the church dumpster for the passing of documents. Have no further contact with me."

He walked to the bedroom. He would forget this annoyance and enjoy a hot shower. As he stripped off his clothes, he thought about his next strategy. It was unfortunate she had discovered his plans. One day, he would be forced to deal with her.

CHAPTER 12

Sitting in my leather recliner in front of a black television screen, I kick my feet up on the ottoman and stretch out. Things with Sydney hadn't gone down the way I expected. After our talk, I watched out of the corner of my eye as she put on a baggy pair of pajamas, settled into bed with a book and gazed at it blankly. I never saw her turn a page.

But things are looking up. With my chair now wrapping around me like a pair of fat arms, I can feel my eyes getting heavy, consciousness slipping away.

A half-hour later, I wake up in the same place. The clock on the wall reads 10:55. I jump up, move to the bedroom, and peer in. Sydney's asleep. I move back into the dimly lit living room, turn on the television, and drop back into my recliner. With the remote slightly trembling in my hands, I bring up the news channel.

It's somewhat of a surprise to see Andria Wilson's face staring back at me. She's on the late evening news, covering a story about the discovery of a dead body found in a Fort Lauderdale neighborhood house. She must be standing in for the usual blonde tonight. No wonder she was so aggressive—this is her big chance to shine. With a quick look behind me, I blow out a breath of relief and turn down the sound. I'm alone. Andria's low, almost gravelly voice fills the room, drawing in the viewer. She gives a quick synopsis of how, when, and where the body of the young girl was found, followed by an interview of the information officer.

He calmly explains the evidence is not yet conclusive on the victim's identity. Andria's image flashes across the screen again. With precise professionalism and just the right hint of emotion, she concludes the segment.

I hear a sound behind me. I turn to see Sydney standing in the bedroom doorway, staring at the television. She crosses the room in icy silence, grabs the remote from my hand and drops it dramatically on the couch after hitting the off button. Her back is ramrod straight as she leaves the room.

There's no reason to feel like I've just got caught in the dark with an old lover. But I do.

Leaning back into my comfortably worn seat, I pat the armrest fondly. *Old boy, it's just you and me.* After a day of stressful work, coming home to some form of routine is comforting. Me, my chair, and the TV. I sigh into the darkness.

I wonder about me and Andria. Was there any real implication of a moral crime? The evidence seems pretty slim to me.

"What's the big deal?" I whisper into the dark.

The silent room absorbs my whisper, returning me to solitude. I'm feeling sorry for myself, but this is not about *me*. What matters are Sydney's feelings. She feels betrayed. This makes me guilty as charged, at minimum of a misdemeanor.

But the real question is … am I guilty of a bigger crime?

Snapshot memories of recent visits with Andria line up into a mental slide show: having coffee at the Urban Cafe—her leaning in close from across the table, accenting her words with soft touches to my arm; lunch at South Port Clam Bar on the intra-coastal—watching her return from the jukebox as our old song lamented the air waves—my eyes lingering a moment too long on her long slender legs; the late afternoon drink we shared at a Las Olas outdoor patio spot. I pause at that memory. Andria had ordered two glasses of wine. I didn't care much for alcohol, but I hadn't argued. We'd met to exchange information on possible leads in the Ford case. The meeting started out as business, but eventually, we somehow lapsed into reminiscing about old times. After the second glass, I felt her leg rub against mine under the table. At first, I thought she'd bumped me on accident. The second time felt obviously deliberate. I quickly turned the conversation back to business, signaling the waiter for the check and went straight home.

These memories assault me, one by one. I begin to recall other things. The subtle fantasies of *what if* lurking behind the casual tone of our conversations. The eye contact that may have been a tad too prolonged. And that night on Las Olas, I hate to admit it, she had my ego in the palm of her hand. Her breathy commentary on my excellent detective skills did far more for my confidence than any self-help book ever could.

With some discomfort, I see my defense of innocence is not bearing up under the evidence. I may not have committed the crime, but I'd certainly considered some scenarios. With some chagrin, I admit to myself certain images of Andria and me together had been allowed to stalk the inroads of my imagination. In my own defense, wasn't I just being a typical guy? These insignificant fantasies never hurt anyone. After all, my imaginations do belong to me, unless I'm being indicted by the thought police. Shaking my head in denial as if to an unseen jury, I try to rid myself of these self-accusations. I blow another huff of air into the still room.

With a start, I realize I must have been sitting there for thirty minutes in the shadowy silence. I pull myself up, quietly pad into the bedroom where Sydney lays fast asleep and slip silently between the sheets. Falling back on my pillow, my hands locked behind my neck, I wait to fall asleep, but my eyes are open wide. I slip out of bed, tiptoeing back into the living room, and grab the remote.

An inner struggle begins as I reason with myself. I turn the TV on. Scanning the channels, I stop at something safe—the Hallmark channel. A scene comes on the screen of some goofball guy and his girlfriend eating candied apples at a carnival. He stops to wipe the dripping caramel from her nose, their eyes meet, they kiss. A moron could write this stuff. I flip off the TV.

Considering other options, the chocolate cake in the refrigerator comes to mind, but I'm not hungry.

Returning to the bedroom, I climb quietly into bed. All is still, except for Sydney's deep breathing. At least someone can sleep. Feeling myself sinking into the soft, clean bedding, eyes and limbs as heavy as bricks, I become groggily aware something's not right. The room seems unusually cold and quiet—except for one annoying noise. The clock ticking. Inwardly cursing, I realize I forgot to set the alarm. I pull myself up and grab it from the bedside table. The clock reads 1:05 a.m. A whispered curse escapes my mouth. I have to be up by six and at the office by 7:45 a.m. to review all incoming reports from the scene. There may also be security camera footage from nearby gas stations or ATM machines to look at. My mind races on. So much for a good night's sleep. Usually, Sydney and I drift off to sleep as we talk about our day. The only things to discuss now are Mary Ford or Andria Wilson. Neither would qualify for the lyrics of a lullaby. I stare at the ceiling.

Grabbing my favorite pillow, I determine to look at the bright side of things. I haven't been sentenced to the living room couch. If I can manage a few hours of sleep, I'll be ready to scope out the original crime scene, the place where Mary Ford was so mysteriously abducted.

CHAPTER 13

Jose Martinez feels the adrenaline pumping in his body. He also feels the darkness, the oppression. He leaves the highway, heading toward Sixty-Fourth Avenue off Commercial Boulevard, and slowly circles behind the sprawling grounds of Central Christian Church. Five different buildings are clustered on the property, all neatly manicured, simple in design. Narrowing his gaze, he slowly pulls into the main parking lot to survey the grounds. Police work comes as natural as breathing. And he could recognize trouble when he saw it. If he couldn't see it, he felt it.

As his eyes flash back and forth over the building perimeter, a sudden movement catches his attention at the east corner of the main building. He eases the brakes and peers into the darkness. A cat emerges into the moonlight, the car headlights catching his gold eyes. He lets out a breath. He never liked cats.

He continues to drive, looking cautiously around him, his senses alert.

Seeing nothing unusual, he breathes out and murmurs a silent prayer. He rolls down the window and inhales the sweet night air and the smell of freshly cut grass. Beside his family, being a cop is the greatest blessing in his life.

He pulls out of the lot to circle the block one more time. Headlights appear as a car turns onto Sixty-Fourth—a city cruiser, patrolling outside its area. He slows to a crawl as he approaches the other vehicle, rolls down his window, and meets the friendly face of Officer Dayton Washington.

"Hey, Sarge," Washington says with an easy smile, "What you doin' on this turf? Aren't you supposed to be off duty?"

"Was in the area, thought I'd do a drive-by. Everything quiet?"

"Yes, sir. Nothing's up, but then again, got an uneasy feelin' in my gut about this one." Washington looks away and back again, opens his mouth to say something and closes it again.

"You have something you want to say, Washington?"

"Just … why do you think the kid's body wasn't left on the church grounds or in the field across the street somewhere? This is one huge place—spreads a good two acres. Lot of places to hide away."

Sergeant Martinez taps the armrest in thought. "Too many possible witnesses. The house he took her to was probably familiar, somewhere he felt safe."

"There ain't no safe place now for that twisted son of a—" Dayton stops himself. "You think he could've been a junkie visiting old stomping grounds?"

Martinez shakes his head as he moves to rest his arm on the window frame. "Could be, but I doubt it. It would take a very clever, sober man to abduct a girl from a church without a single witness."

"Good point, Sarge."

Jose thumps the topside of the car door with his palm. Three times. "Be certain to take note of anything you see … even if it's only slightly out of the ordinary. These types often revisit the scene of the crime."

"Yes, sir. I'll be on the lookout." Washington glances out at the road ahead of him and back. "Well, time to get home. I'm still single and need my beauty sleep."

Jose cracks a smile. "Good night, Officer Washington."

He watches his rearview mirror as Washington's car fades into the night. Pushing the accelerator, he wonders what the young officer was doing out here so late. His shift had ended an hour earlier.

Jose turns the cruiser around, homebound.

A minute later, he begins his finger tapping on the steering wheel again. He quickly moves his left hand to snap the rubber band on his wrist—the sharp sting is adequately distracting.

As he heads for home, Jose prays for Dayton Washington as he does every suit on the force. Everyone except Jet Wholeman, that is. God would have to forgive him on that one.

CHAPTER 14

Hakeem sat on a small steel stool at a metal desk—the only furniture in his small, cramped cubbyhole office. Nothing in the room belonged to him. He did not even have a coffee cup. His training had taught him he could never return to this place—there could be no part of him left behind that would allow anyone to track or identify him. He let out a hiss of disdain. Here, he had an office. That heathen church did not even provide him one. They had no respect for his position. Then again, what did they know? Nothing. Exactly why they would never suspect him. What a trusting mass of Christian sheep filled that place. Even though he avoided even the slightest eye contact with them, many continued to greet him with naive smiles. Their hypocritical kindness sickened him.

He scanned the *Ft. Lauderdale Sun-Sentinel* and *Miami Herald*, almost ripping the local sections to shreds, as he searched for the information he so desperately wanted. He moved quickly because they all had to be returned before they were missed.

The discovery of the girl's body was big news, appearing on all the major TV networks. That pleased him. But the lack of arrests and no mention of suspects or persons of interest angered him. There should have been an arrest. There was plenty of evidence to do so.

He finally found the information he was looking for. The church had been named, but the pastor's name had not.

How could this be?

He quickly raised his hand, about to bring it crashing down on the desk. He stopped, realizing this would draw attention. He fought to control the rage and frustration seething within him.

"These American police." He exhaled through gritted teeth. "They could not find a killer if he was standing in front of them holding a bloody knife."

He quickly refolded the newspapers.

At least the Japanese could find criminals when the proper evidence was left behind.

He left his cubby to return the newspaper to the reception area and searched the coffee table for any additional news sources. Something had to be discovered in the pastor's trunk by now. Scouring the table, he found nothing but religious smut. He thought about the impulsive trip he had made out to the church grounds last night. After seeing two squad cars, he knew he had better exercise greater caution. He shrugged off the thought. No stupid cop would outsmart him.

CHAPTER 15

Once asleep, I slept like a rock as always.

I jump up, expecting to find the early morning sun streaming through the bedroom window, but the plantation shutters are closed, and the room is empty. I open the shutters to find a gloomy, sunless day and then remember last night's conflict—like a bad dream. Hitting the light switch on the wall, I vow to fix things.

I grab a pair of my most comfortable khaki pants from the closet and a short-sleeved, collared shirt—I choose a yellow one to make up for the lack of sunshine.

I head to the kitchen, my mind already focused on the case. I'm anxious to get over to the office, go over the game plan with Tina. Posted to the refrigerator is a note from Sydney saying she has carpool duty and left early for a fast food breakfast with the kids. Definitely not like Sydney. I feel my shoulders sag, disappointed to miss the boys again.

Plenty of time later, I reassure myself. I ball up the note, aim it skillfully at the wastebasket—*bam*. Another perfect lay-up. With an inward smile, I know I still have what it takes. I need to set up time for me and the boys to shoot some hoops together. Another day.

Today, I can't afford to waste time on my usual morning routine—eggs, bacon, coffee, and a perusal of the *Sun Sentinel* sports section.

I've got to get an early start on things at the office. I grab my wallet, strap on my Glock, and grab the car keys off the hook as I step out the door. The air is hot and still, the sky a steel gray, threatening more rain. "What a dismal day," I say out loud to no one.

Tina, at her desk, tosses me the front-page section of the *Ft. Lauderdale Sun Sentinel.* "Front page, top."

I reach for the paper and moan as I catch the headline. The Mary Ford story runs on three-quarters of the page. On the left margin is another picture of her in the pink T-shirt. I scan the article to make sure there's no disclosure of information that could compromise the investigation. The department firmly requested this. Thankfully, there's no mention of where the body was found or the cause of death. We don't want to tip off the killer or inspire any copycat murders. There's still just enough information to make my blood boil.

I see another story has managed to grab the front page. The title reads, "Divers Find Child."

My heart seems to tighten and hesitate within my chest.

As I scan the story, I feel Tina watching me.

"Yesterday was a bad day for kids." She heaves a heavy sigh as she moves toward the coffee pot.

My stomach twists as I read on.

Sheriff's Department Divers retrieved the bodies of nine-year-old Charles Garfield and eleven-year-old Skip Scherer from the canal off State Road 84 and Flamingo Road on Tuesday. A third child, Jody Franks, who used her cell phone to call 911, witnessed the incident. The two children had become entangled in underwater growth and drowned before they could be rescued. They were pronounced dead at the scene. Charles Garfield had first become entangled when he tried to swim to the opposite side in quest of a better fishing location. Jody Franks said the boys had swam the distance many times before. Seeing his friend struggling in the water, Skip Scherer jumped into the canal in attempt to help. The second boy also became entangled, resulting in the drowning death of both boys.

My eyes fog over, fighting that old memory.

I was eleven years old and had been playing with a group of friends off Ninth Avenue and the New River—a popular place for kids at the time.

After several hours, the game broke up and everyone went home. I'd looked briefly for my closest friend, Billy Monnot, but he wasn't around. I figured he'd been tagged early, got bored, and went home. Being a typical eleven-year-old, I rushed home to dinner, knowing I was already in trouble for being late. I didn't give Billy a second thought.

At school the next day, I heard whispers and rumors, mounting like dark storm clouds, on the recess playground. Kids were speculating about how Billy Monnot disappeared. By the next day, his death was confirmed. Billy had been found dead in the river. Apparently, Billy had tried to evade capture during the game by swimming the canal. My guess was that he swam underwater to escape being seen. While in the water, he'd become entangled in the canal weeds and drowned.

I flip to the next news page. The article went on to explain that drowning deaths in Florida, caused by swimmers becoming entangled in weed-choked canals, was not entirely uncommon. I knew that. Every time an incident is reported, I relive Billy's death.

This article, along with the Mary Ford incident, strikes a deep chord in my heart. Pangs of inadequacy and failure.

A dark wave of unforgiveness washes over me. Have I failed Sydney too?

I catch Tina looking at me, her head cocked to one side, questioningly. She's annoyingly adept at reading me. A couple years back, when we were assigned to a case involving a teen drowning off Alligator Alley, I told her about Billy's death. The sympathy in those puppy dog eyes of hers now tells me she hasn't forgotten.

In South Florida, drownings are fairly common, but for me, it never gets easier. As I read today's article, Tina is sensitive enough to leave me alone.

After a few minutes, she returns with two cups of black coffee and hands me a steaming cup. "Hey, old man, when you gonna let go of those archaic newspapers? You look like my grandpa sitting there. What you got against online news anyways?"

I roll my eyes up at her. "I like the feel of newspaper. Call it nostalgia if you want, but if I don't like what I've read, I can crunch the mess up like so and ..." I aim the wadded-up paper at the trash bin. *Bam*. Perfect dunk. "Now that's therapy for you. Try doing *that* with your computer."

Leaning back, I stretch in my chair, ready to refocus on the Ford case.

"We have to keep an eye on those media hawks. They could destroy this investigation—incite an uproar and try and force an arrest. I don't want things rushed."

Tina reaches over and picks up the newspaper. "Preachin' to the choir."

She grabs a pair of scissors from the desktop and begins to cut out the Ford article for a hardcopy file. "Let's make sure we get the right guy right from the get-go. I want this punk gone."

She mutters something under her breath, but my mind is off somewhere else. Unbidden images fill my mind of reporters milling about, cameras everywhere, and then Andria Wilson running toward me, the smell of her familiar perfume …

With an inward shutter, I shut the memories down.

Another rain of thoughts. Sydney. Cold and silent. Her back to me in bed.

I stand up, grab my keys, and signal for Tina, but she's already started for the door. We're on the same wavelength when it comes to work. "What do you say, partner? We take a trip to the church, check out the initial crime scene. There's still unanswered questions about that bathroom. The MP team has been through the place with a fine-tooth comb, but we may just see something they didn't."

"Copy that, Detective."

CHAPTER 16

Upon entering the tent, Hakeem was met by the deafening roar of the diesel generator, an air compressor, and the dirty-water pump straining to keep the water level to a minimum in the ever-deepening hole. Majid came over to him and handed him a set of foam earplugs and a pair of shooter earmuffs to protect his hearing from the high decibel assault. Hakeem nodded his thanks as he quickly twisted and inserted the plugs into his ears and put on the muffs. Even so, his ears were already ringing in protest.

Hakeem observed. At the rear of the tent was a twelve-foot wide hole. A large I-beam spanned the void supported by six-foot tall, steel-legged sawhorses. In the center of the I-beam was an electric winch on rollers. He walked to the edge and supporting himself on one of the trestle legs peered over the edge and down into the hole. Twenty feet down, illuminated by incandescent work lamps, he saw three of his men, each wearing identical shooters muffs, working in ankle deep water. The vibrations of a jackhammer pounded his face as the chisel bit and chopped its way into the keystone at the base of the hole beneath the water. Water foamed from the air exhaust as one man wrestled the jackhammer. The remaining two picked up the pieces of debris and dropped them into the large bucket attached to the winch cable.

Hakeem felt a wash of satisfaction. They would be digging beneath the water table. In Florida, a person did not have to dig very deep before striking water, but the pump kept the level manageable.

He felt his shoulders relax.

He pulled back from the edge and signaled to Majid to follow him outside the tent. Once beyond the walls of the tent, they removed the earmuffs and foam plugs.

Hakeem yelled to Majid over the machines loud roar, only barely diminished. "How far down are we, brother?"

Majid pulled a rag from his rear pocket and wiped his forehead. "Another foot, and we will be ready to put in the bottom plate. We are moving along quickly." He smiled broadly displaying uneven teeth.

Hakeem yelled for all his men to hear, "We are making fast progress. Soon we will have a great victory over the country of Satan." He turned his face to the tented heavens and shouted out praises. The men joined in his exaltation.

Out of the corner of his eye, Hakeem saw Fazel reaching behind his back, swing forward the AK-47 slung over his shoulder, and begin to raise the gun. Hakeem knew Fazel from his time in Afghanistan and knew how he celebrated conquests—firing into the air with hoots of victory. Before he could make another move, Hakeem moved quickly and struck Fazel across the head with the back of his hand.

Fazel fought to regain his balance and then spun around, his face contorted in shock, his weapon held tight. He turned to find Hakeem's automatic pointed directly between his eyes.

Majid was suddenly there, grabbing Fazel's gun hand and twisting it skyward.

"Are you that great a fool?" Hakeem whispered in hissing rage. "Would you call out to the infidels? Alert them with your gun fire?"

Majid wrenched the AK-47 out of Fazel's hand.

Hakeem thumbed back the hammer of the pistol. The metallic click in the still air cried out death.

"Please, my leader." Majid's eyes fixed on Fazel. "Have mercy. He was only trying to celebrate your words of victory."

Hakeem blinked.

"Please, Hakeem, do not kill this fool." Majid grabbed the back of Fazel's neck in a vise-like grip, shoving the thin man to his knees.

Hakeem's eyes bore down into Majid's pleading face.

"My leader?" Majid said, softly. "Have mercy. He is a fool," Majid repeated, "but he is a hard worker and a faithful fool."

Slow moments went by. Hakeem's anger abated. With a sudden turn and the whipping of his gun hand into the air, he cast his eyes back to the massive hole. Soon the job would be complete. He turned back to watch Majid, his hands still on Fazel's neck. Majid's strength could easily squeeze through the muscles until his vertebrae separated. Fazel dropped back to the ground. Majid bent down, knelt on one knee, and leaned into Fazel's face. Hakeem listened closely to hear Majid's words. "The next time you threaten our work, the next time you act the fool, I will seek no mercy for you." Though his fallen assault rifle lay only inches from his hand, Fazel did not move a muscle toward the weapon. Hakeem walked up behind him and laid a hand on his shoulder. Fazel turned his head slightly, his body still shaking.

"You are a fool." Hakeem chuckled. "A very lucky fool. But I spare you for one reason. You are a skilled sharpshooter."

Hakeem watched with disgust as Fazel bowed his head and groveled with gratitude. But he also felt satisfied. He wished all his comrades were as faithful as Majid.

He grimaced as he remembered the conversation from the night before with that unfaithful wench, Meeka. He felt his shoulders tighten as he replayed her insubordinate, screeching voice.

If you were my wife, Meeka, with your beautiful looks and western ways, I'd stone you to death myself. Four large stones were all he would need. His cheeks rose, wrinkling the corners of his eyes. His comrades would agree.

CHAPTER 17

Looking down the church hall toward the crime scene of the Ford abduction, I'm glad to see the bathroom is still cordoned off with yellow tape. It freezes time a bit.

Rubbing my forehead, I look over at Tina.

"Let's treat this like we're the first ones in. Protect the crime scene and step carefully. But before we go in, how about we take a look at the surrounding area? I'd like to get a feel for the layout, and we may find something the MP unit missed."

"Sounds like a plan."

I look to the left, down the wide, long hallway. There are quadruple glass doors fifty feet in front of me. On both the right and left sides of the hall are doors leading to classrooms.

I turn around and step to one side to look around the center of the hallway staircase.

"According to MP reports, she was last seen by her father going through those glass doors." I point to the doors to the right of the stairs. "Mr. Ford took her there just before the service started and watched until she went into the women's bathroom. That last door on the left. He stopped, just twenty feet away, to talk with a friend. Ten minutes passed, and she hadn't come out, so he sent a woman in to look for her. She was nowhere to be found. Simply disappeared."

Tina nods. "According to her mother, this was the only bathroom Mary used. She loved passing by the infant care rooms, so she'd cross the entire church campus to use this particular one."

I turn and put my back to the stairs.

"Right, and it wouldn't take a rocket scientist to know this was the bathroom she'd use on any given day."

Together, we walk the fifty feet to the bathroom door. There's a sign that reads *Women,* accompanied by a stick person in a dress.

I walk back to the glass doors. Passing through, I see a narrow door about fifteen feet from the bathroom. I expect to find a closet, but surprisingly the door opens to the outside. I step into the glaring heat. To my left is a sidewalk bordered by a row of well-manicured, six-foot high bushes that run alongside the wall. At the end of the sidewalk is the eastern end of the church parking lot. Beyond that is a pine tree field enclosed by a chain link fence. Lots of cover for anyone looking for such.

To the right of the door, there are also bushes pressed against the wall, extending past the length of the building. There's a gap in the bushes about thirty feet away. Walking over there, I find a six-foot-high, green metal utilities box attached to the wall, possibly some kind of an electrical box.

We go back inside, greeted by a rush of cold air, and return to the bathroom door. We step under the yellow tape and enter. The room is about twenty-five-feet long, starting with a small barrier room that serves as a privacy feature. On the other side of the barrier, to the immediate left, is a plain, small white couch, followed by four mirrored sinks. Beyond this are eight enclosed stalls, four on each side. The closest two are marked handicapped. Neat and clean, all done in spartan white.

"What do you think?" My voice echoes in the empty room.

"Pretty sterile." Tina shivers.

"Sterile?" I point at the couch. "What's a couch doing in a bathroom?"

Tina snickers. "Haven't been in many women's bathrooms, have you?"

Some things don't require words. I blow her a raspberry.

"Hope the reports include that waste can." I point at a large waste can next to the line of sinks.

"Of course. Nothing found but a million and one tissues."

I walk down the middle of the room and push open each of the stall doors, right and then left, until the final door on the left. The toilet seat is a little scuffed up, some pen marks on the wall, but not much different from the others.

"Well, certainly no signs of a struggle here."

"No. But as you know, often there aren't any in these cases."

"True. And to complicate matters, because this place was well used, any meaningful fingerprints or hair were a long-shot from the start." I shake my head in aggravation.

"Yeah, but they did pick up one partial of the Ford girl's thumbprint."

I nod. "Yep, right about there." I point to an area, just above the interior stall door handle. "But it could have been from a prior time."

"Could have been." Tina gives a sigh of discouragement.

"Three of these stalls have fresh paint. Please tell me they painted before this whole incident."

"The MP report said graffiti was found on the walls and was painted over before the abduction occurred."

"I thought that didn't happen in churches."

"Fresh paint?"

"No. Graffiti."

"Kids are kids, Wholeman. Besides it was just stuff like, 'Billy is hot' and 'Jenny loves Josh'—*tweeny* style."

"Is that what the report said?"

"Yes, minus the *tweeny*."

I turn toward the stall exit. "Let's get out of here, get some fresh air while we take a look around." We leave the bathroom and move to the adjacent exit.

Outside, we find we can't get through or over the thick hedges. But then, nobody else could either, without a serious struggle. Walking the length of the bushes, we scan for any obvious breakage in the foliage. We slow as we approach the outside wall of the bathroom. About fifteen feet from the door, Tina finds something. She motions me over, and we both get down on our knees and peer into the bushes. It's hard to see anything through the dense greenery.

"See?" She points. "Broken branches and some dead spots."

Looking in at the disrupted greenery, I can see she's right. "Could have been an animal, but a pretty big one. Maybe a dog."

I stand up to get a look at the top of the bushes. They're a little above six feet tall.

"There's breakage here too."

Tina joins me and we both stand on our toes, trying to get a better look. Except for some breakage, there's nothing else out of the ordinary.

"Hard to figure. Looks almost like someone crawled from the bottom of the bushes and out through the top." Tina looks at me for ideas.

"Or the other way around." I give her a mysterious look and hum a couple bars from the *Sherlock Holmes* theme song.

She laughs. "You sure know how to lighten things up."

"Sherlock wouldn't give up. Let's try this." I pull my phone out of its holster and press the flashlight app, even though it's still daylight. Scanning the dirt, I find no imprints. Nothing. Then something protruding from the dirt, about an inch from the wall, glints in the light. I return to my knees and, stretching my entire arm and shoulder through the bushes, my gloved hand reaches for whatever lies there. As I pull on the object, I can see a metal-tipped edge of some kind of frame. I tug and out it comes. A small rusted window screen, torn and frayed. With a lot of maneuvering, I manage to move the piece up over the top of the bushes.

"Wonder where this little guy came from?" I hold the screen up for Tina to see.

She examines the piece. "Too small for any windows in this building."

"Well, time will tell. Let's get forensics over here to take a look. For now, we'll bag this screen. Probably been in there for years and finally worked its way out. We'll throw some tape up around here so we don't get evidence trampled by York."

She taps a small bag on her shoulder. "Got it all right here."

While Tina calls forensics, I call to confirm my appointment with Pastor Williams. I've got forty-five minutes to spare, just enough time to do a drive-through at Chick-fil-A.

CHAPTER 18

Tina and I part ways in the parking lot. She's heading out to look at more video footage from gas stations and convenience stores near the crime sights. I've got a date with my stomach.

I gun the car east. It's a five-minute ride for a food fix, but within two minutes I hit a knot of traffic that should break up soon, but for now, I'll just park my brain in neutral.

The blast of a car horn, two or three cars back, brings me back to reality. I release the brake and punch the accelerator, tires chirping on the tarmac as I lurch forward. I meant to put my mind in neutral not in a coma.

I lay on my horn as another car tries to snake its way in front of me. A five-minute drive is turning into twenty, and I'm getting irritable. I should probably turn back, but my stomach growls, reminding me of priorities.

Clouds begin to form, the sun hidden beneath, but the temps are cooler now. Opening up the window, I breath in the fresh, damp air.

Rain begins to fall on the windshield. Heaving a sigh, I lock my mind on the present and stare out at the rain sloshed road ahead. I tighten my grip on the steering wheel and accelerate toward the next intersection, doing my professional best to beat any threatening red lights.

Then I see my destination. Like a lighthouse in a storm. Chick-fil-A.

I turn in and make my order, asking them to hurry it along. Sometimes, it's necessary to flash my badge.

"Official police business." I give an apologetical smile.

The trip back is much quicker, but I need every minute to slurp my Coke and drop morsels of chicken down to the ravenous monster growling in my stomach. The rain starts pounding with such intensity I can barely see two car lengths in front of me. I pull into the church parking lot, cruise up and down the rows of parked cars, looking for a spot close to the building. Spotting a space, I pull in, three rows from the front. The space is bordered by a narrow grassy knoll with a lone shade tree that normally would offer some respite from the scorching sun. Today, the tree just seems to droop in defeat.

I put the transmission in park and check the time on the dashboard clock. I'm ten minutes early. Craning my neck, I try to peer up through the windshield into the downpour, watching the movement of the clouds for a weather clue. The rain is intense, so visibility is low, just slate gray sheets of shimmering darkness. Leaving the car now would be a dumb move, but so is trying to read the weather like a stone-age farmer. I pull up the weather radar app on my phone, which shows rain hovering at the tail end of the city, heading north.

This is Florida. In two minutes, the sun could be shining.

Leaving the engine and air conditioning running, I reach over to the passenger seat and pick up a file, open it, and leaf through the contents. Finding the stapled sheets on Central Christian Church, I thumb through them. Mostly internet printouts. A layout of the church, service times, a list of church staff, and a missing person report.

I look up at the church, barely visible through the pounding slats of water and back down at the file.

The Missing Persons Unit, consisting of only a few officers, had already been by to follow up. They talked to twenty-one staff members, two grounds security officers and three janitors, but now this case is officially a homicide, it's time for me to make additional inquiries.

I grab the manila envelope from the passenger seat and pull the website sheets I'd printed from my laptop earlier this morning. I'd browsed the net, blurry eyed from lack of sleep, searching for any useful material on Pastor Williams and his church. I had no trouble finding articles on the church's numerous community services.

Reviewing the staff details on Pastor Bill Williams, I become increasingly interested. His full name is William Williams. What mother would do that to her kid? His parents must have been a couple of jokesters. I can only imagine what his middle name might be.

I read on. Pastor Bill Williams founded Central Christian Church in 1991 as an outgrowth of a small, home-group Bible-study. After I scan a few pages of information, I can feel my eyes getting heavy.

My body jerks. I must have fallen asleep for a minute. I retrace my thoughts as I suck in a deep breath, tapping my fingers on the steering wheel.

I look at my watch again. Two minutes to go.

My now clearing windshield shows proof of Florida's whimsical rain—all its wet rage exhausted. A lazy drizzle leaves palm trees still dripping under small patches of blue sky. Things are looking up. Time to meet with the pastor.

Turning off the engine, I climb out and trot toward the church offices. I dodge the random puddles, knowing my leather shoes are done for.

CHAPTER 19

The entrance to the offices of Central Christian Church is a standard set up, with two sets of double glass doors, a spacious reception area done in warm tan colors, and a receptionist stationed behind a large wood counter. The room has two modern couches, a glass coffee table, and a few wingback chairs. On one side is a staircase leading to the upper floor—the opposite side has metal, industrial double-doors with opposing, single strip crash bars for an emergency exit.

I make a beeline to the reception counter and nod at the young woman seated there, a plump brunette with a pixie face—Bluetooth attachment in her ear.

She flashes a smile and signals for me to wait a moment as she pushes a button.

"Central Christian Church. Yes, sir. Please hold." She looks back up at me expectantly.

I flash my I.D. "Detective Jethro Wholeman. Fort Lauderdale Police. I have an appointment with Pastor Williams."

She shows no surprise. Police presence has become commonplace here with the missing person and kidnapping investigation going on. MP teams have been out to the church regularly for the past five days.

"Detective Wholeman to see Pastor Bill," she repeats into her Bluetooth.

The church communication systems appear pretty sophisticated. It's a shame more high-tech wasn't put into security.

With a smile, she gestures over the top of the counter to some chairs against the wall. "Please have a seat. He will just be a minute."

Smiling back with a nod, I turn away and do a quick scan of the room. Considering the corporate atmosphere of the reception area, I'm almost expecting to find an espresso or latte machine against one of the walls.

I catch the receptionist's eye. "You wouldn't happen to have any coffee?"

"Certainly. Cream and sugar?"

"Just black." I try to give a disarming smile. I need these people to trust me.

Again, without looking down, she pushes several buttons. "Paul, can you bring up a coffee? No cream, no sugar."

I amble across the room and flop into one of the wingbacks. Nice and soft.

On the glass coffee table are several pamphlets. I pick up one called *The Good News* and page through it.

Out of the corner of my eye, I see a skinny man in his late thirties wearing jeans and a golf shirt. There's a palm tree logo and the words *Central Christian Church* written across his left breast pocket. He enters the waiting room from the side double-doors carrying a Styrofoam cup. As he approaches, a flash of recognition crosses his face.

"Detective …"

"Wholeman, Detective Wholeman," I provide.

"Right. Righto. That's the name."

"It's something I'm usually right about."

He snorts a laugh and hands me the cup.

Placing the cup on the table, I stand to shake his outstretched hand.

"You know, Detective, we met about five years ago. You were investigating the death of Timmy Tyler. You know, that homeless murder over on Tenth Street?"

"Yes, of course. I remember. The case involved two homeless characters, arguing over the contents of a shopping cart. One of them pulled a knife, did some quick abdominal surgery on the other. Were you a witness?" I ask warily.

"Paul Blake." He turns his head slightly from side to side as if he's posing for a booking photograph. "I was the one who had the abdominal surgery."

He chuckles as if it's a good memory.

Fixing my eyes on him, I'm thinking this can't be the same guy. Narrowing my stare, another face just beneath the surface begins to emerge. A similarity? The victim in that particular case had filthy, matted hair—a street denizen who looked to be in his sixties. He'd been found bleeding in foul smelling, greasy clothing that had never known soap. If this was the same guy, there was no resemblance whatsoever, except maybe for the small round eyes and the long thin nose.

A small wave of self-reprisal washes over me—it's my job to remember faces.

Blake grins, his arms held out. "I guess I look pretty different. Things have changed since back then. I'm a new man." He beams with pride. "Pastor Bill stopped me on the street one day, bought me a meal, invited me to church, put me into a rehab program, and the rest is history.

He stops short and leans in a little. "It really is me." He laughs, spreads his arms, and does a three-sixty.

He reminds me of the scarecrow from the *Wizard of Oz* who only wanted a brain.

"I'm really that guy." He gives me a wink.

Hearing the click of approaching feet, we look to our right to see an attractive woman descending the staircase. I glance back at Blake and notice an unmistakable flash of distaste cross his face.

"One of Pastor Bill's secretaries," he explains, touching my arm as if to draw my attention away.

He shuffles his feet a little. "Well, I've got to get back to work. Hope we run into each other soon." Without bothering to make any introductions, Blake flashes a quick smile, turns, and walks over to the receptionist desk.

The woman who steps off the staircase is a tall, dark brunette, somewhere in her late twenties. The swishing movement of her hips suggests she's conducting a silent symphony. Every movement seems designed to capture attention, and I must admit, she has mine.

At the bottom of the stairs, she smooths her red skirt, which seems to struggle to keep the customary two-inch above the knee trend that most professional women adhere to. She crosses the remaining distance and introduces herself.

Smiling at me, she holds out her hand in a slightly European manner, back of the hand upward. A Frenchman would have simply bowed down and kissed it, but being an all-American guy, I take her hand and gently shake it.

"Hello, I'm Meeka, Pastor Bill's secretary."

Her voice is sultry, alluring. Her hand is soft, warm. My mouth goes dry.

In my peripheral vision, I see the receptionist scrunching up her face in disapproval. Not sure whether the look is directed at me or Miss Meeka, I clear my throat and put on a business demeanor.

"Detective Jethro Wholeman, glad to meet you."

Unfortunately, my voice betrays me with a crack. I glance toward the reception area and catch Blake, the former homeless guy, watching us. He has a look on his face that says, *You're pitiful, dude.*

"Would you follow me?" Meeka's voice is breathy and carries a hint of perfume.

She turns and leads the way up the stairs, the silent symphony in full swing. I turn to give a farewell nod to Blake, but he's already gone. He didn't stay to see the show.

As I follow her, I can almost hear the mermaids, calling to the sailors from the jagged rocks. Imagining Sydney's eyes pinned to my back, I keep my eyes on my feet the rest of the way up.

Reaching the top of the stairs, my escort guides me into an open, outer office. At the back of the area sits a woman at a desk topped with a laptop computer, a message machine, a couple neatly stacked files, a full inbox, and a framed picture. On either side of her are two additional doors, one of which is clear glass, revealing a smaller desk— whoever occupies that one must be kept very busy. I move slightly forward and turn to peer through the glass door. There are several, large stacks of files and scads of papers spread across the desk's surface. Meeka surreptitiously follows the direction of my eyes—to what I'm going to guess is her desk.

She gestures to the professional looking woman sitting before us.

"This is Marilyn, Pastor Bill's secretary."

A slight shadow crosses Marilyn's face before she stands, her hand extended in welcome. She gives me a warm smile.

"I'm Executive Assistant to Pastor Williams, Marilyn James." She gives a sideways glance at Meeka. "And, as I'm sure you've been told, Meeka is my assistant."

Something less than love appears between these two.

"Detective Wholeman, I presume?" Marilyn asks pleasantly.

"Right. Jethro C. Wholeman."

She moves out from behind the desk, smiling a patient welcome. She's average weight and height, wearing a dark blue pants suit. Her hair is chin length with a no-nonsense look, face is pleasant in a plain sort of way, no makeup. Unlike Meeka, this woman is closer to what I'd expect for a church secretary. Temperate.

As Meeka leaves through the clear glass door, I take another involuntary look.

A fleeting look of criticism appears in Marilyn's eyes.

"Would you please follow me, Detective Wholeman?"

As she moves away, I grab another look at the picture on her desk. A roasted turkey in the center of a table and a dozen guests suggest the moment is Thanksgiving. One of the smiling faces belongs to Pastor Williams.

Marilyn moves toward a wood-paneled door bearing a flat, simple plaque that reads, *Pastor Bill*. A familial touch.

She gives the door a quick rap and turns the knob.

I steal another quick glance through the glass door at Meeka, who is just finishing a turn around her desk to take a seat. She pulls the chair in behind her, and sits down, her posture surprisingly militaristic. With a long graceful arm, she grabs a file from one of the neatly ordered stacks and begins to type.

"Detective Wholeman?" Marilyn's voice breaks through my train of thought.

"Oh, yes, sorry." My murmur falls flat as I'm ushered into the room.

"Pastor Bill, this is Detective Jethro Wholeman."

A tall, large framed man comes out from behind a desk wearing a pair of baggy jeans and a blue polo shirt.

"Detective, this is Pastor Bill, as we all fondly call him."

The pastor moves toward me with a calm easy smile, hand extended in greeting. He appears to be in his mid-forties, not what I'd call good looking but strong features. He has tousled blond hair and clear brown eyes that turn slightly down at the corners. Puppy dog eyes.

"Nice to meet you Detective Wholeman," he says in a lazy Southern drawl.

His handshake is strong, hands dry, and although his gaze is steady, I detect some strain. He nods at the cup in my hand.

"I see you already have something to drink."

I lift the partly filled coffee cup. "My hourly fix."

He gives an easy laugh, gesturing to three slightly worn wingback chairs for me to sit in. "My caffeine fixes are down to every thirty minutes. I'm trying to drink more iced tea. Can I get you some?"

"I'm good, thank you."

His relaxed style puts a person at ease, but I can't afford to lower my guard. I pick the center seat, closest to his desk, and sit down stiffly. He lowers his large frame into a standard desk chair with wheels.

Watching him, I'm reminded of an ex-football player who's moved past his glory days.

Behind him towers an over-stuffed bookshelf with piles of haphazard books. Well read? Or just for appearances? He leans forward, folding his hands on the desktop.

"I'm really sorry we have to meet under such tragic circumstances. Mary Ford was a much-loved child. She was fourteen but seemed much younger. She was here every Sunday and most Wednesdays with her family. Her father just called me about twenty minutes ago." His eyes meet mine, his voice slightly tremulous. "His heart is broken, as you can well imagine. There's nothing like a father's love."

His eyes redden and water a little.

The emotion looks genuine, but looks aren't everything. Guilty until proven innocent in my book.

"I know the Ford family quite well," he continues. "Of course, your wife also knows them. She knew Mary too, as I'm sure you know."

I give a cough, trying to cover my surprise.

"My wife seems to know everyone."

"Just about. She's well known here for her kindness. We're all very thankful for the support she's given the Ford family. She's one of those rare people who know how to comfort by just listening. And the meal train she arranged for the family was very thoughtful."

"Meal train?"

"Oh, that's what we call it. You know, when church members pitch in to bring meals over each night to a family in need."

"Oh. Yeah, yeah. Of course."

Suppressing my surprise, I swallow down my annoyance this guy knows something about my wife I don't, but should. What else don't I know?

He steeples his hands on the desk. "Our entire church has been praying for Mary for the past five days. And then there's the tragic drowning off 84. I'll be overseeing young Charlie Garfield's funeral as well. A very sad week."

The pastor turns his chair away from me to stare out the only window, a narrow opening in the wall behind his desk. My guess is he's praying.

I give him a moment.

"Pastor, we need to follow up on Mary's abduction."

He swivels slowly back. "Yes, the church will be fully cooperative."

"My department is going to need access to every area of your church, including personnel and their records. Naturally, we would like to see this done without resorting to a warrant."

My statement borders on a threat, but it's the way things get done.

His voice deepens. "Detective Jethro Wholeman. It *is* Jethro, right?"

A slight undertone of anger is in his voice. I suppose this is when he brings down lightning from the heavens.

"Yes, Jethro. But everyone calls me Jet."

His eyes light up a bit. "Jethro, the father-in-law of Moses."

I lean back and cross my legs. "That's nice. But I'd like to think I've got more in common with the all-knowing NCIS investigator, Jethro Gibbs."

He chuckles, nodding his head. "I've watched a couple episodes myself."

Clearing my throat, I push back in my seat. "I'd like to chat, but unfortunately, I'm a little short on time. If we could just …"

"Of course," he says quickly. "I apologize. Let's get back to your request for access to personnel files and records." His demeanor grows serious as he sits back in his chair. "I just want to make it clear, with the exception of our counseling files, which I believe are subject to privileged information, you are welcome to any information needed. You can turn this church upside down and shake it if it helps find the person who killed that innocent girl."

His mention of counseling records jumps out at me. Now, that's something I could use.

He locks eyes with mine, and I find it difficult to look away. His eyes, though deep with grief, are oddly calming. For some reason, I find myself thinking of my favorite spot for bass fishing on the St. John's River.

"There will be no need for warrants," he says calmly. "I believe the police have a God-given authority to do their jobs."

I nod, impressed. "Well, I certainly know now why my wife likes this church."

He leans forward slightly, expectantly, as if a deep question is forming.

Let's not get too personal, buddy. I jump in before he can say anything else. "We also will be needing access to both computer files and hard copies. If warrants are needed, we will provide them."

"I'm not concerned on that front."

There's a timbre in his voice that conveys every confidence a warrant won't touch his church. My cynicism says this sureness isn't in the spirit of generosity, but by some high-powered magistrate in the church, eager to throw his weight around. He and his river eyes won't throw me off the scent. For all I know, he's a con artist clothed in charm and hollow prayers.

"Thank you, Pastor. I'm going to have my people go through all personnel files and talk to everyone on your staff. They'll be arriving late this afternoon and will be here all day tomorrow. Possibly, through the weekend."

"That's fine, as long as they follow the rules of procedure and don't interrupt scheduled services."

This surprises me. I look him in the eye. "This is a homicide investigation, Mr. Williams. We'll have to do whatever's required to get the job done."

His shoulders stiffen a little, but he says nothing.

"I understand your concerns for the church, but with all due respect, Pastor, that's your job not mine. My only concern is to find a murderer."

Even in my own ears, I sound like an arrogant bully, but I've learned from experience people need to know who's in charge from the get-go.

He stands and extends his hand to me.

"Nice to have met you, Detective Wholeman. I don't want to keep you from your work."

That's my cue. I stand and shake his hand.

"Before you leave, Detective, I'd like to ask one more thing. Can you please ask your people to conduct themselves with some patience and discretion during their investigation? There are a lot of hurting people in this church. Mary Ford's death has been traumatic for all of us."

"I understand."

He nods gratefully and looks at me with his river eyes.

For a split moment, I feel like a child.

He leans down to reach for the desk phone.

"I think it would be helpful to you, Detective, if I assign a point person to work with you."

Before I can respond, he punches a number and speaks into the receiver. "Marilyn, would you please send Paul Blake up? If he's not too busy, I'd like him to come up now."

That galls me. "Now wait just a minute."

He stops me, holding one hand up in the air.

"Now, now, Detective. You'll like Paul. He's friendly, easy to work with and knows just about everyone in the church."

"I know who he is. I met him downstairs. And I knew him before he got himself cleaned up. He's—"

"Good," he cuts me off again, "you already know him. There's no such thing as coincidence." He gives me a broad smile.

This irritates me further. What has coincidence got to do with anything? Does he think my previous introduction to Blake is some kind of sign from God?

He puts his hand on my shoulder. "Paul won't get in your way, and I'm sure you'll find him very helpful. If it doesn't work out, just come and let me know."

Somehow, his paternal tone causes me to back down a little.

"Okay, we'll give it a try."

Pastor Bill leads the way into the outer office. Marilyn is just hanging up the phone.

"He'll be right up, Pastor." She smiles.

I peek through the glass door to see Meeka busily typing at her keyboard. I'm pretty fast at transmitting words to a keyboard, but I've got to admit, Meeka makes me look like a snail. She can sure burn up those keys. No wonder they keep her around.

As if she feels my stare, she turns around and looks in my direction.

At some point, I need to question her. For now, I have to deal with Paul Blake.

CHAPTER 20

The dump truck backed up through the open tent flap and came to a stop, the cab section remaining outside. The driver activated the switch that tilted the box. From the rear, as the hinge swung open, large sheets of two-inch-thick steel plate slid out, their heavy edges gouging into the ground. The driver lowered the box, allowing the plates still inside the box to rise in an upright position. He put the truck in gear and slowly moved forward, allowing the load to slide off the rear of the box and drop just inside the tent with a dull but earthshaking thud.

Hakeem stepped forward from the grouped observers, a broad smile on his face. He bent over and affectionately touched the stack of steel plates. Each plate was four feet wide and eight feet long, the same size as a plywood sheet. They had arrived months before in Port Everglades, mixed in with a plywood shipment aboard container ships.

"My brothers," he said in Farsi, twisting himself around to face the men but keeping his hand on the steel. "This will be the weapon that will fire a poisonous dart of fear into the heart of this evil country." He gently patted the steel plating. "We will receive a blessing when we spread the radioactive poison across the whole of this cursed country."

He raised his hand above his head and mumbled in English. "At the least, fear shall return to these infidels."

The driver joined the group, and he and the seven others now raised their hands and cheered, praising their god.

"In truth," Mohammed said in Farsi, "this is the beginning of the greatest day for Islam." He placed his hand on Hakeem's shoulder. "Our prayers will be granted."

Hakeem looked in the man's eyes to find zealous sincerity and fierce pride. Hakeem reached up and put his hand on his arm. Smiling broadly, he said in Farsi, "Brother, we will do this thing together."

Mohammed flushed as he grabbed Hakeem and hugged him. The remaining five men then moved in and huddled together, slapping each other on the backs.

The back slapping went on for several minutes. Hakeem relished the moment, reflecting on the fact that even if they did not cause a break in the nuclear reactor, even if they did not poison the air with radiation, the panic they created would be unstoppable, the victory sublime. But this would not be the only triumph, for he had a personal mission that was progressing masterfully. He would make certain the Christian church was brought low and exposed for its filthy lies. This was his own project—a pet project, as the Americans would say.

As he walked back to his tent, he did not bother to hide his smile. His thoughts were filled with the many ingenious steps he had taken to evade detection by the American police. The first was securing employment in a large network of evil—a Christian church. This provided a great advantage. The job gave him access to all he needed to accomplish his mission. He laughed out loud as he thought of how clever he had been to turn off the surveillance camera at just the right time and to return to switch it back on. All without detection. He marveled at the innovation he had achieved to move the chloroformed body through the small window and into the bushes below. Repairing the wall had only taken him five minutes, using rapid drying caulk and paint. The patch job had blended seamlessly with the rest of the bathroom which had just been given a fresh coat of paint that same day. With much planning, he was able to return less than seventeen minutes later to retrieve the body. His smile broadened as he thought of how he had even returned a third time, in broad daylight, and still escaped detection. To onlookers, he would have just been a common worker, there to do his daily job. But he was anything but common. He was well aware of his genius aptitude. Not only was he clever enough to leave no trace of the daring feat, but there was no one smart enough to catch him. They would never even know his name. But he would know. That is what counted.

CHAPTER 21

Paul Blake leads the way down a hallway to a small office.

Entering, he arcs his hand downward and outward in an elegant gesture of invitation toward the only available seat—across from a small metal desk. As I take my seat, I'm a little taken aback by the tacky mess on the walls—pictures and colorful construction paper plastered everywhere. His desk is filled with books and stacks of misshapen papers. One framed picture peeks out from the clutter.

"Mind if I take a look?"

"Sure, be my guest. That one was taken in India."

Picking up the picture, I see a blond-haired man grinning back at me, surrounded by dark-eyed, smiling children under powder blue skies.

"Everyone has a photo of their families on their desk," he shrugs. "But I have no family. Pastor Bill is all I got. And the church family, of course."

I peer closer at the image and sure enough, the man in the photo is none other than the pastor himself. It's a younger, more tan-skinned version, but still him. He's wearing a red bandana across his forehead, looking out from under the smothering hugs of a crowd of grinning kids.

"Pastor Bill tries to take one mission trip a year," Blake goes on. "That picture was in South Africa. Before he was a pastor, he was a full time missionary. He met his wife, Hanna, on a mission trip to Egypt. She had the heart of an angel. She had to leave her family behind, but like me, she had an entire church family."

I throw him a confused look. "There is no mention of a wife in the reports."

"Oh, she passed away. Died of malaria on a mission trip in Uganda. He's been on his own the last six years. Every unmarried woman in the church has her eye on him." He gives a dramatic roll of his eyes.

I pull out my pad and jot some notes. "They had no children?"

"No, no. Maybe the Lord thought their family was big enough. After all, they helped children all over the world."

"So, Mr. Blake, did you know the victim, Mary Ford?"

"Sure, everyone knew her. She was the friendliest kid you ever met. No one was a stranger."

His description fit with Causeway's diagnosis of Elf Syndrome.

"To your knowledge, did she or her parents ever complain about anyone bothering her, following her, or showing too much interest?"

"No. Never heard anything like that."

"Did the parents have any enemies you know of, or have any conflict with anyone in the church?"

"No, no. Just a nice family. Parents are quiet, kinda shy. They used to joke that Mary found all their friends for them."

"Did you know of any disorder or syndrome that Mary Ford had?"

He shakes his head. "She was a little different, that's all. The good Lord forms people in all different shapes and styles. I believe everyone gets a talent, no exceptions. Mary seemed slow in some ways but gifted in others. Very talented. She played the piano, flute, and guitar. Even wrote music."

I tap my pen thoughtfully on my notepad. A sweet mythical elf came to life only to die.

"Anything else?"

"No, not that I can think of."

I allow a few moments of silence to pass. Sometimes quiet helps to jog the memory.

"Oh, yeah," he says tapping his forehead. "There is something, but it's probably not important."

"Everything is important."

"Well, she got overheated at a church picnic once, fragile little thing. Pastor Bill had to carry her to the pavilion and put cool packs on her head. After that, she adored him."

My attention goes up a notch.

"Did she spend any time with him on a personal level?"

"Not that I know of. But she did want to stop and talk to him whenever she saw him in the halls or at a church function."

"Hmmm, well, I think that about does it for now." I put my pen back in my pocket and stand to shake his hand. "If anything else comes to mind, I'd appreciate a call. Thanks for your cooperation."

"My pleasure. Anytime, Detective. Whoever thought you and me would be cooperating on anything?" He gives a whelp of laughter as he pumps my hand.

Half of my mouth attempts a smile.

As I move to leave, the cluttered wall decorations catch my attention. Just beneath the pictures there's a somewhat scrubby, makeshift timeline wrapping around the room. The ten-inch wide strip of paper, sports colorful child-like caricatures and buildings, bordered with crooked hand-printed dates.

I pause, point to the wall. "Mind if I get a closer look?"

"Sure, sure," he says proudly, following behind me.

I lean in to read the written dates. They start at creation and move through history until a great war called Armageddon. I find the timeline a little obsessive. Maybe even unbalanced. I turn and face him. "Looks like someone put a lot of work into this."

Paul chuckles. "I've got a lot to learn and the more I learn the more I find I don't know."

"Uh-huh."

"And your wife, Sydney, took pity on me and helped me out with some of the artwork. She is one talented lady."

His comment gets my attention, but I say nothing. I'm bothered my wife is hanging around with junkies, and I find it hard to believe Sydney has suddenly developed sketching abilities.

"I'm sorry," I say, consulting the time on my phone, "I have an appointment downtown, and I need to get going."

Paul looks disappointed.

I take two steps toward the door and stop. "Oh yeah, almost forgot." I hand him my card. "Let's exchange phone numbers so I can contact you about anything that needs to be coordinated."

He eagerly pulls out a business card from his pants pocket. "This has the main office line, my direct line, and my cell phone. You can get me on my cell phone at any time, day or night."

I take the card, give it a passing glance, and make my exit. Paul almost jumps in front of me. "Can I get you a soda or something for the road?"

"No, thanks."

"Can I show you the way out?"

"Got it covered."

As I walk down the hall, I turn back to see him still standing in the doorway, his fingertips pressed to his forehead, eyes closed. I get the funny sensation he's praying for me. I shake my head in wonder. Who would ever think a homeless junkie would one day be praying for *me*. Nevertheless, I'm moved by the gesture. Go figure.

Pushing past the traffic, I give the car some gas, blast my horn a couple times, and manage to get to a side road that will wind me back around past the bottle-necked highway. My stomach and I have another appointment with Chick-fil-A, and I don't plan on being any later than I already am. The phone buzzes, screen banner reads *Causeway, Richard*. My stomach rumbles. That's a call I can sit on. Pushing the ignore button, I drive into the fast food parking lot. Ten seconds later, the phone buzzes again. I jab the connect button. "This better be fast, Doc, I got an appointment I'm late for."

"Cancel it. I found something you'll be interested in. Can you come right over?"

"Now?" I look at the time—3:36 p.m.

"The sooner the better. I think it'll help the Mary Ford investigation."

"Okay, okay, Doc. See ya in thirty."

My stomach growls a warning. Don't worry, old buddy, we have a date.

My car lurches forward, straight for the drive-through. My stomach waits for no man.

CHAPTER 22

Heading south on I-95, with the wind hitting my face through open windows, cold air rushing from the air unit, and Caribbean tunes blasting from the radio, I feel this is the closest I can get to an island excursion, at least for now. Another one for the family bucket list.

Unexpectedly, there's little traffic, so I'm free to speed along at a good clip, but rush hour lurks just ahead. Exiting on West Davie Boulevard, I reduce my speed and shove a few fries from my leftover dinner into my mouth. Spotting the familiar medical examiner's office, I make a sharp left into the parking lot and circle around looking for a shady spot. Finding one, I stuff the last of my second grilled chicken sandwich into my mouth and slurp down the remainder of my Coke.

Revived from near starvation, I feel ready to tackle just about anything. As I pull into an empty space, I realize this meeting with Causeway will cut into any time I have tonight for Sydney. Pulling out my phone, I thumb to messages. Nothing. I exhale in relief.

Leaving the engine running, I open the glove compartment, pull out one of Sydney's old church handouts and read the service schedule. There's one scheduled for this Saturday evening. Perfect.

Grabbing my phone, I punch in Sydney's number.

It rings five times before she picks up.

"Hello."

"Hey there. How's your day going?"

"The usual. And yours?" Her voice is cool but cordial.

"Oh, I'm making due. I'll be glad when this Ford case is behind us. Anyways, I have an idea. Wondered if you'd like to meet at church Saturday night? You're always trying to get me there. This is your chance."

A brief silence.

"Okay." She sounds hesitant. "Is this personal or business?"

"You sound suspicious. Can't a man do something right for a change?"

"Okay. I'll meet you there just before six. And Jet? Even if you do have some other motivation, frankly, I'm just glad you're going."

"Me too. By the way, I was talking to Pastor Williams today over at the church ..."

"How did you like him?"

"Seems like a nice guy, but as I was saying, he mentioned you knew Mary Ford. Why didn't you tell me?"

"I tried to tell you ... Anyway, we've not had a lot of time to talk."

"True," I say, not meaning it. Considering my job, her church, and how monumental the entire Mary Ford incident is, I find her statement ridiculous. But I move on.

"So, how well did you know her?"

"Mary and her mother, Melanie, were in the choir, so I'd see them at the practices."

"Mary was in your choir?" This news floors me. "Why didn't you mention this before? I mean we're not talking about the weather here."

"I know. I know. I just couldn't talk about it."

"That's not like you."

Silence.

"It's okay, Sydney. I understand." Of course, it's a lie. I don't get it at all.

"So, what was Mary like?"

"Oh, she was really sweet. Very friendly. At choir practices she would give everyone a big hug. Never left anyone out. She was also very gifted in music. She could sing with perfect pitch and picked up harmonic tones effortlessly. Sometimes she would play the piano for us—played by ear. Her talent was amazing, especially considering she never had lessons. I offered to tutor her in piano at no cost. She was supposed to start next week." Her voice cracked, and she went quiet.

"I'm sorry, honey."

"You know, Jet, I have to admit, I think maybe your survival drills with the boys weren't so crazy after all."

I give a half-hearted guffaw. "How are the boys? I miss them."

"They've been super busy. They've been studying for all the end of the year exams, which they hate, and then of course, they have one activity after another. The Summers family invited them on a camping trip this weekend. They're picking them up early Saturday."

"Sounds great." I swallow down my disappointment. "I want to take them on a fishing trip as soon as this case is over."

"They'd love that."

"Hey, while I still have you on the phone, can you think of anything else about Mary? Anything that stands out?"

"Let me think. Well, her mother did mention once Mary had some type of genetic disorder that caused her to have a weak heart, but Melanie didn't seem to want to talk about it. Mary was obviously different than other teens though."

"In what way?"

"She didn't seem to understand social boundaries and was very innocent for her age, childlike."

"Did her mother ever mention anyone bothering her or the family at church, or outside the church? Or maybe someone who just came off as a little *too* friendly?"

"No. She never said anything like that."

"Ever see any suspicious characters hanging around near the practices?"

"No. Never. This is beginning to feel a little like an interrogation."

"Sorry, Syd. It's habit. Well, if you think of anything else …"

"I will, but I've got to run. Got a class in five minutes."

"Okay, honey, you've been very helpful."

"Jet, one more thing."

I hold my breath.

"I'm still grieving Mary's death, still processing. This hasn't been easy for me."

"I'm sorry, honey. I wish you could have talked to me."

"Another time. I've really got to go."

After we hang up, I exit my car and head toward the ME's office.

It's cloudy out, but I can see the sun just behind the clouds. A soft breeze picks up. I find myself wishing I was somewhere else. Like fishing on a river.

When I enter Causeway's office, he's pacing the floor, deep in thought.

"The blood spatters are all wrong." He doesn't bother to look up, ignoring social convention.

"Wrong? What do you mean?" I can't hide the anticipation in my voice.

He pauses, scratching his head. "The blood spatters bothered me from the very start."

"Well, why didn't you say anything then?"

"I didn't say anything because it's not my style to speak prematurely. My nature is one of exactitude."

"Well *exactitude* me already. I missed an important appointment for this."

"I'm trying to get there, if you'd stop interrupting." He crosses his arms on his chest. "Anyway, I ventured to do some independent study and found the spatters are all the same size. In a natural setting, they would appear in various sizes and shapes. These appear manufactured."

"So, now you're a blood spatters analyst *and* a criminal psych expert?"

"Detective Wholeman, some people have too much gray matter to devote to just one vocation. I dabble in many sciences and at some point, they all connect."

I attempt a good-natured smirk. "Okay, Einstein, what are you waiting for? An energy wave?"

He begins to pack up his medical equipment. "Well, I'd like to hear from serology first, but here's what I'm thinking. The spatters are too uniform to have occurred naturally."

Mental images from the crime scene flash, systematic drops of blood on torso and legs. Causeway is right, too uniform. The crime scene never felt natural, not that *any* of it was ever natural.

I rub my hands together in thought. "So, what this might mean is the killer stood over the body and randomly dripped blood around the scene. A staging of sorts."

Causeway, his medical bag now packed and in hand, motions for me to follow him out of the examination room. The heavy door closes with a thud. I follow him silently down a long, dimly lit hall.

My brain is in overdrive as I try to work through possible scenarios. If the crime scene had, in fact, been staged, what was the reason? Is the killer trying to send some sort of twisted message through the manufactured blood spatters or trying to distract us to an innocent second party?

"I'll show you the pictures I took last night," he says over his shoulder as he picks up his pace.

I lengthen my stride to keep up with him. He turns a corner and without warning, disappears through an open door and into his office.

I almost miss the turn, skid to a halt, and enter the door to find Causeway slipping in behind his desk to pick up a thick manila envelope from a wall shelf.

The office is small, but everything has its place. His desktop is very different from mine. Completely clear, except for one framed family picture. Not even a phone. Empty. If a cluttered desk is the sign of a cluttered mind, what is an empty desk the sign of?

As he grabs a letter opener from the desk drawer, I take a seat in a metal folding chair facing his desk and aimlessly pick up the family photo. The doctor, his wife, and one adult son all look back at me from the picture with empty, unsmiling eyes. Why does this not surprise me?

"I had these expedited," Causeway says as he slices open the envelope. "I noticed this yesterday at the scene."

My left hand begins tapping the desktop, while my right hand goes fishing in my pocket for a magnifying glass. My pockets are like a junk drawer, a little bit of everything and a lot of nothing.

He pulls an inch and a half stack of five-by-seven photos from the envelope and spreads them across the desk, moving with the precision of a blackjack dealer.

"I would do this with a computer and projector," he says without looking up, "but I like working with paper."

He deftly picks a picture from the spread and sticks it in front of my face. "This is the body, as found. Notice the spots of blood?"

I carefully take the picture from his hands. The photo appears to have been snapped from an elevated position, directly over the body, at a right angle. The entire body is visible within the frame, revealing five dark spots on the back.

I swallow hard and steel myself as renewed memories of the crime scene flash in my mind.

Causeway walks around the desk, moving behind me to look over my shoulder. He points with his index finger. "See these?"

I adjust the picture to reduce some of the light glare and focus the magnifying glass on the back of the body. "Five spots on the legs too."

"Exactly. This is where the evidence really gets challenging."

He walks slowly back to the other side of his desk, eases himself into his chair and takes a moment to check his nails.

I grit my teeth and fight my rising irritation.

"Those spatters," he finally continues, "were made from an altitude of about five feet, from a 90-degree angle. All similar in size and dimension. All vertical drops. Notice each of them is a direct hit."

I move the magnifier over each one of the spots. He is dead on.

"And not one of them is on the periphery of the body," he adds.

I look down and search the pictures again, trying to corroborate the evidence with the doctor's theory.

I look over the top of the picture and into his eyes. "What do you make of this?"

He peers back at me blankly. "That's your arena. Not mine."

"Come on, Doc, I've known you long enough to know you always have theories."

Causeway reaches into his desk and pulls out a pack of cigarettes, lighting one with an old, flip lid Zippo lighter. He takes a long drag and leans back into his chair.

"Didn't take you as the type who smokes, Doc."

"I'm a man of many surprises," he says, exhaling the smoke. "Just hope I don't set off any alarms. Now, as I was saying, my guess is the blood does not belong to the victim. As I see it, the blood spatters are inconsistent with any typical patterns I've ever seen. I've got too many years invested in this work not to suspect there's more here than meets the eye. I'm sending copies to the FBI laboratory to have their experts examine the spatters."

Reaching across the desk, he pushes ten more photos toward me. Each of them shows a single blood spatter, a white ruler placed alongside for measurement comparison.

"Those are the ten different blood spatters. Within a fraction of a millimeter, each of the spatters is of the same approximate size and density, even have a similar shape. Life is not that exact. Even two snowflakes aren't exact, and murder is not exactly Mother Nature."

Tapping my foot in thought, I add things up. All the facts are too typical, too expected. A kid taken from a large, middle- and upper-income church, moved to a crack house, left with obvious prints and blood, and no attempt at cover up.

He picks up the phone, dials, and waits for an answer. "Yes. One large pizza, everything on it." He cups the phone. "Would you like to join me?"

"No. The red sauce wouldn't agree with me right now."

"Didn't know you were so delicate, Detective."

Jerk. This guy gets on my nerves, but he knows his stuff. There'd been a time when I was sure the doctor was chemically imbalanced, but it didn't take long for me to find he was the best in his field.

I feel a bump to my arm and look up to find he's already off the phone and pushing another photograph under my magnifying glass.

"Here, Detective. Detect."

With magnification, it's obvious each stain on the back and legs is very similar. Slightly different star patterns, true, but each is approximately the same size. No smears. Just dead center drops with normal drainage.

I skip back and forth through the pictures. "You're right," I finally concede. The blood drops do look pretty intentional."

"Glad you agree. I've had the night to think about it." Causeway knocks the ash off his cigarette. "This could be a—"

"Frame," I interject.

We stare at each other.

"If this is the case, Doc, the perp would be expecting us to track down the owner of that blood. He also must know somehow that the DNA he dropped on the child is on file somewhere."

He gives a thin-lipped smile. "I think you may have hit on an interesting possibility."

"And if he has access to that kind of info, the DNA to frame someone, then he could be someone working within the system. A clerk, a cop, a DCF worker ... the list goes on."

"Hmm, well, DNA will tell us more, but we won't have that data for a while. I'm amazed that computers work globally at lightning speed, and yet DNA test results, at least around here, still takes roughly seventy-one hours."

"Roughly? This could get scary if you decided to be precise."

"Let's just say we have to wait three, possibly four days for the results."

"Well, being you have more gray matter than you know what to do with, Doc, what are your personal theories?"

He takes another drag from the cigarette, close to singeing his fingers, drops it to the floor and crushes it under his foot. A cloud of smoke billows toward me and I fan it from my face.

I noticed how the cigarette litter on the floor clashes with his immaculate desk. He's a strange one. The air is becoming stifling in here, time to leave.

"The truth is, Detective," he puts out a hand to stop me. "I'm not ready to theorize until I have more facts."

"Listen, thanks for your time, Causeway. Gotta move on. Places to go, people to see."

Making a slight move to shake his hand, I reconsider and turn to leave. Never know where those hands have been.

"Listen," he calls after me, "Could you keep me updated with the details … as a professional courtesy? This particular case fascinates me."

Weirdo. "I'll keep that in mind," I throw over my shoulder.

CHAPTER 23

Feeling the first stabs of hunger, Jose Martinez is eager to get home. On Wednesday nights, Angelina makes red-pepper chili so hot it makes his heart pound, eyes tear, and nose run. The concoction is so delicious his mouth waters just thinking about it. As he drives down the highway, he pictures his children laughing, tears dripping from their eyes as they wash down spicy mouthfuls of chili with cold lemonade. But first things first. Before he heads for home, he wants to make a drive-by at Central Christian Church.

He makes the exit off I-95 onto Hallandale Beach Boulevard and heads west. Minutes later, he turns into the church parking lot. He circles around, passing all the familiar church buildings, the worship center, the youth building, the school and then slows as he passes a large stretch of grass where children are playing on a swing-set. A little further on, cheerleaders clad in green T-shirts emblazoned with orange church logos are practicing their gymnastic stunts. A few of the kids stop to look over at his squad car, curiosity on their faces. He turns his vehicle toward the back of the main parking lot and heads for the garbage dumpster area. As he slowly passes, he notices both dumpsters are unusually full. Pizza boxes spill out over the top, along with other cardboard boxes. He wonders if garbage pick-up is late or if there's just been a pizza party somewhere on church grounds. He also wonders why he has never seen anyone out here despite his many drive-bys. There have been many reports by concerned parents of homeless people camping out here. The proximity to the school makes the claims a legitimate concern, but the grounds are deserted now. Accelerating a little, he drives about ten car rows back from the dumpster, parks, and waits.

He moves to pick up his phone to call Angelina to let her know he will be running a little late, but something catches his eye. He reaches for his binoculars, keeping his eyes on a man who has just walked out a back door wearing a green T-shirt, a church logo on the front. He is about ten yards from the dumpster.

The man closes the door and stands there, as if he's thinking. Jose quickly adjusts the binocular lenses, bringing the man so close he feels he can reach out and touch him. The man is looking down, but he clearly has a dark complexion, a short dark beard, and a black ball cap. He clutches a combination lock in his left hand. Jose barely breathes as he watches the man's next move. One that is only too familiar.

With head bowed, the man removes his ball cap and carefully brushes his shoulder with it … *one, two, three, four times*—as if to remove dust or dirt. Returning the cap to his head, the man begins to walk toward the dumpster. Jose begins to count the man's steps—he tries not to but feels compelled. *Eighteen, nineteen, twenty* … he thinks about snapping the rubber band on his wrist, but his hands are tied-up with the binoculars. *Thirty-eight, thirty-nine, forty. God help me to stop. Forty-two, forty-three, forty-four.* The steps stop. The man looks up, studies the heap, and reaches up to grab a white plastic bag from the dumpster's edge.

Martinez wonders if someone accidentally threw something out and this maintenance man was sent to retrieve it. Or he could be salvaging some party leftovers. He inwardly shivers thinking of the dirt and germs involved. The man turns to walk back, bag in hand. *Five, six, seven, eight …*

Stop. Jose cries, but he cannot. In frustration he visualizes snapping himself with the rubber band. *Thirty-two, thirty-three, thirty-four* … After forty-four steps, the man stops at the door, takes off his ball cap, and brushes his shoulder, *one, two, three, four times.* He carefully puts his cap back on, opens the door, walks through, and disappears.

Martinez blows out a breath. That poor devil, he's just like me, except his number is four. *I know how you suffer, brother.* He sends up a quick prayer for the man, and with relief, drives away.

CHAPTER 24

Over the brisk wind blowing through the open window of Hakeem's truck, he could not hear the ring tone, but after some moments he felt the vibration from his hip pocket. He struggled to retrieve the phone and, after swerving the truck slightly, finally got into position to see the readout. He knew the number. He knew who was calling. He cursed himself for missing the call.

Hakeem slowed his vehicle and maneuvered it off the shoulder of the Florida Turnpike. He pulled far enough off so he would not be perceived as a danger should the highway patrol show up. He knew any vehicle pulled to the side of the turnpike would be a red flag to the Florida Highway Patrol, but he also knew he needed to respond to this call.

Once the truck was stopped, Hakeem flipped open the phone. It chirped, indicating he had received a voice mail.

Hakeem went through the necessary steps to play back the message and placed the phone to his ear. In English, Hakeem heard the cold, commanding voice of the emir.

"What do you think you are doing, fool? You have a duty to perform. You do not have the right to jeopardize the outcome with your petty side interests." His voice became cold steel. "You will tend to your job to the exclusion of all else. Do not call me. Do your job."

Hakeem deleted the phone history.

The witch had betrayed him. She had informed the emir of his actions outside of the planned mission. She had, as the Americans would say, snitched him out.

His anger seethed as his knuckles went white on the steering wheel. A disciplined soldier must exercise patience. But when the day came, he would use one of her stiletto heels to—Suddenly, he remembered those stupid pink sneakers. When he had put the girl in the plastic garbage bag to move her from the church to the crack house, her shoes had somehow fallen off. He knew she would be reported missing any moment, so there was little time. The service had already commenced, and with only minutes left, he had retrieved them and thrown them into the truck with the unconscious girl.

Later, when he went to move her, he had forgotten the shoes. He had not remembered them until the following day, after the girl had already been found. The police were scouring the church grounds, and he had seen a police officer in the parking lot, snooping in the trunk of a car. With his pulse racing, he had rushed out to his truck, grabbed the sneakers from the trunk, shoved them into a paper bag, and brought them into the church building. The only place he could think to hide the shoes was the fitness room. The lockers there were too small to hide a body—the police would not search them—but they were the perfect size to hide the shoes.

He had hurried first to the church cleaning supplies closet. There, he grabbed a stack of old newspapers from a shelf and an old combination lock he had found out by the dumpster. He had quickly returned to the locker room where he dumped the shoes and the newspapers into the locker. He almost laughed now at the difficulty he had in getting the lock shackle through the locker hasp, but it had finally succumbed. No one would bother with that large combination lock. How fortunate he had been to find the device and many other useful articles that rich Americans throw away.

For now, the sneakers were well hidden, out of sight and as far as he was concerned, out of mind.

He studied the rearview mirror and pulled back out onto the highway.

A smile swept across his face.

Revenge, it is better served cold.

CHAPTER 25

Angelina pours fresh coffee into Jose's cup as he sits at the breakfast table. She adds some cream and stirs for him. "Today, special treat. Black almond coffee my cousin sent from Cuba."

Jose takes a sip. "Mmm, this is really good. This should help make for a better day." He stuffs a forkful of eggs into his mouth.

"Something go wrong with yesterday?" she asks, taking a seat across from him.

"Oh, nothing really."

"I think something. What happen?" She studies his face.

Jose blows out a breath with resignation. Nothing can get past this woman. "Well, if you have to know, just before I came home last night, I did a drive-by on Central Christian Church. It was a good day. I mean, I didn't ... you know ..."

"Count?" Angelina finishes.

He nods and picks up a strip of bacon.

"What ... how you say ... triggered it?"

"I'm not sure." He shakes his head. "Out of nowhere, it hit me. This guy, I think the janitor, came out of the back of the church, heading for the dumpster. I started counting his steps and just couldn't stop. I tried. I really tried." He began to tap his spoon against his cup. Angelina reaches out and puts her hand over his to stop him.

"God's Scripture say everything has purpose."

He takes both her hands in his. "You are a good woman. I don't do enough for you. When this Ford case is over, I'm going to take you on a weekend trip. Just the two of us. My sister will babysit."

Angelina claps her hands together. "Oh, that would be great fun. Where we go?"

"Anywhere you want, honey."

"Oh, I think hard about this. I will think of something good."

Gulping down the last of the coffee, he stops and looks across the table at his wife. She's still smiling as she takes a bite of her eggs.

"Angelina, something good already came out of it. I mean, that man I saw yesterday."

Angelina puts her fork down. "What do you mean?"

"The janitor at the church. He had the same problem as me. I watched him. He counts, just like me."

"How is this good?" Her eyes are wide.

"Seeing him made me feel like I'm not alone. That I'm not the only one. I prayed for him and will keep praying."

"This is good. See. God's words always right."

Smiling at her, he stands up, walks to her chair, and bends to kiss the top of her head. "It's time to get to work, honey. I love you. Tell the girls I love them."

"I love you, *mi amado esposo*. And our four *ninitas* love you, and the Lord love you *mucho*. He give you big purpose."

"I'm a blessed man, *mi amada esposa*."

Jose collects his things, straps on his gun belt, and walks out the door. As he approaches his car, he puffs out his chest, somehow feeling a little taller. He wonders if it's possible to grow at his age. He lets out a quiet chuckle.

CHAPTER 26

Surprisingly, I wake up refreshed and ready to go get some bad guys. Jumping out of bed, something stops me. Sydney, still sleeping, looks angelic as the morning sun falls on her face.

A wave of guilt hits me. I shouldn't feel so good after another night without my family.

Last night, after coming home to an empty house, there was another note on the fridge from Sydney explaining she was taking the kids to a youth group meeting, and my dinner was in the fridge. I was alone again. Too tired to eat, I skipped my shower like a lone barbarian, fell into bed fully clothed, and passed out.

I have a fleeting memory of the boys giving me a hug goodnight, their sweet smell lingering in the air. Maybe the moment was really just a dream, but that memory is enough to get me through the day.

Humming a toneless tune, I head for the bathroom. As I pass Sydney's side of the bed, I feel compelled to stop and look again. Though fast asleep, her face now has a shadow of a frown. I stoop to kiss her forehead. She stirs but doesn't wake.

After a quick shower and some instant coffee, I'm ready to conquer the world.

My plans are to make a quick stop at the office, rifle through emails, check my inbox, and make some phone calls, particularly to serology and latents. With any luck, I can get over to the courthouse today and get some lab reports.

Once in my car, I get the air blasting and crack the windows to get the air moving. I spot a half-empty bag of Doritos on the passenger-side floor. Stuffing as many in my mouth as I can, I reach for my phone to give Tina a call.

She picks up. "Hey there, got anything new for me?"

"Kind of. Had an interesting talk with Causeway last night. I'll tell you about it later. Can you do me a favor?"

"Maybe. What's that noise?"

"I'm trying to swallow soggy chips. Listen, can you stall the chief on those reports that are due?"

"What do you want me to say?"

"Just make something up."

"I'm not lying."

"I didn't say lie, I said make something up. One more thing, pull up the reports on every case you can find where false blood patterns have shown up."

I can almost see her eyebrows go up, but with a quick thank you, I hit the disconnect button. She always wants to know the when, where, and why and that would take some explaining. Right now, I'm thinking I need to make an emergency trip to the Dunkin' Donuts' drive-through for a cold drink and a veggie-cheese sandwich—something Sydney orders. It'll help balance out the stale chips. Besides, I'm not getting any younger.

Bypassing the order speaker, I pull-up to the first take-out space.

My old friend, Nita, appears at the window.

"Hola, officer, good to see you. You want the usual? Grande Americano, double expresso and five chocolate donuts? Or maybe six today?" She laughs.

"No, no. I'm watching my figure," I say with a wink. "Today, I'll take a veggie and cheese sandwich, some hash browns, a coffee roll, and a frozen Chocolate Coolatta.

"Ooh la la. I hope your wife likes a fat man. You not going to be young forever, Detective." She chuckles again. This time her laugh is a little too loud for my taste.

"Just get me the food, Nita, or I'm going to have to make an arrest."

"Oh. I'm *so* scared." She walks away still laughing.

While I'm waiting the phone rings. Serology.

CHAPTER 27

Weaving my car through twenty minutes of traffic, I finally can spot the Broward County Courthouse.

At one time, this ten-story city building was brightly tiled in aqua, bordered by stately palms, the tallest on the New River—now the structure is a mere dwarf. As the city rapidly grew, a seven-story addition was added, oddly connected by a third-floor crossover bridge. Getting into the building involves finding parking, a long jog over the bridge, and then waiting for an elevator down to the crime lab on the ground floor.

Circling around the garage parking lot until a space opens up is a typical aggravation. Free spaces are about as rare as Fort Lauderdale snow, and sometimes cars will drive up and down crowded ramps for half an hour. Today, I receive a stroke of luck. A parking space appears. I pull in and kill the engine.

I take the hike over the skywalk connecting the parking garage on the east side of Third Avenue to the courthouse on the west. Half jogging across the walkway, my thoughts are on what the lab might have found.

Serology usually gives me the first heads-up call on the job, but getting results from latents so early is unexpected. The initial processing of the crime scene found a lot of smudged fingerprints, but nothing of much use. Considering the heavy human traffic that had muddied up the evidence in the crack house, I hadn't expected any new discoveries. Now, I wonder. To be summoned so quickly means something's up.

I pull open the entry door and wave at the young receptionist sitting in a fishbowl like office. She waves back, looking somewhat vulnerable behind all that glass, even though I know it's bulletproof with a steel reinforced entry door. This may be a little over the top, but everyone is hyper-vigilant these days.

She waves back and pushes the relay release of the magnetic lock. I walk through.

Having passed through the fortifications, she smiles coyly at me, bobbing her blonde waves. "Hey, Jet. You here to see Lou Backman?" She gives me a prolonged glance. In another life, I may have taken up this subtle invitation.

I return the smile and check the time. "Yes. Thank you, Cindy."

She picks up the phone with a little pout and informs Lou I've arrived. A moment later, I see him moving up the hallway motioning for me to come back. He's as muscular and pumped up as usual, his tight-fitting clothes groaning with every stride. He's got to be close to forty, but he looks much younger.

"You got here pretty fast," he says grabbing my extended hand in a powerful grip.

He's wearing a broad, pasted-on smile and, with an abrupt turn, motions me toward the back of the hallway. With long strides, he throws just the right words over his shoulder to make me forget I don't like him. "I've got something very interesting for you, Detective. You won't be disappointed."

We enter a suite of offices with a lone plaque on a door that reads *latents*. Entering, he leads me to a countertop, set against the wall, mounting various magnifiers and computer display monitors. He positions himself in front of one of the monitors, pecks his way through the keyboard to the digital folders, and double-clicks a file. A fingerprint jumps to life on the monitor and simultaneously on a second, larger sidewall screen. The print floats atop other smudges and lesser prints.

"Got a three-quarter partial with a twelve-point match." There's a distinct pride in his voice.

Leaning in closer I let out a whoosh of air. "Now that's the piece of evidence we've been looking for."

In Florida, eight points of fingerprint comparison is sufficient for an I.D. Twelve would be the jackpot.

"Where did you pick it up?"

"On a twenty-dollar bill found under the girl's body." He pushed a printout at me.

"On a twenty-dollar bill? This would be a first. A suspect's fingerprints on a greenback. So, this was on a twenty under her body? But that bill has been through thousands of hands. May mean nothing."

"Or may mean everything. We have an AFIS match," he goes on, waving the report like a trophy. "Appears like this guy either wants to be caught or he's laboring under a lobotomy."

Snatching the report from his hand, I scan the top page. There, center page, snuggled within various encodings, a single name stops me cold and jumps out at me like a Jack-in-the-Box.

"William Barclay Williams." The name shoots out of my mouth like a canon blast.

"Yeah," Backman says with a twisted, cat-got-the-canary, smile on his face. "That big shot minister of the largest church in our fair city."

My mind races.

A crooked smirk crosses his face. "His church has a school on their grounds, so according to policy, the church staff has to provide fingerprints to DCF. That's why they turned up in AFIS. I would have never figured it. You got anything else on this guy?"

"Not yet, he's clean."

"Well, all those guys at a church look clean. Bunch of hypocrites."

"I wouldn't say *all* of them, buddy." Stalling for time, I cross the room, grab a lone metal folding chair laying against the wall and open it with a loud snap in front of me. I straddle it, allowing my arms to rest on the back.

"Listen, pal." My eyes bore into his. "Before you jump the gun, you need to be reminded this greenback has passed through plenty of hands. There's no law against handling money, and just because your print happens to be the only one identifiable, doesn't make you guilty of the crime."

Backman huffs out a single guffaw, shaking his head in the negative. "You sound more like a defense attorney than a cop. If I were you, I'd go after this guy."

Luckily, I'm not *you*.

"I'll check him out." I give a little yawn, even though my heart rate is up and running. "Can I have a copy of this?" I wave the report in front of his smug smile.

Backman hands me an envelope. "That one's yours and here's a copy of the fingerprint."

Grabbing the envelope, I flash him a smile. "Good work, Backman."

"I can't wait to read about the arrest." He gives me a wink. "There's a certain high in seeing a holy hypocrite exposed, ya know? And I don't want my kids meeting this religious kook in a mall or something. Hey, you want a Coke?" He almost bounces as he heads toward a cooler on the floor near his desk. He pulls out two cans and throws me one.

I pop the can's pull tab and take a long swallow of the cold liquid. I'm ready to make my exit, but hoping for some additional information, I decide to delay.

"So, you've got kids, huh?"

"Oh, yeah." He puffs out his chest. "But I got rid of the last little lady long ago." He laughs. "I've got six kids. Four girls, two boys."

Taking another gulp of Coke, I mull those numbers over, discomforting in both size and scope.

"Wow, big basketball team ya got there."

With a proud nod he sits down, leans back, and locks his hands behind his head. "Had four girls right in a row." He blows out a breath of exasperation. "Kept trying for that boy, ya feel me? By the time the fourth girl was in the baker, I told my wife to take care of things, but she refused. But with the luck of the Irish, the second broad I married hit the fertility jackpot—twin boys. So, at least one of my marriages ended on a high note. That is, if you're not counting the screw-job I got on the child support."

He puts his feet up on the desk, while I brace myself to listen. He's obviously getting ready to hear himself talk.

"Women. Can't live with them, can't live without them. But what can I say, women like me and ..."

I tune out his voice as his words rattle off into oblivion. This guy is a bonified jerk.

He stands up and crosses the room, still talking about his female conquests. He slips in an invitation to join him for happy hour at Mulligan's Club.

I nod distractedly. Here I am seeking the killer of a little girl with grief-stricken parents, and this guy is bragging about his own form of female genocide.

I unclip my phone from my belt and punch a recently added speed dial for the church. The receptionist answers.

"Please connect me to Pastor Williams's office." I use my charming civilian voice.

"One moment, please."

Backman goes quiet.

Christian music comes on and then a female voice, "Pastor Bill's office."

"This is Detective Jethro Wholeman with the Fort Lauderdale Police. Does Pastor Williams have time to see me this afternoon?"

"Let me check his schedule, please."

As I wait, I look back at Backman, smoothing his balding hair in the black reflective screen of the monitor. He really thinks he's God's gift to women. He makes me nauseous. His arrogance and disrespect of women reminds me a little of someone, but I can't think of who.

Glancing up at the large, side screen on the wall, I see my own reflection—not a bad looking cat, even with my hair standing on end.

"Detective Wholeman? Pastor Bill is not available, can I—"

I hang up, give a hasty farewell to Backman, and make a fast exit.

Walking to my car, I hit the speed dial.

"Serwathka."

"Tina, I need you to follow up on something."

I heard her typing in the background. "Sure. Hit me with it."

"Central Christian has a school. DCF will have screened everyone on staff. Get copies of those records, including the pastor's."

She exhales into the receiver. "Why the pastor's?"

"Just met with Backman. Fingerprints found at the scene were a match with Bill Williams."

"Hold on a minute. You really just going to drop this on me? That's impossible."

"Fingerprints don't lie. Stay objective, partner."

"I'm not stupid, Jet. Sometimes there *are* mistakes. Where were the prints found?"

"On a twenty-dollar bill, stuck under the Ford body."

"This is messed up. Money passes through millions of hands."

"If you can't stay objective, let me know now. I need you to stay focused."

She lets out a heavy sigh. "I can do this."

"Get the results to the lab and see if they can run DNA and serology comparisons to the blood spatters recovered at the crime scene."

"I'm on it."

"Tell serology I want the results yesterday. DNA comparison should take five days."

"On it. Anything else?"

"Yeah, get me a list of gas stations that run a direct route from the church to the crime scene. Start there, then go for all gas stations and convenient stores within a five-mile radius of both. If you can't get any info on these locations from the abduction files, start from scratch. I want to review any surveillance camera data from the church myself. Might catch something the first team didn't. By the way, you find anything on church footage?"

"Still sorting through it, nothing unusual yet. I did notice on the crime date, a lot of activity around the dumpster area. Looks like some homeless people coming and going."

"Anyone from the church?"

"The church janitor appears once, but part of his job is to dispose of garbage."

"Find anything on violent crimes reports or local pedophiles?"

"Yep. Found two cases of rape within a five-mile radius. One involved a frat party at Florida Atlantic University in Boca. The victim was a college classmate who attends the church. The other involved a woman who accused her boyfriend of raping her in a drunken rage. Both show sporadic attendance at the church."

"Any pedophiles?"

"Yep. Got one. A James Pickens. Served ten years for molesting a twelve-year-old neighbor boy. Address is on file."

"Good work. You're amazing, partner."

"Tell me something I don't know."

"Okay, you know the drill. Send someone over to talk to Mr. Pickens, and find out if he has an alibi."

"Got it."

"Pickens doesn't happen to attend the church, does he?"

"No, Jet. I think I would have mentioned that."

"Yeah right. Any questions?"

"Nope. No time for chatting. Catch ya later."

The phone clicks in my ear. I smile inwardly. The girl's a pro.

CHAPTER 28

After my meeting with latents, I put in a few hours back at the office, writing reports and reviewing those already waiting for me in my inbox.

Now, standing in front of the FAX machine, holding an affidavit and proposed search warrant Tina just handed me, I have to let go of any reservations. Despite the twisting in my gut, I'm ready to feed the documents into the machine to be transmitted to the state attorney's office for review and from there to the circuit judge. Once signed, they'll send them back to me to carry out the search on Bill Williams.

Review of the evidence shows fingerprints on the twenty-dollar bill, confined neatly to one corner of the paper. No other discernible prints found anywhere else. The bill tucked conspicuously under the body of the child as if left there accidentally. The blood spatters too uniform to be natural. The child's body placed in a known crack house. The one incongruency—the pastor's completely clean record and shining reputation.

There are the pastor's conspicuous fingerprints and the unnatural blood spatters but no further evidence to substantiate a staging.

The stacked papers are perched on the feeder of the machine, waiting their turn to be pulled into the document feeder—the hum of the first sheet as it's drawn into the start position has an eerie sound today. The red label, *SAO*

Warrants, seems like a neon sign today. This particular warrant is heavy on my mind.

Perpetrators leave behind evidence—blood and fingerprints. And it's all there. The pieces fit together like a sick puzzle or a textbook crime from the pages of an *Idiot's Guide to Murder.* How tempting it would be to move things along, wrap this case up, and feel good about locking up a crazed killer. There would be major kudos to follow. But easy isn't in my DNA.

Something feels wrong ... but then again, fingerprints aren't about feelings, they're a science.

I tap my knuckles impatiently on the machine top. What would we find at Williams's house?

As the hum of the machine continues, and the dial tone sounds, my thoughts march on.

Pastor Bill, are you capable of murdering a child? A little lamb in your own flock? Could you be so sinister—to use your pulpit to spin a web for the innocent and unsuspecting? Or does someone have it out for you? Someone so close they managed to get a hold of your own blood. Does someone hate you that much or were you just a convenient target?

My phone dings, a text from Sydney. She and the boys are having dinner at her parents' house. The fact I'm not invited is not lost on me. Rubbing my temples, I decide being apart tonight is for the best. I'm not up for any domestic quarrels, just a quiet night at home.

I shake my head and rub my bloodshot eyes as a question begins to form: Can I be completely objective about this case? After all, my wife attends church there, trusts the man. But can I? The machine comes to a halt. Grabbing my copies, I turn and move toward the door.

With long strides down the hall, I resolve to act professionally. I'll be objective and ruthless in my pursuit of the killer as always. I owe at least that much to Mary Ford and her parents.

Right now, there're only two things I can think about—dinner and bed. It's been another long day, but a good night's sleep will help. Who knows what tomorrow will bring?

CHAPTER 29

Friday mornings, I customarily saunter in a little late, but the pressure is on to get things moving on this homicide.

Coffee in hand, I head straight to my office, sit down at my desk and rifle through the stack of papers in my inbox. There it is. The search warrant for William B. Williams. Signed, sealed, and delivered. Conflicted feelings hit me, suspense and dismay, relief and regret, but it's always good to know the criminal system is still working.

At this point, the department can choose to sit on this warrant for up to ten days, but I know that's not going to happen. Too many heads may fall if we mess this one up—there's no room for error. There hasn't been this much press and media attention on a child since Elizabeth Smart was abducted back in 2001. I need to stall this for twenty-four hours, but the boss won't like it.

My computer screen stares back at me blankly. We don't like each other. I bring up my emails, make some quick replies. Next, I bring up today's weather report. A high of eighty-nine with occasional showers. At least the rain will cool things off. I close the computer down.

Tapping my fingers on my desk, I realize I won't be able to relax until I can talk to Tina about the warrant—when and how the search should go down. Until then, I've got some calls to make. The first one will be to Pastor Williams's assistant, Marilyn, to set up an impromptu appointment.

I won't take no for an answer. They can cancel the entire church schedule for all I care.

Just as I pick up the phone, it rings. The screen reads serology.

"Detective Wholeman here."

"It's Sandy, from serology. Got some good news."

"Hit me with it fast. I need a feel-good fix."

"Don't we all. Speedy blood results and my husband's cooking do it for me."

"How do you even put those two together in the same sentence? How about we just stick to blood results. And since when do we get them back this fast?"

"Since someone's been exerting pressure. High profile case and political kudos at stake. Anyway, got two different blood types from the crime scene. One is a match to the victim, type O-positive. The other is type B-negative.

"How uncommon is that?"

"Pretty rare. Only two percent of the population have it."

"Nice work, Sandy. No one knows blood like you."

"If I were a vampire, I might thank you."

Hanging up, things look brighter. With sleight of hand, I toss up the phone and catch it with the other. Time to call the pastor.

CHAPTER 30

Once again, Meeka is the person who comes down the stairs to lead me to the pastor's office. I try to avert my eyes—a self-inflicted morality test.

A flash of her working behind that closed glass door comes to mind. She appears to perform her job well, and yet, the rest of the staff seem to give her the cold shoulder. The more familiar I become with this church, the staff, and congregation, the more unusual this woman Meeka strikes me. She seems out of place, like a majestic giraffe in the Arctic.

Stunning looks like hers have been known to create distraction, even hostility, among coworkers, but more likely, it's the way she uses them. From my view, they may be simply picking up on the way she looks at me … or the other way around. Nah, rule that out. Healthy egos can be misunderstood, the hostility surely goes back before I ever entered the picture.

I twist my wedding band.

First impressions are usually the best ones, so I check off things that stand out about Meeka. Sultry body movement. Lingering eye contact. Breathy voice. All intermingling to produce a certain confidence that's evident in every move. My own sideways glances of admiration are evidence enough. Years ago, under different circumstances, I might have pursued such a woman, but marriage changes a man. Some men anyways. Obviously, Sydney's recent accusations have loaded my conscience with new ammunition. The feelings aren't pleasant.

As Meeka saunters toward me, I vow to monitor my behavior. I have a job to do and distractions like this have made mightier men fall. Names of politicians, presidents, and pastors parade across my mind, all of whom lost everything they'd worked for, including their families, for the fast and furious allure of a sexual opportunity. Sadly, out of all their great accomplishments, the scandal is the only thing people will remember.

One of the keys to solving a crime is eliminating all distractions—like false leads, planted evidence, tainted testimony, and beautiful women.

My investigative brain comes back online as new questions about this woman formulate.

Meeka smiles warmly at me. "Why, Detective, what brings you back again so soon?"

"Business as usual. I hope the pastor didn't have to be interrupted from anything important?"

"What could be more important than this? Just follow me, please."

Following her up the stairs, my conscience gives my mind a job transfer from her hips to her résumé.

"So, how do you like working here?" I try to sound nonchalant.

"It is quite pleasant."

"How long have you worked here?"

She hesitates. "Less than a year."

There's something in her answer ... reluctance?

At the top of the stairs, she halts, pressing the Bluetooth in her ear. "Yes? Uhhuh. Certainly." She disconnects and quickly switches direction, taking a left turn instead of a right. Waving me on, she takes me to a small waiting area with a conversational grouping of chairs and a coffee table covered in religious brochures, magazines, and one dismembered newspaper. As she bends to neatly stack the papers, she looks up at me under her eyelashes.

Clearing my throat, I try not to stare. "Ms. Amari, it would be very helpful if you could answer some questions regarding the investigation. My partner, Tina Serwathka, will be the one meeting with you. Would you mind?"

She hesitates. "I would rather meet with you."

I hold her gaze. "As much as I'd like that, my partner has been assigned to do interviews."

Her smile fades. "I have a very busy schedule, but I will cooperate, naturally." She looks at her watch. "I apologize. The pastor is detained for a few minutes. Could you please wait here?"

"Got nothing better to do." My tone borders on sarcastic.

A slight shadow crosses her face. "Would you like some coffee, Detective?"

"Why not? Have any sandwiches to go with it?"

She pauses. "I suppose I could check the cafeteria, but it usually is not open this early."

"Yeah, could you do that for me? I'd really appreciate that. Waiting always makes me hungry."

She flashes a brief smile, but her eyes are cool, unblinking. A small dent in an otherwise smooth, professional exterior. She turns to leave.

Game on.

"Oh, and when you get a chance could you bring me some matches? Really could use a smoke." I don't smoke, but this request should get a rise out of her.

She stops, shoulders stiffening. Barely turning, she speaks into the air, "I will try, but unfortunately, you will have to take your smoke break outside. That is the law, of course."

Suppressing a grin, I take up the newspaper, cross one leg over the other, and hum loudly as I leaf through the pages. Her sarcasm in that bit about the law is telling, how people act under pressure provides insight. Her response wasn't exactly what I'd expect from a church lady.

Once she's out of sight, I toss the paper, pull out my phone, and punch *favorites* on my contact list. Tina picks up after only one ring.

"Yeah, Jet. Anything new?"

"I was just about to ask you the same thing."

"Nah. Just watching miles of camera footage of people pumping gas. Saw nothing suspicious yet but learned a lot."

"Yeah, like what?"

"Like did you know that three out of five people talk on their phones while they pump gas or that nine out of ten women leave their purses in the car, unprotected, while they wait for the tank to fill up?"

"Geez, lady, you better get Homeland on that one."

"And did you know that at least half of all parents leave their car doors unlocked, children inside, while they're busy sliding cards and punching numbers with their backs turned?"

"Listen, this is all interesting, but I'm in a hurry. I need some feedback on something."

"I'm game, but aren't you supposed to be at the church?"

"Already here. But they dumped me in the lobby like they would a salesman peddling baptismal tanks. Just got the royal escort by that secretary, Meeka. Remember her?"

"How can I forget? You start to drool every time her name comes up."

"Can we stay focused, Serwathka? Anyways, I'm looking at this woman, wondering … how did someone like her get a job at a place like this? You know what I'm saying?"

"What? An attractive woman can't get a job at a church?"

"It's not her looks, it's what she does with them."

"Okay, I hear ya. Go on."

"My impression is no one is overly fond of her. She's just the type we need to keep our eye on. And I'm baffled as to why any staff member would hire a woman who dresses like Paris Hilton and moves like ..."

"Angelina Jolie?"

"Bingo. Now we're on the same page. So, partner, you hang around churches, what's the typical staff woman like?"

"No particular mold, but all the women I've known there have been pretty genuine. You know ... moral, modest, friendly, responsible—the whole caboodle. But I've got to admit, this woman is a little different from the others."

"In what way?"

"Very reserved. All work, no play. Rarely smiles. I've picked up some scuttlebutt about her. Members of the church are usually given first shot at a paid position—they work their way up from the bottom. Meeka was hired from the outside. There's some resentment about that."

"Figures. Staff records indicate she's only worked here for less than a year. And I *definitely* wouldn't put her in the plain or modest camp."

Tina's reluctant sigh comes through loud and clear.

"Jet, putting business aside for a sec, maybe you could stand to think a little less about women's looks. They have souls too, you know."

"Whoa, that's not fair. I'm just saying it like it is."

"Well, maybe you could say it a little less often."

"Point taken. At any rate, why was this woman hired? There must have been some other talented, hard-working woman in the church ready to go up the ladder."

"Maybe her employment was simply a lack of judgement. I hate to say it, Jet, but people in churches aren't immune to stupidity. Who knows, maybe the interviewer was a goggle-eyed male with a sloppy wife who wanted something pretty to look at during office hours. On the other hand, for all we know, she could have come to the interview with her hair in a bun, wearing her grandmother's dress."

"Bait and switch. Got it. I'm also wondering if she's the acting escort for only Pastor Bill's visitors, or more importantly, only law enforcement? And what ties does she have to the pastor?"

"Ties? What do you mean by that? When I was talking about jerks in the church, I didn't mean my pastor."

"Whoa, stay objective, partner. He's not your pastor. For now, he's a potential suspect."

"I hear you. Get on with it."

"Okay, this is the question. Is our Meeka an attractive pawn in the use of some unseen agenda? Or simply a good-hearted woman endowed with certain gifts?"

Before she can answer, I hear the click of heels and look up to see Meeka heading toward me, holding a capped, Styrofoam coffee cup.

"Gotta go, Tina. Call you later."

Shoving the phone back in my pocket, I stand up, a broad smile plastered on my face. "No luck with the sandwiches, I'm going to guess."

She hands me the coffee. "Sorry. Diner is closed. But Pastor Bill might have something for you in his office refrigerator. He is ready for you now."

As we head for his office, I wonder whether it's my imagination, or does she seem a bit more congenial? Cautioning myself, a professor's words from my Criminal Guidelines class comes to mind: "There is a fine line between intuition and paranoia, cynicism and realism. A good detective keeps a balance between them. People are rarely what they appear to be, but not all suspects are criminals."

Good advice.

She takes a quick side-glance at me, as if she wants to determine if I'm looking at her, but my eyes are fixed straight ahead. She slows her pace.

"So, Detective Wholeman, do you have any suspects yet?"

"As a matter of fact, yes."

"Is it someone with a criminal background?" Her tone is casual.

"Can't say. Classified information."

"Of course. Will the pastor be given any updates? He's very concerned, you know."

I felt like saying he's the last person I'd tell.

"No. Not even the pastor," I say evenly.

"I understand."

Was she too inquisitive or just making normal conversation?

As I speed up my pace to match the quick clicking of her stiletto heels, I think again of something I heard back in college. My criminology professor once said everyone is a criminal at heart—they just needed the right opportunity and circumstance. He may have been right. I've found people wear a lot of masks to cover their unsavory motives—my job is to find them.

Meeka abruptly stops at the water fountain. "Excuse me, please," she says, bending over the waterspout.

Still watching her, I'm pleasantly aware my motives are no longer tied to an adolescent battle with testosterone. I feel nothing but suspicion.

"I bet you get a lot of exercise going up and down these stairs," I say conversationally, "with all the visitors a pastor must get."

"Oh, no, this is normally Marilyn's job. I just happen to be available."

My investigative antenna gives a tingle. There's no such thing as a coincidence.

We reach our destination. As she goes to open one of the double glass doors, I quickly maneuver around her and gallantly open it, giving a dumb grin meant to telegraph an ogle-eyed cop with his guard down.

"Thank you, Detective."

Pastor Bill exits his personal office and approaches Marilyn's desk. She's sitting in a relaxed position, smiling thoughtfully, pen in hand. Hearing us, they both look over. The pastor gives us a warm, welcoming smile, but his eyes are edged in fatigue. Marilyn looks wary.

His relaxed expression shows no suspicion of the impending trouble that threatens—that, or he's a good actor, internally sweating.

Marilyn stands to welcome us with a polite but guarded posture. Why didn't she escort me in? She doesn't look very busy.

Pastor Bill hands some papers to Marilyn and turns to extend his hand to me.

"Detective Wholeman, good to see you again."

"Hope I didn't catch you at a bad time. I've got a few things I'd like to discuss."

He nods and gestures me toward his office.

Meeka saunters off, and I glance back to see if the good pastor is looking. He is not.

"Come on in." He gestures to his office. "Sorry for the delay. Mary Ford's mother was just here to discuss funeral arrangements. I'm giving a message Sunday at Faith Funeral Home at 5 p.m., just down the street. If you're interested, your attendance would be welcomed."

"Yes, I'd like to be there. Thank you."

"Glad to hear it. That'll mean a lot to her parents."

It would be inappropriate to state my real reason for going. Funerals and candlelight vigils are a great place to plant an investigative eye. Sometimes killers show up at vigils or funerals of their victims. They have a perverse desire to immerse themselves in the family's grief and suffering, a sick sort of intimacy with the victim. For the killer, it's a sentimental journey as bereaved loved ones tell stories about the deceased's life—their achievements and charities along with their lost dreams and disrupted ambitions. The killer feels a godlike power to have changed destiny, to have derailed an ordained chain of events. What comes to mind is a stone cast into a black river, its steady ripples moving outward, disrupting calm water.

As the pastor moves to close his office door behind us, I take a last look at Marilyn. She's at her desk wearing a worried expression. Either she has good instincts, or she knows more than she lets on.

The pastor moves around behind his desk while I take a chair with a full view of the room, including, peripherally, the office entrance. I never sit with my back to the door, as any cowboy in a saloon knows better. Unfortunately, this cowboy is becoming aware of a need for a bathroom break. I inwardly curse myself for not having gone earlier.

With a last slug of coffee, I lean forward to set my cup on the edge of his desk. "Mr. Williams, you and I need to talk."

"Of course." His smile fades as he lowers himself into his desk chair.

I remove a notepad from the breast pocket of my jacket, open it, and whip it onto his desk, creating a loud snap.

"We have a problem. Unfortunately, Pastor, your name has come under some suspicion."

"What are you saying?" Pastor Bill's eyes grow round, giving a double blink.

I pause, watching him closely. He doesn't seem to have a clue.

"Evidence has been discovered incriminating you."

His eyes blink rapidly in astonishment, his jaw drops. After a moment, he closes his mouth, but his face seems to freeze. I can't tell if he's shocked, horrified, or simply paralyzed.

I reach down, grab the lower edge of the heavy chair and drag it a little closer to his desk.

"Look, I have a feeling you're being framed for the Ford murder."

I let my announcement sink in for a moment.

"New evidence is strongly incriminating."

The initial wave of shock is replaced with a look of confusion. He sits bolt straight.

"No, there's some kind of terrible mistake," he sputters, shaking his head. "That's impossible. What's happening here? I don't understand. The evidence, whatever it is, is wrong."

"Evidence doesn't lie, but people do. But I have to be honest, it doesn't look good."

"What's the evidence?"

"I can't disclose that at this time."

He's now looking at me, wide-eyed, incredulous. He lifts his arms out wide in a helpless gesture of confusion.

"Are you saying you think I'm somehow involved in this heinous crime? That I'm lying?"

He leans forward, his eyes searching mine like a lifeline in a storm.

I don't answer right away. This is the point where I like to just watch and wait. He doesn't show the telltale signs of someone who's lying. I've seen enough liars to know they exhibit a specific checklist of tells—avoiding eye contact, giving a rush of excuses, rambling on about unnecessary details, drawing in their arms protectively, frequently touching their face or throat. Most often, their words and emotions don't match. Words of grief are expressed with blank eyes, or emotions show in the mouth but never reach the rest of the face.

He doesn't show any of these signs.

"I'm a pretty good study of people, Mr. Williams. You don't come off as a liar or a murderer."

He gives an audible sigh of relief.

The lifeline every accused person desperately seeks for is the knowledge someone believes them—the guilty desperately look for that bit of hope, the innocent even more so.

Williams's voice, his eyes, body language, everything I'd been trained to observe, tells me this man is not the typical, arrogant man of power who sees his minions as instruments of his own whims. He appears to genuinely care about people. But should I take a chance on him? It's now or never.

"Listen, Pastor, this may be hard to take in, but I've got a hunch someone planted the evidence. Someone who has a real hate crusade against you. Someone who wants a pound of your flesh."

"I'm not the Merchant of Venice, I'm not a businessman, a millionaire, or a politician. I'm just a simple guy with a simple life. I've got no enemies." He starts to stand up, sits back down. "Are you saying someone, to get at me, killed Mary?"

His body sags under the weight of this morbid possibility.

It wouldn't be the first time a kid was sacrificed for some cheap grudge, but I ignore his question and move on.

"Now, think hard. Have you made anyone angry in your private or professional life? Has anyone ever taken a punch at you, threatened you, broken into your house? Any begrudged neighbors?" My tone is calm, an attempt to thwart the storm that must be gathering in his mind.

He rests his elbows on the desk, hands pressed to his temples.

"Okay, okay." He slightly stutters. "I suppose pastors do make some enemies. We get caught up in what I would call an ideological war. But when it comes to leaders in the faith or anyone for that matter, if you're not making someone mad, you're not doing your job. I preach the Word of God without censorship. My strong suit is not political correctness."

He shakes his head as if to clear it. "For all of history, if a man spoke his convictions outside the realm of conventional thought, he wound up either at the low end of social approval or the high end of a tree noose. Every Monday, following a Sunday sermon, I get a couple hundred emails. Over half of them are complaints about one thing or another. 'You're too judgmental, too narrow, too rigid.' Or, 'You're too liberal, too easy on sin.' The new wave of complaints hitting churches are so-called hate crimes. If you call these people enemies, then yes, I have them."

"Give me some examples of the hate-crime accusations."

"Let me put it this way. I'm a fundamentalist Christian. This means my stand on certain social issues are anything but popular. So, to some groups, I'm a narrow minded hater."

"I get the picture. Any groups in particular?"

He sits back in his chair and looks away for a moment. "Basically, any religion or organization that's offended by the claim there's only one way to eternal life."

"And what would that be?" I'm trying not to yawn.

"Jesus Christ."

"Hmm. I can see why that might come across as a little narrow minded."

"Detective, truth *is* narrow. I'm sure you witness this in law enforcement. Every criminal has a long tail of lies, colorful excuses, and their own version of the truth, but when it comes to the courtroom, the judge isn't interested. He wants the truth, *and nothing but the truth, so help me God.* That being said, if you call this narrow minded—guilty as charged.

"Pastor, I'm not trying to step on anyone's toes here, but lots of people have different ideas about how to get to heaven. That doesn't make them your enemy. I'm trying to establish real motive here."

"Mr. Wholeman, with all due respect, wars have been fought over exactly this type of thing since the beginning of time."

There's a moment of silence.

It's apparent he's now working up to something, so I wait.

"Detective, I don't want to sound like a whiner, but I've been threatened over my faith on several occasions. Twice, I was physically attacked."

I stare at him, somewhat surprised. "Did you discover the identities of your attackers?"

"No. They ran in and out. One time was during a church service, another time was in the parking lot. That's why the church board voted last year for security measures to be taken on Sundays."

"Woah. You have security officers here on Sundays? That's not in my reports."

"We have a security team. Most are church members who are in law enforcement. A couple of them are from the private sector, some are just willing volunteers. On Wednesdays, we cut back to one man because we have a much smaller crowd. But even with security, Mary Ford was taken right off the campus. And now, I'm being accused of this heinous crime. I guess I shouldn't be surprised. When I took my vow as a pastor, I knew the cost."

Crossing my arms against my chest, I lean back in my chair. "Hey, look at President Kennedy. He was taken out even with an army of security. No one is ever completely secure."

He takes in a deep breath, clasping his hands together on his desk.

"But even in this, I know God has a plan." His shoulders square as he draws up taller in his seat. Something in his eyes is just daring me to contradict him.

Stay quiet, don't take the bait, I tell myself. But I can't keep my mouth shut. "I find it hard to believe a god who has that kind of control would allow a child to be brutally murdered. Frankly, Pastor, I could come up with a better plan than that."

He doesn't look disturbed. If anything, he seems to come to life. Now, I've gone and done it. I've awakened the sleeping giant. He smells weakness. The blood of an Englishman.

He looks away as if he's studying something. I look too but see nothing remarkable.

"There's an undeniable evil at work in this world," he says calmly.

"Mr. Williams, with all due respect we need to stay on topic."

"I thought that was the topic—murder and evil," he continues unabated. "Man, since the beginning of time, has traded in what was perfect and true for a passing carnival of thrills. But one day, Detective Wholeman, I assure you, there will be no more sorrow or tears. No more death."

An awkward silence follows. At least for me.

I click my pen button a few times. "Listen, Pastor, we have serious things to discuss. Your fingerprints were found at the scene of the crime."

He leans forward, his eyes widen with astonishment. "I'm sorry. Could you repeat that?"

"There's a fingerprint match."

"I'm sure my fingerprints are everywhere in this church."

"I'm not talking about the abduction site. I'm talking about the house where Mary Ford's body was found."

"That can't be. I've never been there. Can you please have your people recheck this? It must be a mistake." His eyes are pleading.

"Have you ever been fingerprinted?" I'm determined to stay the path.

"I was fingerprinted by DCF as a matter of policy. There's a school on church property."

Of course, I already know this, but I want to hear him confirm.

He clears his throat. "Why would anyone want to accuse me of such an evil crime? I can't understand any of this."

I watch him, waiting to catch the faintest flicker of guilt to betray him.

"Where were you at the time Mary Ford was abducted?"

His body goes rigid. "Should I have an attorney?"

"That's up to you. The system might go easier on you if you didn't, but it's your choice. We have enough to obtain a warrant for arrest and a possible conviction. Is there anything you would like to tell me?"

"There's nothing to tell."

I wait a few moments as I watch him struggling to maintain his composure.

"One other thing," I say in a softer voice, "You're not being taken into custody at this time, even though I've got enough evidence to arrest you. But I want to tell you you have the right to remain silent ..."

I proceed to read him his rights. "Now, do you want to waive your right to an attorney and talk to me right now? Divulging information now may benefit you later."

He clasps his white-knuckled hands tightly on his lap but doesn't answer. He knows the drill—has heard the words before like every other Joe who's ever watched a cop show. He looks down at his folded hands and looks back up. "I have nothing to hide."

"I believe you, but do you waive the presence of a lawyer?"

His eyes blink vacantly. He says nothing.

"Mr. Williams, do you want to talk to me without a lawyer?"

His phone rings and startles him. He picks it up.

"Yes, Marilyn. No, no. I don't need anything. Yes. I'm sure. Thank you."

He lays the phone down, stares at it like a fading lifeline.

"An attorney won't be necessary. I think."

Part of me wants to warn him, but that's not my job.

I tap my pen on the notepad and then stop myself, not wanting to show any sign of nerves.

"Pastor, where were you on the day the Ford girl disappeared?"

"I was at home, sick. My assistant, Pastor Jesse Bennett, gave the message."

"Do you have anyone who can substantiate you were at home that night around 6 p.m.?"

"No, no. I was alone."

"That's unfortunate."

The next question is the one I've been waiting to ask.

"What is your blood type?"

Confusion washes over his face. "What does my blood type have to do with anything?"

"Just a routine question."

"Okay then … let me think. I know it's not typical. Let me ask Marilyn."

As he buzzes her again, I'm wondering if he has her confused with his mother.

"Marilyn, would you happen to know my blood type?"

A moment passes.

"No, no. It's all right, Marilyn. Just routine. B-negative? Okay, thank you." He disconnects.

The room seems to tilt a little. This is big. Real big.

"Anything wrong, Detective?"

"No. Just taking notes."

At this point, I'm tempted to stretch the truth and tell him we have a DNA blood match to his found at the crime scene, a legal tactic used at times to extract a confession when the stakes are high. But something stops me.

I give a dismal shake of my head. "When was the last time you gave blood?"

He scratches his head. "About five months ago. I try to contribute about twice a year when the blood transport van is scheduled to collect at the church."

"How about blood tests? When was your blood last drawn?"

His forehead furrows. "Are these questions really necessary?"

"Please, bear with me."

"Three weeks ago, my regular physician ordered a blood test to check cholesterol levels and some other routine things."

I jot down this information.

"What's the name of your doctor?"

"Isn't my health care private?"

"If you want to clear yourself of any charges, we'll need that information. Listen, I have enough evidence to ask for a bond so high not even your church could raise it, so let's cooperate, huh?"

He looks at me with a vaguely familiar expression. The same expression my father made when he was disappointed in me. This guy is starting to push my buttons. And the pressing urge to get to a bathroom doesn't help.

"Who is your doctor?" I repeat.

"Dr. Liam A. Cooper. His office is on East Oakland, just before the bridge."

I jot down the information.

He pulls out a calendar and traces it with his finger. "As a matter of fact, I have to see him this afternoon."

"What time is the appointment? Let me guess ... you have to ask Marilyn?"

"4:30. They want to retest me."

"Why?"

"For the same routine blood test. Seems there was some kind of error on the first one."

"What went wrong?" I'm all ears now.

"I don't know. Miss James spoke to them." He presses a button on the intercom. "Miss James?"

Before I can raise an objection, Marilyn James cracks the door open a bit, and presses her face through the opening. "Yes, Pastor?"

"Why do I have to go back to see Dr. Cooper this afternoon?"

He sounds like a child, trusting others for his well-being.

Miss James rolls her eyes up and back for a split second. "Remember?" she says maternally. "They lost the last blood sample. They need you to come in again so they can draw another sample."

I turn sharply to face her. "What was that?"

"I'm sorry?" She looks at her boss for further instruction. He gives her a nod.

"Dr. Cooper's office," she continues, "said the sample had been set out for pickup in the night box, but for some reason the laboratory never received the sample. The nurse talked to me. She said all the samples for that particular day disappeared, most probably in the delivery service."

My hand thumps the desk, and they both jump. "Now we're getting somewhere."

"Thank you, Marilyn," he says.

She turns away, leaving the door slightly ajar.

Now I'm in overdrive. But unfortunately, so is my bladder. There couldn't be a worse time for nature to prevail.

"Pastor, I've got to take a quick restroom break, and then we'll continue. This is an urgent development—I mean the blood sample gone missing. Which way is the bathroom?" I try not to shuffle my feet in discomfort.

"Oh, just take a right and it's the third door on the right."

I rush out, trying not to look conspicuous. Once in the bathroom stall, I can't remember such relief, but my mind hasn't turned off. How does a blood sample disappear? Was it lost in the doctor's office? Did it go out with the trash? Was it removed from the doctor's office, lost in transit, or misplaced in the lab ... or stolen?

A frame-up, including stolen blood, is a longshot like Tina said, but all theories have to start somewhere. That lost blood sample could be the very same one found at the crime scene. Drop by drop, it could have been dripped onto the dead body. If this *is* a frame job, I may have just stumbled onto something big.

Follow the motive. The voice of my criminal justice professor echoes in my head.

Still standing over the toilet, I strain to hurry the process along. Way too much coffee.

Okay, what is the motive behind this frame? He's a church cleric. What does he have that somebody wants? Money? Power? Revenge?

Hearing someone enter the bathroom, I look over my shoulder to see a white uniformed janitor pushing a cleaning cart. What timing.

Flushing the toilet, I yell out, "Sorry, I'll be out in a second."

He turns around and goes back out.

Still zipping up, I rush to the sink, wash my hands, and make for the door. Just as I step into the hall, a plastic bottle of Pine-Sol rolls across my feet. Spotting the cleaning guy, already at the end of the hall, I yell out to him. He looks back for an instant and moves on. That lazy son of a gun. I'm in a hurry to get back to the pastor's office. so I gently kick the bottle out of my way. the smell of pine filling the air.

I've got bigger things to clean up.

Upon returning, I find Marilyn and Williams standing by his desk, talking in hushed tones. They look up, concern written across their faces. Marilyn quietly turns to leave.

Taking my seat, I waste no time. "So, who knew you were going to the doctor three weeks ago to get a cholesterol test?"

He rakes his hands through his hair. "Only Marilyn would know that. The appointment would be on her calendar. Can you please tell me how this is relevant?"

"Trust me, it matters. Who else would know?"

"No one."

"Who has access to your calendar?"

"I don't know."

"I need to know."

"Marilyn keeps it in her top desk drawer. No. That's not right. She has a computer calendar now.

"Is there another copy anywhere? Like on your phone?"

"Yes. That's something new we started last month."

"How did you hook that up? I need specifics."

"Marilyn puts the dates into her computer, and it's networked to mine ... then I think it's synced to my phone. I'm not sure." He raises his hands in a gesture of helplessness, looking a little embarrassed.

This time, I'm the one who calls out, "Miss James?"

In an instant, she appears at the door. She either springs out of that chair like a cat, or she's got her ear to the door.

"Yes?" She's smiling, just barely, her eyes look wary.

The pastor speaks up. "Marilyn, who would have access to my calendar?"

She looks back and forth at both of us. I can see the wheels turning.

"The appointment is on my computer, on yours, and Miss Amari's."

My heart skips a beat, and not because of love.

"Anyone else?"

She looks back at me, and then at Williams. He gives her a nod.

"Only if someone were to access the calendar on one of our computers. And it's also on Pastor Bill's phone."

"Is your computer always on? Can anyone look anytime they want?"

She steps across the threshold, quietly shuts the door behind her, and turns back to me.

"No, I have a three-minute screensaver that requires a password. If my computer isn't touched for three minutes, it goes to the screensaver and stays that way until I insert my password."

"Anyone else, other than the three of you, have that password?"

"No one."

"What about your computer?" I turn to Pastor Bill.

"His door is locked whenever he leaves the office," Marilyn quickly interjects.

He nods in agreement as I look over at his computer—the screen is not visible from the door.

"Who else has a key to this door?" I point at the pastor's office door.

Marilyn answers quickly. "Just the three of us."

I turn my head toward the closed door. My mind's eye moves past Marilyn's outer office, through the glass door, and to the desk of Meeka where the busy little bee must be typing away.

"Meeka is the third person. She's my assistant." Marilyn gives me a conspiratorial look before she moves toward Williams's desk and begins to busy herself collecting his coffee cup and a stack of scattered papers.

Her expression tells me she's starting to put some things together. She's a sharp woman, no doubt.

I turn to Williams. "I need you to sign a HIPAA waiver. I'll have it faxed over to you and once it's signed, have Miss James send it over to the doctor's office."

"To Dr. Cooper?" Marilyn looks confused.

"Yes, I want to know what happened to Mr. Williams's blood test."

I stand and move toward the door, and with a sideways glance, I see concern written across Marilyn's face. I make an intuitive decision, stop, and turn back.

"Miss James, thank you for your help. I'm hoping we can develop a working relationship, and I would like to have my partner, Tina Serwathka, talk with you again at some point."

"Certainly. Anything to help Pastor Bill." Some of her guard seems to let down.

"One more question. Have you ever spoken to anyone about the pastor having blood tests done?"

"No. I never discuss anything associated with his personal life."

"Could you do me a favor? Could you make a list of everyone on the church security team and fax it to this email address?" I hand her my card.

She takes the card without looking at it, her eyes brimming with tears.

"If you think of anything that may seem pertinent to the Mary Ford case, please don't hesitate to call."

"Anything to help the Ford family." She hesitates. "And Pastor Bill."

Without thinking, I reach out and briefly touch her shoulder. "I'll do what I can."

Her reserve melts a little. That's a positive. I need her on my side.

I leave with my adrenaline pumping. My gut tells me I'm on to something.

CHAPTER 31

Leaving Marilyn James behind, I almost run out of her office vestibule. The pastor's missing blood sample could be a major lead. I'm so wound up as I turn the corner into the hall, I bowl right into Paul Blake. "Whoa." I grab his arm to steady him.

Paul lets out a laugh as he finds his balance. "I was just coming to find you." He grabs for my hand and gives it a good pumping. "Thought I could give you a hand." He bellows a laugh. "Get it? Give you a hand."

I withdraw my hand with a tight smile. Definitely a scene out of *Dumb and Dumber*.

"So, Blake, we meet again. Marilyn James just told me you are the *go-to* guy for names."

He looks momentarily startled and then cracks a big smile. "Whadda ya know. Your wife must be expecting."

I open my mouth, but no words come out.

"Congratulations. You came to the right guy. I'm known as the baby-name whisperer. I've helped name at least fifty babies in this church and—" He stops short. Probably because of the look on my face. Either this clown knows something I don't, or he's crazy. I'll go with the latter.

"Detective, you *are* looking for baby names, right? I've got a stack of books about that subject."

"No, I'm not. I'm here on business, Blake, not to pass out cigars. I'm looking for any information that could move this investigation along, and I need names to do it."

"Oh. I see …" He shakes his head. "I'm always putting my foot in my mouth. But if you ever do need a baby name⬜"

"I need adult names."

"You mean like staff members?" he asks.

"Anyone who knows the ins and outs of this church. Knows a lot of people. Been around a long time. Maybe even knows something about the layout of the building. Mary Ford disappeared from the church bathroom, and I want to know how."

Blake now looks so fired up I can almost see smoke coming out of his ears. "Oh, yes, sir, Detective. I can certainly help you with that. You should start with Elwood and Mandy."

"Who are they?"

"Well, Elwood Harten has been here since the church started. And Mandy Labber …" He hesitates. "She's a real talker. Knows something about everyone."

"In other words, the church gossip?"

He laughs. "I'll take the fifth on that one. But she means well."

He reaches into his pants pocket, pulls out his cell phone, and starts swiping at the screen.

"Here. Elwood's phone number." He turns the phone to show me the screen. "This old guy knows this place like the back of his hand. He even was a part of the original plans for restructuring the building, about eighteen years back."

I pull out my phone and start to type in the number, but before I can stop him, Blake punches the number on his own phone. He hands it to me, already ringing.

"Don't worry. Elwood always picks up." He flashes an expectant smile.

I turn and take a few steps away, the phone to my ear. After two rings someone answers, "Harten's residence. Elwood speaking."

"Hello, Mr. Harten. This is Detective Wholeman with the Fort Lauderdale Police Department. Do you have a few minutes to answer some questions regarding the Mary Ford investigation?"

There's a short silence. "*Me?*" He sounds confused.

"Yes, sir. Paul Blake gave me your number. He thought you may be helpful."

"Oh yes, Paul." His voice lightens. "He's a nice young man. I'll be glad to help out if I can."

I quickly fill Elwood in on the type of information I'm looking for. Soon, he comes up with a long list of facts and numbers concerning membership, financial challenges, holiday events, and even church building renovations.

Despite the monotony of this information, it's vital to pay attention. Conversations with witnesses can be a lot like winning a bid on an abandoned storage unit. Once you have it, you resign yourself to sorting through heaps of junk with the hope of finding something valuable. That's where I'm at now. In a warehouse of verbiage.

According to Elwood, the church building was once a big open warehouse of portable hot tubs. He explains how he came up with the idea of using a few of the abandoned hot tubs for church baptisms. I got to admit the idea seems clever. He goes on to say that many years back, he'd helped to erect dry wall partitions for the new rooms. The information he gives on the renovation projects are so detailed it's like listening to a YouTube tutorial. He concludes his story by informing me he's now in charge of directing newcomers to childcare classes and to the nearest bathrooms.

This information catches my interest.

"Elwood, are you familiar with the bathroom on the west wing, near the infant care center?"

"You mean the one little Mary was taken from?" His voice saddens.

"That's the one."

"Yes. I'm familiar with that bathroom. I was there when they expanded it. Years ago, that space was just a small, four-by-six-foot room."

"Uh-huh. Can you tell me if you've ever noticed anyone hanging around that bathroom—acting unusual in anyway?"

"Can't say I have. But I can recall the original construction."

"Uh-huh." I prepare myself to sort through some junk.

Well ..." He pauses, apparently taking time to recall the memories. "Back in 1999, it was just a small room with one toilet and one sink. The church wanted to expand the room to fit ten people or so. It wasn't the best location but cheaper to work around the plumbing already there. When you first walked in, there used to be a window just to the right."

"That's interesting, Mr. Harten, but there's no window to the right or anywhere in the room for that matter. Now, if we could just go back to my original question, please. Are you sure you never saw someone acting suspiciously, hanging around that bathroom area? Or did you ever recall giving directions to someone who asked too many questions about the kids or their schedules?"

"No, no. Can't recollect anything like that. But about that window. You see, they decided to wall it in. But there was a second window to the left."

"I'm sure they walled that one up too." I say gently, knowing he's trying to be helpful.

"Not exactly. You see ..." He hems and haws a bit.

"There's no window there now, Mr. Harten. I assure you."

There's a moment of silence. "No. I'm sure there *was* one. Let me think ... It would be where the last stall is now, the fourth one on the right side, just above the toilet."

I pinch the bridge of my nose with my free hand, trying to fight my impatience.

"You see," he continues undaunted, "they always meant to do it proper like, but the guy doing the dry wall got sick. He never finished walling in that second window. So, I just went ahead and did a quick patch job until he could get back to it. I'm no expert, but I'm pretty handy. I duck taped the window up pretty good and covered it over.

I try not to laugh. "Well, there's a solid wall there now."

"Detective, can you hold on a minute? Someone's knocking at my front door. I'll be right back."

"No, no," I say quickly. "That's quite all right. You've been very helpful. I'll call back another time. Thank you, Mr. Harten."

After I hang up, Blake steps in to retrieve his phone. He's probably been hanging on every word.

I give a hasty farewell and head for the stairs. I've got work to do.

CHAPTER 32

Before leaving the church, I decide to take a quick jaunt over to the bathroom where the abduction occurred. Still moving, I send out a quick text to Tina to get a HIPAA waiver for Williams's medical information over to Marilyn James. I take the stairs down to the first floor and turn right toward the east wing. Crossing through the set of glass doors, I head toward the bathrooms. When I get to the women's room, still cordoned off, I crack the door and yell in, "Anyone in there?" I know I should have alerted someone on staff, but I never was one for protocol. Besides, I strongly identify as a man and then some, so I already know I'm not welcome here—in my opinion, no man should be.

I try again, "Anyone in there?" No answer. I look to the right and to the left before I enter. With no one in sight, I step into the vestibule, open a second door and stick my head in. I call out again before entering. Everything looks the same. Eight-stall bathroom, a couch, a changing table for mothers. Neat and clean. Too clean is never good for evidence. One large waste can is standing next to a line of triple sinks.

The theory our division is still going on is that the abductor passed by just as Mary was walking out, grabbed her, and somehow avoided witnesses. But now, studying these empty stalls, I wonder. Someone could have been hiding in any one of these stalls, the one on the end would be my guess because it's the one typically the least used.

But how did he get in, unnoticed, on a busy Wednesday? Is it possible he was dressed as a woman? Maybe it *was* a woman. In all probability, the perp was someone the girl knew and trusted. Someone she went with willingly. Or he could have silenced her with something like chloroform, hid her, and waited for the church to clear out before he moved her. The question remains—drugged or not, how did he get the child out of the bathroom and out of the building?

The old guy, Elwood, said there's a single bathroom window from the original construction that had never been filled in—just covered in plywood. Stranger things have happened so I'm here to check out his story.

Walking down the narrow space between the stalls, I push open each of the doors, right and then left, until I reach the final door, the last one on the left. I shut the stall door and lean back against it. *Were you in this room little girl? And how did you get out?*

Stepping forward, I knock on the wall above the toilet. Disappointingly, the wall sounds solid. The old guy must have been wrong. I run my fingers over the wall. Then I see a crack in the paint. I pull at the gap, peeling away until a foot long, straight line appears. What's underneath looks like freshly caulked plywood. With a small pocketknife from my back pocket, I scrape at the break until it loosens and gives. To my amazement, I'm able to pry off an entire section. As it snaps off, I'm greeted by an amber glow shining through an opening in the wall. There it is. A small opaque window with embedded wire on crisscrossed glass.

"What do you know. Good old Elwood was right."

I examine the window. It's about twelve by twelve inches with tiny gray shreds of something adhering to it. I look closer. Duct tape. The window is too small for an adult to get through but just big enough for a very small person. Hypothetically, Mary Ford could have squeezed through.

Two problems with this theory. First, how could the killer have pushed her out the window and then managed to repair the wall covering before the bathroom was flooded with search teams? Maybe someone was working with him, but there still wouldn't be time. I lean back against the wall, trying to think. According to the father's report, he waited almost fifteen minutes before sending a woman in to look for his daughter. Could her captor have caulked the plywood back in place and painted over it before anyone arrived? No. The smell of paint would have been too strong, too obvious. The second problem with this theory is that the outside surveillance footage shows no movement on the day in question. The window is clearly within camera sites. As far as any visual traces of the window from the outside, the hedges are at least six-feet tall. Those hedges would serve as complete cover.

There must be an answer. I resolve to find it. No modern-day Houdini is getting past me.

I pat my front left pants pocket and breathe out in relief as I pull out a fresh pair of tightly packaged forensics gloves—a good habit I picked up a while back.

Gloves on, I reach over the top of the toilet and push up against the bottom edge of the window. It's sticky, but gives, sliding up into an open position. The window should be really jammed after years of being sealed up, so it's not unreasonable to suspect recent use. This is where forensics comes in. With any luck, prints or hair follicles might be found, or even blood. The abductor could have gotten careless, thinking the window wouldn't be discovered. Like a bolt of lightning, a realization comes to me—the small window screen, the one Tina and I found in the dirt, must be from this very window. I chastise myself. How could I have been out there, looking right into these very bushes and not have seen the opening in the wall? Then I remind myself. An entire team of investigators didn't find anything either. At any rate, why would any of us be looking for something, that as far as we knew, didn't exist?

Sticking my head out the window, I find the view completely obstructed by the hedges. I look down. Sure enough, there's the same sagging bushes we found earlier— broken and parted. He must have pushed her through this window, dropped her into the bushes below and hid her there until later. My heart is thumping in my chest now. Houdini has been uncovered.

I back my head out of the window and carefully pull the steel-trimmed glass back into the closed position. Turning carefully, as if I'm now walking on sacred ground, I open the stall door and gently close it. As an extra precaution this door should be cordoned off. I move to the bathroom entrance, cut off a few feet of hanging, extraneous yellow tape, and return to drape the tape across the stall door. Forensics may not be happy I tampered with evidence, but at least I get things done. As soon as I get back to my car, I'll put in a call.

Leaving the bathroom, I look left and right. To the immediate right is a door marked *Staff Only.* The MP report stated this was a cleaning storage closet. The fresh smell of Pine-Sol seeping through the door confirms that assessment. The doorknob twists in my hand but won't give. Locked. This is where Paul Blake might come in handy—he may have a key. I hate to admit it, but he's been pretty helpful so far. I move to pull out my phone from my pants pocket to give him a call. My pocket is empty. I withhold a curse and run back up the steps, two at a time. Nothing like making a second appearance where you're not wanted, but I've got to have that phone. I pass through the glass doors, down the hall, make a quick left past the sitting area, and then a sharp right. Suddenly, I'm not sure whether the pastor's office was down this hall or the next one. It's not like me to get disoriented, but these offices are set out like a maze. As I'm about to make another turn, I stop dead in my tracks. I duck back behind the wall, my heart thumping in my chest. Carefully peering around the corner to make sure my eyes aren't playing tricks on me, I see them.

At the end of the hall stands the pastor. And Sydney. She's leaning in close to him, saying something, but I can't make out what it is. He has his hand on her shoulder. I clench my fists. She starts to turn away, stepping in my direction. I slide into an empty office and wait. Sydney passes, her familiar perfume assaulting me. I let a minute pass. When she's gone, I head back in the direction she came from. I hear a voice behind me, calling to me.

"Officer? Officer Wholeman?" I turn around and see a young girl I don't recognize. "You are Officer Wholeman, right?" She's holding out a phone.

"Oh, thanks. I was just looking for that."

"Miss James sent me to try and catch you before you left. Thought I missed you."

Absentmindedly fingering my phone, I turn to leave and then back again. "Excuse me, miss, is the pastor still in his office?"

"No, he's left for the day. Do you have any message for him?"

Yeah, tell him to stay away from my wife before I smash his face in.

"No. No. I'll catch him later. Thanks again."

In the parking lot, I look around for Sydney's car. Nowhere. Now I'm wondering if my problems aren't a heck of a lot bigger than I thought.

CHAPTER 33

The rest of the day is a fog as I move on automatic, trying to stay too busy to think about Sydney. My time is spent making calls to the forensics lab, the missing persons unit, serology, and in updating reports. A lengthy call to my boss, Captain Gary Allen, is saved for last—I have a lot of explaining to do.

My priority is to make certain the forensics team gets out to the abduction site as soon as possible. When I call, I make it clear they're not only to look for prints and hair, but to examine both the window and the earlier found screen. If a struggle took place near, or in, that window space, they may be able to pick up blood traces with the use of Luminol. Now, it's about waiting for results.

Not being there aggravates me, but the chief is expecting a comprehensive report on his desk, ASAP. Fortunately, the day is altogether too busy to think about my personal problems.

Shuffling through the stack of papers on my inbox, I find the background checks on the church security team. I scan ten different names. All clean. At least on paper.

I settle down to watch video feeds again with a couple of sub sandwiches Tina picked up. This time, I'm focusing on footage that includes the outside wall of the hidden window. I find no movement. Nothing. Slowing the footage down, I look at it frame by frame, zeroing in on what may be close to the time of the abduction, judging by the mid-morning slant of the sun. At one point, I notice a faint blip between images. Strange the glitch wasn't noticed before. I stop, rewind, and look again. The anomaly could be the wind hitting the camera or some other interference. The blip may mean nothing, but it's not a bad idea to have it checked out. Any tampering with evidence, purposeful or accidental, must be ruled out. I send an email to our tech guy, Sebastien, asking him to go over that area of the footage.

Finally, at five o'clock, the lab calls to let us know they've just received the DNA results. A full report will be submitted first thing Monday morning. I argue for sooner but to no avail. They want a home life just as I do.

On the drive home, I put my mind in neutral. The dashboard clock says six, the day is finally over. The weekend has arrived. There's something heady about Fridays. I can almost hear the collective sigh of millions of employees ready for a weekend of relaxation. For me, this means two full days of guilt-free time to kick back and do nothing. Regretfully, this weekend is shot.

On impulse, I make a quick stop at the fish-bait shop. I'd recently run across a new fishing spot near State Road 84 with plenty of shade trees—a great place for a future family outing. I pick up the phone and hit the speed dial for Sydney, wondering if she and the boys have already sat down to dinner. No answer. I try the landline, no answer there either. They may be outside. No worries. I'll see them soon enough.

With a couple clicks and turns, the radio blasts to life. The song "Time is on My Side" by The Guess Who fills the car. Opening the window and turning up the air, I bellow a few lines while the wind whips my hair. A guy can only think about work for so long. As I gun the pedal, a thought hits me like a bolt of lightning. I break, do a quick lane-switch, and exit on Peters Road, heading toward the Pine Island sports fields. I almost forgot. The boys have another soccer game at seven.

CHAPTER 34

I wave at a vaguely familiar couple on the soccer field sidelines, watching kids go through their warm-up routines. They smile back in bland recognition. Sydney, standing beside me, is making small talk with a couple of soccer moms, alternately waving at parents across the field. Faces I don't recognize. Even the kids look different, bigger. I ignore the small stab of discomfort of being the odd man out.

"Dad, watch this." Max is energized, his feet moving in mock maneuvers as if he were already moving the ball down the field. I keep my eyes glued to the boys when we're at an event. Granted, a soccer field is a friendly enough setting, but large gatherings always have an element of the unknown and are difficult to keep under surveillance. Max has made some disappearing acts before. We usually wind up finding him at the refreshment stand or running around under the bleachers, but even the shortest MIA can seem like an eternity.

"Dad, good foot action, huh?"

"Yeah, yeah, you're a regular champ, but you're tracking slightly to the left. Keep the ball centered."

He works harder, looking up at me expectantly for praise. "Much better."

"Hey, Max, how 'bout some fishing this weekend?"

"We're going camping this weekend, Dad." He continues maneuvering the ball.

So much for that.

I look up and see his coach motioning for him. "Hey, get going. Coach is calling you."

As he sprints off, I yell, "Show 'em who's the man."

He glances back with a big toothy grin, giving me a victory sign.

Turning my attention to Sydney, I see she has moved a few feet away with the soccer moms. She appears happy and carefree. Either she's a great actress, or she has something other than me to be happy about—and I'm not talking about her piano. My line of work doesn't exactly promote trust. Suspicion is my trade.

Looking around for my son Shane, I spot him at the top of the bleachers with his best friend, Jared Summers. I wave, but he and his friend are too busy throwing popcorn at kids beneath the bleachers to notice.

I inhale the brisk air that smells of freshly cut grass wafting on a strong gulf breeze. The aroma of hot dogs coming from the refreshment stand causes my stomach to growl with hunger. I turn to Sydney to ask if she wants anything from the snack bar and stop in my tracks. Sitting on the bleachers, about ten yards to our left, only one row below Shane, is Andria. Her presence is all I need right now. Fuel to the fire.

"Hey, Syd," I say, interrupting a woman who is droning on about some Macy's sale. "I'm starving, let's get some Cokes and hot dogs." I grab her elbow and steer her in the opposite direction.

She pulls back, giving a socially polite laugh. "Jet, get real, you know I don't eat that stuff."

"I hear they just added some kind of tofu thing," I lie, still tugging on her arm.

Not wanting to make a scene, she follows along with a silent glare.

Glancing back, I see Andria laughing with a couple of overweight men who seem to have forgotten their wives. Before I can turn away, she catches my eye and gives me a friendly wink. I return a cool nod and turn away.

What is that woman up to?

When we're out of sight and standing in the crowd around the hotdog stand, I try to casually hold Sydney's hand. She snatches it away.

"I'm not stupid, Jethro, I saw her."

"Saw who?" I ask, knowing I sound like a guilty kid.

"What is she doing here?" she whispers with a hiss. "I know she doesn't have any kids. Is she stalking you? Or is this some kind of clandestine meeting?"

"What? A secret meet-up in public? I swear, Sydney, I have no idea what she's doing here. She probably knows someone here. Or maybe she thinks she can get some information out of me on the Ford case."

"How would she know you were here? Some kind of journalistic hunch?"

"Uh, I don't know. I could have mentioned the kids play here. Or she knows one of the parents. How am I supposed to know?"

"Well, I don't see tofu on the menu, so I'll just be heading back. I better hurry. Andria may be stopping by to say hello."

I wince.

"Or Pastor Bill," I hurl back at her.

With an incredulous expression, she turns on her heel and walks away.

I order three hot dogs and a Coke and don't wait for my change. The game is starting, and I want to get back. I'm not going to let anything stop me from seeing my son play. Stuffing one of the mustard drenched buns into my mouth, I rush toward the sidelines as a cheer goes up from the crowd. Max, first up, just made a twenty-five-yard kick. I let out a whelp of victory, spilling Coke down my pants leg. I down some cold cola, feeling the heat of the day wash away. Everything's going to be okay, I tell myself. Sydney and I have great boys and a great marriage. Just need a tune-up, that's all.

"Jet, you have ketchup all over your shirt." I stop in mid gulp. There beside me stands Andria in a tight red T-shirt and white shorts.

Giving a nervous glance to see where Sydney is, I turn my attention back to the game. I can sense her moving closer. "Andria, this is not a good time. I don't talk shop when I'm with my family."

"I'm disappointed in you, Jet." Her tone is teasing. "I got a tip there's a search warrant ready to search Bill Williams's house. Is it going down tomorrow?"

Out of the corner of my eye, I can see her crossing her arms, leaning around, trying to read my expression, which I'm keeping flat.

She ignores my silence. "And I've heard more. A lot more. Since when aren't you interested in an inside tip?"

"My mind is elsewhere." My eyes are still glued to the game when, from inside my pants pocket, I feel my phone vibrating. Moving swiftly to turn it off, I notice Tina's name flashing on the screen. Good timing.

"Yeah, Tina. What's up?"

"You have a minute?"

I look back at Andria and catch her trying to read the phone's screen name. I take a couple steps away and lower my voice. "Not really, but shoot."

"I reread all the reports, trying to make sense of that window you found … then I remembered. The paint."

"The paint?"

"You know, the fresh paint, to cover the *tweeny* graffiti."

I stop in my tracks. "That's got to be it. You're a genius. The MP team would have missed that if it was reported as a prior repair. Does the report say when the walls were painted?"

"You're going to love this. The entire bathroom was painted the morning of the abduction, eight hours prior."

"Whoa. Let me think this out. The father waited ten to fifteen minutes before sending someone in to look for her. Hypothetically, someone could have slid the cover back over the window, caulked it up, painted it, and had it restored to normal within that time frame. Either someone on the inside was working with him, or we have a colossal coincidence."

"I'll go with the first one."

The crowd begins to cheer as I look up to see Max running the ball toward the goalie. Almost dropping the phone, I run along the sidelines yelling out like a maniac. "That's the way, keep it going, Max." He cuddles the ball between his feet and then, *wham,* kicks it square into the net. "Way to go, Max! You're the man." I disconnect the phone. Priorities.

Andria pipes up, close on my heels again. "Did I hear something about a colossal coincidence? You sounded excited. Are you on to something?"

I turn to look at her. "Yeah, the game."

She gives a pouty sigh. "Oh well, your loss. If you change your mind, you know my number."

As she turns to leave, she throws me a sultry, playful glance, but her voice tells a different story, an undertone of anger. Andria doesn't respond well to rejection. I take another bite of my hot dog, but it's lost its flavor. Hopefully, she didn't hear any more of that conversation. As I cram the rest of the hot dog down my dry throat, I can't help but wonder what the tip was she alluded to? Maybe I should have talked to her. Frustration eats at me. My personal life shouldn't be interfering with my professional. Or is it the other way around?

Sydney and I drive home in separate cars and wind up sleeping in different beds. One step forward, one step backward. On a high note, I fall into a coma sleep. On a low note, I wake up to an empty bed.

CHAPTER 35

Vicki Anderson opens an email, alerting her to attend an impromptu meeting in the FBI conference center. An outsourced advisor on terrorism would be lecturing on NSA phone transmissions. Vicki knows millions of satellite transmissions are received each week involving possible terrorist threats. These transmissions represent thousands of man-hours as attempts are made to trace intricate patterns and systems that often lead nowhere. A needle in a haystack hunt. Despite this, she remains hopeful. She feels it in her bones they're on to something big. She hopes it won't be too late.

After grabbing a coffee, she lumbers into the conference room. The meeting is already in progress. She takes a seat among her coworkers and leans forward to study the lecturer. As he presents his slide presentation of carefully labeled graphs and statistics, shown on a seventy-five-foot computer screen, she is taken by how young he looks, as if he could have just graduated high school. Vicki rolls her eyes. These computer experts are practically wearing diapers these days.

She resigns herself to listen to his droning voice as he points to an image on the screen. His long skinny arm reaches up and lightly taps the image of a US satellite as his voice goes up a notch.

"Fifteen hundred and twenty-two miles above the earth's equator, the NSA Keyhole surveillance satellite, orbiting in geostationary orbit, recorded another of the millions of transmitted cell phone calls of the day, relaying them to a supercomputer in Virginia. The Silkworm software ferreted through all the transmissions focusing on specific Farsi words, *armor* and *detonate,* and the English word *satellites.* As soon as the referenced words were recognized, another program communicated with the cell phone providers and obtained cell phone triangulations on the two communicating phones. Once the approximate location of the callers was established, the sites were then digitally forwarded to a linguist. Within forty-five minutes, the entire conversation had been translated and forwarded to an intelligence analyst. Within an hour of the intercept, the Department of Homeland Security was transmitted a notification by email of over eighty thousand notices received by DHS on that slow Saturday evening. This is just one of millions of intercepted calls, but this particular one is different." He pauses for effect. "This one is local, picked up right here in Homestead, Florida."

Vicki almost drops her coffee. That's only thirty minutes away. It's time some of the local law enforcement take this issue seriously.

Jet Wholeman is the first to come to mind.

CHAPTER 36

Today is the day. Tina and I pull up in front of Pastor William B. Williams's house, a well-manicured structure with a red brick facade over trimmed cinder block. The city of Tamarac is outside of our jurisdiction, so two Tamarac police units are waiting in the grassy swale just ahead of me.

As I park behind the cruisers, Tina is craning her neck past me to get a better look out the driver's side window. She's probably looking for Williams.

Pastor Bill is calmly sitting in a lawn chair on his front patio, bordered by flowering, red hibiscus bushes. He looks as if he's expecting guests for a barbecue.

We both get out of the car and approach an officer who's just exiting his unit.

"Thanks for the response," I say.

"No problem." He gives a half-smile. "All in a day's work."

I glance up at the patio and nod toward the pastor. "Was he sitting there when you arrived?"

"Yep, just like he was expecting us."

"That's unlikely."

I turn to see Tina walking up behind me and give her a quick nod toward the porch. Leaving the officers, I join her in a reluctant walk up the driveway. When we reach him, he gives us a weak smile.

"Good afternoon, Mr. Williams." My voice sounds cold to my ears.

"Good afternoon, Pastor." Tina gives an apologetic smile.

He stands up and offers his hand in silent greeting. I take it begrudgingly.

I look him in the eye and then away with a reluctant sigh, trying to communicate I've got to do my job despite any personal feelings.

"We're here with a warrant to search your house, your car, and the church."

He blinks once, looks away, then back again. "I thought we were going to avoid all this until after weekend services." His voice is calm.

"That was the plan, but there's been too much internal and external pressure. Too many people are getting wind of this investigation … media leaks and such."

He holds up his palm to stop me. "You don't need to explain, and you didn't need a warrant. As I said previously, you can search anything you need to search. Naturally, I never thought that would include my home, but I have nothing to hide."

Tina clears her throat. "So, we have your permission to look around?" she asks diplomatically.

Before he can respond, we all look toward the street as the crime scene investigation van turns into the driveway.

Charlie York steps from the driver's side, walking like a western gunslinger to the front door. Nodding a greeting, he grunts, "Have we got a warrant yet?"

"We have a consent and a warrant." Tina stares him down.

Without another word, York pulls out his phone and calls for an assistant as he heads for Williams's front door. He opens it and walks in like he owns the place.

York takes his time collecting fibers from the house, creeping around and getting into every possible space. His team systematically goes through cabinets, drawers, closets, bathroom medicine cabinets, and bottles of medications.

Every letter, card, photo, form, and bank statement are laid bare. Next, they enter a virtually empty garage and, after poking around in a couple of boxes, proceed to climb into the attic. That turns out to be empty space also, except for one box of tools, an old bicycle, and Christmas decorations.

A careful search of the car begins as they take fiber samples from the interior and then move to the trunk. They finish up by walking the perimeter of the house. Every bush and nook and cranny of the yard is searched. The side-yard garbage can is opened, turning up empty. The neighbors, upon questioning, inform us the garbage pick-up just came this morning. An unfortunate fact. Garbage always has a story. Timing is everything.

Tina and I participate in the search, albeit half-heartedly. Every time I catch a glimpse of York's face, it has a slightly creepy smile, the kind that says, *I know something you don't.*

I suppress the urge to smash the guy's face. This rush of anger disturbs me. Things are beginning to feel personal, and they shouldn't. We're all just doing our jobs.

When all is said and done, nothing is found that stands out as valuable to the investigation, at least until the fiber analysis. We leave without making an arrest. I'm sure York is rankled.

As York and his team pack up the van, I make a hasty apology to Williams for the inconvenience. He shakes my hand, looking vastly relieved.

Tina has a look of victory on her face as we walk back to the car. "I won't say, I told you so."

"Unfortunately, that *told you so* smirk of yours is about to swell. Turns out the pastor's blood test went missing in the delivery process."

"How did you find that out?"

"Last meeting with the pastor."

"And you're just telling me now. You have a partner, remember?"

"Sorry, got a lot on my mind. Besides, I figured you'd get to the bottom of it once you dealt with the HIPAA waiver."

"What HIPAA waiver?"

My head turns sharply toward her. "You didn't."

"Just messin' with you. The waiver's been signed, sealed, and delivered."

With a wave of relief, I chirp the doors open on the Charger, and we climb in.

"Move it, Jet. You can give me rest of the dirt on the drive back to the department. I've got to get my car and head home. Mitch and I have church tonight, but he's down with the flu."

I slap my head with my palm and let out a moan. "Tonight! I'm supposed to take Sydney to church."

"Sorry, bro. Commitments happen that way."

I grumble as I turn the key and the engine comes to life. "I want to go but the timing isn't right. I think I've got myself over-involved in this one."

"A little saying for ya, Wholeman. 'The difference between involvement and commitment is a lot like ham and eggs. The chicken becomes involved, but the pig is committed.'"

"Am I the chicken or the pig?"

"In this case, both."

I rev up the engine. Pig or no pig, I'm dreading the call I have to make to Sydney.

CHAPTER 37

I'm parked in the department parking lot, cool air blasting, as the afternoon sun pours through my windshield. My voice is becoming hoarse as I labor through a call with Sydney. With the phone to my ear, my legs sprawled out across the passenger seat, I stare up at the car headliner wondering why I'm on the defensive. Isn't she the one who is now suspect? But I'm not ready to go there.

"I *am* listening, Sydney. Please calm down. I already profusely apologized for canceling. Do you want me to grovel?"

Her sharp intake of air tells me she doesn't like my tone.

"It's not just about tonight. You're always canceling. And did you really have to wait until the last minute to tell me?"

"I said I'd work on that."

"And you never told me what you meant by that comment about Pastor Bill … at the game last night."

"What comment?" Playing dumb works well for me—it also helps to end an overworked conversation.

"Never mind, Jet. Playing dumb suits you."

"I've never known you to be sarcastic. It doesn't *suit* you."

"A lot of things don't suit me right now. And I'm tired of that air of mystery you carry around like some kind of superhero mantle."

"Don't go there. That's holy ground."

"Your cavalier attitude is disturbing. This is no laughing matter."

"So, you want me to cry?"

"Stop it. This is not a sparring game."

"I saw you in the church hall with Pastor Bill—your heads pressed together in a romantic moment," I blurt out.

I can hear her small gasp of air on the other end of the phone. "What? Is this a bad joke?"

"You tell me, Sydney."

"You mean earlier today? In the hall?"

"You got it."

"We were praying together. That's what people do at church!"

"I'd love to finish this conversation, Sydney, but I've got work to do."

The anger in the following silence is palpable.

Admittedly, what I saw could have been some kind of prayer pow-wow, but the jury is not out yet—I'm not ready to give up my anger. My attitude is bad, obviously, but having seen my wife so intimately engaged with the pastor has uncorked some incivility.

Trying to assuage my guilt, I remind myself the plan to escort Sydney to church tonight was motivated by a need to collect intel. Now that I'm swamped in paperwork, have leads to follow up on, and deadlines to meet, a church visit has become a back-burner project. Despite my line of logic, feelings of guilt remain.

Pressing my fingertips to my forehead, I have a change of heart. "Okay, I'll have Tina follow up on deadlines, and I'll swing by to pick you up. We're going to church."

"No, Jet. I'll go alone. Just do your job."

"Is that really what you want?"

"It's what you want. Soon you'll be running on empty."

"My life is not empty. I have you. I have my kids. I have my job."

The line goes quiet.

"Sydney?"

"I'm here. You know, Jet, we can't side-step our problems."

"I'll fix them."

She gives a heavy sigh. "I think you've forgotten the really good things about yourself, instead of what you've become. Things like your talent, intelligence, magnetic personality."

"I have a magnetic personality?"

"Please shut up and listen. There are a lot of things about you I love, but there are just as many I don't. Despite your best excuses, you *are* seeing your ex-girlfriend. You can call it whatever you want. Networking, insider tips … it doesn't matter. The truth is the relationship may not be love, but at the very least, it's lust."

"I feel nothing for that woman. And what do you mean everyone knows? Everyone is probably that busy body, Gail Summers."

"Gail is just looking out for my best interests. And don't think she's the only one. Just remember, the person being talked about is always the last one to know."

"Are we going to church or not?"

"Jet. Just go. Talk to Tina. She knows you better than I do, anyway."

"What's that supposed to mean?"

"Nothing. I'll see you tonight. That is, if I'm awake when you get home."

The phone goes dead before I can answer.

I'm feeling cold and clammy even in the heat.

My brain is hit with conflicting thoughts, bouncing off each other like bombarding atoms in a nucleus. My job is important. My wife is important. Finding Mary Ford's killer is important. The murder of a child. The loss of my family.

Where should my priorities be?

Is there any truth in what she said about Andria? I can't think about it. Not now.

There's a tapping on the roof of my car. I jump, ready to pull my Glock, but it's only Tina, looking at me quizzically through the driver's side window. I roll it down.

"Problems at home?" she asks with her usual frankness.

"Were you eavesdropping?"

"No-o-o. I've got better things to do, homey. But you look off your game."

My stomach tightens, and a sudden flush of heat rushes to my face. I resist the impulse to snap back at her. "What do you need? I'm in a hurry."

"No way, Jet. Don't try to change the subject. You should see yourself. You're a mess."

Involuntarily, I glance in the mirror. A forlorn unshaved face and a head of wild hair greets me. "Looks like a handsome stud of a guy to me."

"Talk to me, Jet. After all this time, you still can't trust me?"

"What are you talking about? I trust you with my six every day."

"That's not the kind of trust I'm talking about. Listen. I've kept quiet, not wanting to pry into your life, but now we need to talk. You're my partner, and I need to know if my life is in danger, because you're too distracted to have my back."

My fingers turn white, gripping the steering wheel. "Don't tell me I'm not doing my job." With my personal life unraveling, I'm not about to hear about my job performance coming apart too.

I nod toward a couple of nosy pedestrians on the corner about twenty yards away.

Tina lowers her voice to a whisper. "Obviously, your mind has been on other things."

"I've been doing my job, that's all you need to know."

"You messed up, and Sydney found out. Right?"

My head snaps around to face her. "Who told you that?"

"Who hasn't?"

"Who taught you to answer a question with a question?"

"You did," she snaps. An involuntary grin crosses my face, and we both let out a strained chuckle.

"Okay. Okay, let's get everything out on the table. Climb in." I jab my thumb at the passenger seat.

I should've known Tina would get wind of this somehow. Always the investigator, one ear to the wall.

She climbs in, shuts the door, and adjusts the seat for her long legs.

"So, you've been having lunch with the green-eyed tigress who's probably just using you for information."

"Maybe it's the other way around. So, who's been talking?"

She looks me in the eye. "You should know by now the criminal system is a small world. Everyone is in everyone else's business, and the last one to know is always the one they're talking about."

"So, I've been told." I give a grim laugh. "Tina, get real. You know the job demands networking. In this line of work, you have to be friend of all and enemy of none."

"Sometimes we have to draw a line." She shakes her head. "I have your back on the street, but Sydney has your back at home. She's a special girl, Jet. You don't get it. Maybe you don't know what you got."

I sit in silence, mulling this information over, stunned that people in the department are talking about my private life. Years of devotion, hard work, and determination to get ahead taught me to never mix my personal and professional life. I've carefully constructed an iron curtain between the two ... until now. What an ass I've been. Of course, people would speculate about frequent meetings with a beautiful, long-legged ex-girlfriend. It's no secret we used to date.

Tina reaches over and knocks on my head. "Wake up, boy wonder. You know she loves you. Don't you?"

"Andria?" I blurt.

"No, you dope. Sydney. She's hurt and disappointed in you, but she still loves you."

"Hell, I'm disappointed in me."

"Well, that's a start."

"So, you've been talking to her?"

She rubs her forehead. "A little, mostly listening." Tina looks out the window and back at me. "I hate to have to go here, Jet, but someone has to tell you. This whole thing is the talk of the department. Some of the guys think you're hooking up."

She looks away again with obvious discomfort, her hand tapping the armrest. "What did you think people would say, Jet, when they saw the two of you repeatedly meeting for lunch and sometimes even for evening drinks?"

"Oh, come on, Tina. I was collecting information. Those meetings were nothing. I wasn't trying to hide them."

"So, you told Sydney about those meetings?"

"Since when does a wife have to know everything a guy does on the job?" I hang my head, knowing how stupid I must sound. "Okay, you're right, I should've told her."

A silence follows, like she's giving me a chance to examine myself.

"Tina, you know me. I wasn't looking for a hook-up."

"What were you looking for?"

"I wasn't looking for anything. Maybe it's what I was looking at." Leaning back, I rake my fingers through my hair. "Okay, occasionally I caught myself looking … You know, some of those dresses she wears are …"

"None of your business?"

"What I'm trying to say is any normal guy would take a second look. You know me. All bark and no bite."

"Yes, I do know you. And somewhere along the way, you forgot how to respect women. Yeah, men look at women and women look at men, but you don't just give into the glance, you embrace it."

"You're not my Sunday school teacher."

She glares back at me.

"Listen, Tina, how about we bury the axe?"

She nods. "So, was that Sydney you were talking to on the phone?"

"If you must know, yes. I told her I'd go to church with her tonight, but the Ford case is at a critical point. I just can't go."

"Why can't you make it?"

"I just told you. Besides, she doesn't want me to go."

"Yeah, right."

"You know as well as I do, me attending church there is a conflict of interest." I really don't give a hoot about that, but my comment is meant to derail her.

"Nice try. I go there too, so what? And for the record, just because our investigation might point to the pastor of this church doesn't mean I've given up on the church. Two separate things."

My mouth drops in surprise. I'd assumed by this point in the investigation her church attendance would have stopped cold.

"I know what you're thinking, Jet, but innocent until proven guilty, remember? And frankly, I'll need a truckload of evidence to convince me that Pastor Bill is anything but what he appears to be—a godly man." She stares me down, arms folded across her chest. "This investigation isn't going anywhere until tomorrow. Keep your appointment with your wife."

"Hold on there, I have a job to do."

"We're in this together. You go ahead and do what you need to do, and I'll take it from here. Just tell me what needs to be done."

I give her a grin. "You're a real piece of work, partner."

"I'll take that as a yes, boss."

A moment of indecision twists inside me.

"Go home," Tina orders, with a dismissive wave of her hand. "Tell her you love her, and your marriage is more important than your job."

Part of me wants to tell Tina she's busting my boundaries, but another part welcomes sound direction.

Tina opens the door and climbs out of the vehicle. "I'm going back to the office. If you want, I'll get on that report for the chief—at least get that off your mind. I'll email the report to you for final approval."

All I can do is nod.

She leaves as I watch until she's safely in her vehicle.

An idea comes to me. I put the car in drive and pull up beside her just as she gears into reverse and breaks. Motioning for her to roll down the passenger window, I lean out and yell over the engines hum, "Find out what Dr. Liam A. Cooper's office does with blood samples they send to the lab. Is it hand-to-hand or after-hours pickups?"

It feels good to get back to business.

"Do you know something I don't? C'mon, give it up," she yells back.

I pop the car into park and jump out. With a conspiratorial look, I lean into her passenger window, my elbows resting on the door frame. "Patience, grasshopper. Time will tell all. But right now, with the pastor's blood sample gone missing, we need to act. Dig up whatever you can. I want to know if someone snatched that sample from Doctor Cooper's office or in transit to the lab. Find out how it disappeared. If it did, that is."

"I'm on it. First thing tomorrow."

I get back in the car and send a quick text to Sydney informing her I'm picking her up. I head out toward I-95, mashing the gas pedal. A quick glance at the dashboard clock reads 5:45. That leaves me fifteen minutes to make it to the church on time. On second thought, that's cutting it too short. I shoot out another voice text asking her to meet me at the church entrance. An incoming text flashes. Sydney. She'll be there.

My gut tells me things are going to go well tonight. I'll have Sydney introduce me around to some folks, and with a little luck, I'll meet someone who can provide some leads.

Accelerating onto the interstate, I flip the radio to the AM, 94.0 channel for some jazz tunes. A sax with some bass guitar fills the air while a salty, warm Atlantic wind blows through the open window. I'm feeling better already.

CHAPTER 38

Pulling into Central Christian Church, I realize I might have to circle around a couple of times to find a spot, the place is packed—who would have thought—on a Saturday night? I sling the car door shut and start toward the front entrance. The area is well lit, showing the huge, stark-white warehouse shining out of the surrounding night. The front building is bordered in neatly trimmed foliage and small royal palms, but other than that, there's no ornamentation. This is the plainest church I've ever seen. My wife and I are attending church in a remodeled warehouse. My Catholic mother is going to shoot me.

I don't have to look far for Sydney. She's standing by the main entrance doors, waving her arms expectantly. Her face is solemn but somehow glowing. She looks young, hopeful.

For a moment, she reminds me of the same girl I fell in love with fifteen years ago. The young, starry-eyed girl I kissed in my old Mustang convertible under a South Florida, moonlit night. As I get closer, I see her cheeks are flushed and her eyes bright. She's smiling. This is not what I'd expected. At best, I'd foreseen a cool indifference.

Whatever else might have clouded my mind is gone now. And whatever I thought I saw in the church hall between her and the pastor, I chalk up to an overactive imagination.

She grabs my hand and tugs me toward the door. "I'm glad you changed your mind."

"I'm glad you changed yours."

"I took pity on you. Let's grab a seat toward the front before they fill up."

"A seat in the back will do."

"A seat in the front will do even better."

Her attitude is definitely in the positive zone. I wonder though if I've been magically forgiven or if she's just putting her anger on hold until after the sermon.

We walk through the front double glass doors and enter a large vestibule. There are very few people—a wave of relief passes through me. I'm not crazy about going to a crowded church. I like a lot of breathing space.

Muffled music and singing come from a bank of doors to my left. In front of the first door is a young Asian lady, the official greeter, with a handful of flyers. She hands me a pamphlet of information which I gladly grab. Sydney waves one away with a smile, she probably has the thing memorized.

The door opens, and there's a blast of music and singing from a well-lit, monstrous auditorium, packed solid with humanity. So much for elbow room. Everyone's standing, some clapping and swaying in rhythm. There's a thumping of drums and the strained steel of a wailing guitar.

Sydney must have felt me recoil at the sight of all those people, because she tightens her grip on my arm and moves forward with calm certainty.

A guy with a humongous smile greets us, grabs my hand, and gives it a shake. Over the cacophony, he raises two fingers, mouthing the question, "Two?" Sydney smiles back with a vigorous nod. The usher proceeds to lead us down a broad aisle.

This isn't what I imagined. I expected formal clothes, worn white hymnals, the unearthly silence that descends between hymns, and echoes of turning pages and dry coughs. Then again, I hadn't been to a church in decades. I suppose even churches evolve.

As we walk farther down the aisle, I note with some remorse that we're also moving further away from the front door. I make it my habit to sit near a back exit for easier observation of my surroundings … and to leave quickly, if I'm so moved. The usher continues to lead us forward.

Sydney must feel my hesitation, because her grip tightens. No turning back now.

Finally, two-thirds down the aisle, the usher finally stops and points to two empty seats, just a couple of people in. A middle-aged couple, nodding and smiling, press back into their seats to allow us to pass. Cheerfully, I note the chairs are padded, not the wooden pews I'd expected. I'm going to be able to sit in comfort. Sydney places her Bible on her seat and waves at a nearby couple. I notice there isn't a chair in the place without a Bible except mine. I turn and place the church pamphlet squarely on my seat. There, I fit right in.

On the platform stage is a full band: Acoustic and electric guitars, drums, congas, piano, saxophone, and six singers with standing microphones. A deep, pounding rhythm is filling the air with a vibration that goes beyond just sound— the space seems to be charged with enthusiasm. People are gently swaying and singing, while others clasp their hands in prayer. If I had to describe the scene, I'd say it's like they're all a part of a living organism, an energized living thing, eerily charged with some invisible power.

I'm determined to keep my head and not be moved by all the hoopla, but looking down, I notice my foot has betrayed me and is happily tapping a beat. I hear the pure, sweet tones of my wife's voice join the others in perfect harmony. Sydney's warm hand reaches out for mine, the heat of her touch calms me, but I feel something more. A certain, undefinable warmth seems to fill the entire room.

The music slows, and I can feel an intensity building in the congregation. Some of the people are raising their arms now as if trying to reach the heavens, and their voices take on deep, heartfelt tones.

The music concludes, and a man at the piano starts saying a prayer, as if he's directly talking to someone. The room becomes hushed and solemn.

Then things start happening—in my mind. Snapshot images of Andria and me begin popping into my mind. With each memory, I feel my stomach lurch. With each recollection, with each twist of my insides, with the sudden dryness that invades my mouth, I realize now those meetings with her had been anything but innocent. I enjoyed her smiles, her glances, the casual touch of her hand as she spoke. Our conversation may have been about investigations, forensics, crime scenes and criminal motives, but under the spell of her hypnotic voice, I had my own motives. Her words had been velvety, caressing notes, but in the clarity of this moment, the allure was gone.

A wave of nausea hits me. I break out in a cold sweat and let go of Sydney's hand, not wanting her to feel how clammy mine has become.

I breathe a sigh of relief as the prayer ends. A man in a white dress shirt and casual pants comes forward to give the church announcements. Out of the corner of my eye, I see Sydney looking at me with some expression I can't quite identify, but the word that comes to mind is pity.

CHAPTER 39

After the service, Sydney introduces me to one friend after another. The cheerful throng surrounding us are all busy shaking one another's hands and hugging like it's a family reunion. Her friends eye me curiously, all smiling enthusiastically at one another as if they're enjoying a shared conspiracy.

One woman, an overweight blonde, is introduced as Mandy Labber. Now there's a name that rings a bell. The infamous church gossip. She gushes a steady stream of exclamations: "What a cute couple you make. I can't believe he finally came. Miracles do happen." She winks at Sydney and turns to me. "I'm sure your wife told you there are some pretty important people in this church. Governor Gibson attends here, and his beautiful wife dresses just like a princess. Of course, he can't always make it—very busy man, I'm sure." She blabbers on to anyone who may still be listening.

I lean in and whisper to Sydney. "She hasn't taken a single breath. She could qualify for the speed-talking Olympics."

Sydney, trying to hide her embarrassment, turns to introduce me to an elderly gentleman, patiently waiting to be noticed. He smiles shyly as she affectionately pats his thin hand.

"Jet, this is my good friend Elwood. He's one of the pillars of this church. Always ready to help someone. He knows this church inside and out."

There he is in flesh and blood. Good old Elwood. I reach out to shake his hand. "You must be the same Elwood I talked to on the phone. After all, how many Elwoods can there be?"

He ducks his head with a shy smile. "I hope I was able to help some."

"Are you kidding? I'm ready to hire you as an assistant." I try to hand him my card, but he insists on writing his number on an old piece of wadded up newspaper he pulled from his pocket, saying he doesn't want to waste my *nice* cards. I already have his number, but I don't say anything.

"You can call me anytime." He beams at me as he hands over the paper.

A large-set man in his late thirties steps forward and begins pumping my hand and thumping me on the back like we're old friends. "I'm Peter Monterelli. Heard you're a police officer," he says in a loud voice. Some curious heads began to turn. "I bet you have some real stories to tell in your line of work."

"Not any you'd want to hear."

"Are you kidding? Every one of them. I hope you're on the Mary Ford case. You know, the little girl who was stolen right here in this church. *Believe* me. We all want to see that slime ball put in prison."

I'm a little surprised to hear this churchgoer's unsavory description of the perp, but I find his honesty refreshing. My guard goes down a measure.

"Well, a lot of people are on the case," I offer. "Everyone wants this case solved and, believe me, every possible resource will be used. Did you happen to know Mary Ford?"

"I know almost everyone in this church. Been going here for over ten years. I still have a lot of rough edges, but these people never give up on me." He chuckles. "Mary was a sweet little thing. She was in my daughter's Sunday school class. Very talkative. Always gave me a big hug when she saw me. Very friendly."

This man seems jovial and disarming in his own way, the kind kids usually like. Seems like a nice guy, but you never can tell. I take another mental note to send Tina over to talk to Mary's Sunday school teacher.

"This church is like a maze. Where are the kids' classes?" I ask him.

"Five and under are downstairs, six to twelve are upstairs. Upstairs is where my daughter Adaline goes. She's nine. Loves Sunday school. The teens are next door in a separate building on the south side."

This gets my interest.

"Mary Ford was fourteen years old. Why would she have been upstairs with the younger kids?"

"Not sure, but she seemed young for her age. Maybe she fit in better there. All the kids liked her."

Sydney touches my arm. "Hate to interrupt, but we have to get some dinner. I know you must be starving." She looks at me with curiosity.

"Just a moment, honey." I fumble around in my pockets, unable to find the card I just had. "Would you happen to have one of my cards to give to this gentleman?"

"For Peter? Of course. I have a whole stack of them," she says brightly, already digging in her purse. She hands him the card. He looks at it with interest and then tucks it in his shirt pocket.

We say our farewells, leave the auditorium, and head for the cafeteria.

"So, does Governor Gibson really attend church here?" I ask with some surprise.

"Occasionally. But I've never actually seen him."

Sydney leads me down a maze of tan-colored corridors toward what she refers to as a cafeteria but, as it turns out, is more like a full-blown restaurant. Opening the cafe door, my senses meet with a warm hum of contented voices and a blended aroma of baking bread and steaming gourmet plates. The multiple partitioned rooms, with burnt umber walls, Mexican tile, and beige vinyl booths are already filled to capacity.

We wait patiently, at least Sydney does, for the hostess to mark the seating chart and usher us to a small, two-person booth, tucked away against a wall in the back of the room—too far away from the exit for my taste.

I barely slide into the booth when Sydney breathlessly asks, "So, I'm really interested in your take on everything. What do you think?"

The hostess stands at the table a moment too long, as if she too is interested.

I have the eerie feeling that though I know no one, they all know me. Church paranoia?

I nod at the woman, trying to convey a polite dismissal, but she remains rooted to the spot.

"We can take those menus off your hands now," I add.

"Oh, yes, of course," she says with an embarrassed smile. "Anything I can get you, drinks maybe?"

Sydney smiles at her. "Two waters with lemon, will do. Thank you, Michelle."

"And a large Coke, extra sugar, and caffeine," I add.

"Will do." She laughs and turns to leave, giving Sydney a wink over her shoulder.

"Do you know everyone in this joint?"

She shushes me with a finger to her lips and leans forward expectantly. "Well … what do you think?"

"I think operating this place must cost a bundle." I take a look around at the thick seating upholstery and polished oak tables.

Sydney looks around too, as if she's trying to see the place through my eyes. "No, they're all volunteers, and the seating and décor were all donated by various local companies."

"Volunteers, like they work for free type?" I ask incredulously.

"Uh-huh." She nods. "All of the people you see here donate their time and work."

Trumped again. "How about the pastor? Does he get a percentage?"

"No. All profit goes to benefit different charities."

"Did Mary Ford ever help out here?"

She looks away. "Not that I know of."

I do a quick scan of the place. "Anyone with a beard work in here?"

"What kind of question is that? If you haven't noticed, the scruffy look is in these days."

"I'm talking about a fuller beard."

"Not that I've seen. But can we talk about something else? I want to know what you *really* think about this church?"

I stall as I look at the menu. "God 101," I answer flatly.

"That's it? What kind of cryptic answer is that?"

"A little like a university," I add.

She huffs a breath of air. "I guess I'll have to take that as a positive."

I continue to study the menu. I'm not in the mood to give a sermon critique or to admit there was something in the pastor's message that's been repeating in my mind like a broken record. He quoted what sounded like a Chinese proverb. I was only half listening, but the saying went something like … adultery of the heart begins with the lust of the eye. It seemed eerily directed at me. Is that what Sydney and the pastor were discussing in the hall? I put down the menu and begin to snap one of its edges against the table. When I look up, she's still watching me.

"Syd, the service was nice. Real nice." I glance at a passing server with scruffy facial hair.

"I thought it was great." She flips her napkin onto her lap as if she's dusting off my response.

A smiling teen-age girl arrives with our drinks and asks to take our order. Just in time.

Sydney orders a shrimp gumbo soup and salad. I choose a rack of ribs, fully loaded baked potato, coleslaw, and a side order of onion rings.

"Can you bring extra bread?" I ask shamelessly.

"Sure, it'll be out shortly."

"Not short enough for me."

The server gives me a laugh as she collects our menus and leaves.

Sydney leans in, her chin resting on her clasped hands. "If you want to know what I think … the sermon was absolutely captivating. I felt like he was talking right to me."

I blink. "You mean God?"

"No. Pastor Bill."

"Maybe you're right, Syd, but I didn't hear anything in that message for you."

"That's because what I heard was for me. Some of the things he said made me realize I've made mistakes too." She reaches out and touches my hand.

I gulp, not daring to hope she's softening toward me. At this point, I probably should be suspicious. The *too good to be true* adage comes to mind, but it feels good. I'm not about to spoil things by overthinking.

"What I meant by mistakes is my impatience. And I'm quick to judge."

"Ah, honey, you're always patient and kind. If you were any more perfect, they'd have to officially saint you."

"I'm not a saint." Her voice turns firm. "You don't get it. We all fail, we all disappoint. There was only one perfect being who ever walked this earth."

"Mother Theresa?"

"No. Jesus."

"Well, you must come pretty close to Mother Theresa."

"I'm not as good as you think. You don't know my thoughts, my motives, my fantasies."

"What fantasies?" I ask, dumbfounded. Involuntarily my mind darts back to the scene of her and Williams standing together in the church hall.

"Is that all you heard? I'm just trying to say I've made mistakes too."

"So, do those fantasies involve anyone I know?"

She rolls her eyes. "My point is, we both need to try harder."

This is getting deep, but after the last twenty-four hours of frigid communication, it feels more like a campfire chat. I decide to play it safe and stay quiet.

She sits back in her seat. "I've decided to set up an appointment for marital counseling."

There's the catch. A bee caught in honey.

"Sydney, I think two educated, mature adults can figure things out on their own." I watch as her blue eyes turn gray. "But I'll do the counseling if it makes you happy."

"First, I'm not sure there are *two* mature adults here. And second," she continues, "I don't want you to do it *for* me, I want you go to counseling because *you* want to."

"So, now I have to *want* to? Is there some kind of brainwashing app for that? Maybe some kind of online, mind-altering guru I can hook up to?"

She narrows her eyes. "We need to skip the virtual portals. We've had enough of those as it is. We need a real person to mediate. A professional."

"Sure, okay, I want to do it." I cross my fingers under the table. After all, I am in a church.

She seems to fight it, but there it is—a smile of victory.

The waitress arrives with two hot steaming plates of food. I'm smiling now too.

As I tear into the juicy, thick ribs, I realize I'm half starved. Meat heaven. "By the way, will there be food in heaven? Like real meat and potatoes? I'm not talking vegetable and tofu burgers. Or maybe a cold beer? You know, like just one a week? Scratch that. How about conjugal intimacy?"

She laughs and I know the worst is over. For now.

I halt midway between the next mega bite of meat that's just begging to take a trip down my gullet and look at Sydney. Really look. I realize my hunger goes a lot further than my stomach. I watch her daintily eat her salad. She looks so serene, so innocent. Something inside me melts. I realize I'm still hungry, not just for her affection, but her love. How could I have forgotten?

CHAPTER 40

Hakeem pressed the cell phone speed dial and waited for the connection while fingering his pocketed worry beads. The pickup came on the third ring.

"What is our progress, Fazel?" he demanded.

"Do not be angry with me, brother," Fazel spoke in Farsi. "We are moving quickly now the armor plating is being placed in the hole. If all goes well, the explosive device will detonate on schedule."

Hakeem felt the pressure in his chest ease. He had left the site hours ago and had not heard from his compatriots, he had feared they had been discovered and gone underground.

Hakeem suddenly jerked, raging again as he realized Fazel was speaking in their native tongue.

"Watch your mouth," he bellowed in English. "Are you a fool who cannot follow instructions?" He took a deep breath and looked around the vacant church parking lot to make certain he had not attracted attention to himself.

"You know what we have been taught," he whispered into the phone. "You must take care what you say. Those obscene satellites are listening. They could lock in on you." Hakeem tried to control his breathing.

"Ah, yes," came the cowed response in English. "It will not happen again, brother." The other man cleared his throat, attempted to say something, but ended in a nervous stutter.

"Speak. I have no time for stuttering fools."

The nervous man coughed and cleared his throat again, lapsing back into Farsi. "I am sorry, sir, to have to speak of this, but one week ago, my credit card was stolen from my tent. Now, I have received the billing. Women's clothes were ordered and delivered to the post office box in my name … the postal box set up for our mission. This is most shameful, sir, and it must be known I did not order those obscene garments."

"We have bigger things to worry about right now. Burn the papers and do not speak of this to anyone."

"When the clothes are delivered, should I burn those also?"

"It has already been taken care of."

Hakeem terminated the call, started his car, and burned rubber as he left the parking lot.

CHAPTER 41

The phone rings, and I roll over to pick it up before the second ring. The caller ID indicates the caller is the crime lab.

I grunt and rub the sleep out of my eyes.

"Wholeman."

"This is Sandy from crime lab. We're faxing over a report on the vehicle registered to Bill Williams."

"Are you crazy? On a Sunday morning?"

"The rooster already crowed."

"Does the rooster happen to look anything like Backman?"

She lets out a hefty laugh. "You got it. He says an arrest has to be made, and it can't wait."

"Oh, he does, does he? Well, this report better be convincing."

"It is. And Backman and York have been standing over serology like they own the department. If Backman wasn't the duty officer this weekend, I would have told him to go—"

She stops short as a man's voice sounds in the background. I hear her saying good morning with all the charm of a rat snake. My bet is it's Backman. The line goes dead.

Tossing the phone aside, I lay there thinking. I reach over to touch Sydney, but my hand grasps empty space. I remember she slept in the guest room last night—a big disappointment after the pleasant evening we'd shared. When we arrived home, she told me, in a matter-of-fact way, she thought sleeping in different rooms for the time-being was best. I felt pretty stupid for having imagined, the entire drive home from church, all the steamy making-up we were going to do. Women are impossibly hard to understand—full of complex moods and mixed signals.

I get up, stretch my back, and shuffle over to open the shades to blinding sunlight.

So, York and Backman want me to make an arrest. I've got work to do.

I shave, dress, and skip breakfast to make the twenty-minute drive to the department. Tina is not going to like it, but I need to call her in.

CHAPTER 42

Tina sits at a red light, reviewing the list of things Jet has given her to do. With some resentment, she wonders if Jet is still sleeping while she chases down leads on a Sunday morning.

She arrives at Central Christian Church thirty minutes early with the intent to visit Mary Ford's former Sunday school teacher. She hopes to conduct the interview quickly in order to make the nine o'clock service.

At the front desk, the church receptionist gives her directions to the classroom she is looking for—upstairs, first door to the left. Tina takes two steps at a time, her long legs accommodating the stretch easily. Reaching the top, she makes a quick left. At the door marked *Fourth & Fifth Grades,* she stops and peers in. She sees an attractive young woman in her late twenties, placing papers on rows of empty seats, obviously preparing for class.

Tapping on the door frame, Tina catches the young woman's attention.

"Hi, I'm sorry to disturb you. I'm Tina Serwathka with the FLPD." She flashes her badge. "Do you have a couple minutes?"

The girl looks surprised. "Oh, sure. Come in. The kids won't start arriving for at least ten minutes yet." She holds out her hand to Tina. "My name is Jordan James."

"By some chance, are you any relation to Marilyn James, the pastor's assistant?"

She nods with a smile that holds a hint of pride. "Yes, she's my aunt."

"Very nice lady. Pastor Williams is blessed to have her."

"I think so too," Jordan says, with a bob of her head. "Aunt Marilyn watches over Pastor Bill like a mother hen. She even packs him lunches every day at the office. He's become like family over the years. He comes to most of our holiday dinners."

"Pastor Bill doesn't have a family of his own?"

"Not really. His parents have passed away, and his only brother lives in Alaska. No aunts or uncles that I know of."

Tina nods. "That's rough. I have a big family, so it's hard to relate." She taps her pen on her notepad. "Jordan, do you mind if I ask you a few questions? About Mary Ford?"

"Oh, yes. I thought that's why you were here. I'll be glad to help you in any way I can. Please have a seat." She gestures to the first empty row and moves to pull out two chairs, turning them toward each other.

Tina takes a seat, opposite Jordan, setting her notepad on her lap. "Thank you so much for your time. I promise this won't take long."

"No problem." Jordan smiles back.

"Can you tell me anything about Mary Ford you think may be important?"

"I certainly will try. Mary was the sweetest girl I ever met. Very social, but she didn't relate well to kids her own age, so her mother asked if she could join this class. It worked out really well. She was very helpful with the younger children, and always participated in class activities. I know she also participated in the choir. She was very gifted in music."

Tina jots a couple notes. "Did anyone ever visit her in the class you didn't recognize—or hang around in the halls?"

"No. Her parents always walked her to and from class. To me, they always seemed over-protective, but ..." She stops, hangs her head. "But, I guess they were right after all." She looks up with watery eyes.

Tina nods. "Did she ever talk about anyone in particular, outside her parents?"

"She talked about everyone. I mean, in a good way. She loved people."

"She never mentioned anyone was bothering her or too ... friendly?"

"No, not that I can recall."

"So, nothing stood out about her at all?"

"Nothing. I mean, besides the things I already mentioned." Her face suddenly lights up. "Oh, how could I forget? She was very good at sketching. Would you like to see some of them? I still have some of her pictures here somewhere."

Before Tina can answer, the girl swiftly stands and walks over to a long row of white shelves against a side wall. She quickly scans them and bends to pull out a small stack of papers from a bottom shelf. "Here they are." She walks back and holds them out to Tina.

Tina takes the pictures and begins looking at them one by one. They are all sketches of faces drawn in pencil, very lifelike, but with a childish element to them. The one on top is obviously of her teacher, Jordan, capturing her bright smile and laughing eyes. The second picture depicts a young blonde woman—possibly in her twenties—winking her eye and smiling with a mischievous look.

"That one is Miss Philly." Jordan laughs. "She takes care of the three- to six-month-old babies on the first floor, near the stairs. She was Mary's favorite. Her last name is Deen. Philly occasionally took in Mary as her assistant. Oh, how Mary loved those babies."

Pulling out a third picture, Tina can't suppress a smile. This one is obviously Pastor Bill, right down to his shaggy blonde hair and big ears.

"It's not hard to identify that one." Jordan giggles. "Pastor Bill to the tee."

Tina pages through five or six other portraits, all of children, and then stops. A picture of a bearded man stares back at her. "Do you know who this is?"

Jordan leans in to study the drawing. "Hmm, I've never noticed that one. He doesn't look familiar, but to tell the truth, he looks a little mean. It doesn't look like *any* of her other pictures."

"Do you mind if I take these? I'll return them."

"Of course. Whatever you need."

They both look up as a few kids saunter in talking amongst themselves.

As Jordan greets the children, Tina stands.

"Jordan, I'll let you get back to your work. Thank you so much for your time."

As Tina descends the stairs, she can't get the eyes in the picture of the bearded man out of her mind. He looks familiar somehow, but she can't place him.

Hearing her phone buzz, she pulls it out from the outside pocket of her purse and looks at the screen—Jet. She picks up.

"Hi, Jet. What's up?"

"Where are you?"

"At church. Why?"

"Sorry about this, but I really need you over here at the office. There's been a development in the case."

"What is it?"

"I'll explain when you get here."

He disconnects before she can say anything else, and she looks at the phone in disbelief. The nerve. If she wasn't at church, she would be tempted to throw the phone. This was supposed to be her day off.

With quick steps, she moves toward the first exit door, leading to the parking lot. Only twenty minutes ago, the lot was a line of empty spaces, but now, even the twenty rows behind her car are filling up with vehicles. The church service is obviously about to begin.

Moving to cross the road, she recognizes Officer Martinez with his family in a white SUV. He's circling around apparently looking for a good parking spot. She waves at them as she heads toward her car. Just as she reaches her Ford, his SUV drives up beside her.

Martinez rolls down his window and smiles. She can hear the children asking their mother who she is.

"Hello, Jose. I'm surprised to see you here today." Tina flashes them all a smile as she moves to the driver's seat window and leans in. "So, this is your family."

"Sure is." He says with distinct pride. He gestures to the woman beside him. "This is my wife, Angelina, and my children," he explains, waving his arm toward the back seat. "Rosa, Aida, Jami, and Josita. Everyone, this is Officer Tina. She's a detective who works with me."

Tina can't help but instantly like this family as they all exchange warm greetings. "What beautiful children. I didn't know your family attended this church."

"We don't," responds Jose, "but my wife had it on her heart to come here today. So here we are."

"So glad to hear that. You're all going to love it." She takes a step back. "Well, nice meeting you all. I better let you guys go, I don't want to make you late for church."

Just then, Jose's youngest daughter pops her head out of the open, back window, her dark curls blowing in the breeze, her eyes wide with curiosity. "What are those pictures in your hand?" She points a chubby finger to Mary Ford's sketches.

"Josita. Miss Tina is in a hurry," Angelina scolds.

"Oh, that's okay, just some pictures someone drew."

"Can I see them?" the childish voice pleads.

Tina thinks a second. "Jose, do you have a minute? I'd like to show you a sketch of someone, see if you recognize him."

"Sure. Go ahead," he says as he waves a couple cars lining up behind them to go around.

Tina hands the sketch of the bearded man to Jose. "Does he look familiar?"

He studies the sketch and shakes his head. "No. Doesn't look familiar." He holds the picture up for the rest of the family to see. "Anyone seen this man before?"

Angelina and the children all shake their head in the negative.

Josita yells out, "I don't like that man. He has mean eyes."

"You don't even know him, Josita," Martinez corrects her.

"I don't want to know him, Papa."

"Can't say I want to either." Tina chuckles.

Martinez taps the steering wheel in thought and then asks in a hushed tone, "Those pictures related to the Ford case?"

"Yes," she says. "But I'll explain another time. I really got to get going and so do you. Hold on just a sec, and you can take my parking space."

"Perfect. God bless you, Tina."

"God bless you, too." She waves to his family as she steps away.

Climbing into her car, she starts the engine, turns up the air, and hits the radio button for some Christian tunes. As she drives away, she can't help but think—*you can always trust a child's instincts.*

CHAPTER 43

I slide the email in front of Tina. "This is fresh out of serology."

The look on her face indicates her unhappiness about coming into the office on a Sunday. She's made it clear before that this day is reserved for church, followed by a gourmet meal cooked up by her boyfriend, Mitch, a chef at the beachside Le Café Paree. They cut onions and grind fresh herbs for egg soufflés as they watch the telecasted sport event of the day. Sounds like my kind of day, minus church.

Grabbing up the printout, she scans it with a furrowed brow.

"Is this it? Is this why I'm here on a Sunday afternoon. While Mitch watches the game without me? I even left church early."

"Take a closer look. Mary Ford's blood was found in the trunk of Pastor Williams's car."

Her eyes fly open wide and then dart back to the printout, scanning the details. When she reaches the bottom of the page, I slide a picture in front of her, a full color glossy of the blood found in the car trunk.

"Look at the marker."

She focuses on the photo. On the gray carpet, there's a small, dark spot, with a lab inserted ruler to set standard measurement. The ruler reads three eighths of an inch.

Tina twists the picture and squints her eyes, trying to avoid the glare from the lighting.

"These blood drops are the same measurement as the ones found on the carpet at the crack house."

Silence. She taps her forehead in thought.

"So … come on, Tina, what do you think? Could they have been dropped from the same dispenser? Like say, an eyedropper?"

"I say we need to check with serology, see if they agree with your theory. Are the amounts of blood in the house and in the car the same? Are all the blood spatters identical?"

"That's what the ME concluded. And that's not all. The trunk had traces of a dark sand, with a high biological content, consistent with the mucky stuff you'd find in former swamp land."

"What do you think it means?"

"Not sure. Do you know any reason why Williams would be out there?"

She shakes her head, pressing her nails into her palm.

I pick up my phone, scan my contacts, and tap *serology.*

"Serology department," answers a tired voice.

"What a surprise. I thought you'd be home by now."

"Fat chance. What can I do for you, Wholeman?"

Glancing over Tina's shoulder, I confirm the name at the bottom of the report. Sandra Woods.

"I need to chat about the report you just sent me."

"I know. I was ordered to stay here until I heard from you, and it's about time. Hope whatever you need is fast. I got a husband at home, you know?"

"Sorry, Sandy. So, the order is from Backman?"

"That's the one."

I give Tina one of my *it figures* looks. "Listen, I need to ask you a question on this Ford case. Did you compare the blood spatters on and around the body of the child with those found in the trunk of the car?"

"Of course, Detective. We *are* professionals here."

"I know, Sandy, but I'm not talking DNA, I'm talking similarities, patterns."

A pulse of silence.

"And what similarity would I be looking for?"

"I mean, did you compare the size, shape, amount of each droplet of blood?"

Another silence.

"I'm listening." I said impatiently.

"If the blood was planted artificially using some kind of dispenser, then the same pattern found at the crime scene could have been used in the car trunk."

"So, what makes you think the blood was artificially planted?" she asked.

Before I can answer, a muffled voice sounds in the background asking who she's talking to.

"It's Detective Wholeman," she answers. "He wants blood size comparisons for Williams's trunk and the crime scene."

The muffled voice sounds angry, spitting out some expletives. She mutes the phone.

I wait a good minute or so.

"Okay, I'm back. You're now on speaker phone, Detective."

A gruff sigh sounds on the other side. "This is the duty officer."

"What do you know, Mr. Backman. I take it Sandra filled you in on my request for blood sample comparisons."

"Maybe you're the one that needs to be filled in. That pastor freak should have been arrested yesterday. Why aren't you doing your job?"

I feel the sudden rise in my blood pressure. Tina motions for me to stay calm.

"Backman, this is *Detective* Wholeman. If you want to be a detective, why don't you apply to the academy."

In my peripheral vision, I see Tina rolling her eyes.

"And if you want to grow up one day to be the lab duty officer, you need to get busy."

I take a deep calming breath. "Sandy, could you get back to me on those comparisons?"

"You bet." She sounds like she's choking back laughter. "Shouldn't take long."

I stab the disconnect button.

"You got a way with people, Wholeman." Tina smirks at me.

"We have to do something, but I don't want to arrest this guy, not just yet. The evidence for a frame is building."

"So, what are we going to do?"

"We're going out to the church and meet one more time with Bill Williams. We buy time. Ask more questions."

Back to work, we hash out some case objectives and leads to follow up on while we munch on stale donuts from the office fridge. By the time we're finished brainstorming, we've mowed through a half dozen donuts, surprisingly good, especially the chocolate ones. Occasionally, something goes right.

The phone rings. Sandy again, and she sounds excited.

"Okay, Detective, here we go. Preliminarily findings show you're right. The measurements and consistency of the blood spatters are really close, too close to be considered normal. I would be hard pressed to call it coincidental."

"Excellent. Thanks, Sandy, you're a doll."

"A professional," she corrects.

"An expert," I add, with politically correct charm. "Sandy, if I'm right about this, my report will give you the proper kudos."

"Whatever, Prince Charming."

I hang up feeling pretty good at how things are developing.

"Tina, there's work to do, and you're just the one to help me."

"Why not? I've got nothing better to do on my only day off."

"Sorry, partner, but right now, we can't afford to lose the momentum."

As we sort out the piles of reports and evidence, I can't help but feel the pressure of time constraints. Statistically, the more time that elapses, the less chance we'll have of nabbing this guy. Nothing, not even our personal lives can be allowed to slow us down. Except for a bathroom break.

"Tina, I gotta take a quick break."

Just as I take a step, a thought triggers.

"By the way, did you ever get over to the Sunday school to talk to the Ford girl's teacher?"

"Sure did. I was just about to bring that up. The teacher's name is Jordan James. Nothing much to tell. She never witnessed anyone hanging around the classroom or in the halls, and Mary never mentioned anything unusual. She did show me some sketches that Mary made of various people in the church."

"Was one of them of the pastor?"

"Oh, come on, Jet. Of course, there was one of the pastor. It's his face every kid sees at church, not only in person, but on two large screens during every service."

"Careful, Tina, you don't sound very objective. Anyone else of interest in those sketches?"

"Maybe. There were faces of other children, two female teachers, Jordan James and Philly Deen. There was one of a man the teacher couldn't recognize. The man didn't look too friendly."

"What do you mean?"

"Mean eyes."

"And no one at the church recognizes him?"

"I didn't get that far."

"Check that out, would you? Ask around. And talk to all Sunday school teachers on that floor, see if they recognize him. And ask what's-his-name … Paul Blake. He knows a lot of people. Also talk to a Mandy … I think her last name was Labber. Mandy Labber. Or maybe it was Blabber. One or the other."

"Who's she?"

"The church gossip."

"Thanks a lot, Wholeman."

When I return from the bathroom, Tina is reviewing camera surveillance from the church parking lot, taken the day of the abduction. Endless footage of cars and people coming and going drag across the computer screen.

"Looking at that again?"

"Making sure I didn't miss anything."

"Good idea. So, what do you think about the blood type match?"

Without taking her eyes off the screen she answers, "B-negative, that should really narrow down the possibilities."

"Exactly. Listen, I was just doing some thinking. Came up with a theory."

"Is that what you do in the bathroom? Theorize?"

"That's where every guy does his best thinking. You'll agree when you hear what I came up with. This may seem unlikely, but all great discoveries start with remote possibilities. First, Williams's fingerprints are suspiciously conspicuous, possibly planted. Second, the blood spatter is too uniform, possibly staged. If my hunch is right, and Williams is being set up, to what extent would the killer go? A missing blood sample would explain a lot, but let's just say for the sake of argument the sample turns up. Found at the wrong lab. Dead end.

So, the next theory goes something like this. If someone managed to get Williams's fingerprints, isn't it possible they got a few drops of his blood too?"

"Okay, Sherlock, that's a long shot even for you. Find a new place to do your thinking. The bathroom ain't working."

"Hold on now. If it was someone close to him, they would only have to wait for the right moment. Like—"

"Like wait around until the off chance he cuts an orange the wrong way. Give me a break."

"Okay, my theory's a long shot. But let's just say … someone was cozy enough with him that they could have—"

"Drugged him and stole his blood? Wait. You don't suspect a vampire, do you?"

"Stranger things have happened."

"Okay, time to rein it in, Wholeman. DNA results will take a few more weeks, and then, we'll have something more concrete. Right now, we only have blood type."

She swivels in her chair to face me. "Speaking of blood, you'll be glad to know I contacted Dr. Cooper's office. The receptionist said Williams's blood sample never arrived at the lab. Apparently, the lab sends out a carrier van for pick-up. A company called Med Delivery. I followed up on that and tracked down the driver who worked that day. Name was Justin James. He said Williams's sample was logged in but doesn't know where it went from there."

"It must have been stolen in transit. It's the only thing that makes sense. Don't let go of this. We need more follow up. And about the driver … he's not related to Marilyn James by any chance?"

Tina laughs. "It's a pretty common name, but I'll check into it."

"Did the driver have an assistant?"

"Yeah, a young guy about eighteen. His job was to run in and grab the samples while the driver waited at the curb. His name was something like … Kazim Hadaad. It's in my notes."

"Check into him. Get his background."

Something catches my eye on the surveillance footage that's running across her screen. "Stop there. Stop the footage."

She freezes the screen and we see an image of a man driving a black pickup truck.

Tina leans in and studies the scene. "Just a guy and his truck."

"But he's moving from an odd angle. All the parking spaces are to the right of the vehicle. The church is on the right. The angle of the truck suggests he's moving into the roadway from somewhere off to the side." I point to an area behind the back end of the truck that's off the screen. "What's over there?"

"A wall. I believe somewhere in that area is a back entrance into the church."

"Who uses that entrance?"

"Probably just staff."

"Zoom in on him."

She enlarges the man's face, but it comes up as just a blurry profile.

"That shadow around his lower face could be a beard. That's all I can tell."

She rewinds and slowly moves through the images.

"No plates." I punch my palm. "Jethro Gibbs always gets the plate numbers."

"This is a reality show, Jet."

"This guy could be staff, and could have parked the truck near the door, outside of the camera view, for a reason. Is it a coincidence this moment falls within the same parameter of time that the abduction occurred?" I slap my forehead. "Something just came to me. Bring up the footage of the bathroom window, same time frame."

Tina fumbles around in her desk drawer, chooses a labeled jump drive, and inserts it into the laptop. The footage pops up on the screen.

"Forward the video to about the halfway mark and stop there."

"There. What now?"

"Move slowly until you see a glitch between the frames. I noticed it earlier and sent the footage to our tech guy." A still picture of a parking lot and the side of a building, including the bathroom window, shows on the screen.

"There. Go back. Did you see it?"

"Yeah, it's slight, but it's there."

"If Mary's death was an inside job, someone could have turned off the camera—someone who knows the technology—and turned it back on after Mary Ford was pushed out that window. The moment wouldn't have been captured on camera. She could have been shoved in that black truck and transported to the scene of the crime."

"Wow. We may have something here. If so, it's probable two people were working together. I doubt the same person would drop the body somewhere and return to start the camera back up."

"This isn't the kind of crime two people work together on, but we can't rule out that theory either. Find out where the surveillance equipment is stored and who has access to it. Ask around about that black Ford F150, and check that entrance you mentioned against the truck location. Find out who uses that door and why."

"On it. And don't forget, we have a five o'clock funeral to attend. Faith Funeral Home."

"I'll be there. Should I wear a suit?"

"Do I look like your mother? Yes, wear a suit."

"And Tina, don't forget your gun. You never know who might make an appearance."

CHAPTER 44

Dressed in a black suit, I straighten my tie and prepare to enter Faith Funeral Home where friends and family are gathering to memorialize Mary Ford. I expect to see a small huddled group, mournfully clinging to one another in still emptiness, but I'm wrong. The parking lot is filled, and a steady line of people are arriving, but many are engaged in friendly conversation.

Tina is already there, standing in the back center aisle, dressed in a solemn gray dress, a cross-shoulder purse concealing her weapon, and sensible black flats. I nod at her, and we start our watchful vigil of all who enter.

I try to study and memorize faces, but after the first three hundred people, it becomes evident this is an impossible task. I narrow my goal to focusing on anyone who exhibits unusual behavior or appears disconnected from others.

I cross the opening to the center aisle and approach Tina, who has concern etched on her forehead.

"Never would have expected this size crowd," I whisper in her ear. "Today's a workday, for cryin' out loud."

"This is a child's funeral. No one cares what day it is."

People continue coming through the door. The room is designed to hold up to an estimated five hundred people, and it's already over half full.

Sydney appears at the door entrance—her lavender scent reaching me before she does. She's dressed in grave black and freshwater pearls. To me, she's the embodiment of innocence, walking into the wake of evil. Seeing me, she walks over, gives Tina a quick hug, and moves to my side.

"Aren't you going to sit down?" she whispers.

"No, on duty."

"Do you actually think the murderer is going to show up here?"

"Statistically, yes."

"That's a frightening prospect. I'll be praying for you." Sydney starts to leave and turns back. "Dinner is at seven. The boys are expecting you."

She squeezes my hand and leaves to find a seat.

Subdued sobs begin to cut through the silence as Mary's mother waits for the casket to be brought in. Her husband puts his arms around her to comfort her.

I nod at Tina and we move to the back and station ourselves next to the door. I give her a questioning look.

"Nothing yet." She looks around and then back at her watch. "The service is about to start."

There is a commotion at the entry door as eight pallbearers enter, wheeling the small, white casket down the aisle. The sanctuary becomes hushed, all eyes on the casket. I feel like death itself has entered as all movement stills. The only sound is the gurney wheels wobbling on the carpet—a cold, lonely sound, the kind you don't easily forget. Even as I attempt to brush off the feeling, grief grabs my heart.

As two ushers move to close the door behind them, one last man squeezes in, an apologetic look on his face. He sits down in the last row, near the wall.

I turn back and watch as the coffin is positioned at the front altar. Pastor Williams comes forward to takes his place behind the pulpit and opens in prayer. As heads bow, I peer back at the latecomer, sitting to my left, in the last row. His head is not bowed, and his eyes meet mine for just a second, before he looks away.

I elbow Tina. "Who is that man in the last row to our left, seated by the wall?"

She takes a subtle glance. "He looks very familiar, but then so do most of the people here."

The funeral continues as Pastor Williams gives a message on the temporal nature of the world compared to the eternal paradise Mary Ford has entered.

I catch Tina looking over my shoulder, several times, toward the back wall. She quietly clears her throat. "That man does seem oddly familiar, but I can't place him."

"It'll come to you. It usually does."

A sudden, collective gasp sounds from the front of the room. I rush forward to find that Mrs. Ford has fainted, her concerned family leaning over her.

Behind me, I hear the faint swoosh of a moving door and turn to see it closing, a sliver of outside light snaking its way through. My eyes dart to the back wall where the man was seated. He's gone.

Nudging Tina, I bolt toward the door. The glaring sunshine is almost blinding as we run out into the parking lot. We see nothing but motionless cars, no sign of a departing vehicle. I motion for Tina to circle back behind the south side of the building. I go north.

Meeting back in front of the building, we both shake our heads in the negative. I wipe the sweat from my forehead and grunt in irritation. "That could have been our guy, used the distraction to make his exit."

Tina tucks her weapon back in her purse. "Or he was just an ordinary church member that felt it was a good time to leave."

"Did he fly home?"

"Could live in one of those houses." She points to the line of houses on the street behind the funeral home. "This death had a lot of press. Could be a few curious onlookers participating today, but, like you, I don't have a good feeling about it."

The memorial concludes, but Tina and I stick around to ask anyone we can about the disappearing man. Unfortunately, no one noticed him coming or going except for the funeral director who says he didn't recognize him, and he didn't sign the memorial registry. Another dead end.

Sydney and Tina stay behind to support the Ford family. As for me, I'm relieved to make my exit into the bright sunshine. I make a beeline for my car and as the engine roars to life, I turn up the air, punch the radio, and head for the nearest coffee joint. After that, I'm heading home for dinner, do not pass go.

CHAPTER 45

On Monday morning, despite only a few hours of sleep, I feel ready to take on the world. The air feels electrified. Spending an evening with my family was like getting a battery charge.

Heading for my office, I pass by the rows of cubicles where everyone is already busy at their computers. Printers and copy machines hum their tuneless songs in the background. I don't even make it to my desk before I get a call from the duty lieutenant, telling me to take a trip to the big guy's office, Captain Gary Allen.

I trudge upstairs, take the first right, and am quickly ushered into the inner sanctum by Joan, a sour-faced secretary.

"You don't have to sit." Captain Allen's voice is brisk, but his eyes are wary. "This will only take a minute."

I cross my arms against my chest, hoping to look more relaxed than I feel. I'm pretty sure I know how this is going to go down, so I'm not too worried.

He taps his pen on his desk and looks back at me with narrowed eyes. "So, you haven't made an arrest?"

"I guess you've been talking to Backman?"

"And York." He gives an almost imperceptible roll of the eyes.

He comes around and sits on the front edge of his desk. "They tell me you've wandered off the reservation."

I snort out a laugh. "Listen, Cap, we've known each other forever, and I think you can trust my methods by now. An arrest is premature—it won't stick."

"Why not?" There's a hint of interest in his tone. My guess is he isn't going to push me too hard.

"Because … I just know."

He shakes his head, a slow smile forming. "Because you got ESP or you're consulting a psychic?"

"Because the evidence is odd, the facts don't add up, and I got a gut feeling."

"Well, I have to admit you have a good track record, and I've learned to trust you. But you know we got the state attorney's office breathing down our necks too. They're threatening to file a motion with the courts to force an arrest." He stands, angles back behind his desk, and takes a quick glance at his watch. "I've got an appointment I'm late for. Send me your latest reports. I want facts and every lead you got. Give me some solid reasons for this theory of yours. They better be good, Wholeman. Your butt is on the line."

"I'm on it, Cap, and don't worry, I got plenty."

I turn and head for the stairs, feeling like I just scored a goal. I have a reputation for winning around here, but my reputation can only take me so far. This is a high-profile case and I've got to get my strategy right the first time. Taking three steps at a time, I mutter under my breath. I'm determined not to let those jerks, Backman and York, get in my way. Taking a swift left past the cubicles, I head straight for my office. Sliding behind my desk, I'm ready to work.

Tina is already there, and she promptly sets a coffee cup in front of me. We've developed a kind of rhythm, anticipating one another's ups and downs. When we need to talk—friend-to-friend, rather than partner-to-partner—one of us springs for fresh coffee, the flavored, gourmet stuff. When we're just talking business, we go for the free department brand, strong as a black bear.

"Thanks, Tina, strong and black, just what I need."

Tina flops into the padded swivel seat beside my desk, inadvertently slopping some office coffee on the files stacked at the corner of my desk. She jumps to sweep the back of her hand across the top of the Ford file, causing dark streaks on the manila surface. Wet droplets fall to the floor. I watch the drops, all falling in different sizes and different places—just the way they should.

She moves to clean up the spill.

"Forget it. I'll get it later."

"Thanks, I just need to get off my feet for a while."

Normally I'd be venting to her about my encounter with the captain, but something about her demeanor suggests I keep quiet. Leaning back in my chair, I put my feet up on the desk, ready to listen.

Tina settles into a large size swivel chair, pulling up her legs, Indian style. I've never figured out how she does that with those long legs. She begins to slurp her coffee.

"Can you stop that?"

"What?"

"The slurping."

"Mitch thinks it's cute."

"Well, I'm not Mitch."

"And I'm not Princess Kate." She exaggerates her slurp again to make her point. "You'll be glad to know I did some follow up on those two guys from Med Transport. First, Michael James is in no way related to Marilyn James. Second, Kazim Hadaad only worked there for three weeks. He quit, and there's no trace of him. Didn't even leave a forwarding address for his paycheck."

This has got to be the missing link. "Try to find out if he had any friends. Someone has to know something."

"Things are starting to add up, and something came to me last night. Mitch and I were watching the History channel. The program was a special on the Battle of the Bulge."

I can feel my eyebrows go up. This was my kind of conversation.

"A World War II battle," she adds. "Are you familiar with it?"

My mouth twists into a smile. "Does the Pope know his rosary? And since when do you spout history?"

"Don't look so surprised, women like history too."

"Whatever. So, go on."

"Well," she continues, "these Germans dressed up like Americans, infiltrated behind lines, then turned the sign-posts around to misdirect the allied troops. They were wearing GI uniforms and posing like Military Police, sending the military traffic in the wrong direction." She stops.

I try to hide my amusement. "So, the joker throws a riddle. Are you saying you've concluded someone is purposely misdirecting us?"

She looks over her shoulder. "I think we both do. I don't like the way all this evidence is unfolding. It's eerie."

"Go ahead, you've got my attention."

"Look, I don't want you thinking my attachment to Central Christian Church, or to Pastor Bill, has anything to do with what I'm saying. I laid awake most of the night, trying to evaluate my relationship with the church and how it may be affecting this investigation—wondering if it's clouding my vision." She shakes her head in the negative. "But really, I don't think it is. I'm seeing things pretty clearly. You always told me to know the facts, then go with my gut. So that's what I'm doing. I mean, the way the signposts are pointing puts me on edge. I think Pastor Bill has been set up, but for the life of me I can't figure out who or why."

She sips at the coffee, peering over the top of the cup, a signal for me to take my turn.

I put my cup down. "You're preaching to the choir. When the ME first pointed out those perfectly patterned blood spatters, it didn't sit right with me. Then the twenty-dollar bill, found under the kid, turns up with only one clear fingerprint, and the rest of the bill was print clean, another red flag. The crime scene was seemingly wiped clean too." I take my feet off the desk and lean toward her. "But when the search of the pastor's car comes up with blood of the victim, this really shakes things up."

"Out dammed spot, I say," Tina quotes.

Not to be outdone, I quote back. "Yet who would have thought the old man to have had so much blood in him?"

"I'm impressed, Jet. Didn't know you read Shakespeare."

"Only the parts about blood and crime. I'm only part Neanderthal."

"Okay. Let's just stop talking and think." She slurps her drink, again.

I give her the death glare.

We sit silent for a minute or so.

"Tina, 'Something stinketh in Denmark.'"

"Okay, let's stop already with the Shakespeare."

Taking my feet off the desk, I lean forward. "Listen, Williams's blood comes up missing from somewhere between the doctor's office and the lab, only one week before the crime. I'm left thinking, does he steal his own blood? It doesn't make any sense. I've heard of killers leaving subtle clues because of an unconscious desire to get caught, but with all that, he might as well have turned himself in and saved us all the trouble."

"Oh, come on. Williams is not some kind of sadist psycho, Jet. I got a feel for people and I thought you did too."

"You're probably right." I give her a small smile to ease the tension gathering in the room. The knot in Tina's forehead slowly relaxes, she stretches out her legs, and eases back in her chair.

"I thought I was losing it." She sighs. "Glad we're on the same page. You know, we could make the arrest, close the file and walk away, and no one would say we didn't do our job." She takes a long breath and straightens her shoulders. "But that's not the way we work, is it, Jet?"

"Just shoot them all and let God sort 'em out," I say whimsically. "No, we're better than that, partner."

I stand up, ready to pace the floor, get some blood moving to my brain. "If someone is framing Williams, what is the motive? A disgruntled parishioner? Maybe a personal acquaintance outside the church—someone he made an enemy of without knowing it? An affair? A woman scorned? Someone from his past? Is he in line for an inheritance we don't know about?"

"Unlikely," Tina says. "Except for the unknown enemy. Pastors are not always liked. But I'll check out all the scenarios."

I continue to pace. "You could be right, but who would take so many risks, especially in a public place, go to such extreme measures to stage a crime scene, just for a grudge? Why not just kill him and be done with it? Who would be capable of murdering a child and at the same time benefit from ruining Williams's reputation? Who and what would be affected by the arrest of Pastor Bill? Who would benefit?"

"The entire church would be affected. He's well loved and respected but I'm clueless about who this would benefit."

"Is someone out there that's mad at the whole church, or is it more personal?" I continue to pace. "Pinning the murder on him would obviously destroy his reputation. Bill Williams founded the church. According to the church info sheets, and substantiated by Sydney, they began as just a small home-based study group, then moved to a school, and from there to a store front and next to a warehouse, and now to a series of vast remodeled warehouses, and still growing."

"That's right."

"Could there be someone, maybe an associate pastor, who wants to take his place? Become a sort of king over what he hopes one day will be the biggest church in the country. Take all the glory for himself." A grinning boyish face flashes before my eyes. Paul Blake.

"What about that skinny guy Blake who always seems to be at the pastor's right hand?" I ask, watching her face for any trace of suspicion.

"Nah, he's harmless. Besides, he's not in line for a senior pastor by a long shot. He'd have nothing to gain."

"He does have a record of hanging with some unsavory characters."

"That's in the past. Jet, can't you ever believe people change?"

"Try to stay objective, partner."

"Yeah, yeah. Go on."

"Everyone I've talked to makes it sound like Pastor Bill walks on water. If he's the boat on which Central Christian Church floats, then sink the boat and you sink the church. Sink the church and you ..."

"And the people simply go to another church," Tina finishes. "That's the worse-case scenario. Christians aren't looking for just Pastor Bill. They're looking for God."

"I hear you, but for the sake of argument, let's just go with this theory for a minute. The people leave, you got a closed church, empty warehouse. Finances dry up. Unpaid bills. Who benefits?"

She taps her fingers on the arm of the chair. "Maybe someone wants the property ... could have value to them."

"Okay, so check into any requests there's been to buy the property. Any possible mergers or expansions that may be wanted."

Tina leans in, grabs a pen from my desk, and scribbles some notes.

"There's a hospital to the east side of the church. A golf course on the west side. Start there."

She scribbles again and tucks the pen behind her ear.

"There's rumors the golf course is having financial problems—doubt they'd be expanding. And can't imagine a hospital needing any space *that* badly. But I'll check into it."

I continue to pace. "Maybe the motive is less about a single building, or a single person, and more about the institution itself."

"You mean Christianity? Enough to kill a child over? Not likely."

The phone rings. This is the call I've been waiting for— our tech guy. I pick up the phone and punch the speaker button.

"Hey, Sebastien, you're just the man I want to talk to. Have something for me?"

"Game over, bro. The glitch in the surveillance footage shows tampering—high key. Camera was turned off and later, back on again."

"Any indication how long it was off?"

"There's a good ten hours of sunlight on the footage, so can't be for more than an hour. The mystery is, which hour?

Technology on this model doesn't involve a timekeeper. The hardware has an inside lock box, needs a key for access."

I jump to my feet. Begin to pace. "There must be a way to track the time. I need something more exact than the slant of the sun."

"No, not this one. Listen, Jet, I'd like to theorize with you, but I got to take a leak."

"Hold it."

"Whoa, nature versus nurture, dude. I gotta go."

"Wait. The clock. Listen, buddy. I need you to zoom in on a twelve-by-twelve bathroom window on the footage. There's a clock on the opposite wall. See if you can zoom in and get a time reading."

"Woah. GOAT. This sounds almost as good as speed-cubing. Back with you in twenty." The phone goes dead.

Tina jumps up. "Wait. What did he just say?"

"He said the tape's been tampered with. He's going to get back with us."

"I meant the part about the goat."

"I'll get back with you on that one."

"You really think he can get a clear shot of the clock?" Her voice is an octave higher with excitement.

"Why not? The same thing happened on an episode of *Sherlock Holmes*."

Tina laughs. "Okay, reality check. On another topic, have you heard from FBI lately? I heard things are heating up on a national level."

I stop short, run my hands through my hair. Vicki Anderson's words come back to me. *The terror threats have been elevated to orange in South Florida.*

"It's not just national. The threat is closer than you think. And while we're on the subject, churches aren't exactly on a terrorist's friend list."

"Jet, where you going with this? Are you trying to say terrorism is somehow linked to the Ford murder?" She shakes her head. "Last I heard, they blow places up or conduct mass shootings. Not frame people for murder."

"Strategies are changing all the time. After all, who would've thought they'd use trucks in Nice, London, Stockholm and so on?"

Tina cringes. "I hear ya, but this is a real stretch. Too much time involved, too much planning to just smear reputations. Isn't that what Facebook is for?"

"Got a point there." I laugh. "There's something I didn't mention." I sit down. "I got a warning from the FBI that South Florida is under terror watch."

"What? And you're just telling me now?"

"Didn't take the news very seriously."

"Well, things just keep getting weirder and weirder." She crosses her legs and then uncrosses them. "I just don't know. This all seems crazy, and this new brand of terrorism you're trying to sell me is a major stretch. We better keep this on the down low. The department will think we need a state of mind leave."

"I'm not trying to sell anything, just pitchin' it. But yeah, you're right. Gotta keep it real."

But the thought is still stuck in my head like shredded floss between my teeth. A terrorist twist—wouldn't the media have a field day with that?

We hear someone clearing their throat at the door entrance and both look up.

"Hey there, Officer Washington. What's up?" I'm surprised to see him on this floor. "What brings you over to this neck of the woods?

Washington shifts from foot to foot, hat in hand. "Hey, Detective." He nods at me and then at Tina. "How you both doing?"

"We're good," we answer in unison.

"What's on your mind?" I say abruptly.

"Uh, you remember my grandmother, the one who made the report? Lives next door to where the Ford girl was found."

"Oh, of course." I nod encouragingly. "Did she remember something?"

"No, not exactly. But she asked me to tell you something. I know how this is going to sound, but you got to respect your grandmother, right?" he says with a shy grin.

"Right." I smile. "Go ahead, Dayton. I'm all ears."

"Well, she's a woman of faith. She hasn't missed a day of church since I can remember. And she's always thinking of others—"

"She seems like a good woman," I interrupt, not in the mood for a biography. "So, she knows something about the crime?"

"No, no." His discomfort level has increased, the shuffling of his feet now almost a two-step.

Tina throws me a dirty look. "Dayton, come on in. Sit down."

"Oh, no, thanks. I've got to get back to work. I'll try to make this quick. There's no easy way to say this …" He takes a deep breath. "My grandmother gets visions and dreams. Most folks believe these visions are straight from God."

Tina leans in, her face lit up with interest. Her look encourages Dayton and the shuffling feet stop.

"Anyway, she told me she had a vision concerning you, Detective."

I try not to smile. "I hope the vision was about the lottery."

He gives a nervous laugh. "Actually," he continues, still standing in the doorway, "more like a sort of warning. She's had several visions of a bearded man, believe it or not, who wants to bring you down. She said the two of you will soon cross paths."

Leaning back in my chair, I scratch my head, pretending to think about this new information. "Wow. Can't say I've ever had anyone experience a vision about me before." I glance at Tina. She looks like she has a hundred questions and I want to head this one off.

"Washington, please tell your grandmother I appreciate her intel. I'll keep a look out." I stand, giving him a smile. "Well, hate to break this up, but I've got somewhere I got to be."

Grabbing my keys, I make for the door.

"Yeah, right," snaps Tina as Washington backs up to let me through.

Conversation over. At least for me. Looking back over my shoulder, I catch Tina waving Washington back in. No doubt, she wants to explore his religious phenomena a little more closely.

On my walk through the parking lot, my phone rings.

"Sebastien, my man. Tell me you got it."

"I got it. This is epic. Doing what you asked was a long shot, but I figured it out. The clock on the wall, just like you said. It reads 9:24 a.m. before the glitch and 10:44 a.m. after. Someone turned off the camera. Great call, Detective. A real Sherlock Holmes maneuver."

"Great job, Watson. I owe you one. Send me a report on that, would ya?"

"Copy that."

"By the way, there's a new season premiere of the *Sherlock Holmes* series, tomorrow night."

"Retweet. Already recorded. You know, you may be more than just a brogrammer."

As I hang up, I'm wondering what a brogrammer is. These kids speak a different language. But if fingerprints are a universal language, it's all good. Finding some prints on that surveillance box is crucial. This could be a colossal break in the case.

CHAPTER 46

I sit in my car, parked in an industrial lot adjacent to the church. I attempt to wash down a stale bagel left on the car floorboard the day before with a cold cup of coffee. Bacteria must take at least twenty-four hours to form, so I figure the bagel is still good. Beyond my windshield is a panoramic view of Central Christian Church parking lot and campus as seen from the rear of the adjacent warehouse, two-hundred yards away—a good a place as any to set up surveillance. I started out by looking for Pastor Bill's gray Mitsubishi Endeavor SUV, with a *Choose Life* license tag, number CTG08 which I found using a zoom lens on my camera. The car sat at the rear door of the church building, nestled among a half dozen other vehicles.

I glance at the digital readout on my watch. 1:12 p.m. I've spent two slow hours in an uneventful stakeout on a hot, humid day.

Detective work is one-third investigative routine, one-third heart pounding adrenaline, and one-third sheer boredom. But every game has its downside. I find myself distracted by the ripples of heat rising off the asphalt, appearing like a river of clear water cascading through the parking lot. My eyes feel heavy. I give my head a shake without much relief.

Ancient images of my days in the Persian Gulf, like currents of blazing heat, drift across my mind.

Afghanistan makes Florida feel like a cool bath. The heat undulates across the sandy desert with no humidity. Even when me and my buddies found a little shade, next to a Bradley armored personnel carrier, our skin felt on fire.

My eyes jerk open and then dart to the temperature gauge in the dashboard.

Engine still running in the normal range—impressive cooling system for a Dodge.

Movement outside the car causes my body to still.

My eyes snap back to the church campus to a bearded, dirty, homeless guy coming around the northwest corner of the church building. He's pushing a rusty, overflowing shopping cart filled with boxes and food that appears to be in original wrapping, unopened. He's shuffling in a slumped position, his feet adorned in newish Nikes. Moving slowly, he heads toward the church dumpsters, about ten yards from the building. He makes for an interesting character.

The scene creates a classic picture for *Life* magazine, if it still existed. The twenty-first century hobo.

I pull the camera up to my eye, expecting this homeless character to produce a classic butt in the air dumpster dive. With a push of a button, the camera starts shooting, the auto-shutter runs off about ten to fifteen shots. Instead of leaning over the dumpsters rim, the homeless guy releases the cart, grabs hold of the edge of the dumpster, deftly vaults himself up over the top and drops inside, disappearing completely from view. Impressive. This could be a new Olympic dumpster event. Of course, his vault into the dumpster is a violation of city ordinance, but let's not sweat the small stuff. Not my beat anymore.

Another movement to my right. I automatically pan the lens to the right, adjusting the zoom lens of the camera to observe good old Paul Blake passing through one of the back double doors, which closes automatically behind him. I take several pictures of Blake as he proceeds across the parking lot toward an old AMC Pacer, almost disappearing in a heat mirage.

I glance at my watch and make a note on my pad: *P.B. leave, 2:18 p.m.*

I zoom in, focusing on him as he climbs into the vehicle, and trigger a couple more pics. He starts the old piece of junk with a belch of bluish smoke.

Surely a violation of some environmental law. Not my beat.

I take a quick look back at the dumpster and then watch the Pacer back out of the parking spot, proceed toward the lot exit, stop for the traffic light, blinker on, ready to turn east. Could be toward home or to a late lunch.

Turning my attention back to surveillance of the parking lot, I put my camera back on my lap. Nothing moves. I check the dumpster. No movement there either. The diver must still be in there.

The supermarket shopping buggy stands nearby, its pile of collected stuff undisturbed.

Another movement catches my attention, and I grab up the camera.

Meeka Amari comes slinking out the same door Blake just passed through, but she's moving to the left, away from the parked cars in the lot. I aim the camera and trigger off several quick shots. She moves seductively as if she knows she's being watched. Any chiropractor would tell her the human body can't do that without permanent damage to the back.

Meeka moves down the sidewalk and then away from the building. She, too, seems to be heading for the dumpsters.

By instinct, I put my left foot on the brake, and the car into drive, easing my vehicle forward.

She seems to be moving directly for the very dumpster the City Olympian is in. I'm wondering if there's going to be a run in with this guy.

My car continues forward, slowly.

He may just stay in the dumpster unnoticed, never bother her. I don't want to give my presence away if I don't have to. I hit the brake.

Meeka reaches the inhabited dumpster and lofts a white bag—like the ones you get at Walmart—over the edge. The bag plummets into the receptacle, leaving me swearing under my breath. Missed the picture.

The garbage bin shows no movement.

Amari pivots, her hair now a little damp and displaced, and saunters from the dumpster toward the cars in the lot.

The guy within the dumpster remains silent, unmoving. The secretary is safe.

My vehicle is sitting alone in the middle of the parking lot, one hundred yards closer to the church sanctuary than before.

Miss Amari, in full animation, moves toward the back of the lot toward a lone red Mustang convertible, repeatedly flipping her hair from side to side, each turn of her head a seductive movement.

She's attempting a distraction. Game over.

Slowly, covertly, she scans the parking lot while steadily moving toward her car. As she nears her vehicle, she clicks the key fob, and opens the driver's door.

Has she noticed my Dodge Charger sitting in the middle of the parking lot?

I note the time on my watch and log it: *M. A. leaves 2:40 p.m. Dropped bag into dumpster.*

She starts her car but stays parked. There's movement inside her vehicle, but I can't tell what she's doing. Moments later, the convertible roof mechanically retracts. Once down, she and her Ford Mustang leave the parking lot with a loud chirp of the tires.

Was that for show too?

I fire off some zoom-in shots at the retreating license tag.

The mustang waits at the traffic light and turns east onto Commercial Boulevard.

I turn my attention back to the church just in time to see the homeless guy rolling himself deftly back out of the dumpster. Looking more closely, I realize he's not as thin and gaunt as I originally thought.

I fire off another round of pictures hoping to get one or two classic shots of this guy landing on his head but, disappointedly, the dirty, bedraggled figure lands nimbly on his feet and quickly side-steps over to the shopping cart. I continue shooting as the vagrant dumps one singular object—the white Walmart bag—into the cart. This time I'm ready. More pics fire off. Resuming his former slumped posture and shuffling gait, he retreats around the northeast church sanctuary wall.

A ruse. That's no homeless man, and that's got to be the same bag Amari just dropped in the dumpster. Are they working together?

I put the car in drive, mash the gas, and quickly cross the parking lot to the dumpster area. Slamming the shift into park, I grab my camera, jump out and sprint past the trash containers to a corner of the building. With my body hugging the wall, I peek around. Nobody there. I continue my sprint down the sidewalk, almost skidding to a stop at the next building corner. Again, I covertly peer around. There's the shopping cart, still full, standing alone on the edge of the grass. But where is the Dumpster Olympian?

I scan the area. There ... heading away from me, east across the parking lot at a good, healthy pace, no longer bent over. He has a quick gait, close to a trot, the white plastic bag from the dumpster still in his right hand. He's moving toward a blue Toyota Camry parked in the shadows of a large ficus tree.

Pulling the camera to my face, I zoom in on the retreating figure. Medium height, moderate build, long, scraggly hair ... his back is still to me so I can't see his face. Another series of clicks fills the air.

Switching hands, the man pulls open the front passenger door with his right hand and tosses the bag onto the floorboard of the car with his left.

Why the passenger side? The driver's seat appears empty.

I snap another round of pictures.

As he climbs into the car, his right hand comes up and pulls a wig from his head.

There you are, you sneaky slime. I set off another burst of pictures, but his face is turned away. I mash on the camera trigger, allowing the digital to grind off a long burst of shots at the back of his head. "Come on, turn around."

I'm praying there's enough memory left on the camera chip. I remove my finger from the button. Just then, for a split second, he turns, his face in plain view but before I can take the picture, he ducks down. *God, can't you give a guy a break?*

The camera setting is now on auto and clicks away as the man moves around in the car.

There's a lot of glare on the windshield, but something has to come out of one of these.

Internal twisting starts in my gut from a torment of frustration.

The engine roars to life but I didn't see him slide to the driver's seat.

The vehicle moves off toward the east gate. Someone else must be driving—they must have been slumped down in the seat before.

Zooming in on the rear of the vehicle, I get pictures of the retreating license plate. Just before going through the gate, the break I've been waiting for comes. The driver turns his head to check for traffic. I'm ready this time. The camera frenzies into automatic overdrive. Gotcha you devil.

As he waits for the traffic light to turn green before turning east on Commercial Boulevard, toward I-95 and the city, I grab a moment to depress the review button on the camera. Scanning the pics posted in the LCD window, one image jumps out at me—fuzzy, but the driver's face is distinct. My heartbeat accelerates. I want to see this sucker enhanced and enlarged. *I'll find you. Just gotta get you to the right facial recognition expert, my man.*

I grunt in satisfaction as I sprint back to my vehicle. I try to run, and simultaneously page through the pictures without wiping myself out in a collision. Finally, fifteen pictures back, my break pops up: Florida Plate, LTB-326. A break.

Reaching my car, I snatch up my handheld radio and huff into the microphone, "L14."

Radio response. "L14, go."

I start the car, shift into drive, and speak into the radio. "Blue, late model, Toyota Camry, Florida tag Lima Tango Bravo 326, east-bound on Commercial. Driver—dark-haired male with beard, mid-twenties, possibly Middle Eastern descent. Passenger—male, long dark hair."

I crush the accelerator and aim the nose of the car toward Commercial Boulevard, while yelling into the radio. "I need the vehicle detained for any violation observed."

This radio transmission is certain to result in a police traffic stop. No one can drive in South Florida without making at least one violation. Watching my speedometer reach 71 mph, I weave in and out of the traffic as alarmed drivers pull to the right. I'm hoping the Camry is doing its own accelerating. Whether it's speeding, texting, no seatbelt, illegal right turn, missed signal or my favorite, excessive window tint—one of the infractions is bound to catch him up.

I do a rolling stop for the red traffic light, but seeing no traffic interference, speed through the intersection, eastbound.

A female dispatcher repeats my request over the tactical radio.

I continue. "Dispatch, this vehicle may jump onto I-95. Notify FHP."

Hopefully, Florida Highway Patrol will have cruisers already on the interstate. They're normally assigned to patrol that area.

"L14? Repeat, L14."

"L14," I respond.

"Your blue Camry is being pulled over by Charlie 12. Southbound 95 ramp."

I reach down to the transmission hump, feel around to recover the pursuit light. With strobe in hand, and window down, I turn on the blue flashing lights and manage to slap its magnetic base on the roof just as the radio crackles to life.

"All units, all units," the dispatcher's voice barks. "Southbound 95, Commercial Boulevard on-ramp. Shots fired. Late model, blue Toyota Camry, white male, possibly Hispanic, proceeding southbound, tag number Lima Tango Bravo 326."

My heart rate goes up a notch as I push the accelerator through the floorboard determined to beat the others to the scene.

CHAPTER 47

South Florida law enforcement doesn't normally participate in high-speed highway pursuits if there's a chance it could turn into a public threat. This fact worries me as well as I might very well lose this guy. However, now the ante has just been upped, and I feel more confident. When there's a cop-shooter involved, things get serious, real fast. Following protocol, helicopters have already been routed to assist, and every uniform in the area alerted to move toward the pursuit route. But at this moment, catching these guys could still be iffy. Within seconds, every agency from Boca Raton to Miami-Dade will have units turning, hell bent, toward the interstate to apprehend the cop-shooter. There's a growing sentiment out there that the boys in blue don't matter, but to us … we're family.

As word is being passed over radio wavelengths that a brother officer is down, and the perpetrator is attempting escape, the call of an excited FHP trooper, now on our tactical frequency, comes through. Before I can even reach the southbound entrance ramp to I-95, he confirms he's in high-speed pursuit of the blue Camry, south of Oakland Park Boulevard.

I jerk my steering wheel and accelerate off Commercial Boulevard onto the I-95 access ramp, and immediately see the FLPD cruiser, Charlie 12, blue lights flashing, at a stand-still on the ramp shoulder. Nearing the scene, I see a downed officer crumpled on his back in front of the cruiser, two civilians crouched over him. Despite the counter demands roaring in my head to race up the interstate and join the chase, I stomp down on the brake pedal, rubber squealing, and feel the car sliding onto the opposite shoulder.

Surrounding drivers, entering the ramp, are blasting car horns, unaware of the tragedy ahead.

I throw myself out of my driver's seat, leaving the door open as a shield, and pull out my gun from its hip holster. Two civilians are tending to the wounded officer, so I change gears, and holding my hand up in an attempt to slow the oncoming traffic, dart across the road.

Out of the corner of my eye, I notice an abandoned Chevy Malibu rolling slowly into roadside shrubbery—probably owned by one of the assisting citizens.

I jump back as a white semi almost broadsides me, then dodge another vehicle coming up the ramp with no appearance of slowing down. I stare him down, pointing my gun menacingly at his front wheels. He immediately screeches his tires, coming to a smoking halt. I've got no time to play nice.

I sprint toward the downed officer. "Police. Coming through."

A man is applying pressure against the neck of the officer, his hand covered in blood.

"Police." I repeat to the two blood-spattered men who seem not to notice me. "I have first aid training. I'll take it from here."

"No." The young blond man says, busy staunching the officer's blood flow. "I've got this. I'm an EMT." His other hand is on the victim's wrist, taking his pulse. "I was coming up the ramp, saw the whole thing."

"I saw it too," the second man says. "The driver started shooting when the cop walked toward the car."

"Ambulance been called?" I ask.

"Yes, done."

After a second, the EMT looks up, sweat rolling past his blinking eyes. "We need that medical unit STAT, got to get him to the ER. He's losing a lot of blood, but I think I can keep him alive until then."

"Wasn't he wearing his vest?" I blurt, feeling stupid the moment the comment escapes my mouth.

"Hit him in the neck." He leans in to check his breathing.

An anguished screech sounds from the tires of another police unit. The car weaves its way around the stalled cars and skids to a stop off the shoulder of the road behind Charlie 12. A tall, athletic looking officer jumps out and runs toward us.

I wave my hand to catch his attention. "Detective Wholeman. This man is an EMT," gesturing at the kneeling man. "Where is that ambulance?" I yell, trying to keep the panic down in my voice. Witnessing injured bodies, day in and day out, is one thing. Seeing a bloody cop is another. Too close to home.

The road patrol officer hesitates a moment as he cocks his head to hear over the surrounding traffic, the communication coming from the speaker clipped to his shoulder epaulet. "Yes, sir. Seconds away."

The distant scream of an ambulance sounds in the background.

Nodding approval, I turn and run for my vehicle. Over my shoulder, I shout, "I'm heading south with the pursuit."

I can almost imagine the young officer's disappointment— *Why you and not me?*

Back at my unit, I throw myself behind the wheel just in time to hear the pursuit has turned onto 595 West and has accelerated to over a hundred miles per hour. They are six miles ahead of me. I'm well behind, but fully intent on making up the time.

I slam the gas, jumping the car onto the access ramp with a spray of gravel and dirt. The Dodge jumps to life, gripping the ramp tarmac. With a sudden thrust forward, the turbocharge cuts in. My head is depressed into the headrest as I grapple with the seatbelt and watch the speedometer shoot up to eighty mph. I keep the pedal to the floor, with no intention of looking at the speedometer again. This is what I've been waiting for—a chance to let this baby fly. The acceleration continues to press me back against my seat. I'm back in the game.

Catching up to the fleeing vehicle turns out to be easier than I thought. Somewhere north of my position, law enforcement has closed the southbound lanes of Interstate 95, halting the flow of traffic to both protect civilians and to stop them from impeding the pursuit. Most of the remaining traffic has already moved off the road's shoulder. A swarm of police vehicles from the south, blaring their sirens, are joining the chase. My turbojet Dodge Charger is just another one of them.

In the muffled static of radio traffic, I hear, "He lost it. Exit ramp, 441." The excitement in the officer's voice is unmistakable.

I quickly adjust my speed down from one twenty to eighty in order to negotiate the exit ramp onto I-595. Then, I pick up speed again.

Seconds seem to drag by. I pound the steering wheel, mashing the already floored accelerator, and I lean forward, willing the vehicle to move faster.

I'm about two minutes away, which now seems like an eternity.

It's hard to make out all the words with the static and garbled reports cutting in and out on top of each other— what stands out are *Camry* and *hit the guardrail.*

My hands are slick with sweat as I weave through the traffic.

"Shots fired." The static clears.

This could be *another.*

"Suspect is down. Repeat, suspect is down." My stomach lurches.

Ahead of me, I can see blue lights flashing. The approaching exit ramp of US 441 is awash with police cruisers. Within seconds, I'm pulling the car up as close as I can get to the crime scene, now blocked by a jumbled mass of uniforms and police units.

The radio sounds off again, "Be on the lookout in the area of the I-95 southbound ramp, Commercial Boulevard, Middle Eastern man who fled the Camry immediately after the shooting of Charlie 12 …"

The dumpster diver. He's gone.

Jumping out of the Dodge, I sprint the forty yards to the perimeter, where officers stand with drawn weapons.

Despite the distant wailing sirens, the scene seems to be eerily quiet, only a few officers on what appears to be a perimeter, quietly murmuring. I shoulder my way to the front of the group and announce myself. "Homicide. Detective Wholeman."

The body of a man is lying in the roadside grass, but still moving. The officers have taken up a position about thirty feet back, weapons directed at the downed man. I stop, scanning the group in confusion. Why hasn't anyone cuffed this guy?

I freeze as a tortured gasp comes from the body.

I push forward toward the crumpled man, but a sheriff's deputy quickly grabs me by the arm.

"We've been ordered to keep back."

I jerk my arm away.

"His gun hasn't been accounted for," the deputy continues.

"You're joking." I continue forward.

A gurgling gasp comes from the bloody body. The man appears to be on the precipice of death.

"He's dying." I lunge toward the body.

A large, city lieutenant suddenly looms before me, putting out his arm to bar my advance.

"That's right, Detective, but he still has a gun." He gets right in my face. "No one is going near that cop-shooter until we're *certain* it's safe." His face contorts with a slightly twisted smile. "Even if waiting kills him." With a low chuckle, he moves again just enough to block my path.

Standing in this strange stalemate, studying one another, realization dawns. This hulking lieutenant has taken control of the crime scene with obvious plans to let this man die. The rest of the LEOs look on like a passive-aggressive, vigilante posse. Among cops, the shooting of a fellow officer stirs up a passion for revenge, but usually procedure is followed along somewhat legal lines. This is nothing more than a modern lynching.

Even in my anger, I understand this mindset. If you help the fallen perp get back up again, you're only assisting him in lawyering up, standing trial, getting dismissed on a technicality, a release back onto the streets, and the cycle starts over again. Despite this, I still have faith in our legal system, every individual deserves their day in court. Besides, a dead man can't talk, and I have a case to solve.

"You son of a ..." As I push past him, the lieutenant somehow loses his balance and falls on his knees, palms down, onto the gravel.

Boy, you've done it now, Wholeman.

The sidelines suddenly come alive. Officers quickly busy themselves elsewhere, organizing the crime scene, while two others help the EMT get through the crowd. Apparently, they've decided they haven't seen what happened, and they intend to ignore my altercation with the lieutenant and go about doing their job. Boys will be boys.

Before I can stride four paces, one of the motorcycle officers, a young guy, leans in to give the downed lieutenant a helping hand. In the process, his motor boot *accidentally* meets the lieutenant's rib cage with a hard jab. He apologizes, but the lieutenant explodes in angry expletives.

Apparently, I'm not the only one who dislikes this guy.

"Get lost, you sorry excuse for a cop," the lieutenant spits out at the motorman.

I give a mock salute to my new young hero and rush toward the twitching body. More than six feet away from the suspect, I spot a Beretta nine-millimeter. I quickly scoop up the weapon, close the distance between us and lean over the body. There's a gurgling gasp.

He's face down in the sandy grass. I can see a bullet wound, which I suspect is an exit hole, on the left side of his back, under the shoulder. Looking for an entry wound, I roll him over on his back, and spot a puncture wound in center, upper chest.

Nice shot.

"Don't touch him." I hear someone yell at me from behind. Turning quickly, I see three emergency medical technicians running toward us. The lead one is waving me off. Ignoring them, I continue to study the suspect. Dark complexion, moderate, short-cropped beard. My guess is Middle Eastern, not Hispanic. He begins to convulse and lash out with one arm. I grab his hand and immediately feel rough, calloused palms and fingers. A laborer.

An EMT pushes me out of the way which causes me to fall back on my rump. I sit there watching the three men work over the gasping man, while I pretend I love having gravel up my rump. The lieutenant and I now have something in common. Karma some would say.

The bone-thin man is mumbling in a foreign language as he fights for his life.

I pick out one unmistakable word, "Allah."

"Collapsed lung," barks the lead EMT. "He may be bleeding out internally."

The injured man seems to be in good hands, so I move on. I push up into a squatting position, spring to my feet, and hope the maneuver looks as if I've just been enjoying a flash sit-in.

Exhaustion hits me, but I try not to show it. I've been going for eighteen hours, and my adrenaline is fizzling out like a dying sparkler. Straightening my stiff shoulders, I take a deep breath. There's still more to do, but right now I'm just thankful for what I'm sure is a major break-through in the Ford case. This has got to be what I've been waiting for.

I review the facts: a Middle Eastern man spotted leaving the same church where a child was murdered. He takes off with a white bag thrown in the church dumpster, the same bag dumped by Williams's secretary who is also of Middle Eastern descent. This woman is strategically positioned in the church for easy access to the pastor's computer system. The man, with her Walmart bag, flees from police units with a second man, also Middle Eastern, and they are now involved in the shooting of an officer. Combine all this with suspicious blood spatters and the pastor's blood sample disappearance … all this adds up too much to be a conglomerate of coincidences. Finally, I have something concrete to support my theory.

Maybe, there's a God after all.

Strangely, I hear a deep voice that seems to come from every direction. *I am here.*

I blink hard and stand up straight, riveted to the spot. I look around, turning in a circle. No one is even looking my way—all are absorbed in their work. Shaking my head, I realize I'm overtired. Sydney is right. I've got to get more sleep, get off the carbs. I suck the thought up as a random firing of a rogue neuron, brought on by exhaustion.

Dismissing the experience, I move off toward the blue Camry which is now under guard by two patrol officers.

I almost feel sorry for the guy.

Several officers turn to watch the encounter, then turn back to the business at hand, squelching guilty smiles. Another officer, a little more compassionate than the rest of us, elbows a nearby firefighter and motions him toward the ailing lieutenant.

The firefighter slowly looks over his shoulder, spots the prone uniform and runs toward him, calling out for assistance.

There's work yet to be done, so I ignore the distractions and move on.

Arriving at the Camry, I flash my badge to the officers. "Is this the way you found the vehicle?"

"No, sir," a female officer responds. "The engine was still running. I reached inside and turned off the ignition."

I think about this information. The driver obviously abandoned the car while it was still in drive. The car left the road and made impact with the guardrail. There's a line of paint running down a twenty-five-foot stretch of the rail. The passenger side is pressed hard against the guard rail.

My eyes do a quick scan of the area. I nod at the car. "There was another man in that passenger seat?" Maybe the radio transmission was incorrect.

She looks confused. "I was one of the first units on the scene. Only one person got out of that car."

"Are you sure?"

"Yes, sir."

"Were you the shooter?"

"No, sir."

I look at the surrounding area and realize if the dumpster diver had fled the scene up at Commercial Boulevard, he is now long gone. The excitement of the shooting of Charlie 12, and the subsequent car chase, would have provided a cover for his escape.

Moving toward the car, I look first at the driver's door. Through the open window, I see the handles of a plastic bag, emerging from where it had slid up under the heater outlet on the passenger side—the floor is littered with paper.

Noticing the window is also open on the passenger side, I walk around the back of the car, step over the guardrail, move to the passenger side window and lean in through the window. I try to get a closer look. Sure enough, I see the Walmart bag with papers spilling out onto the floor. The first page I lay eyes on is emblazoned with the letterhead, *Central Christian Church.*

I pull my pen from my shirt and am about to move the sheets of paper around with the pen's tip when I hear an abrasive voice coming from behind. "Wholeman. What do you think you're doing?"

Twisting my head around, I see Forensic Technician Charlie York hurrying toward the car.

"This is my crime scene," York barks. He's waving one hand in the air and carrying an orange toolbox in the other. "Leave my crime scene alone."

"Ah, Charlie, give a guy a break."

"Move away."

"Don't think so, Chuck, old pal." My head is still stuck in the window, my attention rooted on the scattered papers laying on the car floorboard. "I'm in the middle of a murder investigation," I yell over my shoulder. "And—

"I don't care what you are." He grabs the back of my shirt and pulls me from the vehicle.

Cops get a little touchy in the line of duty, but unlike other professions we just learn to deal with the quick tempers in our own way.

I spin away around to face him, weariness morphing to anger. I seize Charlie's right thumb, twisting him back away from the car.

York's face goes red. "You son of a—"

"Uh, uh, uh." I slowly wave my left index finger under Charlie's nose. "Let's watch the foul language."

The two young, guarding patrol officers press in to watch. Their faces turn from surprise to silent mirth.

Charlie swears at me.

I apply a little more pressure to his thumb. "Uh, uh, uh. Watch your tone of voice."

"Okay, okay, let go, you dirt bag." York grunts with a hint of submission, jerking his thumb away.

"Don't you ever touch me again, York. Departmental rules—keep your hands to yourself," I say, loud enough for witnesses to hear. Even in my own ears, I sound impressively authoritative.

"You my example, tough guy?" He almost spits the words at me.

I ignore him, move away and lean back into the vehicle to look through the loose papers.

"Look, Wholeman," York says, with quiet venom, "departmental rules say I'm in charge of the scene under the direct supervision of the detective in charge. This is a police shooting. You're in violation."

Not bothering to look up from my search, I let him have it. "This is my case. I called in the initial BOLO. Until you hear otherwise from me, work the other side of the car and stay out of my way. I'm the detective in charge."

The forensic technician steps back and pulls out his radio, calling for instructions.

Moving just the edge of the papers, getting a feel for what's there, I notice a sheet with the letterhead of a Dr. Liam Cooper. *Bingo.* The doctor that ordered Williams's blood test. Another crumpled sheet is filled with hand-printed scribble, but one name pops out—Governor J. Gibson. Addresses and times are noted beneath his name. I realign the paper so I can read the text, but it's snagged on something in the plastic bag. I hook the pen through the bag handle and apply more upward pressure, trying not to tear the plastic. The bag starts to move but becomes stuck again. I gently apply more lift to the pen and the bag breaks free from where it had been jammed under the heater vent.

"What have you got there?" demands an irritated, but tamer, York.

"Plastic store bag." My tone is indifferent, concealing my excitement. This bag is an unexpected treasure cove.

"Hand it over, Wholeman."

I shake my head at him. "When I'm good and ready you'll get what you need to put into evidence."

I should've known York was going to spoil the moment.

CHAPTER 48

Our first marital counseling session is finally over and I can't leave the premises fast enough. Sydney seemed to enjoy airing our dirty laundry to a stranger, but for me, talking instead of *doing* is counterproductive. Sydney and I leave in our separate cars without saying anything to one another. Hitting the accelerator hard, I think about what I saw at the church—Sydney and the pastor. Their body language sure didn't look like praying to me. I suppose he prays with all the beautiful women in church.

I brood in silence, move to hit the radio button, but change my mind. Sydney didn't even ask about the investigation. I just had the day from hell, and she didn't even bother to ask. I decide to give Tina a call to hash out new ideas on the Ford case. The new Middle East theory that's starting to take shape in my mind demands a different motive, a different approach. Tina is my best sounding board. I punch in her number and wait.

"Hey, Jet, I've been waiting for your call. You're the talk of the department."

"I would have called you sooner but had a personal appointment I couldn't miss. Listen, this new development with the shooter could have far reaching implications."

"No kidding. So, what spin do you put on all this?"

I catch a red light, come to a stop and put the window down for some fresh air. "Tina, we both know by now there are no coincidences in this business. South Florida is on high alert for terrorism, and these two clowns arrive on the scene at, where else, the very church where the Ford girl is abducted. I don't know why or how but the two are connected."

"Isn't that quite a stretch?"

"No. Just because someone is a terrorist with religious or political motives doesn't mean they can't have sociopathic drives."

"You know, you're right, Jet. I read in a *Psychology Today* article that it's called *comorbid disorders*. Like having bipolar and schizophrenia at the same time."

"Hmm, I'll take note of that." I yawn.

"Anyway, I get what you're saying," she goes on, "but who has time for so many evil schemes? I can barely entertain a few fanciful thoughts of revenge before I'm interrupted by one responsibility or another."

The light turns green, and I accelerate too quickly, squealing the tires.

"What was *that*? You in a hurry?"

"I'm hungry. Anyway, the key word in what you just said is responsibility. You're responsible to your friends and family and God. Right?"

"You got it."

"So, those are the prime movers in your decisions and actions. Same with the terrorists. They act on their cause first, all else is laid by the wayside until it's played out."

"But wait a minute," she argues, "if they organize all their actions around a cause, then why would they take time out to satisfy a sociopathic drive? The way I see it, abducting, murdering, and molesting a kid sounds like a definite diversion from Plan A. And another thing. Terrorists are quick to take responsibility for their acts of terror. No one jumped out on this one yelling, 'I done it.'"

"Agreed. On all points. But what if somehow the murder compliments the cause? At least in his mind? Someone who is intent on evil can delude themselves into believing almost anything. Maybe a terrorist, an Al Qaeda crusader for instance, with an affinity for murder, but he can't live with himself if he acknowledges it. Instead, he convinces himself the murder is part of the cause. That it'll somehow *help* the cause."

"You know, Jet, that makes a lot of sense."

"I know."

"Okay, Mr. Full of Yourself, go out and do something about it."

"Good idea. Listen, I'll give you a call at the first development."

"Same here."

After we hang up, I arrange my list of priorities. I turn off Pine Island onto Broward Boulevard, heading toward the Broward Mall, just a mile down the street. I'm sure Sydney is not in any mood to cook, at least for me, so I decide to grab some Chinese at the food court. Sometimes, I just like sitting alone in a crowd, watching people. I don't know why, but it helps me think.

CHAPTER 49

I'm doing another surveillance gig from the church parking lot. I started early this morning, and it's been a long day. This part of the job fits into a major boredom slot, but nevertheless, is essential. There's a nearby airport, and the noise is somewhat distracting. I listen as a jet winds up its engines for take-off. The roar fills the air. I can't see the runway from where I sit—it's a quarter of a mile south and buildings block my view, but as I take a deep breath, I sense the smell of jet exhaust.

I muse over the rich smell of jet exhaust and all its associations. In times past, the odor meant the pungent forerunner to a vacation or a reminder of military travels. Now, the smell just means more work.

From my windshield view, I see the boarded-up windows of a run-down house next to the church, adjacent to the warehouse where I set up surveillance yesterday.

I'm reminded of my marriage—boarded up and run down.

Last night's conversation with Sydney, just before bed, is running through my mind like a skip in an old vinyl record. The car radio looks more promising. With a punch of the on button, the radio blasts to life, filling the air with a mournful country tune. Something about sad songs always cheers me up. On second thought, I turn the radio off. Too much distraction.

My joints feel stiff as I try to find a more comfortable seating arrangement. Nothing doing.

Opening the car door, I step out into the brilliant heat. The car remains running, its cool air now blowing out the door. There are some people starting to trickle out of the church building toward the parking lot. Office hours must be over for the day. I scan the faces, looking for the secretary, Meeka Amari, but she's not there.

I stretch a little and get back in my car. Nice and cool.

Tina should be getting back with me anytime now with a background check on Ms. Amari. Hopefully, she's also followed up on any leads that might have come from the bag of papers found in the impounded Camry.

My eyes feel heavy, so I shake my head and stretch out my neck. Normally, nothing keeps me from my shuteye, but last night was an anomaly. My thoughts return to last night with Sydney. Not a good night. One step forward, one step back. She sat on the couch, looking at me from across the coffee table and vented her pain while I wrung my hands in helplessness. She told me she questioned whether or not she ever really knew me. Her words hurt. I looked at her with what I know was the begging eyes of a dog waiting for his master to pet him. She remained still and composed, apathetic.

I tried to take the proper blame, tried to apologize. She didn't seem moved. And then the chastisement began. "I don't know if you get it, Jet. My world has tilted off balance. The person I trusted most in the world has a secret life. You have a hidden world of whispered secrets, tender touches. What is the truth and what is the lie? How can I know if those 'innocent meetings' went further or not?"

I told her she was wrong, those things were in the past, and she was the only one I ever loved. Silent tears ran down her cheeks. I reached out to touch her shoulder. She pulled back. "Honey, I thought we were making progress. You said you wanted to try harder. What's changed?"

She shook her head. "I'm just not sure I can trust you."

Her words are still ringing in my head as the roar of another jet jolts me back to the present. Hours of surveillance gives me way too much time to think. I've got a killer on the loose. I can't lose my focus, but it's getting harder. I'm struggling with guilt about not spending enough time with the kids, and the uncertainty of feeling my wife slip away. Having the chief breathing down my back isn't helping any. I grab the sides of my head and squeeze, as if the action can change the shape of my world. I look around at the blinding sun glancing off the empty cars. The car seems to be getting hotter, and I realize I'm very thirsty. I fumble around the car floor for a bottle of water. Nothing. I'm not one to get headaches, but right now an aspirin seems like a good idea. Wish I had some. I feel a strange constriction forming in my chest. I take a couple of deep calming breaths, but they don't help. Now I'm starting to become concerned. A sudden whooshing sounds in my ears. My eyes start to burn, and I'm short of breath. My chest is getting tighter, and I wonder if I'm having a heart attack. I reach for my phone but stop. This will pass. I just need to relax. But I'm still gulping for breath. I hear myself mutter, "God, help me." I chastise myself. This is ridiculous. I'm not dying. I need to breathe my way through this. I'm going to be okay.

My heart rate seems to escalate. I wait in the silence, hoping for something. But then the contractions in my chest start coming in spasms. A heavy weight descends. I feel pain like I've never felt before. I can barely breathe, gasping for air.

I fumble for my phone again. My shaking fingers try to find the nine key, but I'm quickly sinking into inky blackness.

Darkness covers me, and I feel myself go limp.

A voice like surround-sound comes from within and from without.

You have a choice to make.

The voice has the sound of rushing water but is as solid as rock—more real than anything I've ever heard before. It's the same voice I heard in the crowd, that day on the side of the road, but much clearer.

You are *dying.*

To my horror, I find myself hovering over a deep, black chasm. Everything is in shades of inky black. Below me are shadowy, sharp, jagged peaks. I sense the presence of death. The voice speaks again.

Choose now. Life or death. Me or the world.

Everything goes silent and with the silence comes a growing pressure.

Somehow, with certainty, I know time is running out for me. I hear sand falling as if through an hourglass. I know if I don't make a choice, then the choice will be made for me.

I try to talk but nothing comes out. I'm paralyzed. Trapped in darkness.

The clock is ticking faster.

Out of nowhere, Grandma Elsie's words finally come back to haunt me. For over twenty years, I've tried to remember what she said ... the day I stole her prized pie. The words now echo clearly in my head. "At the end of your life, Jethro, you will be held accountable for everything you've done in this life. You have a choice to make." On that day, my choice had been clear. Eat more pie. But she had more to say. "This is a matter of eternal consequences. Now, what do you have to say for yourself, young man?"

I'd looked back at her in earnest. "That we're all gonna get pretty sick of eatin' pies for eternity."

Thinking about pies scares me at a time like this, when I can barely breathe. Are these the thoughts of a dying man?

Realization hits me like a bolt of lightning—What if there *is* a God and I'm at death's door?

I try to yell out. I can feel my lips moving but no sound. *I want to live.*

I feel something swell up from deep inside. I sense it choke past my lips and I feel nothing else.

I wake up with a start, afraid to move, not sure where I am. Daylight is gone. I put my hand to my heart. It's still beating, and there's no pain. I take a deep, filling breath and peer into the dark surroundings. The sun has already set? I look at the gas gauge and find a quarter of a tank of gas has been burned. The clock on the dash shows I've lost two hours.

I hear the building roar of a jet plane. I push back against the car seat, trying to orient place and time. Peering out the front window, things look pretty much the same. There's the boarded-up house, the airport, the empty church parking lot. But the last time I remember, the sun was still out. Did I pass out? The vision of death is still with me, and I can still see myself hanging over that black chasm. The image is so real I find it hard to believe the event was just a dream. I look at both sides of my hands. Pat my face. I'm definitely awake. I lean in toward the rearview mirror—the same ruggedly disheveled face stares back at me. Nothing's changed, except my hair's standing on end.

Surprisingly, I feel good—energized. Whatever just happened didn't seem to hurt me. No need for a doctor.

I put the car in drive, flip on the headlights, and move toward the nearest exit. When I hit the highway, I mash the gas. I can't get home fast enough. As my headlights merge with the others, I remember the voice. Was it real?

I may have just had a near-death experience. The notion sounds crazy, even to me, but maybe I've been given some kind of second chance.

I roll down the windows. The smell of jet exhaust still lingers in the air and brings the same feeling it did as a kid—the promise of something new.

CHAPTER 50

Hakeem stood at the edge of the abyss filled with elation. He had avoided apprehension by the police and both his missions would continue as planned. He replayed the shooting of the police officer a hundred times. Fazel, fool that he was, pulled his weapon from under his right leg and shot the cop before Hakeem could react. Fazel had then put the vehicle in gear and pushed the accelerator. Hakeem remembered the shock of this man's stupid move and, rather than be a part of the impending chase, had jumped from the car and fled into the bushes on the side of the on ramp. As the police sirens wailed in hot pursuit of Fazel's vehicle, Hakeem had calmly slipped away and boarded a public bus on Commercial Boulevard. He felt certain Fazel was now dead. The reports said he'd been shot by the police. Hakeem understood a police vengeance killing and understood why Fazel had not stood a chance if he had been caught. Besides, he had never returned to camp and would have certainly taken his own life before allowing himself to be arrested. Fool that he was, at least he died a martyr's death.

The master plan was still in place, and only he, Hakeem, could have pulled it off. His leadership, his daring, and his intelligence would be appreciated by all. Even the emir would be pleased.

At the bottom of the massive hole was the fabrication made of armor plates two inches thick. The structure was designed to hold six tons of compressed diesel fuel and fertilizer.

Hakeem wanted to make certain, one more time, of the alignment.

He walked around the edge to the protruding five-foot piece of rebar set atop the hole. On the opposite side was another bar protruding from the hole to the same height. Hakeem backed off from the edge of the hole, about ten feet to the rear of the tent and ordered the canvas flap be drawn back. He squatted, closed his left eye, and aligned the two bars—like sighting down a rifle barrel. He lifted his right arm and pointed his index finger across the line of the bars directly toward the mist rising from the cooling towers of the Turkey Point nuclear power plant. His finger then closed as if pulling a trigger. *Pow.*

Just like the other two now completed locations, the sighting rods pointed dead center at the reactor facility.

He walked to the north side of the tent and sat in front of the computer, double checking calculations. He had done this hundreds of times during these past months, checking both the GPS location for his dig site and for the Turkey Point nuclear reactor and calculating the exact magnetic compass direction between the two. Picking up the digital compass, he went back outside to the dig and again sighted across the hole, aligning the sight bars with the compass. The figure was perfect, eighty-seven point five degrees. Divine progress.

He turned his face to the heavens and shouted out praises. The men around him joined in.

Hakeem felt elated to witness such devotion to his god. He sent up a silent prayer that American law enforcement which had been snooping around the church would not interfere with the fruit of his labor.

"Fill in the hole and load the weapon. We are almost ready," Hakeem ordered.

He watched as the targeting rods were cut from the structure and the backhoe moved to push the dirt and muck into the hole. When the structure had been filled to the last two feet, a steel plate, of the exact shape, was wrested into place.

It had taken only eight hours to fill in the device. Hakeem smiled. A good day.

CHAPTER 51

I'm at my desk for about a half-hour when I hear Tina come in.

"Hey, partner, have a seat."

"You sound cheerful." She pulls up a chair across from my desk.

"Feeling pretty positive. What did you turn up on our suspect?"

"Well, according to the staff, in the last few months there've been quite a few homeless people hanging around the church, including the dumpster area. But that's pretty much the norm for most churches. None of them were reported as being violent or threatening in any way. Also, no one on staff could make an identification from the sketches taken from your photos."

"Someone must have seen him, wig or no wig. Were you able to talk to Miss Amari?"

"Unfortunately, no. Miss Strut-Her-Stuff called in sick today."

I lean back and kick my legs up on the desk. "That's harsh, coming from you. Anyway, I'm not surprised. Timing is about right. What about the Walmart bag York got his hands on? That bag had a copy of Williams's blood results in it, and I want to know why."

"You aren't the only one. I talked with Marilyn James, and she said Meeka has mentioned shopping at Walmart, but then again, who doesn't?"

"Just great. Well, keep on it. Someone must know something. Find out if anyone saw her coming or going from Walmart in the last week. Check Walmart's camera footage. She may have bought something of interest. Last I heard, they still sell ammunition there."

"Got it. But the papers inside may have had nothing to do with what she bought at Walmart. Could've just been a handy bag to stuff with church intel. And our dumpster guy showed up for the hand-off.

"My thoughts exactly. And what about Meeka's background check?"

Tina throws her arms up. "Gone. Nothing in the computer files or in hardcopy. Marilyn looked everywhere. She said they never hire anyone without one, and she's completely stumped by this. I'm having someone check the crime databases as we speak."

"Good work." As I look toward the door, I see the chief pass by and put my feet back on the ground. With my eyes still on the door, I'm hoping he's not coming back.

Tina leans forward and raps her knuckles on the desk. "Got something else of interest. Not sure how this info will help but preliminary findings came back on trace soil found near the body and on Mary Ford's clothes. According to the report, the structure, sediment, and color suggests the soil originated in the South Florida area."

I put my feet back up on the desk and motion for her to hand me the report.

She stands. "Anything else I can get you, your majesty?"

"Maybe a cold drink?"

"Yeah, if you want it in your lap." She grabs the printed report from her desk, returns to her seat and plops down. "I'll read the findings to you." Opening the report, she scans it with her finger. "Here. The sand originated from limestone and is filled with Bryozoan, a type of sea creature, hardened by the long exposure to the sun. Typically found in West Miami. The only other place in the world where this is found is the Bahamas."

"Wow." I punch my fist into my palm. "If these traces came from the killer, it sure narrows things. He's either from West Miami, or the sand has been clinging to his clothes since his last conch and johnnycake in the Bahamas. I'll go with West Miami."

Tina slouches in her seat and lifts her feet up onto the edge of my desk. "So, our killer is from either Coral Gables, Hialeah, Aventura, Doral, Florida City, or Homestead. That narrows down the suspects to only about 100,000 males. And that's only if the sand dropped from his clothing and not someone else's."

"Don't be so negative." I gesture to her feet. "And there's not enough room for two pairs of feet on my desk."

She ignores me. "So, tell me, do you think this shooter is linked to the Ford murder?"

"Come on, Tina. This all can't be one colossal coincidence. A murder and a Middle Eastern-linked shooting coming out of the *same* church? Then we have a mysterious Arabic secretary who throws a bag into a dumpster … a bag that just happens to be retrieved by a cop-shooter."

"I hear you. By the way, I checked out the dumpster thing. The man in question had no prior trips to the garbage bin, at least that were seen. So, in all probability, he wasn't expecting her … unless the moment was prearranged or a convenient coincidence. But doubtful." She takes her feet off the desk. "So, no word yet on who the alleged shooter is?"

"Nothing. I'm worried the FBI has cut us out of the loop. Maybe they think this is bigger than just a local police department."

Tina blows out in exasperation. "Waiting is the worse part. Listen, can we take a different route for a minute?"

"Sure. What's up?"

"About the incident with the lieutenant."

"Oh that," I say slumping down in my seat. "I'm going to guess you're talking about Lieutenant Matthews from Davie PD, the guy who took a fall at the crime scene. He got what he deserved, you know. That pompous clown was just going to let that man die, right there on the side of the road. So … you heard about it?"

"Who hasn't?"

Grumbling, I push out of my chair and take a couple of quick strides to the coffee pot.

"Hey, would you happen to know what a brogrammer is?"

"Sure. It's someone trying to look like he's a techie, but he's really just a salesman. Why?"

"Hmm. Never mind." I stand and take a few more steps. "Want some coffee?" I call over my shoulder.

"No, thanks."

"Good choice. This time of day, you could probably stand a spoon in that stuff."

I slop some brew as I set the mug on my desk and mop the mess up with my wrinkled necktie. "The lieutenant has a god syndrome, you know. Guilty or not, everyone deserves their day in court."

I knew I was being hypocritical the moment the words came out of my mouth. There were a few times in Afghanistan where we weren't in a big a hurry ourselves to supply medical care to insurgents.

I plod on. "I saw it in the lieutenant's eyes. He enjoyed watching the guy die, that sadistic jerk. The man shot a cop and big man lieutenant was going to play judge and executioner. I can hear his argument now. 'It's a waste of time and taxpayers' money to have a trial, and if there's a conviction, we'll wait through decades of appeals before the state finally executes him.' However, Matthews never stopped to think the guy might not have been the shooter at all. There was a second guy in that car, and he could've been the primary shooter. In fact, the real cop-shooter could still be running around out there free." I slump back into my chair. "As I'm sure he is."

"Now you're sounding more like yourself."

"That doesn't sound like a compliment."

I open a file and start to jot down some notes, updating the leads on the Ford case. "By the way, did you ever get a chance to send something over to the hospital … to the wounded Boca officer?"

"Done. Not only that. I paid a visit."

"Good girl."

She shifts in her seat again, tapping her thumbs together behind folded hands. "You seem different. Can't put my finger on it."

"Yeah, I'm overworked and hungry."

"Whatever." She flips opens her laptop and begins to tinker with it.

Twenty minutes go by, and her silence starts to get on my nerves. "What's wrong with you anyway? Don't you have any of your usual social, medical, political, or weather reports to give me?"

"Face it, Jet, I've got skills. And if you don't feel like telling me what's going on with you, then I'll be happy to recite some of those statistics to you."

I hold out my hand to stop her. "Okay, okay, you win. I promise to tell you about it later, but right now I got work to do. We'll grab lunch tomorrow."

"Oh, no, you don't. I want to know why you're acting so weird. I've caught you twice today looking off into space like you're pondering the ways of the world. Not to mention you were sounding pretty philosophical a little while ago."

I straighten in my seat, feeling a new sense of vulnerability. I don't know where she's going with this, but I'm not ready yet for a life and death conversation. I make a show of shuffling some papers around my desk, pick up my cell phone, turn it over a couple of times. "You know, I bet the lieutenant called in sick today."

A slight smile crosses her lips. "Come on, Jet, what's the real reason you're so irked with the lieutenant? I don't think your frustration has anything to do with evidence."

"I already told you. Everybody should have their day in court."

"You never worried about that before. You were more of a guilty-until-proven innocent-type guy."

"Let's just say, I've had a change of heart. I've realized, at some point, we've all been accused of something we didn't do." A moment goes by before I say, "Tina, what do you say we stick to the case. We got work to do."

"I thought you wanted me to talk?"

"Not about me, I don't."

I open my desk drawer to pull out a few peanut butter protein bars and throw one to Tina's already outstretched hands.

She peels back the wrapper and starts in on me. "Did you know that peanuts are high in antioxidants and may reduce the risk of stomach cancer, stroke, and Alzheimer's? Did you also know if you're allergic to peanuts your throat can swell up so much you can't talk?"

"Maybe you should have a few more."

She plucks a peanut from her protein bar and throws it at me. "Okay, I know when I'm not wanted."

"Okay, okay," I say, giving in. "I know what you want me to say. I'm thinking about what's right and wrong, and you're trying to get at why."

With a smirk, she lifts her hand and gives me the victory sign.

"Don't think I didn't catch your pious tone earlier. You don't like the way I handled the situation with the lieutenant."

"You're on a roll, Jet."

"A bad one. But who died and made you my moral guide?"

"Ouch," she says, shuffling some papers.

A beat of silence.

I shake my head. "I'm sorry, Tina, that was stupid. You're right. If there's a god, then there's got to be a moral code also."

Her face registers surprise. "And you believe there's a god?"

"I'm moving in that direction. And don't look so surprised."

"I can't help it. I am."

"Can we get back to work now?"

"Jet, I was making a point."

"That's what I'm afraid of."

Turning back to my computer, I open my email, run down the list, and tap one of them. "Great. Just great. The boss wants a full report about the altercation with the lieutenant."

"You better get on it then." With a sympathetic moan, she slumps in her chair. "For the record, proving you were right in that moment is a battle you won't win. And Jet, one more thing. Don't wait on the God issue. Anyone of us could die before the day is over."

"Aren't you cheerful today," I counter. But her words penetrate.

As I move some papers around my desk, I feel a little dishonest about not telling her about my life and death experience. But I'm still not ready to share the occurrence with anyone.

Tina stands and walks around behind her desk to pick up a file.

"And as for the other thing—just end it, Jet."

I say nothing. She's right. About everything. But I'm not ready to humble myself and admit defeat just yet.

CHAPTER 52

"Wholeman," I say into the phone.

"Jet? Is that you?"

"Yup. You got me." I recognize her voice, FBI agent Vicki Anderson. "You're just the person I want to talk to."

I hear a lot of excited background chatter. "You certainly don't show it. Did you know the extension number on the card you gave me doesn't work?" I can hear the irritation in her voice.

"You must have an old card."

"And your department operator sent me to two other desks?"

"Hey, Agent Anderson, I can't afford the same deep pocket class the FBI has. So, what's up?"

"Remember that conversation we had about terrorists here in South Florida?"

I freeze. This is it. The twist in the case. "Sure, I posted a notice on the bulletin board like you asked. They've been talking it up at squad meetings, but I got a feeling there's more, a lot more."

She chuckles. "You bet, cowboy. You've heard and seen a lot more than you probably know."

"I've got my theories."

"Time to come clean, Jet. That alleged shooter you rescued roadside from our Davie PD caveman … turns out he's connected to Al-Qaeda. Jet, you're my new best friend."

Somehow, I'm at a loss for words.

"Jet?"

"A terrorist? Are you sure?"

"Of course, I'm sure. This is big. The guy in the car, the one you put in your report as a possible suspect in the cop shooting. He's a terrorist operative. Fazel Fahaad. And our captive is singing like a bird. We can't take the intel down fast enough. He's a treasure trove."

"This could be a game changer."

"Maybe, Detective, but at any rate, you did good. Turns out they have something going on down in the Kendall area. An attempt to destroy or damage the nuclear power plant at Turkey Point, or at the least to create a panic about nuclear energy … but that's confidential until the arrests. Keep that one between your ears."

"Nuclear power plant?" I echo, dumbfounded.

"Hey," she cajoled in a loud voice, "Did I just wake you up or something?"

"Maybe you did. To a nightmare."

"Listen, Columbo, you've stumbled on to something big, and this is going to catapult your career."

"I'd prefer Sherlock Holmes, but right now I'm feeling more like Nancy Drew. All this isn't exactly resonating. You're telling me the joker I'm chasing down for murder has something bigger on his agenda—like national destruction and the fall of global sanity as we know it?"

"Something like that." She chuckles. "If you hadn't insured that guy's survival, we never would have extracted this intel, and I'm thinking we're going to find out we've intercepted something huge. Department of Homeland Security has gone code orange and are scouring all areas within a ten-mile radius of the nuclear power plants."

A sudden burst of commotion sounds on her end of the phone.

"This is big. We just raided the sites. Three of them had explosives set up to be detonated. Disarmed them just in time."

"Thank God," I say in relief.

Tina walks over and looks at me, eyebrows raised.

"I'll keep you posted," Anderson says, in a hurry.

"Thanks for the adrenaline fix."

"My pleasure. Got to go."

"Hold on, one more question, Vicki."

"Make it fast."

"Did they get them all?"

"No. Our sources say there's one more out there. Hakeem Ahbad. He's a confirmed Al-Qaeda"

The phone goes dead. I sit there, a little dazed. Tina is staring down at me, hands on her hips, eyes wide with curiosity. I look down at the phone, still gripped in my hand, as if it just gave me an electrical shock.

Tina throws her hands up. "Well, you going to tell me, or do I have to beat it out of you?"

"You're not going to believe this one." I laugh hard, a combination of adrenaline, lack of sleep, and excitement—hitting the still room like bursting popcorn kernels.

Home a bit early, I grab cold pizza and milk from the fridge and move to the kitchen table. Five slices later, I head to the bathroom to get the shower going.

Standing in the shower, still chewing on the last piece of cheese and pepperoni, I enjoy the gush of hot water as it washes the dullness of exhaustion down the drain. I think about my conversation with Tina.

347

I'm bothered more than I want to admit that people are talking about me and Andria—not just strangers, but people I work with. I've never cared much for office gossip, nor for what people think of me, until now.

I somehow feel dirty. Running the shampoo over my head, I scrub hard. Maybe it's time I do something, something that doesn't come naturally. Soul searching. I don't know if my inner monolog is sounding more like a sermon or a girl's chat from *The View,* but whatever it is, I know I can't put it off any longer.

I hang my head, allowing the water to rinse away the soap. I feel ready to admit the truth. I had enjoyed those meetings with Andria. I liked the attention of her lingering glances and subtle touches. What was my real motive? Would I have weakened and given in to her allure eventually? I was playing a dangerous game, telling myself all the while the meetings were just for work, harmless flirtations, but my motive had been much more provocative.

I exhale and am surprised to hear myself asking for forgiveness—the words seem to bounce off the shower walls.

And if you're for real, God, I could really use some help with this Ford case.

It's seems like a good prayer, but something's missing. I add an *Amen.* Better.

An instant later, my mind seems to explode in a succession of images, like a digital slide show. I see the guy from the dumpster, I see his last steps to the passenger side of the car, but this time I have a larger range of scope. I'd been taking pictures, my right eye in the viewfinder to frame the shot but my left eye was open, a trick I learned in photography class which allows for a wider scope of view. Those images are now coming to me in retrospect. I see a man walking, pulling open the door, moving around the vehicle … in a flash, he pulls something from his head—it's a wig with a new look. Instead of seeing just an isolated telephoto shot of the back of his head, I'm now seeing his every move, every action. Then, I catch a glimpse of his face. That must be him. The Al-Qaeda terrorist, Hakeem Ahbad.

I've seen him before, somewhere.

I close my eyes, concentrating, looking for a match. A face. The smell of Pine Sol. A man, walking down the church hall, he looks back at me for one instant. Bingo. There he is. The church custodian.

"Gotcha," I shout, my voice echoing against the walls.

The timing is perfect. Today is Wednesday, and the church service will be starting at six thirty. Sydney will be playing piano, and the boys will be with their church youth group. I pray they're in no danger.

CHAPTER 53

Paul Blake puts his pen down and stares into his empty inbox wondering what he'll do next. He looks at the clock on his desk. 4:15 p.m.

Walking down the hallway, he mentally runs through the tasks he has accomplished today and checks them off against a to-do list. Midway through the list, he remembers Detective Wholeman told him to keep an eye out for anything that might appear out of the ordinary. He smiles to himself. Of all today's responsibilities, this one is a definite priority. To be entrusted with such a duty, after his former life of crime, is a real honor.

As he walks down the corridor, he looks through the windowed doors of each room. He checks locked doors, listens quietly to muffled conversations, and tries to get a feel for the movement in the building. If there's anyone, other than Pastor Bill, who knows this church campus, it's him.

Covering the distance to the church fitness center takes ten minutes. Usually, the trek takes less than a minute, but he takes his time, not wanting to miss anything along the way.

The fitness room light is off, so he reaches over and flicks the switch. The fluorescent lighting hums and the bulbs blink to life. He moves to the bench across from the three rows of lockers and puts his workout bag down. As he starts to unbutton his polo shirt, something catches his eye at the bottom right locker. His fingers linger on his last shirt button as he stares at the combination lock, threaded through the metal fixture.

The lock is much larger than the others and he doesn't remember seeing it last week—he would have noticed this one. The lock is not like a combination lock found on school lockers, fitness lockers, or even bike locks. It doesn't have the regular, rounded hasp that slides through the locker mechanism.

He moves toward the locker to examine the lock more closely and then takes the device in his hand. Heavy. The hasp is hexagonal, and the numbering on the face reaches over twenty-nine, unlike most combination locks. This one is numbered all the way to fifty-four.

He grabs the lock and gives it a tug. The hasp makes a scraping sound as it struggles against the locker holes which are too small. Someone must have really wanted that particular lock, even though it didn't fit. He wonders how long the device had been there.

Paul fumbles for his wallet and pulls out the business card Detective Wholeman had given him. He dials the office number, and, after about five rings, a female picks up.

"Tina Serwathka."

"Hello?" His voice chokes a little. "Is Detective Wholeman there?"

"No. He's away from his desk. Can I help you with something? I'm his partner."

He hesitates. "Yes, this is Paul Blake at Central Christian Church. The detective told me to let him know if I saw anything strange here at the church. Well, it may be nothing, but then again, it might be important."

He goes on to explain the unusual combination lock.

"Well, that really doesn't sound like anything out of the ordinary, but I'll have a patrol officer stop by and take a look. Thank you, mister …"

"Blake."

"Thank you, Mr. Blake."

The phone goes dead.

He sits down on the bench, staring at the locker. Then he calls the front desk to let them know he's expecting the police … again.

Within five minutes, the receptionist calls back informing him a police officer is at the front office.

He quickly covers the distance to the front desk and finds a tall, dark-skinned police officer waiting.

"Paul Blake," he says holding out his hand.

"I'm Officer Dayton Washington. I understand you have something for me to look at?"

"I sure do. Thanks for getting here so fast."

Paul takes the lead, almost running down the hallways to the fitness room. He points out the locker and looks expectantly at Washington's face.

Officer Washington bends down to study the device.

"I don't get it." The officer shakes his head. "What's the big deal about this lock?"

Paul looks disappointed. "Well," he stammers, "this isn't the kind of lock we use around here."

"And?"

"I don't know who put the lock there, and if anyone should know, it would be me. I'm in charge of monitoring the workout equipment and lockers."

"I don't want to sound stupid, but what do you want me to do?"

"I want you to check it out." Paul's voice cracks.

"You want me break the lock?"

Paul begins to shuffle his feet. "Yes, sir, I do. I think we should open this locker."

"Hold on there. It's not that easy. I'll need a search warrant."

Paul looks down and back up again. "Officer, I have a criminal background I'm not proud of, but it taught me a few things. I've got a feeling about this. Something's wrong here."

Washington studies him a moment and reaches for his shoulder mic. "P-21. I need to talk with a supervisor."

The response is quick. "P-21. 10-4."

Washington sits down on a bench, facing the locker, and looks up at Paul. "I'll be getting a call back any second. Who do you think the lock belongs to?"

"Don't know. But Detective Wholeman told me to watch for anything unusual and so—"

Washington's cell phone rings. "Washington, here."

Paul listens as the officer explains the situation to a person on the other end of the phone. After a minute, Washington disconnects and turns toward him. "Mr. Blake, my supervisor will be here in a couple of minutes. Lucky for us, he just happens to be right down the street."

Paul feels his heart rate go up. He steps toward the exit and gestures for the officer to follow him. "Let's head on over to the reception area to meet your supervisor."

When they arrive, the receptionist is packing up.

"Julia, I'll lock up," Paul says as he makes quick steps toward the front door. "We're waiting for another officer."

"Anything wrong?"

"No, no. Just checking on something."

Paul watches through the glass doors as a patrol car pulls up and an officer gets out. The man straightens his uniform, adjusts his collar, pats his right hip, and moves quickly toward him.

Just as Paul opens the door for Julia, the officer walks in.

"I'm Sargent Jose Martinez. I'm responding to the call about a locker."

"Boy, were you quick. I'm Paul Blake. The guy who made the call."

Officer Washington steps forward. "Good to see you, Sarge. I'm running into you all the time lately."

Martinez gives him a cursory nod. "So, what do we have here, Washington?"

"Maybe nothing, but Mr. Blake seems to think it's important."

Paul is already moving toward the locker room motioning to them. "Follow me, officers."

Inside the locker room, Officer Washington points out the suspicious lock and explains the locker situation to his supervisor.

"Look," says Officer Martinez, "Obviously, someone wants their privacy, so they got an extra secure lock. I don't think we have the right to open the locker, and I know we don't have enough for a warrant."

Paul shifts back and forth on his feet. "Can I open it?"

"How do you plan to do that?" Officer Washington asks, an amused tone in his voice.

"I'd get the lock cutters and break it off. Remember, I've got experience in these things."

Blake watches as Officer Washington attempts to suppress a smile.

"I know, I know," says Blake with a laugh, "Old habits."

Officer Martinez is now squatting next to the locker, the lock in his hand. Paul watches as a strange expression forms on the officer's face.

CHAPTER 54

Jose Martinez studies the oversized lock in his hand. He has seen one like it before, an old model—Master Dial Lock Combination. In fact, he has a similar one on the door of his backyard shed, but there's something else about the lock that seems oddly familiar. Continuing to roll the lock over in his hands, he can feel Washington and Blake bending over him, watching.

Suddenly, he remembers the man he watched from his patrol car while doing a church ground surveillance. He can see him clearly. The same bearded man who exited the back door of the church and walked to the dumpster, a combination lock in his hand—the same make as the one he now held. He remembers the way he'd counted the man's footsteps, the number of times he brushed off his shoulder. Then something else comes to mind. The pictures Tina Serwathka had shown him the day he and his family saw her at Christ Central Church. Pictures Mary Ford had drawn. One in particular pops before his eyes—the one of the bearded man. He can still hear little Josita's words, "Papa, that man has mean eyes." A chill runs up his spine as the number *four* repeats across his mind.

Martinez makes a decision. He begins to spin the combination knob. Speaking under his breath, he recites, "Forty-four, four, forty-four." He tugs on the lock. Nothing.

Washington and Blake move in to watch.

"Since when are you a safe cracker?" Dayton chuckles. "You got a past we don't know about?"

Martinez remains silent, still holding the lock. He spins the lock face again but changes the order of the numbers. "Four, forty-four, four." He tugs and this time the lock springs open.

He twists around to see Washington and Blake looking at each other in surprise.

"How'd you do that?" Blake asks, wide-eyed.

Martinez ignores him and struggles to remove the lock from the locker. The metal screeches in resistance as he finally wrestles it free. Placing the lock on the floor, he lifts the locker latch and opens the locker door. They all step closer for a look. Inside, several newspapers are lying on the floor of the locker space.

Martinez would have just left the pile at that, closed the door and walked away, except for one thing. The newspapers are not lying flat. A bulge reveals something underneath.

He lifts the papers and stops cold. A shiver goes up his spine. *Dios mio.*

There sit two pink sneakers. He feels certain they once belonged to Mary Ford.

CHAPTER 55

My Dodge has never been pushed this hard—full throttle, 105 mph, cherry-topped, siren wailing—charging north on I-95 toward the Atlantic Boulevard exit. Weaving in and out of light traffic, I try calling Sydney again on the audio command. Finally, she picks up.

"Sydney, take the boys and leave the church. Now!"

"Why, what's wrong?"

"I'll explain later, but it's not safe. Don't argue."

Another call comes through. Tina. I hang up on Sydney, hoping for forgiveness and compliance.

Tina's voice sounds strained. "Jet. I remembered something."

"Are you in transit?"

"I'm right behind you, keep focused. I've got something. You know the man that disappeared at the funeral? He's the man in the sketch, the one Mary Ford did. The eyes. The same mean eyes. That poor kid saw what no one else did."

"We've got our guy. Let's bring him in."

Another call comes in. It's Martinez. I ignore the call.

Still mashing the gas, with only seconds to my destination, the phone sounds again—Martinez again. He's not backing down. I pick up.

"Make it fast, Martinez. I'm in the middle of something."

"Just leaving Central Christian Church. Was called in about a suspicious locker. Owner unknown. Upon opening the locker, I found a set of pink sneakers, size 6."

I suck in my breath. "We've got him now. Good work, Jose."

I hang up just as the church comes into view.

With wheels screeching, I turn into the church parking lot, Tina just behind me. I bypass the rows of parked cars and make a sharp brake at the curb of the main entrance.

We both exit our vehicles and move quickly toward the front door of the church.

I pull open the main entry door to the church offices, Tina keeping pace with my long strides. The moment I walk in the door, the smell of Pine Sol assaults me. He's here.

"Be careful," the receptionist warns. "The floors are wet."

Flashing my badge, I take off, slipping and sliding.

There's movement up ahead. To my right, a door opens inward.

I stop short and watch as a bare, outstretched arm pushes against the door jamb. A man in a white T-shirt and gray work pants appears. His head is down but there's no mistaking him—the church custodian. He looks up and we lock eyes—in an instant he becomes a disappearing whirl of white and gray.

I touch Tina's arm in warning and then pull my weapon and move toward the door.

Tina nods and pulls out her own gun.

With our weapons drawn, we sprint for the hydraulic closing door.

I curse under my breath, jabbing a finger toward the front door of the reception area. "Tina, cover the parking lot, I'm going in." She nods and moves forward, keeping the firearm low in front of her, her reflexes ready.

I grab at the door handle, push through and into an empty corridor.

I'm chasing a dangerous terrorist, and I can't afford to mess this up. I mentally review the steps of protocol.

I should've called for backup before we entered the building, notified the FBI.

No time now. I can't lose this guy—got to stay focused, not second guess myself.

CHAPTER 56

As I'm standing in the empty church corridor, a quick movement about fifty feet ahead catches my eye. A dark-haired man pops out of a doorway. It's him. He catches my eye for an instant, then turns and runs down a double-wide corridor. Suddenly, he pivots to the left.

I break into a sprint. He's fast, but hopefully I'm faster. Just before I reach the turn, I hear a thud and the surprised squeak of a woman. I come to a sliding stop just before I reach the corner, peer around, and draw my weapon. Just ahead, there's a woman on the floor, surrounded by a dumped box of scattered papers. She looks at me in wide-eyed terror. She appears unharmed, so I nod reassuringly and gesture her to silence. Looking toward the end of the corridor, I spot him. He looks back for just an instant before bursting through the double-wide exit doors with an echoing crash.

I shout, "Police. Freeze." He keeps running.

Now at full sprint, hurdling the fallen woman, my foot somehow catches a sheet of paper, and I find myself skidding in what could have been a perfect slide for third base. Still trying to catch myself, I slam into the wall, catch my balance, and keep going. The door ahead slams shut as the dull sound of gunfire sounds.

My heart pumping in bolts of adrenaline, I make a rush for the door and slam my hip against the crash bar. I somehow lose my footing, slide down to the ground, my weight propelling me across the concrete and partially through the door.

Still on the ground, two shots sound in quick succession. They whiz above me, striking the inner face of the open door. The slugs hit just where I would've been had I gone through the door upright.

I twist myself around just in time to see the janitor turn and bolt across the parking lot into the darkness. Springing to my feet, I exit the door, fumbling for the phone in my pants pocket to call for back-up. "Central Christian Church. A shooter just exited the building. Civilians inside. Need a lock-down on the building, ASAP."

I peer into the twilight, wanting to take a shot at him, but he's put too much distance between us. That and I can't take the chance there's a civilian out there, hidden in the dimming light.

"Jet, over here."

I whip my head to the right. There, twenty feet away, is Tina on the ground, trying to reach for her fallen Glock. In the shadowy light, I get a glimpse of her face, twisting in pain.

"I'm hit," she yells. "It's my leg."

I run to her, phone in hand, and punch a button. "Officer injured. Medical unit needed, ASAP." Squatting down beside her, I quickly examine her leg.

"Jet, I'm okay, I'm okay. Superficial wound. Just go after him." She waves me away. "Don't let him get away." She tries to get to her feet. "Go, go, go."

I make a snap decision. Tina seems stable, so I turn and sprint to the parking lot.

A strained yell comes from Tina. "I'm right behind you."

That crazy woman.

I lean into my run, racing for all I'm worth, and wishing I'd done more early morning jogs.

The chase is moving us away from the lights of the church campus, but I can dimly make out the white shirt ahead of me. That shirt is my best ally right now.

Pitting my mind against my weakening body, I try to turn up the juice.

Without warning, the white shirt rises, disappears, and then reappears as it arcs up into the air. The T-shirt flutters to a landing off to my right. He's attempting to camouflage himself.

I quickly calculate that the fifty or so feet between us won't give me time to aim and fire. The chance of a miss is too great and would give Ahbad a chance to open the distance between us, increasing his odds of disappearing into the night. I wait for a better shot.

Thirty more paces take me past the discarded shirt. As we move farther from the dimming lights of the church campus, tracking him in the darkness becomes increasingly difficult, especially without the white shirt.

I begin studying the layout of the area as I remember it from earlier surveillance. A fifty-foot wide canal is coming up within the next hundred yards or so. There's also a large Florida Power and Light transfer box somewhere off this line of pursuit.

"Duck! Get down." A baritone voice bellows from somewhere. Instinctively flinching, I lower my head, but I can't make out the voice or where it's coming from. Looking around, expecting to find another officer, I see no one. *Got to keep moving.*

"Down. Now." The voice shouts again.

I hit the ground. I realize I'd been a perfect target for the shooter, my body silhouetted against the church lighting. With him fleeing into deeper darkness, using the cover of the canal bank, I could have easily been a goner.

Internal alarms sound. I think Ahbad is about to turn and fire, and just as I'm thinking this, the strange words of the old woman, Bertha Washington, rattle my brain: "You duck when you is told." Suddenly I feel a pressure shoving me, and I'm lunging right. The full thrust of my body is thrown toward the dark shadow of the electric transfer box. A fraction of a second later, the buzz of a first-round of fire whines past my left ear, followed by the booming report of a discharging weapon. I feel my feet touch the ground just twice, and my momentum propels me to cover. Once behind the transfer box, I reflexively fold my body into a fetal ball, reducing target size.

Stay focused.

Another shot explodes off the metal box.

I grind myself into the ground, trying to get lower.

Another explosion. This round rings off the box, whirring off into the distance.

"You lucky son of a gun," I mutter into the night. Or is it just luck? Two warnings to duck, just like Bertha said. I roll onto my right side and peer into the growing darkness. "Where are you?"

There's no answer. In the pale light of the nearby airport, I see no one.

"Who are you? State your name."

"Just stay down." The answer comes.

Another blast as a slug ricochets off the metal box.

"It's Officer Washington." The voice sounds just behind me. "You don't listen too well, man."

"Geez, I thought you were God."

"I've been called a lot of things, but … You been hit, man?"

"No. I'm good. Whatcha doin' here?"

"I stuck around. But now we need to move. You can thank me later."

Twisting myself onto my knees, I peer back around the transfer box. I calculate the location of the weapon flash, correcting for linear movement and sound distortions, jab my arm beyond the edge of the box and fire three successive shots.

I whisper to Washington, "I couldn't get a hit on him, but at least he knows I'm not afraid to shoot back."

"Good move."

The sound of a jet winding up its engines for take-off fills the air, but I can still hear Tina's approach, heavy breathing and sporadic groaning moving closer.

He's obviously under cover now, somewhere over the edge of the canal. He knows he can't stay there. The cavalry will be coming. Got to move soon. Tina will be silhouetted against the lights of the church.

In a crouching position, I call out, "Tina, hit the ground." In the same instant, I hear something that sounds like water splashing.

I jerk back to peer around the corner of the box.

Nothing. Darkness.

Approaching from behind, there are sounds of irregular steps, the dragging of one leg. About fifteen yards away, I see Tina's silhouette as she struggles to walk. Washington has her arm but she's laboring under a painful limp.

"You stay here," Washington orders. "I got his back."

I growl at her, "Get over here, and stay down."

I peer around the corner of the transfer box, but see and hear nothing. "He's either out of ammo, conserving ammo, or on the run again."

I slowly stand up and try to get a higher angle of sight on the edge of the canal, but it's too dark, I can't see a thing.

The sounds of the jet engines are shutting down and the familiar thump of helicopter rotors are approaching. Law enforcement must have shut down the runway so their helicopter could get through. Off to my left, a searchlight flashes, making a clear view of the canal edge even more difficult.

Looks like Tina has called in the cavalry, and with the airport right next door, the first to arrive will be the county sheriff's helicopter. I'm hoping they can get a visual of the shooter from the air before he disappears. If he was laying on the edge of the canal, he would have taken a shot at Tina. He must have moved.

Taking a deep breath, I leave the protective cover of the box and, keeping low with the ambient church lights to guide me, I make a run for the canal, hoping the shadows deter Ahbad's next shot.

Just as I'm cursing the crunching sound of the fragmented coral beneath my feet, I hear the unmistakable sounds of someone swimming the canal.

I lean into another sprint.

The helicopter pilot has detected my movement and his scanning searchlight freezes me in blinding brilliance. The wide diameter of the beam takes in the surface of the canal and before my pupils completely shut down from the intense glare, I see the head of Ahbad duck beneath the water's surface.

"This is the police," the loudspeaker blares. "Stay where you are."

Ignoring the order, I point my weapon at the surface of the water. Temporarily blinded by the lights, I wave my left hand at the helicopter. I point in the direction of the canal, hoping to divert their attention off me and onto Ahbad.

Tina is shambling up closer, still thirty paces off to my side. *She never listens.*

Her weapon is aimed toward the water, and to avoid friendly fire, she holds her badge up high, reflecting gold in the light.

Message received. The beam shifts abruptly to the surface of the water, illuminating the canal.

Knowing he must be blinded by the intense light, I decide to grab what could be my last opportunity. Taking a deep breath, I sprint the remaining distance as twigs and roots grab at my ankles. Coming to a halt near the edge of the canal bank, I use a narrow cypress tree for cover.

Time is passing in slow motion as the blood whooshes in my ears and the sweat trickles down the small of my back. I'm overly exposed and begin to think my terrorist has slipped the light when, suddenly, not a yard from where I'd last seen him, there's movement in the water. Fifteen feet from the embankment. Closing the distance in a few long strides, the dark canal looks back up at me. Looking down, I see silent ripples forming in the black liquid. Bending in to get a closer look, I jump back involuntarily as clawing fingers emerge from beneath the deep, making clawing motions, grasping frantically at the water's surface.

It's him. Only his fingers are visible as he's searching madly for something to grab hold of. His full hand never breaks the surface of the black waters.

My mind freezes. A flash of my young friend, Billy Monnot, left to drown in the clutches of the tangled weeds below, slams me. How many times had I envisioned him panicking in that dark abyss, unable to breathe?

No one came to save my friend—why should this scumbag fair better?

"He's drowning," Tina yells as she hobbles up from behind.

Getting no response from me, she limps painfully past me and edges down the slope of the canal.

"He's drowning. He's going to die," she screams again.

I grab the back of Tina's jacket collar and jerk her back. Her feet slip on the loose coral at the canal's edge and she goes down on her rear, sliding back toward the water. She groans in pain as I pull her up by the collar.

"Stay put," I order sharply. "You're gonna get yourself killed."

In the searchlight beam, I see a dark stain on Tina's right thigh, oozing from the hole in her pants fabric. A look of horror flashes in her eyes.

"You need medical attention, ASAP. Where is the medic?" I punch a number on my phone again. "Got an officer down. Need a medic now."

Crouching down, I rip open her pant leg and examine the bullet wound that appears to have caught the edge of her thigh.

"Stop. Are you crazy? We have to get him outta there."

"He's caught in the weeds. If we go in without the right rescue equipment, we'll die with him." My voice sounds cold and monotone to my ears.

Washington, now at Tina's side, already has his shirt off, tearing a strip from it to use as a tourniquet.

"Washington." She jerks her head toward the water.

"Your wound comes first," he says. "The detective is in charge here."

I'm glad my face is shrouded in darkness. I know it's flat and emotionless.

Washington continues his work silently. The searchlight flashes over the water again, momentarily illuminating the grasping fingers as they slip beneath the surface, for what I'm sure is the very last time.

"That guy is really putting up a fight," Washington comments.

The movement in the water grows still.

Then there's a rustle in the underbrush, about fifty yards behind us. Washington and I both pull our weapons.

"Who's there?" I yell out.

"It's me, Martinez. Your back-up." He closes in fast. "Heard you got him trapped in the water. Is he dead?"

"He's tangled up, probably dead. There's nothing we can do." I holster my weapon.

Martinez speaks into his microphone. "Dispatch? Martinez here. Chopper One on the net? Okay, find out if they have a rope they can toss us, pronto. Emergency unit needed, we have a drowning man and a wounded officer."

"We're on it," the response comes.

They can try all they want to save him, but I know his time is up and I'm not about to sacrifice my life for this sick maniac. Looking back down at the still water, more unwelcome thoughts of Billy Monnot assault me. Pictures of what his last moments may have looked like as he struggled for his young life. I try to shake off the haunting thoughts. I'd rather save Billy, not this deviant.

An inner struggle emerges as lightning quick thoughts do battle. Was Lieutenant Matthew's dealings with the downed terrorist so different from my own? Was I acting as this man's judge and jury? Logic begins to prevail as I'm forced to admit this man is too important to lose. He undoubtedly has crucial intel.

In the shadow of the scanning lights, I make my decision. I throw off my shoes and shirt and lunge toward the canal. I flick open my pocketknife, lock the blade in place and hit the water—its coolness is surprising on such a warm night. He's certainly unconscious now, without air for something close to three minutes. With no time for further thought, I take a deep breath and submerge myself into the black water, moving toward the spot where I last saw the straining fingers.

With zero visibility, I suppress a small fear that he'll revive and grab my feet, sucking me down with him. I shake off the worry and focus on swimming in tight circles. I move downward, trying not to lose my sense of which way is up and which is down. My hand catches something solid and I feel around to discover a human shoulder, then a head, floating harmlessly. I grab the body for leverage to pull myself deeper to the canal bottom where I now feel the thick long weeds, slimy to the touch, that have captured his ankles. In nothing but blackness, with only an occasional flash of the helicopter searchlight, I've only my sense of touch to guide me. My pocketknife still clasped tightly in my hand is my only weapon against the mass of weeds that claw at me.

As I begin to cut away the slimy strips wrapped around one of his legs, I'm surprised at how quick the burning weight in my air deprived lungs is hitting me. Forcing myself to ignore the mounting pressure in my chest, I move to the second leg. With a small current of water, I feel the hold on the body release as it's freed. With my remaining strength, I reach in the darkness, groping for some part of his body. Finding an arm, I grab it and swim laboriously upward, not daring to push off the bottom for fear of becoming entangled myself.

My head breaks the water's surface and I gasp for air. Breathing has never felt so good.

Tina and Washington, illuminated by the searchlights, are already submerged to their knees, their hands extended toward me. I shove the body toward them, and they latch on and pull him in.

By now other uniforms have joined us on the canal edge, all helping to haul the body up the slope of the canal where the EMT guys jump into action, administering CPR and resuscitation.

I yell for someone to attend to Tina's wound. Two EMTs help her to a prone position where they proceed to tear open her pant leg further and remove Washington's makeshift bandage.

"In and out wound, not too bad," an EMT announces as they prepare to lift her onto a transport gurney. Once in place, they move her toward the med unit, parked about twenty yards east of the canal.

"You did good, Jet." Tina gives me a tired smile as I walk alongside, patting her hand reassuringly.

I look over and see two other EMTs are now preparing to zap the criminal's chest with a defibrillator. He looks to be little more than a drowned rat to me. I can't help but feel conflicted feelings of revenge on behalf of the young Ford girl, along with a strangled hope that he'll survive. His testimony is needed to indict any possible accomplices. There's a certain comfort in giving the legal system a chance to serve up its just desserts.

Police cruisers, with sirens whooping, are now driving across the crushed coral of the parking lot. Uniformed men are rushing onto the scene, some FLPD, which I quickly recognize. There are other uniforms that are certainly off their home turf, but I'm surprised to see Homeland Security in their black-marked DHS body armor. They must have come over from the airport. This is quickly turning into a uniformed carnival. Something is up. This show of force is far beyond routine procedure for a local homicide.

"You did good, Jet," Tina repeats, her voice weary with exhaustion as they load her into the medical van.

"You didn't do half bad yourself." The van doors close behind her.

CHAPTER 57

The FBI showed up around 8:45, shortly after the rescue unit had air-lifted Hakeem Ahbad to Broward North Regional Hospital, where he'll be kept until he has stabilized, then off to a federal holding facility in Kendall.

It's now 9:15, and I stand in the shadow cast by a blast of powerful floodlights, a blanket wrapped around my shoulders, feeling my fading adrenaline sucking the energy out of me.

Special Agent Vicki Anderson comes up from behind me. The sounds of her approach as the coral crushes beneath her feet are covered by a roaring generator used to power up the lights. I turn toward her just as she reaches out to touch my arm.

Her face breaks out into a wide smile as she yells over the generator, "Can't sneak up on you, can I?"

"I've got skills, lady." I give her a tired smile.

She looks at me with maternal pride. "Any other time I may argue that, but today, you're Batman, Aquaman, and Superman all rolled up in one."

She grabs my arm and leads me away from all the background noise. "We need to talk."

I'm too tired to offer any resistance, so I allow her to lead me into the gloom, through the taped-off investigation zone, away from the canal, and toward the distant church sanctuary. When we're far enough from the noise and commotion to talk without effort, she stops and looks up at me.

"You know, you're one of the luckiest people I know." Her voice has a tinge of envy. "No, I mean it, really. We've been chasing rumors about these guys for months, and you just fall into it. Then you manage to become the lynchpin in locating an upstart cell that has become the most wanted terrorist group in the nation."

She must see a hint of confusion on my face.

"That guy you pulled out of the drink was the head honcho. He has a female assistant who just happens to be the secretary working at the Ford family's church, where their daughter was taken."

"Meeka Amari, a terrorist? Well, what do ya know. I knew that woman was trouble."

She nods. "She was acting liaison, a skilled agent. Wanted for numerous bombings in Europe."

My head reels, but I remain silent. This may have been in Fort Lauderdale territory, but things have turned topsy-turvy and I'm trying to catch up. Sharing case information typically isn't an option, especially for the FBI. Now, Vicki's substantiating every hunch I had about the link between the murder and terrorism. But ... Meeka, a soldier of terror? This is quite a morsel of intrigue. She's likely the same person who stole church documents and set up the theft of Pastor Bill's blood sample.

We're interrupted by one of Vicki's associates who wants her to sign off on some report, so she excuses herself.

I pivot and move to make my escape, wanting to finish what I started and track down the vamp.

"Hey, I'm not done with you," she yells, catching up to me. "Listen, I know how you feel, us stepping all over your investigation before you could do the follow-up and make your own arrest of this woman, but we couldn't wait and give her time to get out of Dodge."

I twist my face in annoyance and then remind myself the objective has always been to catch the Ford girl's murderer, not to find glory in a one-man show. I swallow my pride.

"So, you already took her into custody?" I ask.

"Hey," she says with a smile, "We're fast and we're mighty, but we aren't God." She looks at her wrist, pressing a button to illuminate the dial of her watch. I lean in to see the time.

I let out a low whistle. "Boy, how time flies when you're having fun."

"My people should be arriving at her apartment right about now," she predicts.

"Anderson, I want to be kept in the loop on all this."

"Oh, yeah," she responds, sidestepping the demand. "Based on intel, this Meeka gal is believed to have been involved in several terrorist attacks in both Nice and Paris. She's a long way from home. But who knows where her home is?"

"Prison soon, I hope."

The fact they're ready to arrest Meeka Amari and my job is suddenly done is a lot to take in. However, I know they won't catch her. She's probably long gone.

I look back again at the canal and the floodlights.

Vicki's phone chirps, and she thumbs it from the phone holster. Pressing the receive button, she barks, "Anderson. Go."

My feet start to shuffle. I don't want to stand there and listen to a one-sided conversation, even if it is good news. I'm beat, I've still got work to do and a report to fill out before I head for home. Home. That word has never sounded so good.

Despite my desire to escape this place, my feet, with a mind of their own, begin to drift toward the canal. A shudder goes through my body as I consider the possibility of Tina or myself having drowned in that canal, trying to rescue a terrorist who holds the lives of others so cheap.

I barely make my escape, when Vicki hisses, "They missed her."

I turn slowly. I'm almost too tired to care, but something screams in my mind. "Can't the FBI ever get it right?"

Vicki frowns. "Her apartment has been cleaned out. Looks like she's fled."

"Maybe there's some clues in her office desk?"

"No. Nothing there. Completely empty. Oh, except for one little oddity." She gives a snicker.

"I'm all ears."

"In her trash can, we found a wadded-up paper. Turned out to be a pencil sketch of a man in long white robes, arms reaching out."

"You mean, like Jesus?" I can't keep the curiosity out of my voice.

"Something like that. I guess that's what happens when you hang around church too much."

I sigh heavily. "Well, if she isn't at her apartment this time of night, she probably jumped ship hours ago."

Cinematic images of Jason Bourne's girlfriends Marie and Nicky come to mind—cutting their hair and dying it black. But Meeka's hair is already black.

"She's probably a blonde already." I throw my hands up in irritation.

Vicki laughs as she turns away.

I continue my trek back to the canal and the mopping-up of the area.

Vicki calls after me, "You're my hero, Jet and one lucky son of a ..."

I keep walking. At this point, I'd be stupid to consider any of this luck. I'm beginning to see a plan emerge out of all this chaos.

It doesn't take long for a whole covey of reporters to show up on the scene, along with the infamous Andria. As her people are setting up the cameras and equipment, I see her scan the area, as if she's looking for someone. Before I can make my escape, she stumbles toward me across the semi darkness, her heels catching on debris. She's extending her pen and notepad out before her as if she's a flag bearer of the sacred arc of the covenant.

One single surge of adrenaline touches me, before I can calm myself. I project Sydney's face, like a film on canvas. With Tina off to the hospital and unavailable as a stanchion of moral stability, I'm on my own. Even so, I ignore Andria just long enough to move into the lights and be near another human being. I need a witness, and the closest person turns out to be Dr. Richard Causeway.

"Hey, Doc, are you finished?" I wonder what he's doing here anyway.

He turns, a quizzical expression on his face.

He's probably hoping I'm about to ask a deep forensic question. Instead, I sidle up beside him, only to meet Andria head on. Even in the gloom, she appears radiant in white slacks and a silky looking sleeveless shirt.

"Jethro, can I ask you some questions?" She looks at me with a sweet smile.

"Hmm, let me think," I say tapping my forehead. "Nope. Answer is no."

She hesitates, not sure if I'm joking.

I look her right in the eye. "All questions concerning ongoing investigations have to be referred to the department. They'll provide any information you need."

She shifts her weight to her other hip, tucks a strand of hair behind her ear. "Jethro, that's no way to treat an old friend."

I give a rueful smile and turn my back on her.

"Jet." She yells after me, a note of pleading in her voice.

I can almost imagine her stomping her foot like a two-year-old used to getting her way.

"Sorry, Andria," I say without looking back. "Our departmental policy doesn't allow contact with the press at this point of an investigation." That felt good.

Causeway, a smirk on his face, shuffles after me. He'd been leaning in, all ears, to grab the exchange, not wanting to miss a single moment of intrigue.

I take a cleansing breath. Shutting her down like that, and feeling nothing, felt better than I could've guessed.

An unexpected ally, I take Causeway by the arm, a witness to my newfound moral fortitude. I point across the gray night, dimly lit by the remaining emergency flares. "Causeway, this could be the beginning of a beautiful friendship."

He throws his head back in laughter. "My favorite line from *Casablanca*. But whatever you say, Jet. It's your night."

CHAPTER 58

I slip quietly through my front door and into the kitchen, placing my keys, wallet, and gun on the kitchen counter. I haven't eaten in over ten hours, but I'm too tired to even open the refrigerator. Well, maybe not *that* tired.

The fridge door seems to open of its own accord, and inside, wrapped in Saran Wrap, is a plate of chicken, a baked potato, some squash, and a slice of cornbread. My mouth salivates. Leave it to Sydney to take pity on my empty stomach. I can't help but smile as I place the dinner in the microwave and hear its familiar hum.

Things seem to be moving a little toward normal.

After I eat, I secure my gun, and pad toward the master bath to clean up. There's Sydney on the bed, sleeping peacefully on her side, her back to me. I know I'm not really welcome in this room, but I'm too exhausted to face the couch.

With just enough energy to shower, I climb out and head toward my dresser for some fresh clothes. Weary to the bone, it's hard to find the strength to even step into my underwear—so I don't. I climb into bed and listen to her soft breathing, feel her drifting warmth through the sheets. There's no place like home. Before I've barely closed my eyes, I'm drifting off to sleep. My last thought is how much I love my wife.

CHAPTER 59

ONE MONTH LATER

I'm driving home on Broward Boulevard and traffic is bumper to bumper. For some reason, the lack of movement doesn't bother me half as much as it used to. I reach for the radio and turn on some tunes. The voice of Chris Tomlin, a new artist I'm into, resonates tranquilly through the car. Glancing at the digital clock on the dash, I see that it's 4:30 p.m. Later, I have a date with Sydney at the evening church service—something that just a month ago, I would've regarded as nothing more than a meeting with a graveyard shift of religious kooks.

Inching along in traffic, my mind drifts off to recent events.

The solving of the Mary Ford case has made me quite the man around town. I know humility is the higher ground, but a guy can't help but be pleased with all the hoopla, hero stuff going on at the department. Not only have fellow officers hailed me the Sherlock Holmes of Florida detectives, but the case has earned me a promotion to Lieutenant Detective.

The murder and combined terrorist plot, now fully exposed, have been extensively televised, rehashed a thousand different ways by every possible talking head. The crime scene piece Andria did at the canal location, on that last night I saw her, went prime time. Of course, her report was banned from our living room or any other room for that matter. She's someone I've de-friended on all levels. Unless my job brings me into unavoidable contact with her, she's officially been ghosted.

Traffic begins to move as the radio blasts one of my new favorites, I sing along in my tuneless baritone.

CHAPTER 60

I hold Sydney's hand across the table at the church campus diner. She looks radiant.

For the first time in a while, I feel confident about our marriage. We easily could have become one more family fatality in the ever-increasing statistics.

Sydney leans a little closer. "Tonight, has been really nice, but I do hope you're done with all the terrorist-capture drama."

"What terrorists?" I say, acting dumb.

A cute crooked smile plays across her face—the kind that makes me want to say anything to keep it there. "You know, honey, as much as I hate to admit it, you were right about the counseling."

She smiles and looks at her watch. "I wonder where Pastor Bill is?"

"Maybe he's with Miss Marilyn." I give her a wink. "I heard through that old guy, Elwood, they've got something going on."

"I'm sure that's *not* how Elwood put it. But I do think that sweet woman has been in love with him for years. Men can be so blind."

"Well, I think he's got his eyesight back."

Looking around, I spot Pastor Bill angling toward our table. I wave him over.

"You're late," I say, with indignation.

Sydney elbows me. "Don't listen to him. Jet has been regaling me with the heroics of his terrorist chase."

"In that case, I'm *not* sorry I'm late." He gives us a rueful grin as he slides into the booth next to Sydney. "I had to go over some things with Marilyn, and the meeting took a little longer than I thought."

I open my mouth to say something but get a swift kick from under the table. Instead, I give him a wink and lean across the table to give his shoulder a conspiratorial fist thump. He smiles, a slight flush on his cheeks.

"I want you to know," I say, "A full ten minutes has passed since I brought up that epic story of how our local homicide team saved the good state of Florida."

"It's been a full ten minutes since I finally got a break," Sydney counters.

The pastor laughs. "Let's just say the timing is perfect."

"Perfect time to order. I'm starving," I announce.

We order dinner, and while we eat, we catch up on small talk. The pastor suddenly frowns and lays down his fork. "Forgive me. I totally forgot to ask about your partner, Tina. Has she fully recovered?"

"Not even a limp. She's back on the job with a fury," I say with pride.

"Then let's celebrate with dessert."

When coffee and dessert arrive, I dig into my chocolate cake, managing to talk between mouthfuls. "Well, Pastor, I've tried to keep the conversation politically correct, but that never lasts long with me. I'm wondering if you miss your former wonder-woman secretary, Meeka?"

He looks up at me over the rim of his coffee cup. "Well, can't say anyone misses her, but I'd like to think she misses us." He gives a wink.

"Fat chance. I hate to break it to you, Pastor, but that's one religious conversion you're going to have to give up on. While we're on the subject, I've always meant to ask you, why in the world did you ever hire her? I mean, she certainly wasn't church material, if you ask me. And her application clearly stated her religion as Muslim. Didn't that concern you?"

"No." He rubs his chin thoughtfully. "I didn't do the initial interview, but I did give the final approval. She had a very good résumé, but that's not why we hired her."

"This I got to hear." I lean back, folding my arms.

He looks down a second as if gathering strength. "My wife, Hanna, was a former Muslim. I met her in Egypt on a mission trip. She was the first person of the Muslim faith I ever led to Christ." His eyes misted. "Hanna had the purest, most innocent heart I've ever known. She was so consumed with love for others that sometimes I was even a little jealous." He smiles sadly and becomes quiet.

"Please go on," Sydney urges. "I've never heard the whole story."

"Well, I couldn't really talk about Hanna until recently. Doing so almost broke me. But when Meeka appeared, I thought … just maybe, she was sent to us for a reason. Yes, I was probably naïve, but time will tell. From the day she arrived at this church, I prayed the truth of God's love would be revealed to her through visions and dreams. Missionaries say this often happens for a seeking Muslim."

I rub my forehead. "That reminds me. Heard something that may interest you, Pastor. When the FBI emptied Meeka's trash can, they found a penciled sketch of a man in long white robes, his arms reaching out. Does that mean anything to you?"

Pastor Bill's eyes light up. "Answered prayer. As I see it, the picture is a vision she can't erase from her mind."

Sydney looks at me, mouth hanging open. "Why didn't you tell me about that?"

"Honestly, I didn't think of it until just now."

The pastor takes a drink of water and pauses. "I'd be curious to know where Meeka is at this point."

"She's flown under the radar, so to speak, and probably is hiding out somewhere in the Middle East. But wherever she is, my guess is she'll be wearing a burka. The outfit works well as a disguise."

Pastor Bill nods and moves to reposition his body as if to read my face better. "Something still bothers me, Detective. Why me? Of all the pastors, of all the government officials, of all the activists, why did Hakeem target me?"

"Good question. But unfortunately, he won't talk. He's been interrogated repeatedly. I don't think he'd talk even if he was waterboarded. But I think it's pretty obvious Hakeem planted himself in your church so he could pull off the frame job. Meeka was there to assist him. Also, you have some pretty influential members here who were attractive to them. We know this intel from his buddy, Fazel Fahaad. Now, that one's a talker. According to Fazel, their focal mission was the nuclear set-up in Turkey Point, but he swears no one else knew about Hakeem's abduction and murder scheme. The general plan was fear and terror. But you, Pastor, well ... you were just a side-job to Hakeem."

"A side-job? If murder is his side-job, it doesn't say much for his career. Listen, I barely knew the man." A flash of anger crosses his face before he's able to rein it in.

"I understand how you feel, Pastor. Who knows what goes on in the mind of a sick guy like that? That's more your field than mine. Incidentally, I asked an FBI contact to do some research into the archives of your sermon podcasts. He found a few references to Jerusalem and your belief the Jews have divine rights to Jerusalem. That's a hotspot right there. I'm sure those ideas were the beginning of the end for any friendship between you and Hakeem."

"But if that's the case, why didn't he just go for me instead of targeting a child?"

"Your ideology. He wanted to destroy your church, everything it stood for. He wanted everyone on the globe to believe that you, a Christian leader of a mega super-church, was a child-killing monster. But I'm sure he didn't have any fuzzy feelings for *you* either."

The pastor shakes his head sadly. "Christianity and Judaism have always been controversial. As for Jerusalem, there's an unconditional covenant in—"

"You know," I cut in, "you've got a gift, Pastor. The way you work a Bible lesson into every conversation."

Sydney gives me *the* look. "You mean the same way you work your job into every conversation?"

We all laugh.

Pastor Bill rests his elbows on the table and taps his bridged fingertips. "I have one more question for you, Detective. Why would this terrorist association go to all the trouble to place Meeka in an office position that required background checks and work history? Was her work here that important?"

"First, that kind of documentation is pretty easy for an organization like the Al-Qaeda to falsify. Our buddy Fazel said Meeka was gathering intel on one of your members, Governor Gibson. Your church holds personal records on him that could have led to sensitive information. We'll know more in a month or so.

"At any rate, Pastor, it looks like Turkey Point was their original target. But the murder Hakeem committed here put the limelight on him. That was something he didn't expect."

"Maybe it's someone like *you* he didn't expect." The pastor gives a shrewd smile.

I can't help but grin. "I'll take that as a compliment, Pastor."

The waitress drops the check off and Pastor Bill grabs it before I can. "My treat," he says firmly. "After all, I have a debt I'll never be able to repay."

"In that case, Pastor, I suddenly feel another wave of hunger coming on."

I waive for the server. "Another chocolate volcano cake, please, with a double scoop of vanilla ice cream."

Later, at home, I'm relaxing with a re-run episode of *Sherlock Holmes* pulled from the recording menu. Sydney walks in and places two cups of steaming herbal tea on the coffee table.

"The boys are fast asleep. Your basketball challenge exhausted them." She blows out with relief. "It's finally *our* time." She nods toward the new 60-inch flat screen Smart TV I'm staring at. "Not that show again. Some things never change."

"What do you mean? I gave up *Burn Notice* and *White Collar*."

"Yeah, right. That's because they don't make them anymore. Now there's only *Sherlock Holmes*, *Criminal Minds*, *Forensic Files* and—"

"Don't forget the zombie shows. A new one starts tonight."

She leans down to give me a warm kiss that lingers just a bit.

This gets my interest more than zombies ever could. I pull her onto my lap, and she snuggles in with a breathy giggle.

"Come to think of it, who needs TV?" I bury my head in her neck, breathing in aromas of warm lavender and fresh soap. She lifts her head to look at me. "You're still a mess, Jethro, but a much better mess." Her eyes show a hint of mischief.

"You make me sound like a refurbished garbage dump."

She laughs. "Let's just say a better man."

"I'll take that. Just don't ask me to give up the Super Bowl, World Series, or any games leading up to those events. And don't even touch *Sherlock* or the *Gotham* series. While I'm on a roll, I'm thinking about getting season tickets for the Miami Dolphins."

She puts her hand over my mouth. "Stop while you're ahead."

I draw her close. "You know, being together like this … well, it's better than."

"The World Series?"

"Don't get carried away."

She snuggles in closer. "I have to say, it's been a great ending to a very long month."

"Just the beginning for me."

"For *us*."

"There you go correcting me. What did the counselor say about that?"

"Shut up and kiss me."

And for once, I do what I'm told.

Just as I'm about to swoop her into my arms and carry her off, my phone buzzes. I try to ignore it, but I can see it out of the corner of my eye, slowly vibrating off the end of the table. Soon, the phone hits the tile floor with a whack.

"Don't answer," Sydney implores.

With a heave of disappointment, I reach for the phone. "Wholeman, here."

"Jet, it's Tina. Got another one. Two bodies washed up under the Las Olas Bridge, east of the intracoastal."

"Timing is really bad, Tina."

"Is it ever good?"

"Got a point. You heading over there?"

She sighs. "Is the sky blue?"

"Blue as it ever will be. Meet ya there, partner."

ABOUT THE AUTHOR

ZANNE MARIE DYER—Before turning her attention to fiction writing, Zanne was a practicing clinical Christian counselor. She is a native Floridian, and she and her husband currently reside in Daytona Beach. Zanne is now busy writing her next suspense novel, volunteering as a counselor at her church, and acting as Chaplain of Volusia County Word Weavers International. She stays actively involved in the lives of her three young-adult children, and their families.

Made in the USA
Columbia, SC
22 July 2020